What people are saying about

No, You're Crazy

Drunkenly dark and magically twisted — as if the spirit of Charles Bukowski woke up in an Elmore Leonard novel and went looking for trouble.
Peter Darbyshire, the award-winning author of *Has the World Ended Yet?* and *The Warhol Gang*

I really enjoyed this book. I'd say I read it in one sitting, but by the time this gritty, inventive novel reached its thrilling conclusion, I was standing on my chair. More than a simple coming-of-age story (or two), *No, You're Crazy* explores how our relationship to our own body bleeds out into the world and leaves pieces of us everywhere we go.
Harrison Mooney, author of *Invisible Boy,* a memoir of self-discovery

No, You're Crazy is a sweeping, shape-shifting saga of connection, loss, and love. It's a wildly ambitious exploration of neurodiversity, acceptance and how we define ourselves. It's an uplifting story exploring good versus evil and free will versus fate. Readers will be captivated by Beamish's unique voice and novel plot lines. You'll never look at the world in the same way again.
Thomas Armstrong, Ph.D. author of *The Power of Neurodiversity*

T0308522

No, You're Crazy

No, You're Crazy

Jeff Beamish

ROUNDFIRE
BOOKS

Winchester, UK
Washington, USA

JOHN HUNT PUBLISHING

First published by Roundfire Books, 2023
Roundfire Books is an imprint of John Hunt Publishing Ltd., No. 3 East St., Alresford,
Hampshire SO24 9EE, UK
office@jhpbooks.com
www.johnhuntpublishing.com
www.roundfire-books.com

For distributor details and how to order please visit the 'Ordering' section on our website.

Text copyright: Jeff Beamish 2021

ISBN: 978 1 80341 216 0
978 1 80341 217 7 (ebook)
Library of Congress Control Number: 2022936002

A CIP catalogue record for this book is available from the British Library.

Design: Stuart Davies

UK: Printed and bound by CPI Group (UK) Ltd, Croydon, CR0 4YY
Printed in North America by CPI GPS partners

We operate a distinctive and ethical publishing philosophy in
all areas of our business, from our global network of authors to
production and worldwide distribution.

Previous Titles

Sneaker Wave

ISBN: 978-0-88982-278-8

For Judy and her infinite support

Ashlee Chapter 1

Missing: Day Two

The man wearing glasses with lenses as thick as a car's windshield plunks himself down pervy close to me on the grey cement bench outside my high school. It's almost like he doesn't see me, which is possible given his glasses and my ability to hide in the seams of everyone else's life. More likely, he doesn't see me as significant, as someone whose presence deserves a little freaking space. But, apparently, I know shit because, in seconds, the stranger starts inching closer, his body almost jerking with curiosity as he turns and stares at me like he would his favorite porn site. A half-dozen times he leans in, his breath on my neck, his eyes on my skull, as if he thinks my head, like his, is packed with twisted thoughts heavy enough to burst through my skull and drop to the ground for him to see.

Before I can drag my tired, loser ass out of there, his lips part and words start tumbling out, *Hello, Miss,* and it's obvious what will follow. Either the usual creepy desires of someone who's spent the afternoon in a windowless bar. Or else the judgmental stuff that comes from people who catch me scolding myself on a packed bus or sitting quietly in a piss-stained alley and just have to ask what my problem is or if I need help, like it's their damn business.

When the man's next words finally sink in, they are almost enough to make me wet myself.

"I am a police officer with the missing person unit," he says, "and I know you are struggling with mental health issues, and I am here to help you."

I steal a panicked look at this random guy in his 30s, who is blotchy, balding, unassuming in a serial-killer way, no taller than me and almost as pale. He wears expensive Asics sneakers

1

that look brand-new and a bright-orange shirt stretched tight over his round belly. Exactly how you would look to put people at ease before locking them up forever.

Even if he wants to help, can't he see that I want to be left alone? That all I desire in this world is to be free of everyone else and the pain that comes with them. So I say in my sanest and most polite voice, without making eye contact, "I think you have the wrong person, sir."

He sticks his phone in my face, its screen revealing a digitized Miami-Dade police department missing person poster with my name and my impossibly joyful and unmedicated face staring back. I release a soft groan. Far better than tossing my head back and letting loose an unshackled wail.

"What exactly are you doing here?" he asks.

Do not look at the train tracks, I warn myself at least five frigging times before doing just that.

The cop's gaze shifts too. To the train tracks across the street. Or maybe to the two white crosses wired to the chain-link fence built around the tracks to keep people safe from fast-moving commuter trains. The fence itself is rusted and fractured with one human-sized hole, hence the two crosses, one for a troubled Grade 8 boy who slipped through last month, one for a homeless guy who took a wrong turn a couple of months before. The cop sniffs the air, like the homeless guy's grim body odor and the Grade 8 boy's familiar stink of sadness still cling to their lingering souls.

The cop turns back to me and speaks my name, *Ashlee*. And as this single word drifts past, my body begins vibrating madly, a low hum tickling my ears, and another commuter train hurtles by.

When the train is gone, when my butt remains safely parked on the bench, I let out a long, relieved breath. Or is it a sigh that's thick with disappointment? The cop's eyes go wide, and I instantly understand what he thinks.

No way is the cop right. But what have I been doing here for the last hour, if not staring with longing at the tracks? If not also learning important things, like how often the trains run, where the gap in the fence is, how fast the trains are moving when they screech past, how the raised stone bed where the tracks sit looks like a sacrificial altar in some ancient civilization, how many seconds it would take a teenage girl, if she felt like it, to sprint across the road, duck through the fence and hurl herself down in front of the fast-approaching steel mass before anyone could stop her?

My body slumps violently like my blood has turned to ice.

The cop says, "My name is Gerry. Why don't we talk for a bit, Ashlee?"

We don't talk, maybe because he wants to give me time to reconsider, to decide that, no, I don't really want *that*? But *that* is obviously a concept my mind considered for a reason. And why not? Is it crazy to hunger for the suffering to end or to yearn for whatever comes after it ends? At best, a complete transcendence of my soul. At worst, a peaceful nothingness that stretches out forever, which is not so bad.

"It's the biggest worry, Ashlee," the cop finally says. "Your history of depression, coupled with the recent loss of someone you love."

Mr. Know-It-All smiles kindly and slouches in his seat, making it obvious he's only just started casting major shade, only just started dragging me back to his reality. His little world where the girl he sees before him has gone crazy with grief and can't quite crawl out of the pit of guilt reserved exclusively for those who managed to kill their own damn fathers.

In my head, I begin berating myself for coming here. For the last two days, I wandered my city's depressing backstreets, disappearing from home long enough to get reported missing, like anyone cares. This wretched journey could have taken me to train tracks anywhere in the city. Instead, here I am back at my school, this place where I stand out for all the wrong reasons, this place where I have always been about as welcome as an STD.

"I lost my father too when I was young," the cop says, trying again. "I understand…"

I raise my hand, surprised when this shuts him up.

In time I say, "You don't look like any cop I've ever seen," hoping that doesn't sound mean.

He grins like he's heard this a thousand times. "Policing has changed. So many of our interactions now are with good people who struggle with mental illness and deserve to be treated with intelligence and compassion. People like you, Ashlee."

"I don't have a mental illness," I tell this Gerry guy. "I'm actually super stable."

I prepare to prove it by giving him the detailed explanation I have rehearsed and delivered far too often these past few months, a six-minute-long lecture, and yes, I timed it. Misdiagnosis heaped upon misdiagnosis by the same confused psychiatrist who loved the word *delusion*. My hyperphantasia, where my mind would conjure vivid images? Diagnosed as delusion. My synesthesia, where each number and letter have its own personality? More delusion. My Great Awakening, where my soul managed to connect with a greater presence, a universal consciousness? Still more damn delusion. My soul transcending from my lame body into a higher being, one that sometimes has visions of the future? You got it. Which all led, surprise, to the same doctor diagnosing me with some batshit crazy disorder called Cotard's Syndrome, where the sufferer, in this case, me, apparently believes she is dead.

I don't, however, believe I am dead. If I did, why visit the damn train tracks today? But I do believe my consciousness has evolved enough to no longer need a crap body. Enough that I have developed, at the very least, heightened intuition, or maybe, at the very most, something far more.

I start to explain everything but decide my explanation would require too much damn effort. Besides, this man likely won't listen either.

It's far better to show him.

"You know, I have this pretty amazing ability to know what people are thinking," I say. "Kind of like intuition."

He smiles. "So, what am I thinking?"

Of course, what he thinks is that I am crazy. Pretty damn obvious, even to those who aren't psychic. Yet there is more. Much more. I don't need to push my way into his thoughts to find out. I just know. My hands begin trembling. Maybe it's better not to answer.

"You are hiding something big," I say, unable to help myself. "And you are dangerous. To me."

He frowns. "Not sure why you would say that," he says. "I am an open book. You need to see that. You need to see the reality of your..."

I raise my hand again, surprised when this shuts him up a second time.

"Don't talk about reality," I tell him.

"Why?"

"Because you don't understand the science behind it."

"Enlighten me."

I laugh. "You don't want enlightenment."

"Try me."

"Okay," I say. "You asked for it." And against my better judgment, my mouth opens and out spills what I have learned about reality: That the two of us and the bench we are sitting on and the sun shining down upon us are all constructs of the mind of the person viewing them because, after all, our eyes don't really see people and objects, they collect billions of bits of light that our brains then process into useful information. And our practical brains don't show us the binary codes and magnetic fields that are actually there. That would be tedious. So they instead show us engaging video-game-like icons that, thanks to natural selection, give us enough information to survive long enough to mate, which in my case has about a zero percent chance of ever happening.

When I am done, his face contorts like he's trying to take it all in.

"So," I tell him, honestly. "Even if I desperately want to be rid of you, or this icon that appears to be you, you may be hard to ditch because you are here for a reason, whatever it is."

"I am here to help you."

No. That's a lie. He's not here to help. We stare hopelessly at one another. The cop who is hiding something. And the girl who people are so sure has broken through the crazy wall, the nerdy daughter of an almost-famous artist father and an almost-glamorous hairdresser mother who both couldn't get enough heroin.

"Where have you been the past couple of days?" Gerry the cop asks, clearly trying to change the subject and make the question sound casual and not like another mental health assessment.

My mind drifts back into the whacked-out craziness of the past 48 hours, and my head fills with guys in rusted pickup trucks hollering *wanna come for a ride, sweetie?*, spandexed moms who catch me talking to myself and sprint off behind giant strollers before this wacky girl eats their babies, a wobbly Walmart toilet seat where I doze off, the filthy yet glorious gas-station sink where, at last, I wash my sticky underwear, an all-night restaurant where time slows like a weighted blanket is smothering the mostly sleeping city. The cop doesn't need to hear about any of this. And not about the blisters, the hunger, the doubt, the soothing yet diabolical voice in my head reminding me there's no need to suffer, all of it almost making me wish I had taken my meds. Or my visit to my grandfather, the one I have never met, the one I was too scared to approach for help.

The cop especially doesn't need me to mention Mom, who in the hours before I left dug her nails into my shoulders and said, *I wish this had never happened to you*, like she didn't already have someone else to mourn.

"Been around," I say.

Gerry nods, and we sit in silence some more. Then he pretends he doesn't understand we are all being stalked by a great evil, and he asks, "So what exactly are you running from?"

"Who says I'm running?"

"Missing people often are."

"Apparently, you think I have finally stopped running."

My thoughts jump to Mr. White, the geriatric cat that me and Mom and Dad all saw tear away from our basement apartment in Miami Gardens back when I was 10. We had watched him run across the street and disappear into an overgrown vacant lot, all of us sure that something, maybe a dog, was chasing him. Turned out our beloved pet was looking for a peaceful place to die.

A group of my classmates struts out from the school wearing matching green practice jerseys and black soccer cleats, their hair in long ponytails. It's our school's Grade 10 soccer team, bitches, and they're walking across the track to the playing field in the middle. And worse, their coach is Mr. Mathews, my history teacher, the former Gulf War veteran who likes to get involved in everything at my school. I pull my hoodie over my head.

Easy to imagine the shit said at school the past two days about me, the girl they see as a sheath of acned skin covering a clot of misfiring brain cells and not as a beautiful, imperfect consciousness bursting with love as it waits to be set free. Bet the hallways still echo with meanness, like: *She's a coward. Left home after her dad overdosed, before she could watch her mom follow dear Dad to wherever dead junkies go.* Or with sarcasm, like: *The poor little freakbox probably got herself trapped in the future.*

The smell of a fresh-cut lawn wafts down from a nearby baseball diamond where a mower buzzes away. It's a comforting scent unless you have read that this smell is actually a distress signal emitted by the grass. It's another reminder of how evolution has shaped our senses to hide the truth.

Gerry the cop continues to watch me. As he does, a thought creeps into my mind. What if he's not a cop?

"Can I see your ID?" I ask.

Do his eyes narrow slightly?

"I already displayed my badge," he says.

"I'm pretty sure that's not true."

"Well, I am pretty sure your illness is affecting your memory."

Rude. And suspicious. I turn away from him and run my fingers along the side of the depressing cement bench. This was where three years earlier, as a 13-year-old, I would each morning collapse my disappointing body, the one without a thigh gap. Beside me, a familiar and dangerous presence usually lingered. And I would sit and watch the same people, each day dressed in the same dreary clothes, as they labored around the track like they had seeped in from a zombie movie and gotten trapped, like the rest of us, in the same-old three dimensions of space and one dimension of time. This isn't real, I would tell myself. Life really can't suck *this* much. I didn't know it at the time, but life wasn't so bad back then.

It's still more than an hour from dark, yet the lights above the playing field begin popping to life. The cop looks past the lights and at the grey clouds racing past. "Is that a storm coming?" he asks.

"Yes," I say. "Some rain. You know, I better go."

He shakes his head. "Not an option. The two choices are going with me to see a nurse or going home to your mom. Either way, we'll need to get into my car, which is parked behind us."

Wish I could ignore him and simply stand and leave. But even if this man and his words are not exactly reality and are a construct of my mind, he must still be taken seriously, just like the danger presented by a train barreling down the track or a poison symbol on a bottle's label.

My alleged savior has obviously pored through a thick file about me because he leans forward and asks, in what could pass for a kind voice, the million-dollar question, "Don't you want to be with your mother at home where you'll be safe, where you'll both be happy?"

A strange, distant sound reaches my ears, apparently leaking from me. Laughter, or cackling. Because it is kind of hilarious to suggest anyone is safer or better off in any way being around other people.

"You need to be back on your medication," Gerry says.

He even knows about that? About the Seroquel?

"I'm not on any medication," I insist.

"You're supposed to be. That's what your mother told me."

He extends his arm, and in his palm rests a single white tablet that isn't the shape or size of my usual prescription. "You could take one to take the edge off," he suggests. "To quiet your mind a little."

"Even my parents stopped making me take my meds. I needed a clear head to help support our family."

He will scoff at this. But he doesn't. He says, or at least I think I hear him say, "You mean to help them with the gambling?"

Anger surges through me, and I nearly leap to my feet and bolt. Because he must be mocking me. He must think it's funny that someone believes she has special abilities that can be used for gambling. But there is nothing funny about any of this shit. Just ask my dad. Oh wait, he's dead because of the gambling. Too late.

I stand and start walking away.

Mr. Supposed Cop calls my name. Seconds later, a voice shouts a question that's probably not rhetorical. "You truly believe you will get away, don't you? What is it you think you have? Luck or something more divine?"

I turn to this man and see he's standing. His face is no longer kind and thoughtful but as overcast and agitated as the sky, his true identity slowly being revealed. I want to say, *You are the darkness that exists to destroy the light, or at least absorb its powers.*

But I don't want him to know that I know.

"I can help you, Ashlee," he says, sticking to his story.

Then, without warning, he closes the distance between us with startling speed. He extends his hand and says, "You need to accept who I am and what I say."

In my eyes, he must see something saying this girl will never submit because before my feet can move, his sweaty palm and fingers have wrapped themselves around my wrist like a too-tight manacle. "You are coming with me," he says firmly, walking toward the parking lot and dragging me with him like I am a giant puppet he's forced his stubby hand into.

It's tempting not to struggle and just close my eyes and let whatever terrible thing that is about to happen really happen. But even if I don't fear death, I don't want it to come brutally at the hands of this strange man. So I try wrenching my arm free, which makes everything worse. He tightens his grip, and soon he's picked me up and is carrying me awkwardly under one sweaty arm.

I scream, not just *Help*, but *Rape, Murder, Child Killer*, and he cups a hand over my mouth, and I bite down hard on a couple of fingers. The word, *bitch*, reaches me. I am still screaming when the man repositions me in both arms like a heavy package from Amazon. When he does this, I can see the soccer girls watching, their perfect lipstick-heavy, blowjob-giving mouths open wide, and Mr. Mathews, who's still built like a soldier, or maybe a tank, charging across the field like he's gone nuclear.

My wannabe abductor must spot Mr. Mathews too. He hesitates and turns his gaze toward a small bright red compact that looks nothing like a police car. He's obviously making a calculation. Then, instead of easing his grip on me and awaiting Mr. Mathews' thundering arrival so he can show his badge like a real cop would and explain about apprehending me under some mental health act, he drops me. Hard. On the cement. And it's clear he plans to run to his vehicle, where he will jump inside and lock the doors in the seconds before Mr. Matthews arrives.

With everything confirmed, I pick my bruised self up and, bye-bye, book it in the other direction. Anyone listening can probably hear Mr. Mathews yelling as he pounds and maybe kicks at the car's windows. Next will come a screech of tires, though I will be long gone by this time. My quick legs have already put me on a path leading to another street.

I run four blocks to a busy six-lane road lined with shops kept safe by rusty black bars on their windows. No one has followed me, not the fleet-footed soccer girls or the persistent Mr. Mathews, who probably chased the red car and the imposter out onto the street and down the block in the other direction. In the distance, a police siren or two grow louder. I duck into a pawn shop's doorway at a bus stop and catch my breath. The half-dozen hotel maids waiting for the bus in peach-colored aprons don't give me a second glance, and when the bus arrives a few minutes later I fight off an urge to step in front of it. Instead, I climb on and take a seat behind the driver and stuff my hands over my eyes and start humming out loud to drown out the voice telling me I have got everything wrong.

Mike Chapter 1

Missing: Day One

The woman's arrival, like any decent sneak attack, came in the sleepy first light of dawn, the gunfire-like clacking of her high heels shaking me from my poolside trance. As she drew near, I listened carefully to her footsteps, at first dismissing them as uneven and without purpose, like those of the heroin addicts who haunt Miami's Overtown. Then slowly, I sensed the misdirection, the cloaked truth that there was nothing arbitrary about the way this intruder walked. I sat in a collapsible chair with my back to her, a pre-breakfast Southern Comfort and ginger ale nestled in my hand, a sprinkling of languid strangers around me on the pool deck. And yet without seeing her face, I knew the offensive sound of her steps would stop the moment she reached me, the moment our shadows became intertwined. I tried to recall ever experiencing such precognition, even once in a lifetime where the occasional sense of foreboding may have come in handy.

The woman's footsteps slowed, and as expected, she came around to face me. One look was enough to tell me she walked like a drug addict for a reason. She truly was one, no surprise in this neighborhood of cheap extended-stay motels where disheveled people would wander off the street looking for a handout or a place to crash.

"Whoever your dealer is, he's not here," I told her before she could speak.

She removed dollar-store sunglasses from her bloodshot eyes and squinted in my direction, even though the sun blistered down behind her back.

"Better keep your feet moving," I warned.

She was Hispanic and may have recently looked like she was

in her mid-30s. She swayed from side to side on blocky wooden heels she had no business wearing and said, "You're the guy I'm looking for. I can tell by the tattoo on your neck."

I stood, convinced any man of any size didn't look imposing nestled in a peach-colored cloth chair while drinking from a transparent plastic cup emblazoned with flowers that could be pansies. "I don't have a tattoo on my neck," I told her, struggling against dizziness from standing too quickly.

She stepped back and shook her head. "You tried to get rid of it, but the scar... it's still there. I can make it out. A swastika. It's pretty damn offensive."

Her voice, both sloppy and precisely grating, all with an accusatory undertone, struck me as more than a simple irritant. It was the familiar sound of trouble, and it threatened to join a long list of other suspiciously innocuous sounds that turned out to represent so much more: my childhood footsteps fast on a dark road leading from the place that was supposed to be home; a gentle late-night knock on my bedroom door by someone I was expected to trust; the fake pleasantries of a married woman I would try to impregnate while her husband watched; a mustachioed head meeting concrete following a righteous scuffle; a handful of trucks skidding to a halt on loose gravel in a distant land where only armed men possessed vehicles with dependable brakes; and, most recently, the gentle coaxing of my inner voice, that usually trustworthy old friend, to ignore my ringing phone one more time.

The woman regarded me like she expected a response to her swastika remark. What she got was my finger pointing to the chain-link gate she had wandered in through. And a simple reminder tailored to the drug-addled, "The exit's that way, in case you've already forgotten."

"Mike," she blurted. "You're Mike Baker, right? I know this is your address. The taxi driver helped me find it."

I grabbed her wrist, careful to avoid the heroin-activated

scabs. With my other hand, I took her elbow, giving it a slight twist, and began leading her across the cracked pool deck, which, given it was 8:30 a.m., was surprisingly full of people, mostly either recovering from a hangover or starting on the next one.

"I need your help," the woman protested as she struggled to stay atop her heels.

"You think if I had any money I'd be living here."

I opened the gate and started to push her through, only to see the fingers on her free hand wrap themselves around the wire mesh, almost like she believed she was being forced through a portal and into a dimension where shakedowns weren't allowed.

"Wait," she groaned, her droopy eyes finding their first hint of urgency. "I don't want money. I need your help."

"You've got 30 seconds," I said, meaning it.

She took a deep breath. "I am your son's wife."

I reached up absentmindedly to make sure my sunglasses remained in place. "I don't have a son," I said.

She shook her head. "You're right. Not anymore. He died last week."

I leaned forward and stared not into her eyes but at them, confirming her pupils were tiny, which told me how wasted she was, which in turn confirmed that every brazen word she spoke came together to form one colossal lie.

Unfortunately, my supposed daughter-in-law seemed to draw energy from this eye contact, from my sudden hesitation. She forced out a grin and asked, "What, you're not going to shed a tear for the child you lost, for the husband I...?"

"Time's up," I said.

I tugged at her arm again, though too gently to dislodge her from the fence, which was another mistake. We stared at each other until a man wearing a green Miami Dolphins cap called out from the path that led to the parking lot. "Excuse me, mister, but the lady told me you'd pay her fare. You're Mike, right?"

When I returned my gaze to the woman, her strength had drained away with bewildering speed. She no longer clung to the fence to prevent me from tearing her away but instead grasped it with blood-starved fingers to keep from falling. She let go and collapsed to her knees, puking up a mouthful of clear vomit. I grabbed a white plastic chair from the pool deck, placed it in the shade of the withered palm tree garden outside the fence and pulled the woman to her feet and dragged her to the chair, where she settled with her head between the legs of her faded jeans, her right hand scratching madly at a sore on her left arm. Only then did I turn to the taxi driver and ask how much she owed him.

Once inside my building, I walked past the elevator and climbed the stairs to my fourth-floor room, hoping a little exercise would kick my brain into gear. Upstairs I removed a stack of bills from an envelope I kept assuredly in a paperback copy of *The Color of Money* because, after all, thieves don't get irony. They probably don't open books either. I drifted to my lone window, a sliding door that offered a view of the pool, and saw the woman remained where I left her, as if she argued her persistent presence gave the slightest credibility to her words when everyone who overheard our conversation knew how far she would go to pay for her next fix.

"Okay," I said to the driver after returning downstairs. "Here's the $60 fare for getting her here, plus another $60 for taking her back home, plus a $40 tip."

I turned to the woman, who muttered softly to herself, her face only glancing in my direction for a second. "And here is $50 for you to score when you get back to wherever you came from and another $50 to fry your brain enough to forget you ever came here."

Into the front pocket of her jeans I stuffed the money, unsure if a single word I said registered with her but confident the cash would. I helped her to her feet and half-carried-half-walked her to the taxi, where she fell upon the filthy back seat.

I leaned into the vehicle and used my cell phone to photograph the driver's photo ID card before stepping close to where he stood by his door. "If you drive a couple of blocks and take the money from her pocket and dump her at the side of the road in the vulnerable state she's in, I'll hear about it. Understand?"

He shook his face, the wrinkles around his widening eyes growing deep. I waited for him to voice objections like, *You of all people question my integrity.* Instead, he said nothing and climbed inside his taxi and slammed the door.

At that exact moment, the back door flew open. The woman's face poked out, and with a crooked mouth, she gasped, "It's your granddaughter. She needs help."

She sneered at me and added, "Maybe you both need each other's help."

Before she could say more, I pushed the door shut and pounded on the roof, and they disappeared as abruptly as they arrived. I stared at the heat rising from the pavement where the taxi had been parked, thinking a greater sense of relief should consume me.

Back at my apartment, a crumpled piece of paper sat on the hall carpet against my door. How had I failed to see it 10 minutes earlier when I came to get the cash?

I scooped it up and brought it inside and read it by the light of the sliding glass door. It was handwritten on the back of a long and wrinkly Burger King receipt and said,

Hi. I'm your granddaughter, Ashlee. I know, SURPRISE. Anyway, please forgive my mom and her condition. I think you understand how tough it is to lose someone you care about. Speaking of that, I know we've never met, but I can see we have lots in common. I can see we've both had enough. I wanted to approach you today, but I got scared. Not scared for me but scared for you. Because I am like a curse on other people. And everyone should get to write their own timeline. So I guess this note is my hello and my goodbye. Take care, Granddad.

It was signed *A*.

I cursed, like someone who had twice stepped in shit. I would treat the note the way you would any poorly conceived lie. By tossing it in the trash and not giving a second thought to a woman so high she'd actually think I would believe that my imaginary granddaughter had written the ridiculous note when in reality, Little Miss Heroin had scrawled it herself before approaching me at the pool.

I walked to the trash can but instead deposited the message in the nightstand drawer. Then I sat on the bed and tried not to give my supposed new-found family a single thought, which was tougher than expected.

Ashlee Chapter 2

Missing: Day Two

When I can bear to face the world again, I pull my hands from my face and hit the Exit button and step off the bus in what looks like an emptied-out industrial area near downtown Miami. There is a vast rail yard nearby, and when I spot it, I turn and head off in the other direction.

As I cross the street, a car horn blares behind me, making me jump. It's like a reminder to focus and get out of my head and shake loose the unproductive thoughts that consume me. Right now, I couldn't even answer the tiniest questions, like whether my friend Gina's new crop top from Forever 21 is too slutty to wear to school. So how will I ever answer the bigger ones, like, if he wasn't a cop, who the fuck was that guy on the bench? And does it really matter?

When I realize I am staring at the flattened body and spine of a small bird in the gutter, lost in thought like any number of the perma-fried passing by me, I want to scream.

I have never bought drugs in my life, but soon I am haggling a tall teenager with shockingly clear blue eyes down to eighty bucks for four hits of heroin. He then points me to a needle exchange where I get a kit containing a syringe, an aluminum cooker, a packet of citric powder, a small bottle of clean water and a rubber tourniquet, plus a sympathetic smile from a public health nurse who says, *Stay safe.*

I wander some more, looking for a place to rest. The sun is dipping low, and as I walk, I spot a paper version of my missing person poster, this one stapled to the wall outside a youth shelter. I rip it loose, with some difficulty, and as I do, my eyes fall on a woman with bright red hair watching me from inside. I turn and run.

A few blocks away sits an abandoned warehouse I passed the day before. It's in a neighborhood that's neither good nor bad, one where people swarm to the coolest bars and restaurants and nightclubs and where balding middle-aged men cruise by in minivans in search of damaged girls who, for a few wrinkled dollars, will offer up whatever they have left. This ruined building is covered in graffitied plywood sheets that don't quite reach up to its broken skylights. Out front sits a sign promising some new condo project. I don't see decay before me, but rather a damaged soul awaiting its rebirth, its glorious transformation, and I know this is exactly where I need to be.

There is no obvious way in, and I am circling the building when my intuition flairs up again. Before me approach three twenty-something girls in clingy dresses, their faces thick with makeup, their high-heeled steps eagerly taking them out for a night of funsies. When my eyes stop on the girl wearing a blue dress and large hooped earrings and a pretty smile, the dread that races through me is instant.

"Don't go out tonight," I blurt out, blocking her way. "Something bad will happen."

Her nose twitches like a bad smell bombards it. "Fuck offfff, weirdo."

One of her friends says, "We're not giving you any money, so go."

I start walking backward so I can watch them, almost sure a car will jump the curb and smush the one girl. But it's me who goes down when I trip and fall on a tree root bursting through the broken sidewalk. That's okay because it's right then two guys and a girl peel back a sheet of plywood and squeeze inside the warehouse.

I follow, cringing as I wind through a maze of damaged rooms and broken people before finding an empty room and a patch of cement floor that doesn't reek too much like ass pie. Around it lays a free-for-all of torn-apart arms and legs and torsos and heads, some smashed or burned by lighters, all mundanely naked. Someone has attacked these mannequins with nasty anger. In a corner of the room sits a twisted heap of yellow rain-proof coats, a few dozen toques and several crushed cardboard boxes stamped *Miami Rescue Mission Shelter*. I kick aside a tangle of spent syringes and bent spoons and, ugh, a dead rat, and sit down on my tiny sliver of fertile sanity in this great desert of madness buzzing with unholy energy.

It starts raining through the building's shattered skylights, and even though I have my new weather-appropriate coat with its most handy hood, I am more done than ever. The only thought that gives me even the smallest piece of comfort is the darkest one of all: if I choose, I don't need to endure this much longer.

When the contents of my mind become too much for me, I turn my attention to, ta-dah, the mind-numbing heroin.

I am definitely not into drugs. I have never shot or smoked or even snorted heroin. I have only done drugs twice in my life, once with near-disastrous results. Yet how many times have I sat in a room full of fucked up people and watched them do what I am about to do? Enough that I am sure I can draw the cooked drug through a filter and into my syringe. Enough that I can tell a vein from an artery.

I lay out my supplies and get to work, only resting once the needle is ready. Good thing, because soon the daylight fades, leaving me alone in the dark and rain. Alone except for one voice. The fucking dangerous one. The one that reminds me how much I have lost and how much suffering is still to come unless I do something. The one that points out I don't need to wallow in pain anymore.

I tell it that I will soon peacefully transcend. That I just need to give things a little more time.

The voice whispers that death must come before rebirth. That all paths lead to the same place. As proof, it points out that I have settled somewhere it would be oh so easy to fatally overdose alone. And that I have loaded a single syringe with all four hits of heroin.

I almost jump when my eyes fall on the four empty heroin packets scattered on the ground next to the very full syringe. The dangerous voice tells me to pick up the needle, stick it in my bony arm, and finally shake the physical weight holding me down. Just like my childhood cat, Mr. White, I have finally found a quiet place to leave this world, it whispers.

And the voice is right. It's not how I would choose to do things, but how often do we actually get a choice?

I pick the needle up and whisper to it like a family friend.

Tonight when it's dark. Then we will see where you are going to take me.

I stroke the needle, my mind rewinding through the past few weeks. Dr. Gregory, the psychiatrist I didn't want to see, trying to hand my defeated mom my prescription for anti-psychotics. Mom refusing, like she was rejecting the diagnosis too. Me explaining to Mom and Dad that everything's fine because some people have been given the spiritual gift of prophecy. That split second when they look at each other and want to say, *Our little girl really is fucking crazy,* but don't. Something later changing in their expressions. Maybe from the hit of heroin they took after disappearing into their bedroom. Maybe from realizing that believing me beats the alternative. Maybe from the power of the truth. *Predict something,* Dad saying. Our little game, me announcing who would walk by our apartment building next. Mixed success is still success. Dad taking me to the casino because, wink-wink, he couldn't leave me alone in my condition. Him giving me money for the video arcade, but only after I pointed out the *winningest* slot machines. How his lucky streak was really *my* lucky streak. How newly flush Mom and Dad never ran out of heroin. How heroin at the time in Miami was often cut with deadly fentanyl. Now me sitting alone in a warehouse beneath the failing light and laughing about possessing the power of prophecy but not a future to peer into. About not needing to be clairvoyant to know that my beautiful soul and the shitty tangle of flesh and bone that people call Ashlee cannot together survive the guilt that is slowly suffocating us.

I look around the room for a distraction while I wait. I pick up a mannequin's leg, and then an arm, and a torso, and go to work. It's like a giant jigsaw puzzle that forces me to concentrate on something other than myself.

Once done with the mannequins, I sit down, and my thoughts immediately go to yesterday, when I watched my grandfather by his apartment's swimming pool. How I had wanted to approach this stranger and ask for help. But I now see I really wanted to ask him to help end my suffering. I chickened out and wrote him a lame note, all the while imagining him holding my head underwater in his pool, my last gasps of life drifting to the surface in cheery bubbles.

It's almost dark. I add my urine scent to a corner of the room and wipe the blood from my lower lip, which I always bite when nervous. I am sitting back down when a sound that doesn't quite belong reaches me. Maybe it's me inventing a distraction. It fades, replaced by sirens wailing on the street, two men in a distant room arguing over a score of crack, the air around me thrumming, my dully incessant heart beating well past the point anyone wants it to.

The sound comes again, and my first thought is that I have managed to slip into a fourth dimension where space and time work differently.

The strange sound starts as a whisper and is followed by hushed laughter in this place where no one laughs.

Through the doorway is a sight that perhaps only I can see, because maybe it does hang out in a fourth or fifth dimension, which scientists believe exist, even if these realms usually can't be detected by our eyes. It's a beam of light from a flashlight or phone or some unearthly object, and it's moving through a distant hallway.

More whispers, like whoever's talking doesn't want to be heard or seen in this primitive world.

My body stiffens. I stand and move behind the eight mannequins I have reassembled and dressed, just like me, in yellow coats and toques and other discarded rags and arranged in a phalanx of thin-bodied soldiers that now shield their always-retreating queen. My mind scolds me for this choice, for even caring what happens to me, though I guess fear is a hard habit to break.

The flashlight beam strikes the floor outside the room where I stand. I want to shrug and say *whatever*. But I stoop down and pick up the syringe I had set aside, the one with a deadly dose of heroin, and conceal it in my hand and wrist, like a weapon. Just in case. And I stand perfectly still in a glamorous pose like my mannequins, hoping not to be noticed. Just in case.

The flashlight beam, which turns out to be a very common cellphone beam, swings inside my still room. And I am noticed.

"What have we got here?" a voice explodes. "Looks like a junkie and her homeless friends, all of them making America suck."

Three men. Two of them shout with delight as they begin knocking my mannequins back to the ground while the third one lights up his companions with his phone. When the mannequins are down, one man gently grabs my chin and leans in, staring into my eyes. "She's in La La Land," he shouts. He smells like expensive cologne and the same Dove men's soap my dad used. His breath is like peppermint and tequila. Even in the phone's dim light, his face is clean-shaven, maybe handsome, probably a few years older than mine. He's dressed in a clean buttoned shirt like someone going clubbing, not someone living on the street.

Which means I will be left alone so I can return to my deathwatch.

I think this right up until he grabs my neck and forces me to my knees. The man beside him moves behind me and slaps the back of my head, which is still covered by the hood of my new yellow raincoat. "Okay, junkie," he says. "At least you were smart enough to dress for the conditions."

Nothing happens for a few seconds. Then water begins raining down on my head and back as the man starts pissing on me. Their laughter is more upsetting than the urine spray bouncing onto my jeans. I lower my head and want to cry, and when a hand pushes my face back up, it becomes clear that they are filming me.

While they laugh and shout and say some of the worst things I have ever heard, I repeat the same words, *This isn't really happening*. And when they mock my words, I know something really is happening and that salvation won't come through begging or even praying for a miracle. It will come from understanding that good conquers bad and remembering that this flawed gift from God that I inhabit may be full of limitations and may not be what it appears but is more than capable of plunging a needle into the enemy's heart.

I wait until one of them reaches down and shoves a handful of bills in my face. He says, "So, junkie whore. Are you ready to suck all three of us off for fifty bucks? Or will you do it for ten, just enough for your next hit?"

I pull the syringe from my sleeve and slam it down at his neck. Only it's like he expects this, or maybe I'm just too slow. He grabs my hand and twists the needle loose. Their laughter is gone, and just as quickly as they disarmed me, one of them clutches the hair at the back of my skull and uses his other hand to slap my face. They take turns slapping me, not like I am a worthless mannequin but something worse, which seems to raise their spirits because they begin laughing again. Each time they slap me on the face or the side of my head or somewhere else, one of them shouts, "Reject all drugs, junkie."

All I can do is close my eyes and wait for it to end.

Like always, time makes little sense, and who knows how long they attack me. Something deep inside me shifts and detaches. I move, yet I don't move.

On their own, the men stop. They lean in, maybe trying to hear the words I moan over and over. When the words return to me, like in a loop, raw determination surges through my voice. *Harder, harder,* I say. *Hit that bitch harder. Kill her.*

The men are probably surprised because they begin laughing hardcore. Their feelings, though, are nothing compared to mine. My joyful heart is about to burst open. What has been revealed isn't just my newfound conviction but something equally unexpected: a complete separation of body and spirit where a soul shakes its earthly shackles and drifts high and guilt-free into the night.

A voice calls out from the hallway, *Someone need help in there?*

An older man enters the room, followed by a second man, who wields a pipe.

My attackers back out of the room and are soon gone, their laughter trailing behind them.

The filthy girl with the bloodied face rises to a knee and shouts at the fleeing men like the prideful, foul-mouthed sinner she is. *I guess I'll see you never, assholes.*

The two new arrivals study her, their bodies shaking with addiction from beneath their filthy coats. The older man asks, *You okay, girl?*

She stutters, confused. She understands that part of her is missing, but she's unsure what part. Or how. And as duality is not a concept an unconscious creature can figure out, she will never know. So she asks, *You can still see me?*

The man's voice is deep and sad and kind. *I can see you there, girl.*

And he may be right, though not for long. Even the girl knows she will soon fade to nothing, like the spots you see after staring into a great light.

The girl glances up at me, and even though I now exist to shine love and purity down on others from a safe and heavenly distance, I have nothing for her. The two men follow her gaze, squinting up into the darkness and seeing nothing but more darkness because casting your tormented eyes on a transcended soul takes a shitload of faith that most people don't have.

Mike Chapter 2

Missing: Day One

For an hour or so I turned the crumpled note in my hand like a great work of fiction, trying to decide which of so many things bothered me most about it. The false identity. The accusation I had given up on my life. But there was something even more disturbing hidden in the words. It was my supposed granddaughter saying goodbye like there would never be another hello.

This led to the question that was hard to shake: Could the woman who harassed me by the pool, in her condition, written words with a dash of subtlety that hinted at suicide?

It was almost a relief when I remembered I had left my glass, chair, towel and phone by the pool. I hustled downstairs and was surprised to find none had disappeared in the lawless disorder that often accompanies even the smallest commotion.

As I waited for the elevator in the lobby that reeked of the cigarette smoke that had years ago pervaded the carpets and plaster walls and ceiling, I tried yet again not to let the word "granddaughter" permeate my head. More than that, I struggled not to think about how I possessed the skills to track down the taxi driver and his passenger, allowing me to investigate her story and draw my own conclusions. But would they be my own? The diabolical nature of the human mind was well known: it is drawn to mysteries, the more outrageous the better; it is enticed by other people and the inherent danger that comes with them, like it has forgotten the need to survive.

My stomach made a gurgling sound, another unwanted internal stirring. I studied my wrists, the right one sore from dragging the woman to the taxi, even though she didn't weigh much. I lifted my hand to my nose, taking in the lingering scent of her skin, her familiar-smelling perfume. Don't go there, I told myself, letting my hand fall gently to my side, forcing my thoughts to slip away from this dangerous moment.

To my relief, two young men swaggered into the lobby with a loud and crude series of observations about their Denny's waitress and her ass. They stabbed at the elevator button with stubby fingers protruding from heavily inked and disproportionately muscled arms. They turned and stood facing me. The taller of the two men, his smirk wide, nodded at me and my poolside stuff and said, "Hey, it's the dude who's too scared to go anywhere. Did you get all anxious and shit out by the pool?"

As they awaited my response in full slack-jawed glory, they surely saw only a tall, grey-haired man, his face weathered, his slightly muscular body no longer able to conceal a droop, his spine compressing under some great weight only he could imagine, his solitary wish for the day to pass into the next one without too many hassles.

Of course, it's one thing to have a dead-end life at my age. But what was their excuse? I could picture the tall man in a mustard-stained green Subway uniform, his already-balding friend in an ill-fitting security guard outfit with a black tie that fell six inches short of his strained belt, both immersed in the rancid stink of failure. If they were lucky, all they would ever regret about their shitty lives would be the many things they never managed to do, rather than what they actually did.

I stepped forward, turning my body to face them. A fearless grin began hijacking my mouth while an empty look pressed out from my eyes. It was an expression I had absorbed studying the most dangerous inmates in a maximum-security prison and augmented years later by staring into the barren eyes of two imposter Iraqi soldiers who five minutes later would detonate their suicide vests inside the gate to Baghdad's green zone.

I let my gaze shift from one man to the other, hoping to

convey the look of someone with nothing left to lose. To my surprise, it worked. They shrunk back just enough for me to see, and they were done. The taller one muttered something about being tired of waiting and moved past me to the stairs, his friend trailing behind. Seconds later, they were gone, leaving me alone to think about what happened.

The elevator button's light blinked out, and the door began inching open with a dull chugging sound. I stepped inside, and the elevator shuddered like it could somehow fall further than the ground floor, before beginning its slow, slightly dizzying ascent against the pull of gravity. I placed a steadying hand against its graffitied walls.

Inside my apartment, I poured myself a drink and sat on the end of my bed, which wasn't really my bed. Every piece of worn-out furniture in this shithole came with the room: the rickety table with the two chairs covered in cracked orange vinyl, the two bedside lamps with mismatched shades, the chipped dresser where a picture-tube television was bolted down, as if someone would steal it.

I waited for my new obsession with the possibly fictitious note-writing girl to finally recede, like floodwaters that left behind little trace other than a lingering stink. A half-hour later I was still waiting. I kept pouring drinks until they nearly poured themselves. Finally, when my back ached and the ice cube trays in my freezer were empty, I glanced at my watch, not so much to check the time but to confirm its hands still limped forward because, in my head, time barreled backward. Of course, time never did that. After all, it would be too easy if you could return to a war-pocked street in Afghanistan, or maybe the steep concrete stairs outside a group home for teens, and erase a single mistake. No, time always crept ahead, for reasons the world's greatest physicists couldn't explain. Time also defied definition, maybe because you couldn't see it, or hear it, or touch it. It could touch you, though, and when an afternoon lightning storm lit up my gloomy room, even the poorest eyes could see my hardest years had perfectly chronicled themselves in the glowing white scars on my tanned skin and in the shake of two weathered hands that never quite looked clean.

Mike Chapter 3

1976–1978 Bellingham, Washington

On nights when the walls closed around me like I was a rat in a narrowing drainpipe, I would push open my bedroom window and drop to the ground below. My feet would land with the slightest sound, though any noise seemed wrong, given that in neighboring homes, children slept soundly and sometimes, I was told, under the gaze of parents who watched over them for no other reason than to see if they lay safe. My steps ballerina-light, I would wind through the yard and out onto the road. And then I would run. As fast and far as time and energy allowed, my battered sneakers silent on the empty asphalt, my legs never faltering unless the distant rumble of an approaching car pushed me back into the shadows.

The first time I snuck away, I was 11 and living in a so-called historical house in Bellingham's Fairhaven neighborhood. That time I didn't wait until the house grew quiet. Didn't wait for my tears to dry. I climbed onto the roof and dropped to the grass and ran three blocks to an empty park where I nestled into a swing and, for a change, didn't fantasize about seeking bloody revenge against the world. The wind blew strong from the southwest, its roar rising and falling through the thick cedars at my back. The trees rustled violently like a monstrous force tore through them. In my mind, shadow monsters huddled at the treeline, spiked steel balls on chains dangling from clawed hands. I found the courage to spin around and face the noise and whatever creatures it brought, and I understood for the first time that this was where you wanted to be when an enemy came at you in the dark: outside in the open where the streets were wide and empty, and the quick and resourceful always survived.

A half-hour later, when I strode home prepared to face a well-deserved beating for wandering off, a second discovery presented itself: no one missed me when I snuck out.

I won't claim I never got caught, not at that house or the next one or the one after. But when I did, it usually was because a cop spotted me in full flight on an empty street or skulking through someone's side yard. Six times I was returned by six different police officers, including a pretty cop whose name tag read *Fox*, whom I mistakenly called Officer Foxy, drawing from her a belly laugh. The father at one house nailed shut my bedroom window, ignoring my protests he'd created a fire trap. The next time I crept down the hall and snuck out the back door, which I of course discovered was easier anyway.

Even if I was caught a few times, dozens and dozens of nights I was not. So many that in time I found the courage to leave the silence of my sleepy neighborhood and explore the sharper edges of the downtown, where I soon became the youngest member of the nighttime street scene.

It was difficult to believe anyone else other than cops wandered the city late at night, at least until I ran into Two-Wheeled Eddie, like really ran into him, as he rode his bike up a quiet residential street while peering into parked cars.

"What the fuck," he muttered as our nocturnal paths collided, knocking him from his bike and sending a dozen 8-Track cassettes tumbling from his backpack.

We stared at each other in disbelief before going our separate ways. Two weeks later, I encountered him just before 4 a.m. in an alley behind a 7-Eleven, still on his bike, his hair tied in a neat ponytail, his arms and legs too long for the grey tracksuit he wore. On his back, a set of golf clubs, a guitar and, of course, his bulging backpack all fought for space.

He almost jumped when his eyes adjusted to the dark enough to take in my shape as I stood statue-still in a clump of evergreen bushes twenty feet away. "You again," was all he said.

He didn't ask why I was out so late. Instead, he said, "Watch my shit while I run inside."

And, "What kind of Slurpee do you like?"

We sucked on lime green straws as he talked about spending nights plundering unlocked cars of their treasures, teaching their owners to be more careful, a valuable lesson.

Two nights later, Eddie would introduce me to a collection of other miscreants. The city's homeless, the unwanted, perhaps even the unloved. They were, in many ways, worse off than me, a detail strangely comforting. None ever struck me with a ping-pong paddle or called me "idiot" like it was my real name. None ever did the worst thing of all: shrug and walk away when they saw I needed help.

There was Alice, who claimed she was retired and wintered in California. She counseled me on how to avoid the police patrols and a few of the street people better left alone. She knew I was a foster kid and would pull me close for a hug when the night's darkness began to soften, whispering in my ear with wonder, "Time you returned to wherever you're from."

There was Bernie, a young-but-bald man who panhandled outside downtown liquor stores in the day and bars at night. He was known as the best dumpster diver in town, and sometimes I accompanied him on his nighttime rounds behind grocery stores and restaurants, where the goal was to beat the rats to the bounty.

And lastly, Parker, who loved to sell and smoke weed and lived in his broken-down van and each day ate the same $2.50 meal at Burger King.

There were other drug dealers, too, including one who pestered me to sell drugs for him at my school. Each time I refused, he stuck his tongue through his missing front teeth in disbelief and asked: "You think it's wrong to ease people's pain?"

The first time he tossed out this question it struck me I knew little about right or wrong or what motivated me. I did know a little about house rules that needed to be obeyed because every home I ever lived in had a long list of them, usually containing the word *Don't* in capital letters. But those lists didn't apply once you stepped onto the road, and no one ever sat me down and said, *Okay, here is what you need to know to survive out there.*

While far from perfect, my street friends became more like the family I had always desired. And they rarely demanded anything other than my continued presence, like I represented a crucial part in an engine that kept chugging along. So, when one rainy night they asked for my help in "something illegal but morally acceptable," I couldn't refuse.

Alice needed a ride to Portland to say farewell to a friend dying of breast cancer. Because Bernie and Two-Wheeled Eddie wanted to accompany her for support, hitchhiking was ruled out, given getting a ride for one person was difficult enough. And when they came up short on the cash needed to buy Greyhound tickets, Eddie floated an idea. In his travels, he had spotted a Cadillac in mint condition parked in a locked garage next to a stately Eldridge Avenue house that overlooked the ocean. Eddie said the car worked fine; he'd seen an elderly man drive by occasionally. Best of all, the man left the keys inside the vehicle's ignition. For the man's reward of such kindness, his car would be left nearby in good condition on the completion of the Portland trip.

After presenting these facts, Eddie added, "There's only one of us who can get into the garage though. Its side window, well, it opens just wide enough for a small child to fit into."

Because I never thought of myself as a child, it took a few seconds to realize he meant me.

"I'll do it," I answered to three broad smiles.

From there, everything happened quickly. An hour later Eddie helped me squeeze through the window, holding my feet as he lowered me to the ground. I unlocked the garage door as Eddie had instructed and rolled it up. We climbed into the Cadillac and were gone, secure in the knowledge not a single light had come to life in the house.

We stopped at a downtown red light on the way to pick up Alice and Bernie, and ten seconds later a police car pulled up alongside, an occurrence Eddie later called a stunning stroke of bad luck. Eddie had once told me every cop knew every street person by face and name, and he had been right. When the cop looked over at Eddie sitting nervously behind the wheel, the cop's head jerked in recognition. Eddie panicked, throwing open the driver's door and yelling, "Run." Eddie disappeared into a narrow alley and the cop, who had come around to the front of his car to give chase on foot, ordered me to stay put.

I knew what I needed to do and didn't hesitate. I slid onto the driver's seat, honked to get the cop's attention, and slipped the car back into Drive. I put the gas pedal to the floor like I had seen in dozens of movies and had experienced in the most expensive race-car games at the video arcade. The engine roared, and the car swung side-to-side as it accelerated on the slick street. Fishtailing, Parker would later call it. Appropriate because I shot up the road like a fish bouncing from rock to rock in rapids. First, I hit a lamppost, followed by a parked car and then, right before I was about to ease off the gas, the Cadillac whirled around, giving me a glimpse of the cop chasing me on foot. As the car spun out of control, I didn't think about how much this would hurt and the trouble that would follow. Instead, I grinned that for once I was about to take one for the team because, finally, I had a damn team, even if this perfect family stuff was messier and more dangerous than I ever dreamed.

* * *

In the summer of 1978, five weeks after the car crash that separated my shoulder, cut my face, totaled a once-mint Cadillac and ended my short stay with a family who suddenly saw me as a budding criminal, I stood on the street outside a home that I hoped would become lucky number 9, because, after all, the first eight weren't very lucky.

My caseworker, Mrs. Thomas, a heavy woman with a cheery voice, drove me cross-town to the group "home" where I would not be the extraneous child who failed to fit in. Here, all five of us would be wards of the state.

The house sat on a lot thick with cedar trees in a neighborhood of once-grand homes on Washington Street near the corner of Grant. Mrs. Jennings came out when we pulled to the curb, shaking my hand with enthusiasm that didn't drain away the moment Mrs. Thomas drove off after the briefest of introductions. She wore dressy pants, a white blouse, a half-dozen bracelets and a sweet-smelling perfume, which all suggested she treated her group home responsibilities with the professionalism of an office worker.

"Do you prefer Michael or Mike?" she asked.

All my life people had called me Michael, the name on my birth certificate and in my file.

"Mike," I said, surprising myself. "I prefer Mike."

"Well, Mike, welcome."

The introductions began: Mr. Jennings, who wore a security guard uniform and grasped a lunch bag with a banana sticking out the top and who with a grin announced there were lives in need of saving, or at least protecting, at the hospital where he worked; Kimberly, my age, a ginger and hot, who looked up from her *Tiger Beat* magazine with a disinterested expression that seemed like a mask; Richard, who at 12 was the youngest in the house and so wild about *Gilligan's Island* reruns he barely turned his head away from the living-room television to acknowledge me; and, finally, the two biggest shitheads at my high school, Jim Rowland and Scott Mayes, who I knew were in the system though I had no idea lived in this very house.

I unpacked quickly and, unsure what to do next on that August afternoon two weeks before entering Grade 9 at Bellingham High, grabbed the book I was reading, *The World According to Garp*, and went out into the backyard. I sat my long-and-lean body, five-foot-nine and 120 pounds and growing fast, on a swing and pretended to read.

Kimberly soon stood before me in a mundane outfit of jeans, a plaid shirt and white North Star running shoes that she made look exotic. She folded her arms across her breasts, which I couldn't help noticing were about as full and round as I had seen on any girl her age, and started laughing. "*You* read for pleasure?"

From a corner of the yard, Jim shouted, "I fuck gingers for pleasure."

And Scott added, "I shit-kick bookworms for pleasure."

Kimberly gave them both the finger and said, with an impressive toughness, "Get lost, losers." She turned to me and said, "Okay, so tell me, what do you think that book, which I have read, is really about?"

At that moment, I saw with some accuracy how the summer would play out in long-awaited House Number Nine: Richard would stay the fuck away from the rest of us, Jim and Scott would try to make things difficult for everyone, and the Ginger Goddess would keep me from killing Jim and Scott, or more likely the other way around.

That night, Kimberly remained in my thoughts. Especially as I lay on my bed in my new bedroom, which resembled an oversized closet, though it did boast a door that shut and did sit in a basement which offered a little privacy.

I imagined her leaning close, her lips brushing across my neck. There was a knock on my door, and I jumped. Because an erection kept me from leaving the cover of my sheets to answer it, I yelled, "Come in."

Before the door swung open, I knew it would be Kimberly,

who would sit on my bed in the darkness, small talk turning more torrid as she slipped off her top. A figure opened and closed the door. Seconds later the bed creaked under a body's weight. My growing erection nearly creaked too.

Mrs. Jennings said, "Just checking up on you, Mike. Making sure you're exactly where you should be because, well, I heard you like to go out and wander at night."

The surprise that smacked me quickly turned to disappointment and then embarrassment and finally an unsettling emotion better not named.

"I'm okay," I said.

She moved forward and stroked my face. She kissed my forehead and said, "I'm so glad. I know your life hasn't been easy."

Hard to say how much time passed between the moment she kissed me and the moment she reached under the covers and expertly located my erection. It could have been 10 seconds or 10 minutes because the shock of what she did distorted time. Apparently, it also strangled any objections from me. Perhaps I had waited my entire life for someone to come into my room at night and treat me as someone capable of being loved or at least desired.

Either that or I had waited forever for someone to touch my cock.

And she had it in her hand, and she whispered I must have been thinking happy thoughts before she arrived and I deserved some tenderness, some mothering. In less than a minute, I had ejaculated all over the sheets. She took my head and pulled it into her soft breasts.

She whispered how this needed to be our secret and cuddled me long enough for my embarrassment to shrink. Before she slipped away, she spoke the kindest words possible, "You are loved, Mike."

She returned the next night and the one after and the one

after that. She stopped, of course, the two nights Mr. Jennings was off work. Then she returned the next five. The first few times, she jerked me off. Later, instead of only using her hands, she added her mouth. The time after that, she stripped down and let me touch her. Two weeks following our first encounter, I was putting on a condom and full out screwing her.

Each time, she would pull me close after we finished and squeeze my mid-section with her arms. A few times, she cried, not for long. No more than a few tears, followed by assurances I brought her much joy.

I knew what she did was perverted and more than a little illegal. Strangely, that made me value her actions, and the risk she took, even more.

In her arms, I would tell myself that this was what had been missing from my life: love and sex, all of it in one package. One 36-year-old blond former Avon saleswoman who sometimes starved herself to try and lose the 20 extra pounds she said she carried around her hips and who each day tried to teach five foster kids life lessons, one of them of course not being to never fuck a minor in your care.

In the months to come, I almost never snuck out at night, though I still managed to see my street friends occasionally after school. One day I ran into Alice for the first time in weeks as she panhandled outside a restaurant. She looked at me in near shock, like she saw a ghost returned to his former life.

"Well, I'll be," she said. "You must still be mad at all of us over the Cadillac. Either that or you've found yourself a girlfriend."

I laughed hard, and even street-smart Alice couldn't figure out what was so funny.

Ashlee Chapter 3

Missing: Days Three and Four

Free from my earthly constraints, I quite simply just am. Which means I don't stand or sit or eat or shit or regret anything, especially not my less-than-stellar past, or crave anything or even see anything other than the glorious light of our shared consciousness, which swaddles me in purity like a baby. Without time, my new state of being stretches on for eternity without pain or suffering, only love, which I shine down on others from up high, where I am untouchable.

Except that this love isn't enough to soothe the tortured souls of most warehouse misfits, who make such a fuss that their noisy dysfunction rises from their physical world to reach me in my deeper cosmic reality.

Like, for example, the teenage girl who loudly fought an invisible enemy until I made her think she felt my calming and loving arms wrapped around her thin shoulders. And the mangy heroin addict who was noisily departing this world until I convinced him I was giving him a lifesaving Narcan shot that his buddy was too wasted to give. Even the two men who chased off the nasty cellphone-wielding trio are a little high-maintenance. Their names are Gerome and Sam. While they were unable to witness my glorious transcendence, they did glimpse my departing physical presence, and it obviously left a strong impression because they still delude themselves into believing they see Physical Ashlee, even though she has like 99 percent vanished.

And so they also imagine they see me accompanying them on a morning walk to their favorite panhandling street, a trip where they tell stories about potential employers slamming doors in their faces and about sleeping in roadside homeless camps and standing at highway onramps for hours waiting for a ride toward Miami, this seaside paradise where their luck has changed far less than they hoped. It's sick to think about people looking at them and their black skin and right away taking in something other than their kind hearts.

We reach the busy pedestrian street, and they arrange me, or the ghost of conformity they see as me, in a prime panhandling spot next to the cardboard sign they'd made with the black Sharpie from my purse. It reads, FORTUNE'S TOLD, TEN DOLLARS. I don't mention the errant apostrophe in the word *fortunes*.

And yes, I can communicate with Gerome and Sam and anyone else; my thoughts exit through the chatty mouth of the disgusting girl they believe they see. The truth is I have already imparted too much on my two new friends, starting with when I mentioned my psychic abilities, and they asked me to predict their futures, which I did. Sadly, their so-called futures are much like their so-called pasts and their so-called presents. I wish I could have lied to them, but I couldn't. That's why I'm happy to help soften their disappointment by having my physical sidekick collect a little cash for them.

My lingering physical presence sits there alone for most of the morning, while my higher presence, my true being, uses meditation to expand its connection with the conscious universe. Gerome, the older man, panhandles across the street, where he can make sure his new teenage pal doesn't get hassled.

Most people walking by ignore the physical me, likely because they don't behold a physical entity leaning against the wall outside a Starbucks. Some do, though, and they smile at the sign and drop a few coins or bills into the jar at the feet of the girl they think they see. One rude man asks if the girl sees him fucking her in the near future. Four people sit down and get their fortunes read. For these four, the true me gets involved, pressing my presence forth. First, I look at their auras and, next, based on the colors I see through my synesthesia, tell them exactly how they feel right now, which is the easy part. Then I place a supposed hand on theirs and drift far into their futures, usually getting a glance at critical moments in their lives. I use my intuition to confirm what I have seen, and finally, I reveal their futures, not with words but with thoughts my customers believe are words spilling from a teenager's smart mouth.

One woman, who coincidentally has the brightest future because she's about to land her dream job and meet a kind guy at her yoga class, thanks me by dropping sixty dollars into the jar. The other three don't like their futures quite as much, though they see enough truth in what I've said to pay me, and tip me, for my services. Like with Gerome and Sam, I remind all three that we possess free will; that with a little work and an open mind, we can all change our path.

Gerome and Sam need a break, and my lingering physical presence manages to buy monstrous slices of pizza and bottles of Coke before the three of us return to the corner of the warehouse they call home. We split our panhandling cash into three equal shares, and Gerome and Sam almost gasp at how much I collected, with Sam proclaiming that *white girls rock*. They leave so they can score and *recharge their souls* as a celebration of their newfound fortune.

While they are gone, I float through the warehouse, this messiest of interfaces, this loudest of my mind's projections. I need to ditch this place. What's keeping me here when my soul could be soaring somewhere more scenic and peaceful? Something whispers that I must stay a bit longer. That *something* is either my intuition or a voice from the higher consciousness. Who knows? There is so much we don't understand.

The messed-up blond girl I comforted last night is struggling again. Like the warehouse that half shelters us, she heaves with misery, her hundred-pound body pulsating with heaviness.

I allow my true being to descend until it hovers next to her.

Then I search for an uplifting memory, one that's funny, one that offers a little divine inspiration. What floods my thoughts is more bittersweet than uplifting, more a collection of memories than a single one. I don't know why I've picked it, or maybe why it's chosen me. It is a story of gritty persistence. Maybe even survival by those unsure if they want to survive. And at its heart is a glamorous party and an awkward girl who finally gets to wear a beautiful dress.

The blond girl's eyes are closed, but I am sure this story can reach her and maybe give her a few moments of relief. The words she imagines she hears are soft like footsteps on a beach littered with broken coral and shells. Soon the warehouse's walls fall away, and a happier version of the world floods in, though we all know looks can be deceiving...

It's three years ago, and I'm 13. It's not the Pink Floyd music in an endless loop that draws me from my bedroom just before sunrise. It's the lack of voices, of any human sound. The living room is full of lifeless people, all coming down from a night of pills and powder that my father generously bought with some of his artist's grant money. It seems as if everyone fatally overdosed. But they look peacefully content too like they have gone somewhere else, and suddenly I want what they have. Maybe not an epic night of coolness, not really, but something half-interesting to tell my friends the next day, other than how I spent two hours cleaning up spilled drinks and puke before putting Mom and Dad to bed. I know where to find what I'm looking for. Two baggies in my sleeping father's shirt pocket. I remove the two prizes without waking him, pop a pill into my mouth and swallow it down with vodka. Then I shake a dime-sized clump of powder onto the coffee table and snort it like so many people have done in our home.

Time leaps, and I balance on top of the outside balcony's railing, my raised palms resting on the peach-colored stucco ceiling, my toes tilted slightly toward the street far below, my lips vibrating in what could have been a mad laugh. I can't remember climbing up there. All I know is I should have done it long ago because the perspective from up high is stunning, a single pink balloon drifting past a distant backdrop of downtown Miami skyscrapers. *Ashlee.* A voice soothing and slurred croaks behind me. I don't turn but know it belongs to my father's best friend, Sanders. He stumbles forward into my vision, his body crashing into the railing and nearly sending me tumbling forward. Two hands wrap around my waist and pull me back inside the apartment. A filthy finger forces me to puke out my stomach's contents on the carpet. My mother wraps me in her arms like a baby as I sip water from a plastic cup and shake like in the throes of a Red Bull overdose. Two days later, I am at counseling, explaining my *sad feelings* over and over to a stranger. Soon my life isn't mine to control, and I am spending four days on suicide-watch at a nuthouse, or state mental health facility, after I can't stop crying and can't slow my racing heart.

Back at home and finally cleared to return to school, I say to Mom, *I can't go back. What will I tell Gina, Becky, and Sophie and everyone else?*

Tell them you had the flu, she says.

That's lying, I counter.

It's okay to lie when it's for your own good.

Her words etch themselves deep inside me.

Two years later, and I am making breakfast. While I use my tongue to wipe a mix of toast and peanut butter from the inside of my mouth, a presence behind me makes itself known. It's the heroic but horrendously hung-over Sanders, who I turn to see is rather intently watching me as I lean over the kitchen counter.

Before I can even say *Mornin' loser*, the kind of friendly banter I enjoy with my protector, he lurches forward, grabs my ass and starts to run a hand between my legs in *that* area while his lips and tongue press at my face. So gross. I jump back, push his hand and face away and kick at him when he tries again.

I'm sorry, Ashlee, he whines, *but you're such a beautiful young woman that you made me do that.* Then he adds, desperately, *Don't forget, we have a special bond, you and me. So please don't tell your parents.*

I am done, and I whirl away and hurry to my room, where I stare hard into the dresser mirror, hoping to see what he just saw. The young woman grinning back, chest rising and falling rapidly in the fight-or-flight exertion that didn't take her far, catches me more off guard than the creepy hands of the man who once saved my life.

A few weeks later and only days after my sixteenth birthday, my father takes me to a fancy party at a Miami Beach hotel as a reward for *the sacrifices we had all made* in the years he tried to launch his career as an artist. Earlier, Mom had taken me shopping for what she called a new dress, and I didn't bother to point out that technically this wasn't true, because I didn't own a single dress, so saying this was a new one implied I had an old one. We went to Marshalls, and she helped pick out a dark blue gown that she said would look amazing on my long pretty body, which, again, wasn't entirely true because I had just reached five-foot-three and was still, in my opinion, covered in baby fat.

Why aren't you taking Mom? I ask Dad while we drive to the hotel in his new Kia Rio, the first car our family has owned.

He smiles. *Because Mom came to the launch of my new exhibit last month and next week she's accompanying me to another party. So, this is your turn.*

Dad always has a way of making me feel special. At the hotel, he tosses the keys to the valet, opens my door and escorts me inside by the arm. In the lobby, I expect someone to shout that I don't belong here. No one seems to notice us, and I tell myself, *I can do this. I am such a cuuuute party girl.*

We ride the elevator to the penthouse suite, where a smiling woman meets us in the hall and sticks name tags carefully on my dress and the lapel of my father's jacket.

I'm nervous, I say when we enter the vast suite with its views of South Beach, and Dad keeps me at his side as a woman who identifies herself as an Art Basel hostess introduces us around. We meet three NBA players I have never heard of and one rapper I had, plus all sorts of other people who look rich and a few hipster-types like Dad who look like they wouldn't mind getting rich.

Two of Dad's paintings sit on display in the center of the room along with a dozen others from different artists. Dad is asked to stand with his works, which are, he tells me with a laugh, *perfect examples of contemporary art masterpieces.*

People parade by marveling at his paintings, and Dad is expected to humblebrag. A few people ask actual questions, like which emotions he tried to capture in his work, especially the one that shows a twisty bare tree silhouetted against a bright background of summer colors.

In time, the party begins to change. The lights dim, the music's beat grows louder, and the focus drifts away from the paintings. I finally leave Dad's side when a teenage boy invites me onto the balcony, which he calls *the terrace*, to admire the nighttime view. His name is Riley, and he is rich and cute, a great combination if he wasn't such a dick, a one-upper who spends most of the time bragging about his private school and his sports car and his father's courtside seats at Miami Heat games. He says shit that he thinks is brilliant, and I smile and coolly say, *I know, right?* He asks me one question, *Who did you come with?* And when I answer, *My father, the famous artist*, he grunts unimpressed, the way you would expect the son of a banker to grunt.

Dad always says rich people hate being corrected, so when I point out to Riley that South Beach is merely a neighborhood in the larger city of Miami Beach, and not a separate city as he claims, he gets a little petulant, like I've committed a party foul. He remarks out loud that the terrace is getting *really, really boring.*

A tall, glamorous lady with long earrings walks by carrying a tray of glasses filled with red and white wine, and when Riley and I both take one, she waves a finger at us like we are naughty children and smiles before whispering, *You didn't get those from me.*

The woman is stunning. Riley, who isn't much taller than me, stares directly at her boobs, conveniently at eye level. When she leaves, he turns back to the view of the city, like nothing else on the terrace is worth his expensive gaze. Will I ever grow to be as tall and gorgeous as the woman? Will I ever have plump lips that speak engaging words? It's easy to think I have already reached the peak of my beauty, as mundanely disappointing as it is.

Not that Riley still listens, but I excuse myself to go to the bathroom, and when I come out, I go hunting for Dad. I wander the suite's grand rooms for almost 10 minutes, ignoring the looks of a half-dozen men who each seem to seriously check me out before, I guess, realizing I am nothing more than a kid, though this fact doesn't always make their intense eyes back off. It's all so disgusting, though not entirely.

I find Dad in a bedroom with a group of people huddled around a table covered with piles of white powder, much of it arranged in long, straight lines. I know what the powder is, like I knew exactly what my father meant when he described this party as my reward for the sacrifices our family had endured when he couldn't sell a single painting and my mother's job cutting hair at Great Clips all went to pay the rent and, sometimes, to buy a little weed or blow *to keep the artistic spirits from getting too low.*

One man snorts a line and hands a straw to Dad, who is a wizard at anything drug related. It's during the exchange he sees me by the door.

I turn and run, unsure why anger rattles around in each step.

Soon I am out by the elevator, which an older couple has just entered. I step in with them, and as the door closes, my father comes running after me, too slow like always.

I hurry through the lobby and out onto the street. Unsure where I am going or why, I turn left and soon find myself in a small beachside parking lot, the pounding of waves coming from the other side of a line of thick trees. I run up a set of paint-chipped wooden stairs and onto a promenade where two street people sit on a bench drinking beer from tall cans as lovers stroll by holding hands. Past them I go, down more stairs to the sand. The beach is dark and empty, and I kick off my new shoes, which really are my new shoes, and leave them lying there. I run across the sand nearly forever until it gives way sharply to the water's edge. Down I step to the damp hard-packed beach below, and when I turn and look back toward the promenade, a wall of black sand fills my vision.

A wave breaks behind me with a boom, and I almost jump. I stand there and look out at the lights of a departing cruise ship, wondering if everything my father and mother told me about our new lives with my Dad's newfound success is a lie.

When his voice reaches me, I really do jump.

There she is, my sweet girl. I refuse to turn around. I fight an urge to ask, *What are you even talking about?* When I sense him move close, I take 10 steps down the beach, counting each one in my head. My father sits on the sand above me, and when I turn to face him, he motions for me to join him. He always motions the same way: three quick circular gestures with his right hand that say, *please hurry to me.*

I shake my head and say, *I don't want to get sand on my dress. It's the only one I have.*

He pats his hand on his lap, and after the passage of enough time to show my outrage, I sit like a little girl and not a grown woman who men are starting to notice.

I was panicking because I couldn't find you, he says.

Sure, I say.

You mean everything to me, he says.

Sure, I repeat staring out at the beach, determined not to hear another lie. His body begins shaking, and I look back to see he's sobbing.

I want to cry too, but someone needs to be the strong one. So, I ask, and it's the hardest thing I have ever done, *Do you love me more than your drugs?*

Yes, he says without hesitation.

I want to make him choose, once and forever, between me and his addiction. I want to make him promise he will never again get high. Even I know that each time he gets wasted is like taking another step through the surf and out toward the dangerous open ocean. But I don't want to make him speak the words we know would be a lie. I place my arms around his head and hold him tight, like part of me learned long ago how fleeting this moment would be.

When his tears dry, he picks me up and carries me across the sand. We understand, of course, that he will soon disappoint us both. But not tonight. Not on this night when we celebrate how wonderful life could be.

Back in the warehouse, it's drizzling again through the broken skylights, and I get Physical Ashlee to cover up the girl with one of the yellow jackets I found on my first night here. I want to tell the girl the rain is my father's sweet tears falling gently upon me once again. But the gushing sentimentality and nasty guilt that usually surrounds any memory of Dad seem to have lifted like a fog, revealing our tender moment on the beach for what it really was. A sickness passed from father to daughter. A sickness disguised as love

The story over, the girl finally stirs, her eyes twitching. And I hit her with the final words she needs to hear.

You must figure out how to survive on your own. Because your parents aren't coming to help you. And if they were, they'd only make

everything worse.

I have barely projected these last words at my new friend when my now more enlightened brain interjects. It points out that *making everything worse* is exactly what I am doing with Sam and Gerome. That once again, I am helping give money to addicts, who will happily keep accepting it until it finally kills them.

Oh my God, I groan.

Almost on cue, Sam and Gerome stagger back into the warehouse, mumbling something to me about resting their eyes before we do a little more panhandling.

Wisdom begins swirling around me, enough even to penetrate the blond girl's drug-drenched mind. And I am sure she now understands the heart of her problem is not addiction, because we all have our weaknesses. No, it's fucking dependency.

Mike Chapter 4

Missing: Day Three

The girl circled me patiently as I moved through a ruined building, always keeping her slender form in the shadows, always searching for an opportunity, like hungry wolves did around the nighttime campfires of long-ago hunters. I lowered my eyes and pushed across the garbage-strewn ground, sidestepping two hooded figures sharing a needle as they squatted in a pile of broken glass, their young and tattooed limbs exposed in desperate anticipation. The filthy plaster walls around me grew close, and soon I wound through a tight maze of closet-sized rooms. Overhead, the sun beat down with such force I had to be outside in the Florida sun, though I knew I was indoors with the same certainty I knew I was dreaming. Panic began to eat at me as I stumbled from cubicle to cubicle, never to escape this prison of my own making, and it wasn't until my eyes glanced up that, finally, I bumped against a thick door. Behind it, I was sure, lay a voluminous room where, at last, the woman-child waited.

My hand trembling, I pushed open the door and entered. The girl stood on a chair facing me, the palms on her outstretched arms open to the secretive sky, her face alight with a wide teenaged smile that reminded me of a challenge. She had dark black hair, a face as pale and acne-free as a porcelain doll, an expression of innocence that almost called you to wrap her safely in your arms and cry heavy tears for every injustice she suffered.

She looked beautiful in a way that deeply aroused me. That was until she spoke.

Hi, Granddad. I've been expecting you.

I started turning my eyes away to hide my shame but

stopped, fearing she would be gone when my gaze returned. At this hesitation, her smile grew wider, like she knew my every emotion and could read my thoughts and see straight into my heart, which was impossible because, again, this was a dream, my dream.

I waited for her brown eyes to turn away, for the girl to be shunted off by the next random sequence from my twisted subconscious. Instead, she grew closer and clearer, like she possessed all the power. Like I was living in her dream. She reached for my shoulder, and her touch left me pleading with myself that it didn't feel real.

She smiled again like she wanted me to believe she meant no harm, and she spoke words as clear as any I had ever heard: *It's my Granddad, often talked of, never seen.*

I tried to shout myself awake. Tried to move one limb, one finger, knowing that was how you defeated the frozen terror of sleep paralysis. My thoughts went to Henry Fuseli's terrifying painting *The Nightmare* which depicts an incubus-like creature on a sleeping woman's chest. Did such a demon hold me down?

My groans were met by a comforting voice in the distance. And by an idea claiming to be the truth: that this girl had visited me before in my dreams, always fading from memory as I awoke, just like now. Even this thought began to crumble as my eyes popped open and Maricela, who apparently had fallen asleep beside me on my cramped double bed, asked, "You okay, Mike?"

The digital clock beside my bed read 1:40 a.m. The dream's strange images had retreated, my mind fixating on a more immediate matter. That Maricela, by remaining at my side, had broken what had become a most convenient pattern of her rising and going home after sex.

"I'm fine, but it's late," I said.

"We both fell asleep," she said.

I turned on the bedside lamp, and Maricela began collecting

her things: the obvious like her denim shorts and her bright orange tank top and her cheap rubber flip-flops, all of which she pulled on with the groggy precision of a sleepwalker. And, of course, the less obvious like the envelope that contained five $20 bills and the bassinet on wheels that held her seven-month-old daughter, Estefenia.

I opened the door to my suite, and she pushed the bassinet into the hallway. She dug into her shorts and produced the key to her suite directly across the hall from mine. She pushed her door open, and I followed her inside, towing the bassinet. It was a series of movements we had made enough times to turn them into a routine.

In the darkness of Maricela's suite, it was impossible to see what she was doing, though I knew just the same that she was checking her daughter to make sure the harsh hallway lights had not awoken her. I could almost sense her smile when she saw Estefenia slept soundly.

"Night, Mike," she said, kissing me softly on the cheek, a kind goodbye that always made me feel like a shit.

On my way back across the hall, the usual thought reared up, another newly formed habit, perhaps: how Maricela never complained, a near impossibility for a 24-year-old broke single mother of a colicky baby.

It was her baby who had thrust us together in the first place. I had returned from the pool one day to find an *Out of Service* sign stuck over the elevator button and a woman, who later introduced herself as Maricela, sitting against the wall rocking the largest baby stroller on earth.

I started up the stairs but stopped, probably surprising myself more than I did her.

"You need help with that monstrosity?" I asked.

She shrugged, her eyes playful. "You mean the baby or the stroller?"

She removed her daughter, and I collapsed the stroller to a

more manageable size and began my struggle up four flights of stairs. I followed her down the hallway, curious to see which suite would be hers, and looked suitably stupid when she stopped at the door across from mine.

When she saw my expression, she smiled and said, "Hi, Neighbor."

I stood awkwardly as she leaned down and struggled to find her keys in the stroller's side pouch. Her breasts pushed against her bra and the low-cut shirt she wore. They transfixed me, right up until the moment she found her keys and her eyes rose suddenly to mine.

I stepped back toward my door and mumbled, "Um, sorry."

She looked at me as I searched my pockets for my key and surprised me with her words: "You could have a little of that for $75."

"Make it $100," I answered without hesitation.

"You're a shitty negotiator," she said.

"So are you."

Twenty minutes later, after putting Estefenia down for a nap, Maricela had pushed open my unlocked door and entered with a baby monitor and a sheepish grin. She told me she had only ever slept with kind men, a category she hoped included me. And, oh yes, she had never slept with one for money. I didn't know whether to believe her.

The sex was good, if not a little gentle, likely the result of her saying while she undressed, "Haven't done this since the baby came. Curious to see, you know, if the doctor put everything back the way it had been."

I didn't ask about difficult births or extend the conversation in any way. I just took in her breasts, her strong and smooth legs, the curve of her hips. She was compact, no wasted space, no inefficiencies, a body shape that suited her.

When we finished, I wasted no time relegating myself to the bathroom to get dressed. By the time I returned, she had slipped back into her clothes, and I pointed to the envelope on the nightstand. She collected it and the baby monitor and, before leaving, said, "So I hear that, you know, you don't leave this apartment building, except for the pool. That you get everything delivered. Must make you kind of lonely and desperate for some company. Anyway, you know where to find me."

The words "lonely and desperate" became my code for requesting more time with her, usually about twice a week in the four months since we met. Our time together did evolve, the most significant change coming about two weeks in when I said I didn't trust her shitty baby monitor and suggested she wheel her daughter's bassinet into my suite and leave it by the door, out of sight of the bed.

Next, we started incorporating an early dinner into the session, with me ordering from an eclectic mix of nearby restaurants, from Thai to Cuban. I would spread an old comforter on my filthy carpet, and we would sit down picnic style, Estefenia crawling between us as we ate from paper plates and downed a few beers or a bottle of wine.

I enjoyed our conversations. It wasn't that Maricela was well-read or well-traveled or well versed in anything. But she was frigging smart, the type of smart I had often found overseas in people who had to hustle to survive, people who were born with a brain and little else and knew how to put it to work. Maricela had a way of boiling everything down to its essence, of cutting through the bullshit. That's why it was unwise to let her start analyzing what she called *my situation*.

As someone who truly almost never went out and ordered in everything I needed, my time with Maricela represented a welcome diversion from the way I typically spent my days in Fort Lauderdale: lying by the pool, reading in my room and, occasionally, taking the three-minute round-trip walk around our apartment grounds. It was a routine that began before coronavirus, though the pandemic had made it look nearly normal. Most days, my contact with Maricela represented my only interaction with another person.

"It's a good arrangement for both of us, isn't it?" Maricela asked one day.

Which had made me think about a soldier I met at a U.S. military base in Djibouti, a tiny country in Africa. Over drinks at a bar near the airport, he entertained a small group with his story about screwing a scrawny teenage girl of no more than 13 or 14 who had been propositioning personnel outside the base. He regaled the raucous table with descriptions of the many positions she knew, or at least submitted to, because, after all, in Africa, they started them young. When he sensed my distaste, he looked at me and exclaimed to great laughter, "What? She needed the money."

So, I had become that guy.

* * *

On the morning after Maricela had awoken me from my dream, my door rattled with an impatient knock. When I opened it, Maricela wandered in balancing Estefenia in her left arm and an empty coffee mug in her right and sat down at my table. She did this, appeared abruptly and invited herself in.

"I'll have a dark roast today," she said, and I took her cup and grabbed a pod and got the Keurig working. I had once thought of buying her a Keurig of her own, though had dismissed the idea for reasons I couldn't recall.

"Do you remember what you dreamt about last night?" she asked. "You were, like, making a lot of noise. Guess that's why you always kick me out of bed right away. So I won't have to hear that."

I took a seat across from her and said, "I don't kick you out of bed right away."

She snorted. "Okay. You stay and lie close and talk for about five minutes now. That's all the intimacy you can stand. I get it. But back to the dream. Is it tied to what you've, you know, seen through your work?"

I would tell her I don't remember. Simple. Yet this dream, I realized with alarm, hadn't entirely slipped into the shadows the moment my eyes popped open; it remained defiantly in sight, daring me to acknowledge it, like a slightly disturbing cell phone photo you see the morning after a party. I heard myself say, "I dreamed about this pale-faced girl standing in a broken building and claiming to be my granddaughter as she stared me down with these freakishly smart eyes."

This answer appeared to jolt Maricela.

"So, in those few minutes when we talk after doing the dirty, and in all our meals together, you have never mentioned having kids. Definitely no mention of grandkids. In fact, you told me more than once you have no family. Like actually none."

I shrugged. "I think I only dreamed it because some loony woman approached me by the pool the day before and put that thought in my head."

"So you're saying there's no chance you have kids, maybe grandkids?"

"No. I'm not saying that at all."

* * *

That night I would make one of those seemingly mundane decisions you later realize amounted to much more than you first thought. My right knee sore with arthritis, I took the elevator instead of pounding down the stairs as I headed out for a walk around the apartment grounds

As the elevator doors began closing at their usual glacial pace, the sound of loud and joyful female voices crept in. I pumped the close-door button and cursed when this did nothing. The second before the doors touched together, a long, bare arm pushed inside followed by a woman in a tight red dress. She smiled at me as two more joined us, the others probably Cuban like the first, all in similar party attire, one of them, upon closer inspection by my mediocre eyes, Maricela.

As we slowly descended, it was easy to notice how good Maricela looked. Her short dress clearly announced she had lost most of her pregnancy weight on those long walks with Estefenia, and tonight she wore makeup, a lot of it, for the first time I could recall. She appeared unburdened too, maybe by the freedom of a real babysitter and not her mother, whom Maricela told me loved to utter the phrase "I told you so" about the endless list of what went wrong in her daughter's life.

I waited for Maricela to introduce me, and when she didn't, it was obvious she hadn't told her friends about me and our arrangement, which suited me fine.

The elevator, awash in the smell of cheap perfume and hairspray, was soon overcome too by their conversation.

"Oh, girl," said the girlfriend wearing the shiniest shade of blue one could imagine. "We are gonna get you some tonight. All those months clutching the statue of Saint Maria Goretti and praying for forgiveness when what you needed is to get laid. Like really laid."

Her other friend howled and said, "Oh, and your sugar daddy, he don't count, not from what we've heard."

At this, Maricela turned to me, her eyes round and almost apologetic, her lips trying to form words she couldn't speak.

Her friends noticed, and the one in blue looked at me and said, "Oh, sorry for our language, mister. Just excited for our friend is all."

As they laughed, I half expected Maricela to speak up and explain that in fact, her sugar daddy wasn't an exotic person from a better part of town. He was the neighbor across the hall, the man in this very elevator, the one who apparently didn't fuck her properly.

But she looked away, and the elevator bumped to a stop on the ground floor, and as the door opened, an emotion both desperate and unexpected stirred in me. It wasn't overwhelming; in fact, it barely registered. But it had registered enough for me to notice, enough for me to remember what I needed to do.

In Seattle, the rainy winter had given way to spring. I could give my neglected house a good cleaning and stop drinking for a few weeks and, who knows, maybe accept an overseas assignment that would reboot my career and unstick my life. And as a bonus, never hear anyone use the words "your granddaughter" and "trouble" in the same sentence.

I followed the women out into the lobby, aware I had made my decision to leave Florida in less than one minute.

When they reached the door, Maricela's friends exited into the humid air. She paused and held it open for me with fingers adorned by jewelry and brightly painted fake nails that my eyes had never seen. I stopped abruptly and gestured with my hand for her to go on. She gave me her comforting look that said everything would be okay, and I knew she would be right, having learned long ago not to get caught up in painful longing. She turned and hurried to catch her friends, the door between us swinging shut with a dull metallic thud.

Mike Chapter 5

1980 Bellingham, Washington

Kimberly wore jean shorts and a halter top, a hint of light brown clinging tenuously to her pale skin, as she and four others burst out of the Douglas firs and climbed down a sandstone formation to the rocky beach below. She didn't look at me or any of the three dozen other teenagers who knocked back Olympia beer while a ghetto blaster discharged The Clash loud enough to keep others from exploring this isolated shoreline stretch of Larrabee State Park. She had probably arrived in a car with Scott and Jim, or Jimmy as he liked to be called, as if he had changed in any way decent.

When Kimberly finally noticed me, she smiled before spreading her towel on a boulder and coming over to where I sat on a log and giving me the briefest of hugs. It was a Saturday afternoon in late July, and we hadn't seen each other since our final days of Grade 10 a month or so earlier.

"Hey, stupid," she said almost shyly.

Kimberly and I hadn't exactly become estranged. We just never grew close in all the ways I wanted in the 23 months since we met in the group home on Washington Street. We had only lived there for five months before the Jennings decided, one could assume, that looking after five foster kids wasn't the windfall they expected and not without its difficulties. One by one, we were relocated in the days before the Jennings moved away in search of a better-paying job for Mr. Jennings. Jimmy and Scott left first, followed by Richard, Kimberly and finally me, an order likely running from least to most popular. Of course, I was surely the only one who fucked Mrs. Jennings, our last coupling coming with a flood of tears on the night before I would leave to join an older couple on the north end of town.

In the months to follow, me and Kimberly occasionally hung out at school, remaining close-but-distant friends. We shared conversations about practically everything, except one taboo topic: how we had wound up in the foster care system. I always suspected she never told her own predictably sad story, which had remained a secret, because it would oblige me to tell mine, and everyone knew that no one had a crappier story than me. So we talked about other things, and I sometimes put a hand on her arm or leg while giving her a longing look. She usually smacked my hand away, affectionately calling me stupid, making sure none of our intimacies ever turned full-on physical.

Even as I spoke to her on that Saturday at the beach, I worried, like always, that she saved the most intimate parts of herself for someone else, though there were never any signs of this, and she possibly remained a virgin. A hot ginger virgin.

"Hey, spaz," Jimmy hollered. "How's little Mikey?"

"Actually, it's still Mike."

"Actually, you should shut the fuck up."

Already tired of his company, I joined a group of classmates who stood in calf-deep water drinking warm beer and tossing rocks at nearby boulders poking from the water.

In time, I found myself smoking a Maui wowie joint with a girl at the edge of where Kimberly, Scott and Jimmy loitered with a few older teens I didn't know. Kimberly drank and laughed while not joining in the conversation much, even though she always had plenty of intelligent shit to say.

I had driven to the beach with a guy named Thomas who had signaled he needed to leave for work. Which sucked because I wanted to sit down and reconnect with Kimberly. I stood, intending to say my goodbyes, when I heard Jimmy say to her, "Time to pay your debt, girl."

She shrugged, not moving. Jimmy flicked her arm with his middle finger and began to climb the rocky hillside that looked over the beach. Kimberly followed without reacting to the smirks from Scott and those who remained behind.

My joint finished, I needed to find Thomas and head out. Instead, I made my way towards the woods where Kimberly and Jimmy had disappeared. They hadn't gone far. Halfway down a rugged trail they had stopped, and for a second it was like my eyes, or maybe my brain, had malfunctioned. Kimberly was bent over a stump, her shorts at her ankles, taking it from Jimmy, who looked relaxed and almost a little disinterested as he thrust into her, his ass cheeks contracting and releasing.

I winced and began drawing back so they wouldn't notice me. Yet something told me to move forward, which I did. Kimberly heard my footsteps on the rocky ground and turned her head my way. She stood up straight, grasping for her shorts with panicked hands.

"What are you doing?" Jimmy hollered before he looked at me and shrugged. "Get the fuck out of here, Mikey. And you, Kim, get back on the business end of this thing."

She rushed past me, her hand stuffed across her mouth. I turned and followed, leaving Jimmy alone with his wasted erection.

I caught up to Kimberly as she climbed down the last few steps to the beach. She grabbed her towel and a plastic bag she'd brought, and when I reached for her arm, she gave me a shove. She wouldn't look at me, and I let her go because, like always, I didn't know what else to do.

From up above the beach came Jimmy's voice. "You little fucker."

The boom box played a Supertramp song. Almost everyone turned to Jimmy, anxious to witness the entertaining shit that would ensue once he closed the final 30 feet to where I languished at the water's edge. I leaned down and picked up a softball-sized rock and waited.

For me, time had nearly run out, and what little remained would fly by in a panicked rush. Yet the opposite happened.

Time slowed, and maybe my heartbeat too. My thoughts became focused. It hadn't been fucked-up lousy luck that put me here with a rock in my hand. Not at all. This was precisely where I needed to be.

Like a brushed-back baseball batter charging the mound, Jimmy sprinted the final 10 feet while pulling his right arm back in the mother-of-all-punches, which he threw at my head. I ducked and stepped to my left, and as his punch tore by my right ear, I swung the rock at the side of his head with all my strength. A hollow cracking sound rang out, and he staggered back.

I didn't wait for him to regroup. I stepped forward and pounded his face twice more with the rock, catching him above his left eye. His legs failed and he went down, blood spurting from a gash on his forehead.

Jimmy's friends would be on me in seconds, which was too bad. I wanted to keep pounding his head until his skull opened to reveal his tiny lizard brain. Scott appeared first and what he did shook me from my rage. He stared down at his friend, his face without expression.

He turned to me and said, "Fucking party wrecker."

A girl arrived with a multi-colored beach towel and applied pressure to Jimmy's forehead. They helped him sit up, though his head bobbed up and down.

The rock slipped from my hand. My eyes searched the beach for Kimberly without success. Someone slipped a different cassette into the boom box, and a small cheer came up when the first pounding drumbeats of AC/DC's *Highway to Hell* began. The pop of more beer cans opening sounded in celebration. By now, Scott and a couple of guys had stood Jimmy up and were, with some difficulty, escorting him up one of the flattest trails leading from the beach to the parking lot.

Thomas had left, so I began looking for Kimberly. For the next half hour, I searched the parking lot, the bandshell, the boat launch, the main beach and a handful of the trails around the park. No Kimberly.

I walked up to Chuckanut Drive, intending to hitchhike home. A girl's voice struck me like a slap. "I hate you, you know." Kimberly sat on a rock in a clump of waist-high grass, her head barely visible.

She stood and walked past me to the road, where she crossed and stuck out her thumb. I took a place beside her and stuck mine out too.

"I could get a ride a lot easier without you standing next to me," she said.

"Guess there's all kinds of shit you could do easier without me around."

We didn't talk for the next few minutes, and my eyes began sizing her up. Kimberly had somehow both filled out and lost weight at the same time, and she now stood on long bare legs bent forward slightly at her slim waist as she stuck her thumb out. Her freckled shoulder blades protruded so sharply from her back they could have hidden a pair of angel wings, though apparently, she was no fucking angel.

A Buick full of guys slowed down and hollered a lewd remark about Kimberly's tits before speeding away, horn blaring. Her raised middle finger found nothing but exhaust fumes. I started to tell her she had earned that type of treatment, before clamping my mouth shut and wondering what was wrong with me.

Kimberly grew impatient and began walking down the road toward Bellingham. I followed, raising my thumb at the sound of each oncoming car. The road was narrow, winding and enclosed by a thick evergreen forest on each side, meaning there was almost no shoulder to walk on and cars seeing us had few places to pull over, even if they wanted to. Dozens of cars passed dangerously close without slowing, and when I had almost resigned myself to walking all the way home, a 1960s-era pickup truck rounded the corner and stopped, and from inside grinned the relaxed face of Tim Kolchuk, who had also attended the beach party.

Through the open window, he shouted, "Do you have a death wish or something?"

"Jimmy got what he deserved," I said.

"I'm sure he did. But do you two have a death wish walking on this road? Get in."

We eagerly climbed in, Kimberly sitting in the middle of the bench seat next to Tim, someone I knew little about, other than his father owned the largest lumber yard/hardware store in Whatcom County.

Kimberly, intent on ignoring me, thanked him and pointed to the tape sticking out of an 8-Track player mounted underneath the dashboard.

"What's this?" she asked, forcing a slight grin.

Tim bit his lip and then shrugged. "You know. That fucking movie from a couple of years back."

Kimberly pushed in the tape, and the disco beat of *Saturday Night Fever* exploded.

Tim laughed and grappled for the volume knob to turn it down, or maybe off, in embarrassment. He surprised me by cranking it up and singing along, his grinning mouth emitting a high, piercing sound. His wacky presence was a welcome distraction, even when he shouted, "When you play music, you need to go all-in like Mike does when he fights."

We reached town, and Kimberly asked to be dropped off downtown near the courthouse, a 10-minute walk from her home. I jumped out too, in spite of Tim's offer to take me a mile or two closer to where I lived. We waved goodbye to Tim, and I began following Kimberly as she crossed Whatcom Creek on Dupont Street and took a trail along the creek's banks.

"You stalking me?" she asked when she saw I hadn't turned off toward home.

"Just wondered if you want to talk," I said.

She stopped walking and gave me a shove. "So, are you here to get the same thing from me as Jimmy. Because we both know that's all you've wanted since we first met?"

"I don't want anything other than to say I'm sorry."

Kimberly took a few steps towards an evergreen tree stretching out of the creek. "Over here," she called. "You want to fuck me up against this tree? I'm serious, Mike. Let's do it so you can finally leave me alone."

"Funny, you pick this as your route home?"

She rolled her eyes. "Stop feeling sorry for yourself. This is the fastest way. Besides, I didn't ask you to follow me."

Kimberly knew better than anyone how I hated Whatcom Creek. For years it drew me in repeated frustration thanks to a single black-and-white photograph of my teenage mother standing in a shallow strip of flowing water as she clung to a baby that was supposedly me. At least according to the photo's back, which was dated September 23, 1964, and contained my name and that of my mother. My dad, I assumed, was sort of in the photo, too; a single blurry finger cut across the top right corner of the image.

Like the other two photos I possessed showing my family in happier days, meaning everyone-still-alive days, my mother's smiling face always captured my attention. Was the smile forced or real? And if it was real, what had gone so terribly wrong in the years to come?

With my fingers anxiously wrapped around this one thin fragment of my earliest life, I had spent countless hours walking the banks of Whatcom Creek in search of the exact spot where the photo was taken. Once I had found the location, I would know much more about my parents. Maybe it was shot in Whatcom Falls Park, where a happy couple with a newborn could find peace in nature's beauty. Or maybe it was snapped at the point the creek flowed fast into Bellingham Bay, a place, if you found the courage, you could place your baby's head underwater, release the body into the current and watch it get swept out to sea. The answer, or answers, never came, even after repeated visits where I covered every inch of the creek's winding route, twice with Kimberly at my side, our sneakers and jean legs wet as we waded out into the water hoping to match the image captured on paper with what lay before us. Last year I finally gave up, renouncing the creek and the devious fucker who had written Whatcom Creek on a photo so obviously taken somewhere else. I also renounced the obviously fake smile on my mother's lying face. And in doing so I had taken the photo and dropped it into the fast-flowing creek, watching it spin away. Finally, her presence did exist somewhere in the damn creek, even if only on a piece of photo paper doomed to rot.

Now, all these months later, I found myself back at this place I swore I never wanted to see again. I turned from the creek, from Kimberly, and sat on a patch of gravel-covered dirt.

Kimberly surprised me by taking a spot next to me. We sat in an agitated silence for a good 10 minutes, the first hint of evening dew bringing a sudden coolness. She leaned close, her shoulder touching mine in what would surely be our last moment together, and said, "It was right there. That trail up from the creek. The second time I helped you try to find the spot where the photo of you and your mom was taken. You walked up that trail and swore you would drop the whole thing forever."

I nodded, surprised she remembered. "So. I was right," I said. "We aren't here by accident."

"Nothing's ever a damn accident," she said, shifting on the hard ground. She studied me. "And have you dropped it?" she asked.

"You know I have."

"So, you see it is possible. To toss aside a hopeless infatuation."

I turned away and thought about the afternoon I left the creek for the last time. How, like now, I struggled to look at Kimberly, my face so consumed by emotions that left me embarrassed and confused. She had taken me in her thin arms, her eyes searching mine from beneath the brim of her baseball cap, and squeezed me hard like she understood everything.

Maybe that was when my longing had shifted from a teenage mother I would never know to another teenage girl I would forever struggle to get close to.

Kimberly touched my arm, a jolt back to the present. "There is an endless number of reasons why I would fuck an asshole like Jimmy and not a decent person like you," she said.

"How about one good one?"

"I'm tempted to give you all of them. Just to shut you up. But, okay, I'll give you one, and you will agree I'm right."

"I'm listening."

She took a deep breath. "You and me, we both know first-hand that sex is exploitive. That it's an act one person inflicts on another, and it messes them both up forever, so it's not something two good friends should ever willingly do."

I took her words and began processing them. I squeezed them hard, like a hug from Kimberly where every raw emotion and bone and muscle in her body were laid bare. When I turned back to Kimberly, it was her turn to look away, and I couldn't tell whose shame made her hide her eyes.

"How did you find out?" I asked.

"Old house. Thin walls. The way you and Mrs. Jennings both acted. I don't know, I just did."

"And what about you? How…"

She cut me off. "Before you ask that, let me throw a question at you. Did what Mrs. Jennings did to you make you happy or sad?"

"I guess you'll think I'm some sick, pathetic fuck if I say happy? That it made me happy, but maybe not for the reasons you think."

She considered my answer for much longer than I expected. Finally, she said, "No. No, I won't think that. But if you liked it for any reason, it's proof."

"Of what?"

"Proof it fucked you up inside, and you don't even know it."

I shrugged, unsure what else to do.

She faced me and crossed her freckled legs. "I liked Mrs. Jennings, but she was lucky I didn't call the police."

"Okay," I said. "Enough about me..."

She brushed a strand of hair from her face, and I was sure she would use her superior brain capacity to shift the conversation back to me. Or she would stand and walk home alone, and this door that had swung wide open between us would slam shut forever. She didn't move, however, and we sat in silence, our universe slowly returning to the shape it had once been.

When she spoke, I jumped.

"I'm going to tell you everything. About my stepfather, about the 'accidental' touching that grew into something more. About the Bellingham cops who tried to make it sound like it was my fault. About my mother, who knew but did nothing and even tried to cover it up and went to jail too. And you're going to sit there and shut up and not cry a single tear for me, because you went through the same thing with Mrs. Jennings, even if you were too stupid to know it and to fight back like I did. And when I'm done, we're going to get up and go home and never speak of it again."

"You don't need to tell me," I said.

"Yes, I do. So shut up for once."

Even before Kimberly began telling her story, I knew exactly what would happen when she finished. I would get up and go home silently as she wanted, but I still wouldn't regret what had happened with Mrs. Jennings. The changes in me would come in other ways, in ways Kimberly had not intended, because even as stupid as I might be, I could see how much pain it took for her to relive her story.

She brushed her hair back, and as she started to speak, every cell in my body ached more than ever to slide closer to her.

Ashlee Chapter 4

Missing: Day Four

Gerome and Sam tell me they are ready for some more panhandling, their hands shaking with anticipation. For once, I do the right thing. I explain I must leave and let my soul travel to a glorious destination it has longed to visit. Their smiles fade quickly, which sucks, but at least it won't be me who kills them. Besides, maybe without me and the extra cash, they will become desperate enough to try for a spot in the state-run detox program they keep talking about applying for.

They do badger me with kind questions, like where I will go and whether I have a home or friends I can lean on. I am deliberately vague, telling them I have looked into my future and seen my soul connecting with others in an Arizona desert. This leads to them asking, a little desperately, if I require more panhandling cash for such a long trip. I tell them no.

Before we say goodbye, I promise to give them a gift far greater than cash: the big, satisfying story of my Great Awakening, with a side dish of everything they need to know about time and space and reality. They look at each other and nod, and we leave the warehouse and buy three more Cokes and find a spot on a bench.

They imagine me beginning with these words: *My awakening happened, according to our species' time construct, a few months ago in the office of my beloved therapist, Rachel.*

Sam says he likes the name Rachel, and then he and Gerome fall mostly silent like the good listeners they are.

Partway through the story, I get a little sidetracked when I start talking about the great ideas and inspiration I have gained not just from Rachel but from books, even if it meant many lonely, nerderiffic nights lying on my bed and reading the latest non-fiction work on the nature of reality or the newest blog on what the universe is made of. I especially liked reading, I tell them, about how science, over the years, has exposed the greatest untruths of our existence. That the earth is flat. That the universe revolves around our little blue and green planet. That time and space and everything we see are real.

I love it, I gush to Sam and Gerome, that kick-ass scientists are questioning what we experience in our day-to-day lives, arguing that our false beliefs about our perceptions prevent us from solving the greatest mystery ever: what is consciousness? My two new friends listen closely to the theory at the heart of this belief: that our eyes don't actually see the various people and objects we think they see, because none of it exists, so our minds instead create icons like birds and trees and rocks and the homeless guy down the street, all of it to help our species survive.

Sam and Gerome exchange a few glances but seem to understand what I am saying. I know this because Gerome asks, possibly blowing his own freaking mind, *if nothing exists unless we are there to construct it, then did the Big Bang begin with human observation of it?*

They have plenty of other questions, too, like how it is possible I am not sitting next to them on the bench when they so clearly see me. Sadly, none of this talk gets us closer to defining consciousness and understanding why we are here and where the fuck *here* really is.

Anyway, I finish the story of my Great Awakening, and Gerome nods politely and whispers, *Okay then.* For him and Sam, it may not be a revelation as big as the fiery collision of stars that spawns a black hole, but it's a start.

They both gently hug the physical presence they think is me, and we say a muted goodbye. I am sure they understand it's for the best we're apart because everyone knows that great darkness always follows the brightest light.

My physical sidekick has gone less than a block when Sam appears at her side. He's holding the fortune-telling sign and asks, *Can you tell me exactly what you say, you know, when you read people's fortunes?*

You mean, how I do it, how I actually read their fortunes? he hears me ask.

Well, yes, how you believe you do it. And especially how you tell them you do it.

Sam imagines we sit on a low brick wall where I offer a detailed explanation about fortune telling, one that is interrupted when my soul focuses its attention down the street and sees Gerome quickly approaching with the red-haired woman from the youth shelter. And, of course, I understand in a heartbeat that these two kind men believe they are helping me by trying to haul me back into a world that's supposed to make perfect sense but never does.

Physical entities that have guzzled down two bottles of Coke are damn fast, and soon this one's left behind Sam and Gerome and the red-haired woman and retrieved her purse from the warehouse and taken a seat inside a nearby coffee shop full of edgy urban white and Hispanic girls drinking expensive spiced lattes. The baristas don't want her there, maybe because they know there's something commonly temporal about her, but she buys three expensive drinks before she looks out the window and sees something that would stop my own damn heart if I still had one.

Ashlee Chapter 5

Twenty Weeks Before Missing

My awakening begins in the office of my beloved therapist, Rachel. And it comes in the form of a six-word inspirational quotation that I am not meant to notice as impressionable little old me leafs through a book full of *much more appropriate* quotes, which means less bat-shit crazy quotes, during my final session with her.

Rachel never squeezed my hand in a patronizing way and told me I was *special* because my synesthesia allowed me to experience so much more of the world than most others. She never pushed anti-depressants on me either, at least not successfully. And best of all, at least according to my parents, she was free, her services provided once a week to me and Miami's other vulnerable teens, thanks to a rich benefactor's generous donation.

Unfortunately, all nourishing things have a shelf life, and this would surely be the case with Rachel. A woman of her obvious talent and grace would eventually build up her practice enough that she no longer needed to perform cut-rate sessions with fucked-up kids when she could do the same at full price with fucked-up wealthy adults. I knew it was nearly time to say goodbye once Rachel had relocated from the back of a dingy shopping mall, where she answered her own phone and wrote out her own receipts, to a fancy office with a beautiful secretary who always blanched when she remembered the freaky girl named Ashlee was a charity case.

I regret not opening up more to Rachel in our sessions. I avoided the worst of my secrets and fears, the ones that seemed to announce to the world what a whiny little loser I had become. Anyway, I always told myself I was working up to talking about them. Just the same, Rachel was great, sometimes even sharing her difficulties with me, usually loneliness, hard to believe, because she was so smart and pretty. When I would tell her I couldn't believe she wasn't in some exciting romance-novel relationship, she would say something wise, like, *Life doesn't always work the way you think it should.*

That makes me sad, I responded once, leading to a long discussion about *tempering one's expectations.*

In my very last session with Rachel, she spends the first 15 minutes talking up her replacement, a woman named Belinda who hasn't yet grown her practice enough that she could afford to jettison the subsidized cases like me.

She's a friend of mine, and you'll love her, Rachel says. *I've told her all about you, and she can't wait for you to set up your first appointment, which I keep telling you that you need to do right away.*

Rachel tries to get me to call right there from her office. I refuse, saying I forgot my cell phone, which contains my jam-packed calendar. Can Rachel detect my iPhone's faint outline in my hoodie pocket? She studies me for a little too long and then writes out Belinda's name and number on a piece of paper, for the third time that month, and pushes it into my damp palm.

We spend much of that final session reviewing my so-called progress, with Rachel, for a change, doing most of the talking. She focuses on one of her favorite topics, the inner and outer worlds we live in. *Remember,* she says, *the inner is the thoughts and feelings and perceptions that make up your own personal reality, the outer the more concrete physical world that makes up our shared external reality. The two are connected, and each can affect the other, right?*

I nod.

Like if you got hit by a bus on the way home. That would be the external world impacting your internal world. Might make you forever scared of buses, right, assuming you survived?

I nod again, wishing I had never mentioned how much I hate

taking the bus to see her.

So, can you give me an example of how your inner world could affect the outer world of the oncoming bus in a positive way in this same situation? How your feelings or thoughts could change something in this exterior world?

I think carefully, pretty sure this is like a final exam question that will give me access to a more enlightened world, pretty sure, too, that I will disappoint her. *I guess I could use psychic power to move the bus. You know, make it fly into the air over my head at the last second, so I don't get hit.*

How about something a little more plausible and grounded in reality.

I push further into my brain. *I could go into the future, see that I'm about to get hit by a bus and take a different route home.*

Or, she says, *you could make sure you have your shit together. That you're mentally in a good place so you don't have your head lost in thoughts as you step off the curb, or worse, so you don't deliberately step out in front of the bus.*

I like it when she swears. It is her way of telling me she means business.

You need to keep working with a therapist, Ashlee. There are no shortcuts. You need to get stronger to endure the difficult world we live in. Or else you will never be safe from that bus.

She's right about the connection between what happens in my head and in the outside world. But even she must admit my answers about how this works are far more interesting.

As my session winds down, Rachel hands me a book of inspirational quotes. *Pick one that resonates with you, read it to me, and we'll see if we can both use it in the weeks ahead to change our worlds, internal and external, for the better.*

I'm not trying to be a little shit. But many of the quotes are so sucky. I find a good one from Einstein: *The true sign of intelligence is not knowledge but imagination.* But screw it, at the last second, I substitute it with something even better.

I lean forward and say, *It's by Pablo Picasso.* "*Everything you can imagine is real.*"

Does Rachel sigh like she wishes she had ripped that damn page from the book? Can I almost hear her familiar words, *delusion can't save you,* trying to claw themselves to the tip of her tongue? *Listen, I admire your creative mind,* she says, *but I can think of more appropriate quotes. Maybe for discussion with your new therapist, you can find one about perseverance through difficult times.*

She stands, and I leap to my feet and hug her before she can stop me. I know therapists aren't supposed to get emotionally attached to their patients, especially the suicidal ones. She squeezes my back gently, more than I expected.

You've really helped me, I tell her as she steps back.

This remark will surely make her smile, even if we both know it is an exaggeration. But instead, her eyes look the way I suspect they would when she watches a sad movie curled up alone on her couch. And as I leave Rachel's office for the last time, it's painfully clear how right she is about my feelings having the power to impact the outside world. About this mysterious correlation.

On the way to the bus stop, the piece of paper with my new therapist's name and phone number makes itself known from inside my jean pocket. The damn thing is heavy like a rock. I remove the paper from my pocket and a pen from my purse and, oh yes I do, scratch out Belinda's name and number with a flurry of blue ink. On the other side, I write the Picasso quote, *Everything you can imagine is real,* before stuffing it back in my pocket.

The same homeless guy sits in his regular spot outside a liquor store with Georgie, his glam but dirty white-haired poodle. Funny, I don't know the guy's name, but I do understand he needs cash to feed himself and Georgie, and he hasn't had a drink *for going on two years,* even though I have more than once peeked back to see him go inside the store after receiving the usual three dollars of my babysitting cash. Of course, everyone knows we all sometimes need to take the dangerous little shortcut that never gets us where we are expected to go but does give us a teeny bit of pleasant distracting relief from the exhausting shit.

In the distance, I can see my bus, a small square of vivid blue that pops out of the surrounding dull expanse of sun-bleached grey, like it is screaming to me, *Remember, girl, what you learned today*. And I do remember.

Just then a rotten smell reaches my nose from the overflowing garbage container to my left. The supposed garbage container I can smell and see and even touch if I choose to get closer.

As I plug my nose, I consider the Picasso quote, *Everything you can imagine is real*, and marvel at how this genius had years earlier come to the same conclusion as today's scientists. Everything we imagine *is* real because that is all we do: we construct in our minds the world we live in, including all the people and objects and animals. It is real to us, even if this reality is a big fat lie, or maybe what Rachel would call a delusion.

The garbage bin looks and smells and probably feels so repulsive because it is filled with germs that can make me very sick. My brain and eyes and nose and fingers all want to keep me safe. But they also want to keep me from discovering and messing with a deeper truth because some of the best scientists agree there is something profound hiding next to the electrons and magnetic fields and all that stuff that we choose not to see.

And what is that more profound truth? What is the correlation between my inner world and the outer world where I live? What is this one bit of mystery in our otherwise dull lives? I am surely on the verge of figuring this out, this one answer that would allow my very existence to suck far less and maybe even become bearable.

The bus stop has no bench or shelter, and I sit on the ground meditation-style, avoiding most of the spit. I stare down and think, like really think. Nothing happens other than my bus passing by. I don't know how many other buses pass or how many long breaths I exhale in fear and frustration or how many times I rock back and forth or how many strange looks I get or how many times I pray for Mom or Dad to show up and take me home before a burst of anger surges through me, and I like it. Right then, I quit thinking and start feeling. Which is way better, even if much of what I experience is a dull pain rising through the concrete and into my tired body. My legs are crossed, and near the spot where my open-toe shoes come together, a clump of dandelions grows defiantly from a dirty sidewalk crack. There are three yellow flowers that look like tiny umbrellas and a third that has gone to seed, its white globe joyfully perched atop an erect stem, eagerly sharing itself with the world. People call dandelions a weed, douse them in poison, rip their heads off, try anything to destroy this unexpected beauty they can't control. These dandelions, I sense, have deep roots and screw-you grins and kind souls. Tough little motherfuckers.

As the sun drops low, I stare at them, my fingers and eyes caressing their soft flowers, whose colors grow brighter in the twilight. It's the strangest thing; it feels like they're staring back at this girl who is the pesky dandelion of the human world, often judged for taking root where she shouldn't, frequently trampled on by careless others, usually never seen for what she is. This thought makes me smile, and then something even stranger happens. The dandelions start moving, their straight stems swaying like tall trees in a storm. Only there is no storm. Just a late-day calm, a sticky heat crying for a breeze. I cup my hand around the dandelions, the way you would protect a match from the wind. Again, there is no wind. And they keep moving, locking and popping like hip-hop stars doing a happy dance they surely want me to notice, parachute-like seeds floating up and catching in my hair and on my eyelids.

My new friends move until they are spent, until the three

flowers and the once-seedy globe pull close for the long night ahead. I close my eyes, stretch my back and don't so much think about what I witnessed as let it wash over me. What engulfs me is a gently loving natural world that is aware of my presence. That is making me aware of its presence. It comes to me fast, a sudden rainstorm, and I cry out because it's too much, then it slows, a warming sun on a winter day. I want to analyze it with my conscious mind, with my wildly spinning three-pound brain, though I understand this is not the way. So I take it in like you would a hard kiss or comforting embrace.

At first, it communicates only in feelings, welcoming and loving, until a voice heavy with the experience of infinite lifetimes abruptly puts these feelings into words. It whispers, *Your gracious soul needs to understand that humanity is a blight and family is a blight. You must free yourself.*

Then it says, *It's not safe sitting here so long after sunset. You need to get up and go home.*

I open my eyes to see that darkness has fallen like a giant eyelid dropping over the earth. The busy street has gone ghostly quiet except for the occasional passing car or groups of noisy people lurching home from a bar. No one has checked to see if I am okay, and no one will. I am on my own, except I am not. I have my new connection with the natural world, this universal consciousness older than time that I have been allowed to join.

I nearly crap myself when my phone reveals it's past 11, which means my bus is no longer running and, worse, I have been gone almost seven hours without getting a single call or text from anyone. As I stand and start the long walk home through the human-created outer realm of my city, the collective inner world opens wide for me with more hard-won knowledge. *Take the busier street a block up; it's safer. You need to stop to eat and pee at the all-night McDonald's on the right. Don't make eye contact with that shirtless man standing on the corner. Don't let your beautiful, beautiful heart grow heavy.*

By the time I reach home and climb the stairs to our apartment, where music blares, it's clear I have tapped a source of support and knowledge that will allow me to exert some control over my life. More than that, I have become part of a far truer world that most people have been conditioned not to see.

I go inside and stand in the middle of a whacked-out Friday night gathering that smells like cheap wine and puke. Everyone, especially Mom and Dad, is too wasted to notice me; it's like I am not there, which is possible. Mom's ginger-haired friend Zoey finally sees me and pulls me against her pregnant belly and starts dancing, if her crashing around the room in bare feet can really be called that.

I should be mad at my parents, but I am not. Because, like most other people, they are simply a weight on everything good and authentic in this world. More so because I love them and am tied to them like a leaky boat paddled deep into the Everglades.

So when super-blitzed Mom finally lays her bloodshot eyes on me and rips me from Zoey's arms and whispers that she loves *her girl* and spins me around like we are sharing some precious mother-daughter time and not just stumbling through another messed-up night of epic hurt, I don't even bother telling her about my Great Awakening and how I no longer need her.

Mike Chapter 6

Missing: Day Four

When the knock came, I knew it would be Maricela at my door with her baby and an empty coffee cup and an almost-sincere apology for what had happened in the elevator last night with her two friends. I wouldn't answer, denying her an opportunity to see my packed suitcase. Instead, I would phone her from Seattle and tell her she could borrow my Keurig and my car while I was gone, which wouldn't be for long, except that last part would be a lie.

I sighed. She knocked again. I waited for her to holler, *You're not at the pool, so I know you're in there.*

She didn't shout out but continued banging, which should have been a clue. I opened the door to face the woman who claimed to be my dead son's wife. She was clearly high because, well, a leopard always has spots.

Her voice, however, sounded a little more down-to-earth than the last time we met. She calmly said, "Let's start again. My name's Kacey. I'm your daughter-in-law. We need to talk."

I stepped out of my suite and closed the door behind me. "You need to leave. Right now."

"Hear me out, and I'll go. You can decide whether you want to help your granddaughter or whether you want to continue being a selfish fucker."

I laughed, comforted that by tomorrow she would need to fly to Seattle if she wanted to arrive unannounced at my door. Maybe that's why I confidently led her into my suite and showed her my packed suitcase and my emailed boarding pass for a 7:15 p.m. flight. I even pointed to the Seattle Seahawks jersey I wore with departed quarterback Russell Wilson's number 3 on its back, more proof I had already checked out of Florida.

She studied the boarding pass before turning her eyes to me.

"My God, now that I'm not so high, I can see it clearly. You look so much like him, like my Joshua."

She lowered her head and spoke the next few words staring at my filthy carpet. "I'm glad I got to see what he would have looked like if he had been able to grow old."

For a couple of reasons, this was the verbal equivalent of hitting below the belt. I took her elbow, gently this time, and pointed to the door.

"Acting is not your strong suit," I told her. "And neither is writing notes supposedly from my granddaughter."

She feigned surprise. "You got a note from Ashlee? When? Can I see it?"

"Oh, I think you've already seen it."

"I didn't write you a note. It must be her. Ashlee. Please show me."

I removed the note from the drawer and handed it to her. "Why don't you take it with you."

The woman read the note and shrieked. "That's her handwriting. She must be close. When did you get this?"

"I think you know," I said, trying to herd her toward the door.

"Wait," she said, reaching into her purse. She removed her phone and scrolled through God knows what before a sad smile emerged, one possibly sincere. She pushed the device toward me.

"That's her," she said, waiting for me to take the phone. "Ashlee. Your granddaughter."

I stared at her outstretched hand.

"Here," she said. "Take it."

I didn't and said, "I haven't figured out exactly what your game is, though I suspect it ends with you asking me for money."

The intruder began scrolling madly through her phone again. When her fingers stopped, she said, "Here, look at this one. This is Ashlee and her father. Your son."

She held the device out again, and as she did, she added, "Ashlee looks much more like her father than me, which means she resembles you slightly."

I surprised myself by accepting the phone and looking at a photo of a man with his arms around what I presumed was a teenage girl. Did the man in any way mirror me from several decades ago? Possibly, though you could say the same about any number of people. The girl, however, intrigued me a little more with a vague familiarity.

I tried to recall what the girl in the dream looked like. Did she have long, straight black hair like this one? And pale skin, in spite of her slightly darker mother, assuming the woman standing before me, the one I refused to call by her name, was even her mother?

"She's much paler than you," I said.

"You think? I'm 100 percent Dominican. She's only 50."

I studied the girl's photo again, unsure why.

"So, will you help me?" the woman asked, her words startling me.

I handed the phone back. "Let me guess. She needs money. A college fund, perhaps? Little something for her mother thrown in?"

Anger flashed in the woman's eyes, a genuine emotion at last.

"She's suffering from depression, and she's run away. If that's not urgent enough, it sounds like someone tried to abduct her. And then something even worse happened. The cops are doing nothing other than giving her photo to some patrol officers around where she was last seen. You seem resourceful to me. I want you to help find her."

"No," I said. "Leave it to the trained professionals."

"You don't understand what's going on. Someone tried to abduct her when she revisited her school. A teacher stopped it.

The cops are the ones who told me about that. And then… and then there's this."

She began scrolling through her phone again while I moved to my apartment's front door and opened it wide. She had to come right up to the door to show me her latest revelation.

"It's some social media app I never heard of," she said.

She hit play on what appeared to be a video. I reluctantly retook the phone and read the caption under the video: *Miami Junkie Thinks She's Turned Invisible After Getting Set Straight About the Dangers of Drugs.* It was disturbing footage of three guys, faces pixelated, who were harassing a girl wearing a yellow rain jacket in some dark shithole. They grew increasingly belligerent and then violent, acting like they were doing a hilarious public service by provoking a junkie and then slapping her around as they ordered her to renounce drugs. The video ended with the bloodied girl rocking back and forth and repeatedly moaning, "You can't hurt me because I'm no longer here."

It should have sickened me, even if I didn't believe this girl shared my blood. But it didn't stir up any feelings in me. What sickened me was this woman believed this was her daughter, and maybe it truly was. Which meant she wouldn't stop hounding me until I helped.

* * *

My guest sat in Maricela's usual kitchen chair and even drank the same blend of coffee. I took a seat across from her and stared at a Miami-Dade police department poster that in red capital letters read "MISSING PERSON" and below that in blue "Juvenile," followed by the girl's name, description, where and when she was last seen and, of course, a photo of her.

I went to the police department's website to confirm the poster was authentic and up-to-date. I even called the number on it and requested an officer update me on the girl's status.

"Are you family?" the police clerk asked.

When I answered, "I'm her grandfather," the woman who calls herself Kacey didn't even try to suppress a grin.

The update was there truly was a girl named Ashlee Sutton, and she was still missing. The clerk did confirm the abduction attempt while volunteering few details. She also confirmed police were investigating a videotaped attack on a girl they weren't completely sure was Ashlee, despite Kacey's insistence. They also hadn't tracked down the location where the video was made, though they believe it was posted from a Miami IP address. Finally, the clerk told me of a possible Ashlee sighting near the downtown by a counselor at a youth shelter.

"I'm sure you have a car and hours before your flight," Kacey said. "Let's go for a drive and look for her near the youth shelter where she was spotted."

I ignored the suggestion. "I still think my connection in this is bullshit, but I am sorry if that's truly your daughter who's missing."

She in turn ignored what I said. "We could cover a lot of ground. It's not a great area, but I will go anywhere on earth to find Ashlee."

"I don't go out for drives. The car is there for emergencies. I'm not even sure it will start."

She rolled her eyes. "This *is* a fucking emergency."

"So her last name is Sutton? Was that your husband's last name too?"

Kacey's eyes brightened, as did the intensity of her ever-present smirk. "At last, he asks the question. The grandmother question. Who did he fuck all those years ago to bring into the world a son he never once met?"

She leaned forward as if she had me and said, "I promise to give you her grandmother's name if you help me find Ashlee."

I rubbed a hand over my eyes as I thought about being trapped in a car with this woman. But she was right; this was an emergency because she would hound me forever if I didn't help her.

"Okay," I said. "I'll help look for the girl for a few hours if you promise *not* to give me the name of Ashlee's grandmother. And if we don't find her, I'll leave town, and you will never bother me again. Deal?"

* * *

When we reached my car, it had a flat. I didn't want to sit and wait for AAA, so I changed it myself and washed my hands at an outside tap. The car did start, barely, and soon we were on the highway to Miami, my hands clenching the steering wheel to keep them from shaking.

The last sighting of Ashlee was near NW 20th Street, a few blocks east of Interstate 95. The primarily industrial area abounded with empty warehouses and homeless shelters and vacant lots strewn with garbage and sidewalks covered in graffiti and the occasional sign promising a better tomorrow in the form of residential development. Street kids loitered about, too, making it a perfect place to start.

On the drive, Kacey gulped water from a plastic bottle and repeatedly opened her window and leaned out.

When she saw me eyeing her, she said: "Just beat up from all the stress."

"Uh-huh."

"You're one to talk. You look like you could puke before I do. What's that about anyway?"

"Just a hangover," I said.

"Uh-huh," she replied sarcastically.

"So, how did he die?" I asked, hoping she wouldn't notice me wiping a patch of sweat from my forehead.

"Who?"

"Joshua. Remember? The son who looked just like me."

She shook her head. "A sad death. Overdose. Heroin. Laced with fentanyl. I don't believe it was his doing, though. We had a regular dealer who looked out for us. I think someone purposely set Joshua up to OD."

I tried to decide which I found more predictably laughable: the way he died or his wife's argument that it wasn't his fault.

"So why would…"

"Did you want to pull over?" she interrupted. "To take a minute to compose yourself after hearing how your son died."

"I'm fine."

"I know. It's just that you shouldn't be."

I ignored this and asked, "So why would someone set Joshua up to OD?"

She took a long drink of water like the question had slipped from her mind alongside a clot of dead brain cells.

"There's a lot of suspicious shit going on. A lot of interest in, well, in Ashlee."

We pulled in front of a drop-in center for street kids where the counselor had spotted Ashlee, or so she believed. My plan, I told Kacey, was to cruise this neighborhood in a grid. If that turned up nothing, we would do it a second time while showing Ashlee's poster to anyone we passed.

She nodded her approval. She was a little less positive about the next words out of my mouth.

"What was Ashlee using?"

"I don't understand the question," she said.

"You know, what was she on? Heroin, cocaine, ecstasy?"

Kacey gave me the same hard look as some of the street people we passed. "So, you figure because the parents use, the kid does too." She turned and stared out the window. "She doesn't use. She's a good kid."

"Most good kids don't run away unless there's, you know, issues at home that have messed up their lives too."

Kacey turned back to me. "Just help me find her, okay. Don't make me justify my life."

"Well, that video you showed me. It looked like the girl in it tried to stab her attackers with a needle."

"Doesn't mean it was hers."

"And the guys. They obviously went somewhere they thought they'd find junkies."

A guy pushing a shopping cart wandered in front of the car, and Kacey nearly conked her head on the dashboard when I braked.

"Anyway," I said. "It would be useful to know what she was struggling with in her life."

"We'll find her by searching, okay."

"Boyfriend troubles?" I suggested.

"No."

"Maybe a boyfriend who, you know, intended to exploit her."

"What are you saying?"

"One who wanted to profit from her."

"You dickhead. You're saying she has a pimp?"

I shrugged. "Kind of sounds like the so-called abduction attempt was her pimp trying..."

"No," she almost screamed. "My daughter doesn't even have a boyfriend. She's never been on a date. She's still a virgin, so don't you dare call her a whore."

"Okay. The abduction attempt could have been over a drug debt."

"There you go again. Would you shut up and watch the road."

I couldn't shut up, though. "What did you mean when you said there is a lot of interest in her?"

"She's a little different, that's all. You know, in a special but very unusual way."

I shook my head. "Well, that seems to run in the family."

She turned to me. "Yeah. Apparently so."

It took 40 minutes to cruise the grid mapped out in my head. By then, I wanted to race home and lock my door. But I had made a deal. So we began driving the route again, this time with me doing the very last thing I wanted: getting out of the car each block or so and brandishing the poster and trying to engage in meaningful conversation with an assortment of people so fucked up some probably thought they imagined my presence. A few answered respectfully that they hadn't seen the girl, one asked if I was her pimp, two more said they didn't talk to cops, and one demanded to know how long I had worked for the CIA. If nothing else, they served as a perfect reminder why I rarely went out.

I was standing partway down an alley trying to connect with a confused-looking Cuban man when I spotted a building I had failed to see from the street. Three-storeys tall, white, though the bottom floor was covered in colorful graffiti and full of broken windows mostly boarded up. Something about the building caught my eye. Maybe the two stick-thin figures prying back a piece of plywood and slipping inside. Or more possibly the dome-like collection of broken skylights on its roof.

It took only a few minutes to locate the loose plywood and squeeze inside. Greeting me was a warehouse full of small rooms and cubicles, all without ceilings, all flooded with natural light from the skylights. I would need to move through this building, which took up half a city block, like a rat in a maze.

This first room was empty, if you didn't count the crack pipes and needles and beer cans and other garbage littering the cement floor. The place stunk like piss. And shit.

The first person I encountered lay in a pile of debris, a spent needle resting on his lap. I prodded him with my shoe, and when he didn't move, I placed two fingers on his neck, finding a pulse. A second person, wearing what looked like a dozen layers of ragged clothes, staggered past oblivious to my efforts to get his attention. I pushed forward through more of the same.

When I finally decided I had seen enough and began making my way out, another thought slipped into my head like a piece of paper deposited neatly in a cardboard file folder: *She's in the next room waiting for you.* I paused, confused, and when I found the… what was it, courage?… to enter the room, Ashlee Sutton stood on a sun-drenched patch of floor, scolding me with a grin like I was late to her party.

The girl wore the same clothes as in the poster, though her black hoodie was now dirt-stained and tied around her waist, her jeans filthy and her low-cut black boots scuffed with God knew what. Her face looked even paler in real life than in her photo, and her brown eyes were so round they seemed almost cartoonish, though one of them was still black from an injury. Her very full lips were swollen and bloody, and her neck and chin displayed a mix of cuts and scratches that looked another day from infection.

I waited for her to repeat her greeting from the dream, not that I remembered it, and was almost disappointed when she said, "Finally. Nice to meet you, Granddad."

As I approached her, my mind delved into accidental drug exposure and whether I had picked up something from Kacey or the stash in her purse because the floor seemed to shift like the deck on a boat cutting through rough water. And what took place over the next twenty minutes would do nothing to convince me my second-hand drug fear was ridiculous.

"Hi, Ashlee, my name is Mike," I said. "I'm here to take you home."

"I'm surprised you can see me, Granddad."

"You're standing right in front of me."

She laughed, and a sadness gnawed at me when she asked, "Am I?"

I reached out and took her wrist, perhaps ignoring an urge to check for the same needle marks possessed by everyone in this shithole. "You feel very real to me."

"That's awesome, but you should know that it's just your eyes and brain tricking you as they struggle to make sense of how you are speaking to someone who's not here in physical form."

"I see."

"No, you don't, but that's okay."

The girl moved close and studied my neck, which made me flinch.

"Oh my gosh, how cool is this. I so recognize the scar from the tattoo you got before going to prison and tried to have removed. Grandma told me all about it."

"I'm not your grandfather," I said.

She looked exhausted and even a little defeated, though she still had enough energy to give me a huge smirk. "Grandma also told me about your thing for pushing people away."

I let out a nervous laugh. "Says the girl who ran away from her family."

"Ouch, Granddad. I did say in my note we have lots in common. That's why I'm sure we will meet again soon. Maybe where the big cross and the vortex come together."

I didn't understand what she meant about the cross and vortex. But I was interested that she claimed to have written the note.

"So you're saying the note was you and not your mother?"

She almost rolled her eyes. "I did want to approach you, but I chickened out. And then Mom arrived, and I didn't want to have any part of two wasted people having an epic pre-breakfast fight in public."

"I wasn't wasted. But that doesn't matter. Right now, you are going to reunite with your mother. In my car. Outside."

"I'm happy you got to meet your daughter-in-law while there's still time," she said. Her eyes turned sad at an alarming speed, and she added: "I'm sorry you never got to meet your son."

"I know. But your mother, she's right outside the door."

"For now. But I bet you have figured out the same thing as me. That sometime very soon she will join my dad."

I shuddered. "Don't talk like that. She's safe in the car and only a little high. Why don't we go out and talk to her so you can see everything will be fine?"

"Will it? You might wanna look forward in time before you try to guess what will happen next." Her teenage smile had returned, and she added: "Remember what the White Queen said to Alice, 'It's a poor sort of memory that only works backwards.'"

"We need to get out of here," I reminded her.

"Not a fan of this place, Granddad?"

"If I ever wanted to visit a replica of Hell, well, now I have."

"Granddad, it isn't like Hell. It is Hell, at least for most people. Hell and Heaven both exist on earth; they're not someplace you go when you die. Even the Bible explains this. In Luke, when Jesus says, 'The Kingdom of Heaven is in our midst.'"

"I see."

"No, you don't, Granddad. But, again, that's okay."

I took a backward step toward the door, hoping she would follow. She didn't. Instead, she went on, "You know, I have already experienced great darkness here. And it led to great light."

I wanted to ask her about the videotaped beating, which I was pretty sure did feature her as the victim, though that discussion was better left for outside in the car.

"Okay," I said. "So why don't we look for the exit?"

She nearly giggled. "You act like I'm lost in here. I'm not like the others. I pour my love on them each day because they have been deserted by their families, their friends, the people who are supposed to love them. They have no one. And Granddad, the saddest thing is that most of them are better off alone, given what their families did to them before they left."

With those words, she stepped forward and placed a hand over my heart.

"I am sorry, Granddad, that your life has turned to shit. That you are living in your own hell in your apartment complex with the swimming pool. But once your money runs out, you will find yourself in a hell just like this one, so maybe it's good that you've gotten a look at what awaits."

My eyes settled on the inexplicably needle-mark-free skin of her bare arms.

"I'm not high," she said, startling me.

"Well, you aren't making a lot of sense."

She grinned again. "Or am I making too much sense?"

I ran a hand over my throbbing forehead. All I wanted was to find my way out of this stench so I could sit in the fresh air and regain my bearings and escape the girl whose words attached themselves to me like shit.

"Listen, Ashlee. I am taking you to your mother, even if I have to drag you. I've heard enough crazy talk."

"What's crazy, Granddad, is how people keep thinking small-minded thoughts and expect their world to be anything but tiny and dull."

I took a firm grip of her hand, and she deliberately bit her bottom lip, which she seemed to do often, like she had a tick. Finally, she said, "You can't take me to your car, Granddad, because I have already transcended. I told you, the physical entity you see is not really there."

When I sighed, she squirmed free and picked a brick out of the rubble on the floor and placed it in my hand.

"I want you to take this very solid item, which you see as a brick, and slam it as hard as you can against the forehead of the departed soul before you, which you see as a girl. I bet the body you see before you will simply vanish because it's not there. At the very least, it will die a bloody death and then vanish, but either way, you will still be able to communicate with me, with my true being, which is no longer tied to that body."

Sixty seconds, I thought as I let the brick fall to the ground. That's how long it would take to toss her over my shoulder and carry her outside. And it was going to come to that.

"There's a second reason, Granddad, why you won't get me to your car," she said, wrongly thinking I was still listening. "It's because this is my story, not yours, only you don't know it yet."

As I stepped forward to lift her, a high-pitched wail descended upon us, seemingly from all sides. I listened carefully, deciding the noise came from the hallway.

"Don't move," I told Ashlee sternly. "I'll be right back."

"Like I told you, we will meet again, Granddad," she said, her grin wider than ever.

In the hallway, a teen almost as young as Ashlee rocked back and forth as she cursed and howled and swatted at an imaginary presence out of her reach. I tried to calm her but couldn't, and she soon tired herself out and slumped against the wall, her eyes rolling back.

I shook the girl, and when she didn't react, I searched for a pulse, which I didn't find. I began giving her chest compressions, which, thank God, may have worked, judging by the long groan she let out. I called 911, and a dispatcher bombarded me with a series of not-urgent-enough questions.

"She's fucking dying," I finally shouted, unsure if this was still true.

While I waited for the paramedics, I studied the girl, wondering how the fuck someone so young could be allowed to slip so far away. Matted hair as yellow as the rain jacket she wore. A jagged scar above her chin. A bony chest that, mercifully, still rose and fell. *How had I managed to find someone even more in need of help than Ashlee?* With that thought, I turned and raced back into the room where I had left my supposed granddaughter.

And when an empty room greeted me, a long, deep laugh rose from my belly.

* * *

The next several hours scrambled past in a complicated mess, which started not when I grew tired of waiting for the paramedics and carried the blond girl out to the street, but when I stumbled upon Kacey wandering outside the plywood opening and claiming she sensed Ashlee's presence. When I told her that I had found and lost her daughter inside, she rushed into the opening she'd seen me exit through, which compelled me to follow her because of the danger, though not until help had arrived for the other girl. The police rolled up shortly after the paramedics, and Kacey would become their responsibility. However, they apparently saw me as their responsibility too, wanting to talk even after I argued I would miss my flight if they took up any more of my time.

By the time I finished informing the cops about both girls, my watch confirmed I would be spending another night in Florida, exactly as I had feared. Annoyed, I said goodbye to Kacey, reminding her I had done my part to narrow the search and demonstrate her daughter still roamed the earth in one nutty piece, meaning Kacey needed to honor our deal and forever leave me alone. Instead, she demanded details of exactly what Ashlee had said.

We sat on the hood of my car across from the warehouse where my routine 911 call had turned into a rousting and rescuing of junkies. The emergency lights of three cop cars, two ambulances and one fire truck lit our faces in a psychedelic collection of colors.

On the sidewalk, a stout man wandered by, his eyes darting between the warehouse and me and Kacey. Maybe another cop. Perhaps a curious passerby. As we started talking about how I wound up in the warehouse with Ashlee, he seemed to listen until he noticed me watching him and moved on.

"Your daughter said a lot of shit, and some of it didn't make sense," I told Kacey.

"But some of what *your* granddaughter said did make sense I bet," she countered.

"To be honest, I don't want to recall some of it. Stuff about Hell. About how she wasn't in the room with me."

Kacey laughed, one of the saddest sounds ever. "That's my Ashlee. I didn't tell you because I was worried you wouldn't help if you knew."

"Tell me what?"

She crossed her arms over her chest and stared up at the night sky. "Ashlee has been diagnosed with Cotard's Syndrome. It's a rare disease that makes people believe they are dead. Only she doesn't exactly think she's dead. She thinks she is evolving from her physical body into a higher form, into pure energy, part of a bigger consciousness connected by love."

"Oh," I said, sure these were the most genuine words she had spoken to me.

She studied me with an expression that for once didn't deploy full-out contempt. "You don't like or respect me. I get that. But you should at least understand the heartbreak of having a child with a mental illness who's too sick to know she's sick." Her eyes fell. "Especially when both parents were consumed by a sickness of their own."

We sat in silence, serenaded by the occasional shouts of cops and the rumbling of three-legged shopping carts full of untold treasures. Over the years, I had learned that if you give people enough time to talk, the truth eventually spilled out because most people couldn't help themselves. Kacey had more to tell me about Ashlee, perhaps about some abuse or other extreme dysfunction that drove the girl out onto the street, though what she eventually said was unexpected.

She stared into the shadows for a long time. When she finally spoke, the sharp edges were gone from her voice. "The moments I feel the saddest about Ashlee, and I do feel sad all the time, even if you think I'm a shitty mother… those very saddest moments don't come when I picture her in a warehouse filled with junkies. Or when I think about her disease. Not at all. It's when I picture the happy times in her life, and there were many once. Her friend Gina braiding her hair in our cramped bathroom. Ashlee in a spaghetti food fight with me and her father at the kitchen table. The anticipation in her eyes on her first day of high school. How everything was joyous, like it would never end. Only it did end, and I'm terrified it's gone forever. All because I never noticed the one misstep. The exact moment it all went off the rails. If only I had seen this and corrected it, well, none of us would be here."

Kacey straightened and said, "Anyway, now you understand that me and Ashlee, we come from Crazy Town, her with her mind, me with my drugs. Only there's more to it than that, and you need to tell me everything she said because…"

She paused.

"Because she's right about so many things. It's like some crazy good intuition comes with the illness. She seems to sense what may happen next. Not always. But sometimes. So you need to tell me all the crazy shit she said. It may help us find her."

Maybe this woman had finally worn me down. Or maybe she deserved to hear what her missing daughter told me. So I gave her that, minus what the girl had said about me. And minus what the girl had said about her mother soon dying.

My end of the bargain delivered, I dropped Kacey off outside her apartment. Before she climbed from my car, she asked, "Can you help again tomorrow?"

"I'm catching another flight tomorrow," I said.

I braced for another nasty attack on my character. She said nothing, the sting of her silent stare worse than words. She rose, a little unsteadily, and disappeared into a stairwell.

Maybe I needed to go after Kacey and take her aside and impart a certain set of facts on her, so she would understand why she must stop dragging me into the steaming mess that was *her* family. Yet even the act of explaining myself felt like more than I owed her. I hurried home, rebooked my flight and prayed to never hear from Kacey Sutton again, even if it meant she would overdose like her husband, making Ashlee's morbid prediction come true.

Mike Chapter 7

1980–1982 Bellingham, Washington

If God failed to deliver Kimberly into my arms in my final two years of high school, he did give me another gift. Good hands for catching a football. And fast legs, which began growing long and strong that summer before Grade 11. Our school's football coach, who also taught my gym class, one day instructed me to run a pattern he scribbled on his clipboard and to turn around and look for a pass from him. When I pulled it in effortlessly, he nodded to himself. By the end of that year, I was on my way to six-foot-three and a starting position at wide receiver.

In my senior year, I entertained dreams of a football scholarship. I never got one, though I would discover football had opened another door, one unexpected. Tim Kolchuk, who had become my best friend, told me about the opportunity, though he admitted it left him torn.

"It's either the best job in the world or… well, okay, it's not the worst, not even close, but I haven't figured out what the catch is," he told me one day. "I'd do it in a heartbeat, but they don't want me; they want you, the football star."

So, one day in the spring of my senior year, Tim accompanied me after school to a meeting of sorts at the Royal Fork Buffet, where we met "his guy," who paid for an early dinner for the three of us to talk business. Tim's friend was named Walter, and his thick beard suggested he was a few years older than me. He looked soft enough around the middle to be a regular at the buffet.

As I loaded my plate high with roast beef and potatoes and barbecue chicken, Walter sized me up from across the aisle. I turned to Tim and said, "Your friend's giving me the creeps."

Tim laughed as he dumped gravy all over his dinner.

"Actually, I don't know him that well," he said. "I know his girlfriend. She's a family friend. But you'll want to hear what he has to say."

We ate before getting down to business, Walter pushing me for details about my football stats, like total yards offense and average yards per reception, before taking a moment to say he'd been a linebacker on Bellingham High until his graduation four years ago.

We all returned to the buffet for seconds, then thirds, and Walter nodded and said, "My girlfriend, Cheryl, she works in a fertility clinic north of Seattle. Every day she's dealing with women whose husbands don't have what it takes to make a baby because of, you know, low sperm count or weak-swimming sperm. But artificial insemination, well, the procedure is expensive, kind of a pain too, and not always effective, even though the sperm are dropped in near the end of the line. And for some women, there's a bit of a stigma using the clinic's services, especially if their church and family don't approve."

Walter sat back and took a large drink from his Coke. "So. My girlfriend made a few very subtle inquiries of a few women. What if we could find a young, healthy guy with lots of strong sperm and good genes; say a very athletic and good-looking high school football player? Would you pay for such a service from a live donor?"

I began to laugh. "So, how exactly would my sperm get inside them?"

Now Walter grinned like he'd hooked me. "Some women want you to make the donation into a cup, in a neutral location like a hotel room, and they inject it into themselves with a needle-free syringe. And others, they want it injected the old-fashioned way."

* * *

101

I met the first so-called customer in a mold-specked motel two blocks from Interstate-5 in the neighboring city of Mount Vernon. The woman, Walter told me over the phone the previous night, had wanted me to come by her home in Bellingham's Fairhaven neighborhood and "bang her right there on her own bed," Walter's words, I'm sure. However, her husband worried about neighbors getting curious. So off we went to an early evening rendezvous down the highway.

Walter drove me in his '69 Buick Skylark, his favorite album, Jackson Browne's *Running on Empty,* serenading us as we cut through the forest and farmland separating the two towns. On the way, he spoke about the economics of our arrangements, detailing my cut and how I may have to screw a few women numerous times until they became pregnant. And if they didn't, how neither of us would get paid. In what he called an act of charity and good faith, he would pay me in advance for the first few customers, although it would be weeks before he would see any money.

Walter also went to great pains to describe what a total prick the first woman's husband was turning out to be. How he refused to accept test results showing his shitty sperm count. How he tried to blame his wife for their lack of progress on the pregnancy front.

"That said," Walter added, "at least there is a husband, otherwise you could be hit up for child support down the road. Don't worry, though. I've considered the legalities of this work, and I'll make sure each woman is legally married, so you're off the hook."

Walter turned to me and smirked. "Now, with husbands come other issues, and I guess I should mention now how this particular one wants to be in the room to watch, to make sure there is no monkey business."

I snorted and looked at Walter. "I'll be screwing his wife. What other monkey business does he think could happen?"

We parked at the far end of the motel's cracked parking lot and walked past dozens of rooms and a smattering of parked cars until we reached #102. Walter knocked politely, and the door flew open, revealing a man wearing a big-collared disco shirt and an accusing expression.

He nodded in my direction, almost as if I had already fucked his wife. "That him?"

"Yep," Walter said, and I followed them both inside.

Peggy, or Mrs. Hauser as the husband instructed me to call her, rose from where she sat on the queen-sized bed and shook my hand warmly. In the next few minutes as Walter outlined what he at different times called "the rules" and "the agreement," Mrs. Hauser looked me over with a much more approving set of eyes than her husband.

"Anyway," Walter concluded. "Mike is a good kid. Clean. Comes from a successful local family, so great genes. Very professional and clinical in his delivery. And the most productive live donor in my business."

I debated which lie sounded the most outrageous.

An envelope changed hands, Walter departed, and Mr. Hauser took a seat on the room's other piece of furniture, a sagging green armchair in the corner. His mustache half-covered his pursed lips. He leaned forward in anticipation of something.

Mrs. Hauser took my hand in hers and even this bit of contact made me grow a little hard. She was thinner than Mrs. Jennings and gave off a more finely featured beauty. Younger too. Maybe late twenties. Maybe a little shy.

Or so I thought.

"Let's get undressed," she said, her hands wasting no time undoing the buttons on her blouse, starting at the top. Never once as she stripped off her clothes, or in the 45 minutes that followed, did she glance at her husband, even when he spoke, which he did at regular intervals.

I had thrown my clothes off quickly and stood waiting with

a serviceable enough erection. She smiled, leaned in and kissed me on the lips.

"No kissing," Mr. Hauser called out. "Nothing that would create an emotional attachment."

At this, she stopped abruptly, wrapped her ringed fingers around my cock and knelt to take it in her grinning mouth.

Mr. Hauser shouted that we put aside all foreplay and get down to business. She shrugged and laid back on the bed, and when she directed me between her legs, I was more than ready.

Her husband grew quiet, at least at first, when she took me inside. Within a couple of minutes, she had me roll onto my back, and she took her place on top, which prompted Mr. Hauser to almost leap from his seat. "No. No. No. That's not a good position for pregnancy. The penetration's not as deep and some of the sperm could leak out when he comes."

I expected her to defy him, but she nodded for me to return on top. Mrs. Hauser began to moan, perhaps a little too loudly for her husband's liking, and this sound excited me enough to soon deliver, with what I hoped was an impressive force, my first possibly paid sperm shipment.

Mrs. Hauser held me in her arms, her eyes round and warm as they looked into mine and whispered for me to stay put.

Then we did it twice more for good measure. Mr. Hauser's stream of objections, which ranged from "You're both enjoying this a little too much" to "A little less moaning would be nice, Peggy," faded away like background music or maybe the constant hum of a dentist's drill.

Once we were done, I went to the bathroom and had the briefest of showers. When I returned, anxious for a satisfying goodbye from Mrs. Hauser, an empty room awaited.

Walter said nothing as I climbed into his Buick. He almost discreetly waited until we rumbled out of town before asking, "So. Best guess. Do you think a seed was planted?"

It was, of course, a judgment I could never make. In the

weeks that followed, I provided my happy little product to 13 women. I would get paid for impregnating 11 of them, a pretty remarkable accomplishment, even if they were all at the ideal time in their cycles. For five of the 11, including Mrs. Hauser, one session would be enough; the other six required a little more attention. Of the two who didn't get pregnant, one was a sour-faced woman from Burlington whom I fucked joylessly on four separate occasions until we both agreed enough was enough. Of course, almost all the women, at least initially, lacked the enthusiasm of Mrs. Hauser, especially one from Marysville who lay beneath her sheets when I entered her bedroom and, after much awkward discussion, finally revealed her bare legs and hips, instructing me not to dare touch her body with my hands. She guided me in, with much obvious pain on her part, and lay still, no doubt praying I would finish soon, though I didn't, and in time she took my hands and pulled me close and positioned them over her breasts while she nodded encouragement. Only one of the women opted for the syringe, despite Walter's suspect advice that natural insemination, statistically, proved 300 percent more effective, and even she switched to a direct deposit after two failed attempts. None, other than Mrs. Hauser, had a husband who insisted on being present.

Unlike Walter, I rarely left these sessions in motels or a client's bedroom focused on whether I had succeeded. My thoughts mostly swirled around the sex itself. Not whether I enjoyed it or even whether the woman had. But whether we connected in a deeper way than what each woman experienced with her husband, given how my skills as a lover steadily improved.

I did occasionally consider the money and for good reason. In May, I would turn 18, which meant I would age out of the foster care system on the day I graduated from high school. While the money Walter paid me for each impregnation was decent, it amounted to little more than what I made in a week at most of my minimum wage jobs washing dishes or pumping gas or helping at Tim's father's lumber yard. It would, however, give me a small safety net after graduation while seeking a place to live and a better-paying full-time job.

I would entertain these short-term thoughts about the sex, the money, whether Mrs. Hauser groaned louder than Mrs. Beckett, the youngest and hottest of all the women, but rarely did I consider a more everlasting subject: the babies I helped create.

In late July of that year, I would experience one such moment when my attention drifted further forward than my next paycheck. By then I was living in a tiny basement suite and lamenting the unfortunate end to my sperm donation career, thanks to Walter's girlfriend getting fired from the fertility clinic after her boss heard rumors she was siphoning business away to her boyfriend's enterprise. But the venture had allowed me to scrape together enough money to build up my bank account and buy and insure a piece-of-shit 1972 Ford Pinto, which in turn made it easier to hang out with Tim and a few other friends and to travel to my new job. I had found employment painting houses, decent-paying work that unfortunately would dry up when summer ended. The workdays were long, productive and maybe satisfying when I would stand back to admire each house's colored transformation. It was an okay life, perhaps a little mundane. And a little incomplete in ways I didn't yet understand when contemplating such things while stuffing myself with Kraft dinner straight from the pot while standing alone in my closet-sized kitchen.

Some days after work, I would buy a chocolate milkshake from Boomer's drive-in and walk the few blocks up to the edge of Sehome Hill Arboretum, a forested park with a fancy name. I would stare up at the imposing hill, the tall green cedars contrasted against the deep blue sky, before locating a trail, disappearing inside and beginning my hike up and over and finally down to Western Washington University and then back again.

Sometimes Kimberly joined me, her red hair stuffed inside a purple Washington Huskies cap, her thin, freckled legs moving as quickly as her mouth as she plunged into topics she would discuss with me and only me. I could listen to her talk forever, warmly content in her company, and in those bittersweet moments, I would convince myself we had both received a gift greater than anything we had given up.

When alone, I would wander the old brick university campus and pretend not to be a little regretful that a post-secondary education wasn't in the cards for me. Sometimes during my walks, I would find a place to sit and catch my breath and tell myself I formed a tiny piece of something more significant. That was what I had been doing one July day when I spotted a familiar figure walking through the campus. I was sitting on a curb in the university's back parking lot when Peggy Hauser strolled by alone. Only she wasn't alone; she carried a bump in her belly that, I assumed, represented my motel handy work.

She moved in the direction of the arboretum trailhead, and I pleaded silently for her to turn and notice me. When she didn't, I stood and...

"Leave it," a voice behind me barked.

I turned to face Mr. Hauser, whom I guessed had returned to their car to claim the water bottle he held.

Before I could speak, he looked in his wife's direction and said, "That's my baby, not yours. There is no proof you had a hand in it, though I was kind enough to see you got paid. But if you ever approach my wife, I won't be as charitable."

His eyes bulged with hate. He pushed past me and hurried to catch up to Mrs. Hauser, not looking back.

I sat back down, and a bewildering thought came to me. I had spent nearly 18 years in foster care where hardly a day passed when I didn't believe that life had screwed me by abandoning me in a series of fake family homes. And now that I had served my time, I was learning the outside world had even less to offer, if that was possible, while at the same time being filled with more complex emotional attachments, which everyone knew usually led to trouble.

A block away, Mr. Hauser had caught up with his wife and apparently mentioned my name. She stopped abruptly and looked back to where I sat. Her right hand absentmindedly stretched across her swollen belly, caressing it. I could imagine her pushing aside her husband and making her way to me with the same passionate expression she displayed in our hotel encounter. Instead, she spun and walked away.

The truth pressed down on my chest like a great weight: I would never lay eyes on the baby I had helped create; I would never see Mrs. Hauser again; and my lasting memory of her would not be her hustling in the other direction with one arm wrapped around her husband's waist. It would be her scowl as she regarded me before turning away.

Back in the forest's shelter, my thoughts shifted away from me, away from her, and toward the life she carried in her belly. The life of someone I would never know who would likely grow up to one day bring into the world a son or daughter who would also forever remain a stranger to me. Ten other soon-to-be mothers also walked the streets of the Pacific Northwest, all of them one accidental meeting away from reminding me what would never be.

For the first time, I lost my sense of direction in the forest. I remembered Kimberly's emotionally delivered theory that all sex was exploitive. I laughed out loud at what a stupid fuck I had become because if she was right, and she usually was, I had managed to find a way to exploit myself.

It took ten minutes to find the trail that would lead back the way I had come what seemed like forever ago. Soon I left the forest and wandered downhill past homes where parents readied dinner for kids who rode bikes carelessly in circles as they called to friends who climbed higher in cedar trees than was safe. It all looked so idyllic, so perilous, so unfamiliar.

On a residential street around the corner from the drive-in restaurant, she waited faithfully where I had left her. My Pinto, which stuck out in too many ways to name. If I were lucky, she would start with her usual explosion and shudder forward across the pink hopscotch court drawn in chalk on the road and take me home in anything but anonymity. She may have been the ugliest car ever created, and she came at a heavier price than I could have imagined, but she represented almost everything I had.

I climbed inside. The fucker started, and I tore out of that place where even the youngest set of eyes watching my departure knew I didn't belong.

Ashlee Chapter 6

Missing: Day Four

While finally ditching the warehouse, I do the one thing I swore I wouldn't: I stop and watch my grandfather, who is working frantically to help the blond girl. My metaphorical heart almost bursts with love at his surprising compassion toward this stranger, which makes me wonder if I'm wrong to believe I don't belong at his side, at anyone's side. This girl is my cue to leave this dark corner of Hell and find the vortex and cross, just like I carelessly told my grandfather. Not that it matters what my grandfather may have heard; he will never find me, even if finding each other is what we were born to do.

Because my grandfather and I are bound in so many ways, if he turns, he'll spot the physical representation that he surely believes is me, which would be a hassle. So, while I float up through the warehouse's broken skylights on the start of the coolest journey, I instruct the worldly creation below to quietly sneak behind him while he's screaming at a 911 operator. She moves quickly past, and once we are both far enough away that he can no longer sense us, and create us, Physical Ashlee finally vanishes, poof, gone forever, taking with her my final link to the messed-up, artificial world below. Even if I exist beyond human emotion, this moment leaves me conflicted, like someone who just lost a long-suffering elderly aunt who was close to her.

I drift over the street, where I pause, confused. I had thought that once I transcended there would be unity in my voice, but doubt lingers. Doubt that reminds me I am not just forever fleeing my grandfather but also my mother. Of course, I know exactly where Mom is waiting in a car one block away. That's because the former keen-eyed physical me, while sipping expensive coffee in the hours after her panhandling career ended, saw dear old Granddad park his car and climb out and walk by on the street before he noticed the warehouse and went inside.

I retreat into the blinding late afternoon sun, a perfect place for pure light to hide, and counsel myself, *Hey girl, don't go near that damn car*. Yet soon, I am right above it, and the disunity in my head is deafening. One internal voice pleads for me to open the car door, wake my mom, and climb onto her lap like a little girl, even if this is physically impossible. But a more intelligent voice speaks up, pointing out that if you're not present to witness something horrible happen, then it doesn't really happen, at least not in your heart. It wins out. I order my presence to linger only for a moment outside the passenger door where Mom's head and shoulder are slumped. I am careful not to disturb her, not to enter her thoughts. She twitches, and that's when I notice the tear-streaked handprint on the outside of the window where her tired face rests. That's also when the not-too-distant echo of a girl's sobbing voice reaches me: *I'm so, so sorry. I'm so, so sorry.*

And it's clear that Physical Ashlee isn't gone after all.

* * *

As I slip into the coming dusk, sirens approach, their wail painful, urgent. But it's a false urgency because you can never beat time. You can't even compete with an opponent that exists only to give structure to an imaginary world where everything we create is doomed because it comes with a ticking clock.

Almost everyone, my grandfather included, believes time only runs forward, never backward, but no one stops to think about the greatest moments of our lives and how they are filled with nostalgia and yearning. How they are somehow ending and arriving at the same time. How the past, future, and present collide in one glorious juncture.

That's how it was with the crazy so-called dreams, or maybe visions, that started my transformation in the weeks after My Great Awakening. These visions were new and terrifying and exciting. And the second I began having them, they began to feel as familiar as an old friend. Suddenly I understood that the end of these awesome experiences had already planted itself within sight on the horizon; that these unforgettable moments that were only just beginning were already spiraling towards their end.

Physical Ashlee jerks me from this abstract memory, which is a surprise because there's no one else nearby who cares to conjure her into existence. No one, of course, but me. She's sitting on a bench at a bus depot, where it looks like she went into my purse and removed some panhandling profits and bought a ticket so she can join me in Arizona. It also appears she is now passing the time until her bus's departure by reading from the sketchbook she removed from my purse. The sketchbook where, months ago, I jotted down a timeline of my important life events before running my eyes down the list in dismay and whispering to myself, *How lame is this*, my head falling back onto my faded Barbie pillow in dramatic fashion.

Physical Ashlee isn't reading the timeline but something else I detailed in this book: the crazy days after My Great Awakening. I want to call down, *Hey, Bitch, get out of my shit*, but there is something about her that's easy to admire. She's like a cockroach that can't be crushed. A smart little cockroach with a crazy-active mind that allows her to stay one step ahead of me.

I read along with her and see she's at the part I had just been thinking about, as if she's trying to make sense of how we got here. In my words, which are her words too, there is something comforting, maybe because they're so linear and uncomplicated like we think our lives should be. And each word rings with an undeniable truth: that faith and love are the same thing, just like madness and clarity, birth and death, and who we are and who we think we are.

Nothing good ever comes from reliving the so-called past, but it's hard to help myself. So I read along too.

Ashlee Chapter 7

Seventeen to Eleven Weeks Before Missing

The dreams begin a few weeks after My Great Awakening, that moment when my soul connected with a powerful and helpful consciousness. While this discovery had helped eliminate much of my sadness, or at least make it more bearable, some nights I would still go to bed thinking that it wouldn't be a big deal if the morning never arrived. On those nights, I would fall asleep and soon find myself shaking free from sleep paralysis, which I would later learn exists as a door keeping the unenlightened from going where they're not ready to go. Each time, I would wake up in my bed, float to the ceiling and, no fucking way, look down see my curled-up body asleep on the twin bed below. Then I would calmly hover, consumed by the same questions. Do dreams have the same rules as everything else in the universe, like, duh, you can't be in two places at once? And if so, do I exist in the physical body of the timid girl on the bed or in the restless soul of the girl floating above? Which one is most legit? Or better yet, which one do I prefer? To no one's surprise, I would always make the earthly choice, the safe choice, the quintessential Ashlee choice, falling back to my bed and waking up inside my body, which would shake with mad energy.

These dreams repeat for weeks, long enough for me to relax and find them to be cool and all, even if a little unsatisfying. Long enough for me to think they might, in some way, be connected to my synesthesia AND to my hyperphantasia. Not one or the other but both. And not my regular synesthesia, where, for example, numbers and letters would take on personalities, with say the letter F being playful and the letter K snobby and mean. No, I mean the mirror-touch synesthesia, where I would see a person in pain, and my body would buckle with a hurt I couldn't trace to a specific body part. Of course, I had once thought everyone's senses overlapped like this. Then one day, in kindergarten, my teacher overheard me talking to students about the *nice* letters and the *mean* numbers, which led to many hours with school counselors before they diagnosed my so-called gift. The hyperphantasia is a separate ability I also thought was common, until in middle school I realized other people couldn't read a dull passage from a book and recreate it in their mind in such detail that it would take on a life of its own, like a movie clip where you didn't know the ending until you saw it. This talent I tried to keep to myself.

Anyway, the theory I develop is this: when I am in emotional pain, these two talents team up with my sleeping mind to create a movie clip of my soul leaving my body, which brings some relief because the pain remains with my body and its many senses and not within my buoyant soul.

It's a theory that sounds right. Even the part about it not being real. But next time I dream the dream, enlightenment comes shortly after I reach the ceiling and get a little cocky. For once I don't rush all scaredy-cat-like back to my body. Instead, I listen to the guiding voice of my soul, which asks *What do you really want from the universe?* A simple answer explodes from inside me: to break free from all my fears so I can finally see reality as it is. So, I choose to let my soul wander a little longer around the ceiling of my bedroom. In return, I am rewarded with new insight because I study my surroundings and see that darkness comes in many shades and that the shadows on my ceiling are not all the same. The blackest, I notice, are more than the usual flat chested silhouettes. They have gained another dimension and push forth from the plaster in unworldly shapes whose darkest recesses soon reveal themselves as holes, or more precisely, as exits.

I reach up and claw my way through one, like someone

parting the upper branches in a tree's canopy so she can see the sky above. And as my head and body rise out of my bedroom, and my eyes take in what's before me, something uncouples in my head, opening a space where panic rushes in.

Suddenly I understand this can't be a dream because I'm not really sleeping. I am also sure it's not some stupid fantasy either. It is maybe the most authentic moment of a pretty lame life, a thought that suddenly terrifies me. I squeeze my eyes shut and scream, only no sound leaves my mouth. I don't open my eyes until my gasps flood my nose and head with the familiar and comforting scents of my room: the lavender Mom sprays on my pillow to help me sleep; the sweet stink of vehicle exhaust from the six-lane street outside. I lay trembling on my bed, whispering the same words over and over. *What the genuine fuck?*

I tell no one about my experience, though before my afternoon English literature class, I use Google to research hallucinations and astral travel and other dimensions and stuff like that, and even crazy examples of synesthesia and hyperphantasia, finding nothing that exactly matches what happened to me. That is until I type *out-of-body experience*. Bingo.

It's three more nights before I find the courage to push my way through another breach, another exit into the great unknown. Slowly I climb out of my bedroom and find myself drifting in the night sky above my apartment as if the ceiling existed only in the constructs of my drab imagination.

It's an understatement to say my discovery brings stress. Crapping myself would better describe my reaction to this world without constraints, this world that's not behaving in the way my mind's been trained to expect. I expect this fear to drag me down to earth like fear always does. Yet I overcome it enough to rise a little higher above my apartment building. The wind laughs in my ear. A passing gull whoops with delight. I discover I can glide forward by merely giving thought to where

I wish to go. I don't get far because the terror storms back. I close my eyes and return to my bed, where I lay like a bird whose body has been stretched long by gravity's pull.

A few nights later, I find myself drifting over the port of Miami and the cruise ship terminal, the night air warm on my skin. *How cool is this*, I think. When I return to bed, I spend far too much time searching for an exact explanation of my out-of-body experiences. Are they a quantum leap of faith or a run of madness? God's hand or the lure of something darker? And will I ever know?

For hours I read about our three spatial dimensions, width, depth and height, or put another way, left/right, forward/back and up/down, and how scientists generally agree there are more dimensions, though we aren't aware of them because we never evolved to see them. This begs the question, when I leave my body and enter the breach, am I going into another dimension? Other questions follow. Is this other dimension looped because somehow I always find my way back? Does time behave differently in such a place? Why wouldn't it, after all? Is it the true world?

Of course, anyone hearing about these trips could argue that rather than *having* out-of-body experiences, I am simply *dreaming about having* out-of-body experiences, or even *imagining dreaming about having* out-of-body experiences. And, instead of traveling into another dimension, am I merely shifting into Crazy Land, as any therapist would surely say? So I keep my mouth shut.

One night the voice of the shared consciousness reassures me like it often does. *Don't be afraid. Liminal moments are always rooted in great confusion.* Of course, I don't know the meaning of the word *liminal* until I look it up on my phone's dictionary app after waking.

Some nights when I emerge from the breach, I am no longer above my apartment in my neighborhood but somewhere distant and unrecognizable, dark rooms where ancient clocks tick loudly like in conversation or eerie streets bustling with strangers who all seem to be casually watching me. These places hum with a presence I can't quite see, an awareness that leaves me unsettled. So, after several times being hurtled into these places, one night I am overcome by the realization that these are my journeys, meaning I call the shots. And just like that, I am standing on the soft rubber surface of the playground Mom would take me when I was five, leaving me skipping like a kid again. The next night I visit my grandmother's bedroom, where I watch her sleep, her wrinkled hand gently touching my grandfather, or the man who helped raise me as my grandfather.

Some nights, of course, it's a struggle to control what Mrs. Sampson, my favorite teacher, likes to call *the narrative of our lives*. In between the places I want to go, I am occasionally propelled into random scenes like the ones my father surely stumbles upon while high, and each of these leaves me struggling to interpret what I see.

Tonight, I watch a young girl swing her feet out of a high-rise window and light a cigarette. She leans too far forward and falls to her death, though only after our eyes meet, like she's sharing some critical insight. That's fucking weird. I return to my bed and cannot forget this violent scene as real as anything I have ever seen. At school, I spend most of my history and algebra classes trying to figure out what it means, if anything. Is it a falling away of the part of me that has become irrelevant, like useless childhood tendencies?

As I leave school, this answer further evolves. Was I witnessing my desire to transform into a woman and become sexually active, like my toxic-mouthed classmate Maria Perez, who some boys say gives the best blow jobs in school? While I entertain this thought, Maria materializes in the flesh perched outside the school's front door, and I stand back and study her. Not just her trashy crop top or her full blow-job-giving lips that are covered in a dark shade of lipstick and making an appropriate duck face, but her very presence itself, like I had conjured her.

Maybe I'm not as stealthy as I think. Maria notices me watching her, and she calls out, *What the fuck are you looking at you ugly little lesbian whore bitch*?

I do what I always do at the first sign of trouble. Run. Fast. I hurry down the stairs past her, though as I rush by, she lunges forward and punches me hard in the back of the head, sending me stumbling. She follows me out onto the street, ready to beat my ass, only I am too fast. The extra salty Maria shouts the word *cocksucker*, kind of ironic, and then, before turning away, lets loose the other C-word. Nice.

I head off in the wrong direction before looping back home on an unfamiliar street, my thoughts focused on the pain in the back of my head. In a cluster of shops, a storefront window boasts bright orange painted letters that read, *Friends of the Seven Signs*. Next to its door is a poster that says, *What Do Your Dreams Mean? Plenty. Come Inside and Ask.*

My out-of-body experiences clearly are not dreams. But they do happen after falling asleep. Inside I go.

I am greeted by a fifty-something lady named Cynthia who doesn't even bother to dye her grey hair, which she keeps tucked in a simple ponytail. She sits on a large sofa next to a much younger woman, Tasha, who others later say is an environmental activist. One so pretty that any man who walks through the door will want to join the group or sign up for $75 private one-hour meditation lessons or at least ask for her phone number, which she never gives out.

The sign said I should ask about my dreams, I say. They both motion for me to sit down between them, and it feels nice to be welcome somewhere. We hit it off, a regular bramance. They talk about how my dreams are spiritual journeys based on my subconscious thoughts and how they can be mined for information on my feelings and what's on my mind.

I will, of course, learn that while they are partly right, their advice is shallowly incomplete. But I do like their term *spiritual journey*, and the following week I find myself again in the shop, where Cynthia talks with me for more than an hour about my beliefs and how I can reach down deep into my humble soul and discover more faith. It turns out the answer is by committing $50 of my babysitting profits for a seat, or mat, at a spiritual-belonging session with Lucas, the group's spiritual leader.

Nine of us attend the two-hour gathering the following week. I am the youngest, though that doesn't mean that Lucas, who like Cynthia has grey hair tied in a ponytail, ignores me. He takes my hand, stares into my eyes and tells me my soul gives off a powerful vibration. He keeps my hand clasped in his and begins talking about my consciousness, his intense eyes growing cringeworthy. It's tempting to say *Creep much*, but another woman appears, and he finally releases me. I find a mat to sit on far enough away that he won't be tempted to get gropey while I'm stretched out in some compromising position that he's requested.

While Lucas is a bit over-the-top enthusiastic toward me, I do love the session with him. It's life-altering in exactly the way he promised because he confirms what I felt in my Great Awakening: that the world we live in is not the fixed place we think we see and there is much more to it than most people realize. He also makes me more confident that there is more to me than my far-too-active mind and my not-too-attractive face and body that one senior boy once labeled as *merely fuckable*.

In that first session, Lucas tosses out so many ideas that, when I get home, I sit up past midnight writing them down in my sketchbook, which has become part diary and part collection of interesting and inspirational words. Among my favorites from Lucas: how if we properly exercise our free will, we can change our reality and our future; and, most of all, how nothing ever will mean more than this moment we live in right now.

It's clear he's right about so much. But again, I can already see there is much he fails to understand. Even the trademarked seven signs of an enlightened life that he presents are not, at least in my opinion, the most important to seek. An outrageously conceited thought rises from my soul when Lucas takes my hand and stares deeply into my eyes as he says goodnight. *Pretty soon, the student will become the teacher.*

Mike Chapter 8

Missing: Day Five

The plan was simple: Turn off my cell phone, don't answer my door and when 3:30 p.m. rolled around, quietly go downstairs and climb in my pre-ordered taxi and go to an airport bar where I would have plenty of time to enjoy three or four different tropical-sounding drinks while waiting in comfort for my 7:05 p.m. flight. Nowhere would I converse with anyone in the Sutton family.

A good plan, one blown out of the water at 10:40 a.m. with a constant pounding on my door, which I did ignore. Of course, Maricela had a key, and she let herself in, walked past where I sat in bewilderment at the kitchen table, glanced at my packed suitcase and put the Keurig to work.

She took a sip of coffee and got straight to the point as always, "Sorry about what happened in the elevator the other day. I had been telling my friends our sex sucked, but only so they didn't think I was lame. I do like our time together."

"You don't need to explain yourself," I said.

"And I don't want you mad at me." She paused and tilted her head toward my suitcase. "Going somewhere?"

"Back to Seattle for a few weeks."

"Not back to work?"

"No."

"Is it because of what happened in the elevator?"

I stood, not doing a great job of hiding my annoyance. "Everything isn't always about you."

"Okay. I'll stop flattering myself."

"Here." I handed her an envelope. "I was leaving you a note and some money for when I'm gone."

"What does the note say?"

"Just what I told you, I have some matters to take care of in Seattle."

She sat at the table. I remained standing.

"Does it have anything to do with that Hispanic woman I saw you leave with yesterday? Must have been important for you to go out somewhere."

"No."

"And you're not mad at me?"

"No. And I have some more packing to do, so I need to say goodbye."

She studied me.

"You know what you need?" she asked.

"No."

"A woman your own age."

"Thanks for the advice, Ann Landers."

"Who's Ann Landers?"

When she stood without the envelope, I picked it up and thrust it at her.

She wouldn't look at it. She said, "I feel you have lots of money. You own your place in Seattle, right?"

I shrugged. "I'm pretty well off, yes."

"So why do you even live in this dump? If I had your cash, I would be so long gone from here. And I would never come back."

I pushed the envelope forward. "Speaking of money..."

She asked, "So is this it? For us?"

"Of course not," I said.

Maricela nodded, more to herself, and turned to go.

"The envelope," I said.

She turned back and stared at it with a blank expression.

"How much is in there?"

"Eight hundred."

"And you're saying you're gone for a few weeks, huh?"

I didn't answer. She took the envelope from my hand, and I

didn't think any less of her.

* * *

At 3:20 p.m. I waited in the parking lot, hoping the taxi would be early. No such luck, but it didn't matter because I filled the time making a couple of calls related to something I had seen the night before in the warehouse. While I talked on the phone, my eyes were drawn to an unmarked police cruiser, from which two men exited, one tall and white with a slight stoop in his shoulders and the other black, likely a little older, his dark suit a sharply tailored fit, his gaze menacingly alert.

The tall man studied his cell phone's screen, which likely contained an address, while his partner reviewed the collection of arrowed signs that pointed to my mid-rise building and the half-dozen neighboring low rises, all teeming with miscreants.

From my shady spot under a palm tree, I said, "Can I help you find an address?"

When their eyes fell on me, they shook their heads in disbelief. My breathing became labored.

They approached, the older cop's walk deliberate, like a cat sneaking up on its prey. And I knew they came for me and why, however impossible that was.

"We're looking for Mike Baker," the tall man said. "Would that be you?"

I nodded slowly.

His colleague stepped forward. "My name's Detective Douglas. My partner is Detective Sweeny. Is there somewhere we can go to talk?"

I pointed to my suitcase. "I'm waiting for a cab to take me to the airport."

They looked at each other. Douglas turned to me and said, "You need to delay your trip."

* * *

We sat at my kitchen table, and when Douglas put on a compassionate look and told me Kacey Sutton was dead, I did my best to act shocked, though my acting probably sucked as much as my alleged daughter-in-law's.

While it was the wrong time to become emotional, my body did go a little slack with sadness at Douglas's words, my eyes cast down on the table's coffee-mug stains as I considered Ashlee with one mental illness and zero parents. Inside my head, however, my reaction was much less calm; in fact, to employ an expression Maricela loved, I was "fucking freaking out."

"Do you have anything you wish to tell us, Mr. Baker?" Sweeny asked.

Other than Ashlee's spectacularly accurate prediction, which would make me sound insane, no, there wasn't much I wanted to say. Not even how I didn't like the sound of this conversation.

When I didn't answer, they began to release further bits of information, perhaps like you would let out a rope with a noose on the end, starting with how Kacey died: a fall through the third-floor bedroom window in her apartment to her death on the sidewalk below.

They told me about their suspicions: possible signs of struggle in the apartment, the recent death of Joshua, Ashlee's disappearance and a possible attempt to abduct the girl, and finally "other events" they didn't immediately divulge. Douglas fired up his laptop and showed me a photo from a surveillance camera of me dropping off Kacey last night about 9:30, saying I could have been the last person to see her alive.

"Other than the person she may have struggled with inside," I interjected.

This, of course, prompted a reaction, though not the one I wanted. Douglas clicked to another photo, this one showing the back of a man wearing a Seattle Seahawks jersey, number

3 stenciled on it, as he entered the building minutes before midnight. Kacey had taken her fatal fall at 3:10 a.m.

"When did that person leave the building?" I asked, pointing at the picture.

"Don't know," Douglas said. "Multiple exits."

"And you think that's me?"

"We hoped you could tell us," Sweeny said.

"The reason why we ask," Douglas said, "is that hours earlier, a detective with the missing person unit interviewed you at a warehouse where you had allegedly located Mrs. Sutton's daughter, and he recalls you wore that Seahawks jersey."

"Not that one," I said emphatically, pointing at the photo. "One *like* that one, because that is not me."

The two cops sat back in their chairs and considered my denial. Douglas looked from me to my low-rent room, like he struggled to hypothesize the connection between the two.

Unlike Sweeny, whose unshaven face suggested he rolled out of bed this morning and headed straight to work, Douglas looked neatly groomed: His hair clipped tightly to his scalp, his face clean-shaven. Even his eyebrows looked like they had been recently trimmed. All this preciseness left me uneasy.

"Let's talk a little more about your timeline last night," he said.

After this awkward discussion, we moved onto, among other things, Kacey's state of mind when I dropped her off, her drug use, the family's finances, how I had tracked Ashlee down to the warehouse, if I was aware the two detectives had both met Mrs. Sutton for the first time a week ago because she was convinced her husband had been killed and she had marched into a police station with her suspicions, which turned out not to be credible. An hour later, I told them I could still make my plane and would be more than happy to answer any further questions from Seattle.

"You need to cancel that flight," Douglas said, "because

there is more we require of you."

That's how I would wind up at the sprawling Miami-Dade County Medical Examiner's office, better known as the morgue, identifying the body of a woman I had only met twice.

But before we left my suite, before I called to cancel my flight for a second straight day, I took my last misguided shot at partly extricating myself from this mess. I said to the two cops, "Shouldn't a family member identify her body?"

They did what they always did. They looked at each other.

Douglas finally answered, spelling out the facts like he lectured an idiot. "Kacey Sutton's family is in the Dominican Republic, not exactly nearby. Her daughter Ashlee Sutton is missing. Her husband Joshua Sutton is newly deceased. Joshua Sutton's family is small, with the man who raised him residing in a care home in Bellingham, Washington, with early-onset dementia. Of course, Joshua Sutton's biological father, we have reason to suspect, lives right here in Fort Lauderdale. That would be you."

"I told you I only met this woman a few days ago. She's not, how would I say it in my profession, the most credible source, so I'm not confident we are related as she claims."

Douglas nodded. "We understand. But, again, we have reason to believe you have family ties. Why don't you identify Mrs. Sutton's body, and then we will deal with that secondary issue immediately afterward?"

"Shouldn't," I said, "the body be identified by someone who is not, apparently, a suspect in her death?"

Douglas smiled. "We never said you are a suspect. Never even said anyone harmed Kacey Sutton. Only that we have a few suspicions we need to rule out."

"So, this isn't just another made-up-yet-difficult exercise that allows you to observe me some more as you look for inconsistencies or something like that?"

At this, Douglas sat back in his chair. His smile remained

wide, his eyes joining in with the same delight. He wasn't an imposing man: Probably about five-foot-ten and 160 pounds. His voice carried the hypnotic smoothness of a singer you could listen to all day. Even the way he sat seemed inviting, legs open, arms never crossed, palms skyward. Every part of his demeanor should have put me at ease. It didn't, and I couldn't figure out why.

* * *

The morgue, a young male attendant with thick glasses proudly told me, could hold 555 bodies.

"A 747 jumbo jet could go down, and we would have enough cooler space to handle all the deceased," he boasted as he led us down a long corridor.

My fists clenched at this man's suggestion that my daughter-in-law, and it looked increasingly like that once-wild claim could be valid, was in her death merely one of the masses, someone so insignificant her slab number had three digits, so unimportant the person chosen to identify her didn't even know her middle name or favorite song.

In a viewing room, six photographs sat face down on a table.

"Why didn't you just bring the photos to my apartment?" I asked.

Sweeny smiled. "Bureaucracy. We can only obtain a copy of morgue photos when a criminal investigation file has been opened, and we're not quite there yet. Might not ever be."

Unsatisfied, I asked to see the actual body, but the attendant said they don't do that anymore, not even in police investigations. I countered that I had witnessed far more death than either of these police officers, perhaps as much as some who worked here. While the attendant dismissed this statement with little thought, Douglas leaned in slightly like he wanted a better look at me.

When the photographs were laid before me, I instantly recognized Kacey Sutton, though I said nothing. My eyes were drawn to the bloodied crown of her head that I assumed had hit the ground first. Then they went to her eyes, and I nearly ejected a short laugh and sob all at once. In death, her eyes looked as cold as when she regarded me in life. That said, there was something likable about Kacey. Her persistence, her loyalty, the loving way she spoke about the daughter she had absolutely failed. Of course, all these admirable traits had melted away each time she regarded me. I considered the contempt she harbored for me, about what she saw when she looked into my eyes: the ultimate deadbeat father and grandfather. Like she believed a sperm donor should be accountable for his offspring.

"Yes, it's her," I said finally.

* * *

We reconvened upstairs in a small boardroom reserved for law enforcement.

"Before we tell you about your family connection, we have a few more questions about the elusive Ashlee Sutton," Douglas said.

I laughed, a noise that sounded wrong in this building full of death. God, I needed a drink. "She has a mental illness; you must know that?"

Sweeny nodded. "We are aware of that. We've talked to our colleagues in missing persons."

"I'm not sure what I can add."

"When you met her, did she say where she was going, what her plans were?" Douglas asked.

"No."

"Did you know," he continued, "that your son, Joshua Sutton, won almost $100,000 at several Miami casinos over several nights the week before he died? And that, in more than one, his daughter was spotted in his company, though of course only in the areas she was permitted by law: teen video arcade, restaurant, hotel lobby, hotel room, swimming pool?"

I shook my head, a little tripped up by the word "son." "Maybe he was, you know, parenting. Watching over her. I heard she was depressed."

"Could be," Douglas said.

"Mrs. Sutton," Sweeny said, "told an officer investigating the girl's disappearance that Mr. Sutton believed the girl had a gift. Most would call it luck. Maybe intuition. According to his wife, Mr. Sutton called it a psychic ability, you know, the ability to see into the future far enough to know what number would come up on a roulette wheel or which slot machine was about to pay off big."

This was interesting, though at its heart lay a disturbing question: who was crazier, my son or my granddaughter? Or maybe these two cops wasting even a single minute investigating it?

Douglas thankfully kept the conversation moving forward. "Of course, when one analyzes the supposed miracle of their winnings, given the brief period they occurred in, there is nothing extraordinary about it. Ever heard of Littlewood's Law?"

"No," I said.

"It suggests a person can experience a miracle, defined as odds of one in a million, about once a month. This theory is based on the typical person experiencing about one 'event' a second in their lives, meaning about one million events occur every 35 days. So, if a miracle is a one in a million event, they happen more frequently than we believe, and that's the crux of the theory: with a large enough sample size, there is a probability that outrageous things will occur. Now, stack a few of these miracles up close together, like a few big slot machine wins, and it may seem like there's something else at play here, even though that's not true."

"Impressive for a cop to know such a theory," I said.

"A Master of Psychology degree from the University of Florida hanging on my wall suggests it's not that impressive. Well-versed in philosophy as well."

"And you're working as a cop instead of getting rich in private practice."

Douglas smiled like he genuinely enjoyed this line of conversation. "My family's doctrine going back generations has always been to give back to the community first, while you're young. Then make money for yourself as you grow older. But always the community first. It's like another law, the law of karma."

"That's impressive too."

"So," Sweeny said, putting us back on track. "Apparently, these gambling wins provided lots of money for Mr. Sutton to get high, so high, well, sadly, you know the rest."

With that, I hoped Sweeny was wrapping up our conversation.

"How about this New Age group Ashlee belonged to?" Sweeny continued. "The one that put up a $10,000 reward for her safe return. Do you know about them?"

"No. I wasn't aware of any reward."

"Mrs. Sutton didn't mention them or the reward to you?"

"No."

"Did she ever give you money?"

"No."

"Do you know this man?" Sweeny asked, placing a video-surveillance photo of a chubby man before me. "This is the man who tried to abduct Ashlee a few days back."

I studied the photo. "No."

"Do you have a name?" I asked.

Sweeny shook his head. "Not quite. The video isn't the greatest quality. The teacher who chased him didn't get a great look at his face. And the one person who got a close-up look at this man is still missing."

"So no suspicions who this is?" I asked.

"We have a couple of people in mind. One's a sex offender, one's a petty criminal, one's a neighborhood man that the teachers at the school find creepy." Sweeny paused. "That's why it's important to find the girl. Well, that and the vulnerable condition she's in."

I studied the photo again.

"What?" Sweeny asked.

"He kind of looks like a man I saw at the warehouse where I stumbled upon the girl. In the moments after I lost her, while I talked to her mother outside on the street."

Douglas leaned forward. "You sure about that. Based on this crappy photo."

"Who knows?" I said, unsure of anything.

I waited for the detectives to show the video of the men assaulting Ashlee in the warehouse. When they didn't, I asked, "Aren't you going to ask me to identify the three men in the social media video?"

"Do you know them?" Sweeny asked.

"No," I said.

"Well, we do," Sweeny said. "Or we think we do. We don't believe they're related to her disappearance. Just some rich assholes. But they may face charges when we're through with them, yet another reason we need to get a statement from the victim."

While there was much I didn't want to share about the girl, there was one thing I did want to pass on to the two of them. I reached into my jean pocket and pulled out a small, printed flyer.

"What's that?" Sweeny asked.

"I found one of these in the room where I met Ashlee Sutton and a second one, this one actually, near another girl in bad shape, the girl I called 911 for."

The paper read, "Don't despair. If you want a safe place to sleep AND a little money in your pocket AND a chance for a brighter future, give us a call." A phone number was below.

Douglas shrugged. "Lots of charities help the street kids. So what?"

"Well, something bothered me about this flyer. The promise of money for drug addicts. So I called around. Most agencies who work with downtown street kids say it doesn't belong to any reputable group. They figure it's more likely the work of a cult or something else nefarious. A pimp. A pedophile."

Douglas snatched up the flyer, his eyes crinkled with annoyance. "I will share it with our officers in the child exploitation unit."

He slipped it into a folder and abruptly asked, "So I want to ask. What's your sudden involvement, Mr. Baker, with the Sutton family? You were estranged from them, or so you say, for their entire lives, and you show up on the scene the moment everything is spiraling out of control."

"Is that a question or an accusation?"

He smiled again. "And at the same moment they finally possess a little cash."

"Again, a question or accusation?"

"Either way, you haven't answered."

"I told you, Kacey sought me out to help find Ashlee. I had no contact with the family up until then, wasn't aware of their existence, and I'm still not convinced I am related. No evidence has been provided."

Sweeny picked up his phone, scrolled for a minute, and said, "Detective Willett of the Bellingham police department called you several times on your cell phone last week. Left voicemails. You never called back. He asked our office to dispatch officers to pass along a message to you in person, though they didn't find you home. The detective was calling with information about your connection to this family."

I had received the messages and decided the last fucking people I wanted to speak to on any matter were the Bellingham police.

"Been busy," I said.

Douglas grinned. "Well, if you had found the time in your busy schedule, Willett wanted to talk to you about a historical sex assault and child exploitation file from the 1970s."

"Jesus, what the fuck are you accusing me of now?"

Sweeny, always the serious one, finally cracked a smile. "No, Mr. Baker, you're not the suspect. You are the victim. The suspect is a woman named Carol Jennings."

* * *

If the past 48 hours had not been bone-jarring enough, the next half-hour would jolt every atom in my body to its core.

The two officers described in bare-bone terms the events set in motion by the death one year earlier of a woman named Carol Jennings. While their account lacked details, the story would gain bits and pieces in the days to come until it finally read like this: After Carol Jennings' death, her husband, Don, who had been living in Pompano Beach, Florida with her, flew back to his birth town of Bellingham and took residence in a seniors housing complex. His memory waning and his conscience heavy, he one day walked into the Bellingham police station and reported a series of crimes that happened decades earlier while they operated a foster home for children. The wrongdoer, in this case, was his wife, who had years earlier, in the late 1970s, confessed to him to sexually assaulting four male children in her care, the last one managing to make her pregnant, which brought the entire sordid affair to light, or more accurately, to his attention.

Because he loved his wife and believed she was sick, Don Jennings had agreed not to go to the police and not to abandon her but instead to remove any chance of it happening again by closing their foster home. In fact, they moved to Florida, where they decided she would have the baby and they would raise it as their own. They had always wanted children but never managed to conceive.

Joshua was born and grew to have his own family. A few years back, Don Jennings had worried about the physical differences between him and his purported son and feared Joshua would find out on his own that Don was not his biological father, destroying the trust between them. So one day, Don and Carol confessed to Joshua, explaining that Mrs. Jennings had an affair that resulted in the pregnancy. Joshua, Kacey and Ashlee were all told by Don that the biological father was a nasty, vindictive man and should not be contacted under any circumstance. They were not informed that at the time of conception, the father was in fact a 14-year-old boy living under Mrs. Jennings' care.

That boy, living in foster home number nine, was of course me.

"So," Sweeny said after providing just enough facts that I understood what he was saying, "for what it's worth given the accused is deceased, Detective Willett has tracked down all the victims except for you. They were reluctant to talk about it these many years later, but the story seems to stand up, or so he says. The detective would like you to get a blood test to show you are Joshua Sutton's father, which would provide at least some physical evidence. And then finally this case can be closed, as much as any crime resulting in a baby's birth can be closed."

The two officers awaited the many questions that would surely spill from my curious mouth. Yet nothing came out. Their story, which was my story, made such perfect sense it left me staring at my hands. When enough strength crept back for me to stand, they led me to the door and gave me their cards.

"And one more thing," Douglas called. "Please don't go to Seattle during our investigation of Mrs. Sutton's death. Give it a few days. We need the autopsy results and toxicology report, need to interview a few more people."

"So I am a suspect."

He smiled and said goodbye.

* * *

Fifteen minutes after my return to my apartment, a knock sounded on the door, followed by Maricela's voice.

"Mike? That you in there?"

I opened the door, and she took a long look at me and came in, Estefenia resting on her hip.

"You look like shit. What happened? You missed your plane again."

From the fridge, I took two beers, offering her one, which she took and immediately began knocking back.

"You wouldn't believe me if I told you," I said.

She sat at the kitchen table and moved Estefenia to her lap. "Try me."

"It's a long story."

"Does it look like I got better shit to do?"

I wished I had never opened the door. I also wished Maricela would remain in the chair and coax me into telling the entire story, which was what she did.

"It will help, you know, to talk," she prodded. "Just start by opening your mouth, stupid."

The way she said "stupid" was not without affection, and my mind wandered back to another world where a red-haired girl constantly called me that name, usually with a wide grin on her freckled face. I could almost feel a clump of withered synaptic connections in my brain spring back to life, and there was Kimberly sitting so close our legs nearly overlapped as she whispered a smattering of crude words into my ear. There she was leading me under a canopy of trees high above Bellingham, asking me if I liked football more than girls, telling me I drove the ugliest car she had ever seen, even occasionally being kind enough to show me that all I knew about the world and what a fucked-up place it could be was at least partly wrong.

Estefenia had fallen asleep in Maricela's arms. I turned off the harsh hall and kitchen lights, and took a seat across from them, glad to be basked in darkness.

"You asked for it," I said, telling her what I had wanted to tell Kacey and more, another two beers each more, to be somewhat exact.

"Oh, my God," Maricela said when I finished.

For a moment, she regarded me with a different expression, almost like she looked at someone else.

"So why do you think someone would harm, what is her name, Kacey?"

I shrugged. "Usual reasons. Love and power don't seem to fit. So maybe money?"

"So, what are you going to do?"

I laughed at this question, which seemed to assume I had more than one option.

"The very last thing I want to do."

"What's that?"

"Get out and look for my damn granddaughter."

Mike Chapter 9

1982 Bellingham, Washington

None of us had dressed for the October chill as we huddled in the McDonald's parking lot off Interstate-5, killing time by trading bad jokes and checking the night sky for pre-Halloween fireworks. Kimberly hadn't brought a coat, so she bundled herself in an old jean jacket Tim found in his truck.

"You sure you don't want to get in my warm car while we wait for Tim's magical surprise?" I asked Kimberly, suffusing the words *magical* and *surprise* with all the sarcasm I could muster.

"I'd have to be freezing to be seen in something so ugly," she said. "It's even uglier than Tim's jacket."

Even Tim, in his first year of the Bachelor of Arts program at Western Washington, wasn't safe from her prodding. While he became enlightened, I worked at his father's lumber yard, as did Kimberly, who was Tim's father's favorite cashier because she knew all kinds of useful shit like the difference between treated lumber and regular cedar boards.

Kimberly was three weeks away from her eighteenth birthday, which meant she would soon age out of the foster care system and be on her own. On our last hike, she had told me she had saved enough money to move in with two girlfriends and take a couple of classes at the community college while she worked. Her goal, which she revealed to me with enough wide-eyed enthusiasm to make me jealous, was to become a cop and push from Bellingham's police department at least one of those old fuckers who years earlier had mishandled her sex assault complaint.

We waited almost a half-hour that fall night for Tim's surprise, and when, finally, he said, "Wait. That's it, off to your left," Kimberly and I strained our eyes before giving each other a puzzled look.

I saw nothing other than a McDonald's employee carrying two oversized bags of garbage across each shoulder.

"Right there," Tim said more urgently, pointing at the worker.

The person in question walked slightly stooped with his head down, yet it didn't take me long to figure out his identity. When he reached the dumpster, we heard a grunt followed by a thud, sounds that repeated themselves seconds later.

"Hey, Jimmy," Tim yelled.

Jimmy spun around, looked at the three of us, and began retreating toward the restaurant's back door.

"Thought by now you'd be the manager, not still the low-life garbage boy," Tim said.

I pushed away from my car, wanting Jimmy to react. He didn't. He kept plodding forward, though noticeably faster. As he entered the restaurant, he raised a middle finger and slammed the door behind him.

Kimberly, her mouth wide, turned to Tim. "You brought us here to see *that*?"

Tim laughed. "Two years of hearing how he was always coming for Mike, blah, blah, blah. I wanted to give him his chance when we were all together to enjoy it."

"That was so bad," Kimberly said, gently slapping Tim on the chest though unquestionably appreciating the kindness he had offered.

With the slamming of the McDonald's back door, the three of us moved into another chapter in our lives. Perhaps, a more grown-up and intelligent chapter, as demonstrated by Tim inviting us to meet him later that night at a party one of his more learned friends was hosting near the university.

Kimberly gave Tim a long and almost awkward hug before she tossed him his jacket and climbed inside my ugly car and made a series of mock puking noises.

* * *

The party took place at an old house on a hill on the western side of the university. By the time we arrived, The Stones screamed and thumped from three-foot-high speakers, and the house swarmed with a mix of WWU students, their working friends like me and Kimberly and a few older people I later learned included a mix of local firefighters and cops.

This public safety presence may have explained the drunken fireworks show that began shortly after midnight when a large cache of illegal fireworks confiscated by police was lit and sometimes tossed a little too dangerously close to those who gathered to watch. It also explained why the party got a free pass when a police cruiser arrived to investigate noise complaints.

Kimberly was dancing with one of the firefighters, and as I watched her, Tim stopped at my side, nodded at him, and said, "That's Todd."

"Who's Todd?"

"You know, Todd," Tim said. "The foster home Kim's lived at for the past 11 months. Todd's the firefighter husband of the woman who runs the place."

A few hours later, as the party mellowed to an REO Speedwagon album, a couple of firefighters began making out with co-eds on the back porch. One disappeared to his El Camino, where he and his new friend became nothing more than moving shapes behind an opaque window.

Tim's buddy Jack stood beside me and nodded to the car with a head thick with frizzy shoulder-length hair: "Those firefighters got quite the life."

I agreed.

"You heard some of them got a regular fuck-fest going on at one of the stations?"

"No."

"Oh yeah, each person on one of the shifts is responsible for bringing in one girl a month for gang bangs. They love the young ones. University age good. High school even better. They call the sessions 'station tours.' Lucky fuckers."

For the next hour or so, I made a few not-so-subtle inquiries about our town's apparently not-so-noble firefighters, hearing a wild assortment of rumors that initially made me angry and then a little unsure if any of them could be true.

When the party wound down, I found Kimberly and an equally high girlfriend named Dawn lying on the hallway carpet listening to the druggy sounds of Pink Floyd. I roused them, and they both clawed their way back to reality before accepting a ride home.

Being pretty messed up, I drove slowly and somehow found Dawn's house, even though she didn't know a single street name in her neighborhood, her only directions a slurred "go left" or "turn right." Later, when I pulled up in front of Kimberly's group home on Virginia Street, I needed to wake her.

"Thanks, Mike," she said, squeezing my hand.

"Nice not having a curfew, huh? I hear you have a good arrangement worked out with your guardian?"

"Sure, Mike. Goodnight."

She opened the car door and zigzagged up the sidewalk and a tall flight of concrete steps before seeming to collapse inside the front door.

* * *

In the more than two years since I had pounded Jimmy's head with a rock, I must have wondered a million times why no one came after me. Ever. I had once asked Kimberly's opinion. Did Jimmy and his so-called friends leave me alone because: A) Jimmy was a coward like his friends, and they all knew he got what he had coming? Or. B) Because my mother, when I was two, killed my equally violent father in a drunken and bloody knife fight, and everyone suspected I too possessed the capacity for such a horrendous act?

Kimberly regarded the question like a great weight she couldn't drop fast enough. "No one thinks of you like that, so it must be A," she blurted.

A few weeks later while we walked up Commercial Street in a light rain, I asked her another awkward question, this one about the death of my mother in the fifth year of her prison term, a shank to her kidney when I was seven, ending the sad timeline of her life. Pregnant at 16, a mother at 17, a convicted killer of her husband at 19, dead at 24.

I asked Kimberly, "Do you think no one ever adopted me in the years that followed because they looked at my file and saw how my parents died and said, *Fuck. Stay away from that one*?"

"Of course not, stupid," she said.

Like me, she sucked as a liar.

* * *

By early November, Kimberly had about a week left before aging out of foster care and would soon be moving in with her friends. So why couldn't I leave it alone?

One Friday afternoon, we took our lunch break together and walked the few blocks from the lumber yard to the Kentucky Fried Chicken. We sat bundled up outside on a cement table, and I asked, "You gonna miss everyone at the foster home where you live?"

Her hand slowed as she brought a greasy chicken breast to her mouth, though I could have imagined it. "Sure," she said. "But moving around is what I do."

"So I've heard."

Her glare told me to drop it, but I pushed on anyway.

"I've heard a few things about the husband at your foster home. Todd, right? That he takes girls for special tours of his fire hall. Shows 'em all the hoses."

Kimberly looked about as uncomfortable as I had ever seen her.

"You're not very chatty today," I said.

"If you have something you want to ask me, Mike, just hurry the fuck up and ask it?"

"Okay. Are you fucking your guardian?"

"Yeah. I am, okay."

I had expected another lame lie, so when she answered, it left me speechless. I picked up a piece of chicken, my teeth ripping at the thick breaded covering until I recalled her once scolding me about Mrs. Jennings. She was, as always, a step ahead of me, and when I began bringing up her disapproval of my relationship with my former guardian, she interrupted.

"We're both older now and better able to make decisions."

"You're letting yourself get exploited. Again."

She threw a chicken bone into the white and red box her food had come in. "I don't want to be judged by someone who impregnated half the women in the state who married impotent husbands."

"Well, at least I got some money out of that. Well, maybe you do too."

She bared her teeth. "You ever call me a whore again and you'll be sorry."

"So, what do you get then?"

Kimberly stood and began cleaning up her scraps, which she dumped in a nearby bin. She would surely leave. Instead, she sat back down

"What I get is to live in a place where the adults are caring. Where they hug you, where when they ask how you are, they are really asking and not just being polite, where the kids are happy, where I'm respected like one of the adults."

"Does his wife know?"

She hesitated, and when she spoke, her words sounded weary. "I'm not sure. They have some kind of open marriage."

"And do you sometimes get gang-banged at the fire station?"

Anger flashed in her eyes and disappeared. She didn't bother to lie. She stood, tossed back a single strand of hair from her eyes and began walking back to work with me trailing behind like that day we hitchhiked on Chuckanut Drive after a disastrous beach party. And like then, I studied her as she walked, unsure exactly who I saw.

I worked the rest of my shift, my rage gaining in mass with each passing hour. When I left, I barely looked at Kimberly, who was ringing in a plastic bag full of nails at the front cash register.

On the drive to her group home, I told myself how, in time, she would see she was wrong about so much. Like her claim she wasn't being exploited by someone much older. Or her belief that two close friends couldn't become a happy couple.

It was bad luck for Kimberly's guardian, and for me, that he was home. A girl a few years younger than Kimberly answered the front door, and I asked for Todd. He arrived on the stoop far too quickly for me to spawn anything resembling a sober second thought.

He was shorter than me and muscular with thick, wavy black hair and a mustache too large for his square face. He smiled like a person sure that whatever arrived at his door was good.

"I hear you got a thing for fucking kids in your care," I said.

"Who the fuck are you?" Todd demanded as he shoved me hard, a dangerous and provocative move given I stood on top of a steep cement staircase.

For my safety, of course, I countered his attack with a shove of my own. Soon his arm was around my neck, and mine his, and whatever I had come for had begun. Our limbs intertwined, we lunged back and forth like some two-headed beast. Before either of us could disengage, we lost our collective balance and began tumbling, rather painfully, down the stairs. Our newfound connection ended when we reached the bottom, where only one of us hit his head on the sidewalk with a sickening pop.

"Shit," I whispered to myself.

* * *

Two days later, after my first court appearance, Tim Kolchuk's father, Ron, paid my bail, and I walked out into the fresh air for the first time since the confrontation.

I liked Ron. He was a good boss and, from what Tim told me, a good father. He always backed up what he said. Kimberly and I always suspected he was the anonymous donor who made sure each foster kid had a gown or tux for our high school's graduation ceremony a few months back.

I also appreciated his old-school, no-nonsense approach to everything, from work to life, and deeply valued his opinion. So, the relief that surged through me was unimaginable when he and Tim met me outside the police station after my release, and Ron slapped my back and said, "Don't you worry, Mike. You've done nothing wrong. He's the one fucking children in his care, and he's the one who came at you when you called him out."

While they drove me home, I listened to how Ron Kolchuk would dismiss the public defender and hire me a real lawyer and pay for it. How in his day someone wasn't criminally charged just because he won a fair fight; how the cops and firefighters were all in cahoots but that means nothing to the judges hearing the cases.

When they left, I wanted to call Kimberly. Tim had told me the State had arranged to put her up in a motel room for her last few days in the system. When I asked which one, he shook his head. I understood.

Todd, from what I heard, had suffered serious head and back injuries. I didn't know it at the time, but he would never work as a firefighter again. Not that he would ever be given his job back. Our confrontation had, it appeared, become big news in town after *The Bellingham Herald* newspaper wrote a few stories that managed to link his injuries to allegations of "sex parties involving teenaged girls" at Todd's fire station. Todd himself faced charges of sexual exploitation. It was, simply, a terrible fucking mess for everyone involved, from Kimberly's caseworker, who had personally recruited Todd and his wife as the new more relaxed breed of future foster care providers, to the fire chief, who found himself defending men he surely wanted to strangle, if for no other reason than getting caught.

Some regarded me as a hero who challenged the cozy boys club that secretly ran the city, or so they told me, sometimes stopping me on the street to offer support or penning lengthy letters that found me even without a correct address. Others, unfortunately, stared with distaste at the spawn of two violent parents, perhaps sure I would soon supplant my mother or father for the title of the family's most savage member.

But Kimberly possessed the only opinion I truly cared about, and she didn't offer it from wherever she hid. She had arranged to be transferred to a small hardware store partly owned by Ron Kolchuk, meaning we no longer even worked together.

One night I finally coaxed the name of the hotel where she lived from one of her friends who worked at Boomer's drive-in. Ten minutes later, I parked outside the aging motel off I-5 on the north end of town.

For nearly three hours, I waited, frequently starting my car's engine to warm my hands over the lukewarm heater. An old Toyota glided through the parking lot almost silently on four small cylinders. It stopped in a space near a row of numbered doors, and Kimberly climbed out the passenger side. The night sky was a blanket of blackness, though enough light fell on the parking lot for me to see she was bundled in a cream-colored knit wool jacket that mostly covered the red shirt and brown pants that made up her hardware store uniform.

Soon the driver leaned at her side, kissing her neck, wrapping his arms around her and squeezing her ass like he owned her. He looked like one of the firefighters from the party near the university. Or maybe I just wanted him to be another firefighter.

They turned and began walking toward the wooden staircase that led to the second-floor rooms. I called out to Kimberly, a little surprised to already be out of my car and closing in on them.

While Kimberly would never fully condone what I did to her so-called guardian, I did hope at least to salvage something from what had happened, even if just getting her to admit she had needed my help.

To his credit, the maybe-firefighter stepped forward in front of Kimberly. His bold body language was belied by the fear that arrived in his eyes the moment he probably guessed my identity. He muttered something about me not needing more legal trouble. My pace quickened. I had already decided where to hit him and how hard and how many times, aptly using the skills and rage that made up my entire inheritance.

As I drew my right arm back, Kimberly jumped in front of the man and tried to give me a shove, though my momentum took me into her hard enough to almost knock us both to the ground.

"Why do you need to ruin everything?" she screamed like all my anger had transferred to her on our clumsy contact.

Before I could find words, the other man spoke. "Let's go inside, Kim, and have a beer. C'mon."

She looked at me, then at him, and shook her head. She turned and began climbing the stairs alone. Her friend called after her a couple of times before moving toward his car. My eyes followed Kimberly as her steps echoed along the outside corridor before falling silent.

I stood in the middle of the parking lot, my hands, ears and cheeks turning red from the cold. My warm car beckoned. I didn't budge, and I wasn't sure why. My thoughts clung to, of all things, Kimberly's final steps to her motel-room door, which had involved no backward glances. Maybe my mind played tricks on me because I swore Kimberly had stepped with a harsh finality that screamed, *Take a good look. It's the last one you'll ever get.*

* * *

Two weeks before Christmas, I met with Ron Kolchuk and my lawyer, a pudgy man whose name I could never remember but would in my mind call Mr. Grey for the way his hair perfectly matched the color of his suit. In the cramped lumber yard office, he updated us on my suddenly less-positive-than-before "situation," his every word or gesture deflating Mr. Kolchuk to the point that the face on my always optimistic boss grew as grim as the masks on the scarecrows sold downstairs. The state prosecutor, Mr. Grey advised us, believed he could get a conviction and would seek a four-year sentence, based on legal precedent, the victim's injuries, the fact I had confronted him at his home. If this wasn't bad enough, Mr. Grey believed the state had an 80 percent chance of winning.

"I've discussed a plea bargain with the prosecutor where you would plead guilty to a lesser charge and serve only one year, likely less with early parole," Mr. Grey continued. "The plea bargain they offer is a better-than-usual deal because, I believe, too many institutions would find a trial of this nature embarrassing. And this better-than-usual arrangement is what I would recommend to you."

Most of the ensuing discussion involved Mr. Kolchuk and Mr. Grey. I stood and went to the window, so deep in thought

I didn't realize I had risen until I found myself surveying the lumber yard and the industrial street where my beautiful brown Pinto awaited. The criminal record that came with a guilty plea scared me much more than the time in prison. It told the world I was guilty of a violent crime. It told the world I was like my parents. Far better to fight for my innocence than agree to be forever branded a criminal, even if this legal fight came with a risk.

My mind was made up, or so I thought.

Todd's name fell from Mr. Grey's mouth once more, followed by a depressing list of injuries, which for now trapped him inside a damaged body that couldn't yet climb from its hospital bed or force out a single coherent sentence.

As I sat back down in my wobbly chair, a voice in my head asked the one question ignored by everyone in the room. Who would pay for what happened to Todd if not me?

Mr. Kolchuk and Mr. Grey finally exhausted their words. Lost, they turned to me. I stared at the wall calendar featuring a stunning bikini-clad model wearing a Santa hat and brandishing a mocking smile that suggested she knew exactly what someone like me thought. I surprised everyone by saying, "I guess one year beats four."

* * *

The judge had court time available the week before Christmas, and it seemed all parties wanted to wrap up my case before their holiday break. I was given several days to get my shit in order because the moment the judge agreed to the plea, I would be immediately convicted, sentenced and transferred to a prison, probably Washington State Penitentiary in Walla Walla. I used some of this time to pack up my meager belongings, which Tim would store at his home. Once again, I tried to engage Kimberly, who refused to return my phone calls.

Two days before my court date, someone knocked on my door, and I rushed to it expecting Kimberly. No one greeted me except a blast of frigid air, though Two-Wheeled Eddie eventually materialized on my doorstep from wherever he lurked. I invited him inside, and though he declined, he lingered on the front step long enough to explain he had heard about my plight and wanted me to meet two people who could help ease my time in prison.

"They're skinheads who recruit potential skinheads," he said, climbing on his bike. "But they're cool. For the most part."

* * *

The skinheads met me the next day in a video arcade downtown. With shaved heads, piercings and jean jackets emblazoned with the name of the band No Remorse, they greeted me with warm handshakes and introduced themselves as Thomas and Frank. Their tattooed hands folded politely before them, they spent the next 40 minutes earnestly explaining the culture of their burgeoning white-pride movement, which they claimed was no more racist than government policies allowing our state to be flooded with illegal Mexican farmworkers. They talked about the groups they admired, like the Aryan Nations, which worked to turn Washington, Oregon and Idaho into white-only states.

"I think they're too late," I pointed out, not wanting to seem too ridiculously naïve.

In time Thomas and Frank turned their attention to my situation, which they had heard about from a cop who thought I was "getting screwed over" by the legal system. The cop had known I knew Eddie, and he was approached to contact me. Because I would likely wind up in Walla Walla, Frank was interested in how we could help each other. The skinheads in the Aryan Brotherhood prison gang, Frank and Thomas claimed, ran the prison and always kept an eye out for more good men.

I only needed one suitable tattoo and the name of their contact inside the prison, and no one would dare touch me, meaning I would effortlessly fly through my time.

"Take a few minutes to think about it," Thomas said, his eyes falling, with noticeable disapproval, on the Asian girl at the concession stand who wrote food orders on a small pad.

As suggested, I walked outside and around the block. I considered returning to my car and my empty apartment and forgetting every word I had heard. I was no racist shithead. But I couldn't stop thinking that, in extreme circumstances, we all needed someone to watch our backs. And who better than a group of guys who had no complicated emotional attachments?

I worked this through my mind until it sounded acceptable, and I returned to the video arcade, nodded at Thomas and Frank, who led me two blocks away to a tattoo parlor where I received the required marking, a solid-black swastika that went on the side of my neck and looked alarmingly larger than expected.

The next day in court, my fingers repeatedly pulled my shirt higher, like they alone wanted to hide the swollen, offensive symbol. As the judge reviewed the plea bargain, I took one last look around the courtroom for Kimberly. She wasn't there.

"Bitch," I whispered to myself.

The judge approved the deal and sentenced me not to one year but two, with the possibility of parole in 14 months, at the McNeil Island Corrections Center on the other side of the state from Walla Walla.

"Bitch," I repeated, this time out loud.

Ashlee Chapter 8

Missing: Days Five and Six

Do transcended beings dream? I guess so because I dream I am a physical entity riding a bus through a flat desert at night, my full bladder aching, yet not enough to wake me. Bright stars wink down like we share a secret. The vortex and cross lie ahead like my grandfather was told in the warehouse. It will be somewhere there, in the desert, that all will be revealed, even the one who hides in the darkness behind a mask of purity.

My dream quickly turns into a nightmare. Suddenly the stars begin collapsing into blackness. And I cry out as I tumble alone into this darkness and desolation, this emptiness that echoes with loss. A man's face, wrinkled and weathered from countless hours stooped in outdoor labor, appears before me, his kind hand on my shoulder. He must understand I am now an orphan because he leans in and whispers, *Even if they're both gone, they left you so many good things. I can see all of them shining in your eyes.*

And suddenly, my dream returns to the calm night desert, the bus rocking gently in the first gusts of an approaching shitstorm, one that will test my faith and the faith of so many others. The darkness seeps back gently, and this time I let it wash over me until I melt away.

Later in a bus-stop diner, I find Physical Ashlee, who is reading again. Don't get involved, I tell myself, but I glance down, and the very first word fills me with longing, which means it fills me with weakness too, because we are always stronger on our own. I start reading and again become trapped in my own words, trapped in a time when everything is pirouetting out of control.

Eleven to Seven Weeks Before Missing

Dad has sold all his paintings, *even the early and less refined ones,* for a *substantial amount of money,* so, whoo, it's party time, with him and Mom often entertaining a bunch of newfound friends and a few old ones. At least they bought me a snazzy Apple laptop and got me a Netflix account, meaning I do my homework in my room and watch *Breaking Bad* episodes with my headphones on to drown out the noise coming from our apartment's kitchen and living room.

Breaking Bad is amazing. Maybe it's the cute Jesse or, more likely, the comfort that comes from seeing how mine isn't the only life impacted by drugs. I binge-watch the entire series, sometimes taking a break for several days each time an episode especially moves me. One such episode is the one where Walter lets Jesse's heroin-overdosing girlfriend, Jane, choke and die on her own vomit to prevent her from blackmailing him. *Shit,* I think.

As I power down my laptop that night, I decide this scene represents the exact moment when Jesse and Walter change places, with Jesse becoming the show's moral conscience and Walter a cold-hearted fucker consumed by the evil and greed we all possess to varying degrees. Before I drift off, I decide this isn't wholly true. That nothing ever happens all at once but instead bit-by-bit over time, like the slow trickle of blood from a wound that you swear isn't big enough to kill you.

A few nights later, Jane's deadly vomiting scene comes to me during a supposed dream, only my mother is Jane and my father is Jesse and I am Walter, burdened with the responsibility of deciding whether Mom lives or dies. I hesitate at the critical moment when she begins choking on her puke, and by the time

I crawl across their bed in agonizing slow-mo, it's too late. I wake up, rush into the kitchen, turn on the light and start sorting through the garbage under the sink. There I find what I had seen earlier that day while throwing out a banana peel, though my brain didn't fully recognize what it had taken in. It's a needle, and as I uncover it beneath some paper towel, it nearly pricks my hand.

I race into Mom and Dad's bedroom and turn on the lights and climb between them, immediately seeing that:

1) Both are breathing.

2) Both are high enough that my voice and my hands shaking them and the light flooding their room all fail to wake them.

3) Another needle rests on Dad's nightstand.

Mom is sleeping on her back, like Jane when she choked, so I push her on her side, and even this doesn't wake her. *Breathe*, I coax myself.

The digital clock reads 3:07, a reminder of the long night ahead. I take their pillows and put them against the headboard and sit up. I turn off the light, stick my feet under the covers and stroke my Mom's hair back behind her ear. It's stunning how many important signs are made available if we only look for them. For hours I watch over my dependents, even missing the first two school classes that day.

Dad stirs first, groaning as he opens his eyes and feels the assault of the light through the thin blinds.

I don't scold him. Instead, I say in a matter-of-fact voice, *You need to get sober and get your ass down to your studio and start working.*

He doesn't jump at my voice. He turns slowly and struggles to focus his eyes on me. His words ooze slowly like his mouth is full of sweet molasses. *There she is, my little girl.*

I am not your little fucking girl. I am a young woman with important responsibilities.

Yes, okay, he says.

Dad glances past me at Mom and with great effort swings his body around and puts his feet on the floor. I'm guessing that's when he sees the needle in plain sight on his night table. He stands, sweeping it up with one hand as if I hadn't yet spotted it, before disappearing into their bathroom, where he takes the longest pee in history.

While he showers, I sit with Mom. I should be mad at her for allowing herself to follow Dad's lead and should turn my body away to let her know how I feel. Instead, I curl behind her and place my right arm around her waist. She's wearing one of Dad's old T-shirts and nothing else. It rides up her hips. I reach down and try to pull it toward her legs. I kiss the back of her head. Finally, she wakes.

Unlike Dad, it takes her a good 10 minutes to get her bearings and find her way back into this world where she has a daughter and a job at Great Clips and a husband she loves but shares the same sickness with.

When she turns her head to face me, her eyes tremble like she's facing her greatest fear. I understand exactly what she's thinking. I don't know how but I can hear her thoughts, which don't stretch out in a traditional combination of words forming a phrase and then a sentence. They come to me as a detailed set of facts and feelings that enter my mind as one whole concept, like a painting. Mom isn't thinking about how the heroin is hurting her; she's worried her drug use will rub off on me.

Don't worry, I tell her. *I hate fucking drugs.*

She leans in and kisses my neck. Her breath is less than stellar, like the general smell of their room. I don't care. She starts playing with my hair.

You're overdue for a cut, she says, *Why don't you come by the shop after school today and I'll look after my beautiful girl?*

I don't question out loud whether she'll make it into work today. Or whether she still has a job. Or even how long I can do this for. Because it's all out of my hands.

* * *

So, apparently, I have no friends after Maria Perez told Gina today she would *destroy* her and Becky and Sophie if she ever spotted them with me again. Gina took the threat seriously, wasting no time texting me the news in her typeractive glory, along with a reminder that Maria's father is a well-known gangster and former soldier from Nicaragua and that Maria has rearranged the faces of a half-dozen girls and even a couple of boys.

It's more shitty racism, texts the blond-haired blue-eyed Gina, who likes to say the white girls in our school are the minority and are often subjected to abuse.

Tonight, she tries to conclude our texting with a my-period-is-late anxiety-ridden signoff, *Still luv u girl but can't risk gettin seen with u now that that bitch Perez runs our shit.*

I respond, *U r such a loyal friend, said no one ever.*

Gina takes offense, or so her ensuing passive-aggressive texts indicate, like I care. I am spending more time with my New Age friends, and earlier today, Lucas invited me to a private spiritual session with him tomorrow night. Before bed, Gina texts an apology and suggests the drama with Miss Nasty will *blow over*.

Still, the next day my friends avoid me. And at lunch, my enemy approaches in typically aggressive Maria Perez fashion, as I sit alone in the cafeteria eating the peanut butter sandwich Grandma made with the fresh bread she picked up with some other groceries to restock our empty fridge and cupboards. Before I even see Maria, I notice her purple-black weave, always a legendary sign of trouble in our school. When she sees me by myself, her dick-sucking grin is instant and wide and savage.

Poor little cunt. No one will sit with you.

I give her a kind smile, hoping to point her toward the peace of her inner being, the place where purity lives, assuming the

Great Evil has not already found its way inside her like so many boys' dicks have into her filthy fuck-stain mouth.

Of course, it fails to have the desired effect, judging by the ten minutes of abuse I suffer until the bell rings for class.

* * *

That night at the Friends center, Lucas sits me down across from him in a meditation room, and we stretch. He cuts to the chase, and for the first time, he uses the words *psychic* and *prophecy* in the same sentence as little-ol' me. I laugh because everything I have read about extrasensory perception says there's no scientific evidence to support it.

Lucas begins reminding me about what happened two days ago after I fell asleep in a group meditation session, my body twitching wildly, all to everyone's amusement. When I awoke, someone asked if I had been dreaming. I told them I had a short dream about meeting Jesus, who came into the Friends center to lead a prayer service, though he spent most of his time drinking coffee from a bright red cup and lecturing me that the group wasn't following God's narrow path.

So, Lucas says. *I know Cynthia told you the dream could be analyzed as a simple manifestation of the fears you may have that our group's beliefs don't align precisely with the Bible and mainstream religious teachings. I would agree with her assessment, except what happened next changed everything.*

Lucas tells me that twenty minutes after I went home, a homeless man came inside and said he was interested in learning more about us. He wore sweatpants and a ripped hoodie, and the hair on his head and face was the same length and style as Jesus's hair in many historical paintings. Someone got the man a coffee, in a red cup, and he sat on a sofa listening to Cynthia's description of the group and its beliefs and how it has hundreds and hundreds of members who support each other

157

and follow Lucas's lead and raise money to spread peace and understanding to the masses.

Lucas grins. *The homeless man, who did bear a striking resemblance to depictions of Jesus, listened patiently until Cynthia finished. Then he launched into a lecture on blasphemy and how we need to follow the word of God.*

Then Lucas delivers the real surprise.

I don't think you were dreaming when you conjured up Jesus. I think instead you were having a symbolic out-of-body experience. And I'm sure it wasn't your first.

Okay, now you're just making stuff up, I almost tell him. Because even if I already knew I frequently have out-of-body experiences, the symbolic stuff, the suggestion they mean something, is a big fat twist.

I immediately hit Lucas with the most pressing question. *So, where do I go when I have these experiences? Could I be traveling to another dimension of space and time?*

He considers this like he's wondering if this is what I believe. *I don't profess to have all the answers, though I will say that's entirely possible.*

He spends forty minutes explaining concepts I don't fully understand. He talks about how prophecy has been observed in many cultures and religions for thousands of years. He mentions Corinthians 12 from the Bible, where Paul talks about the Holy Spirit routinely bestowing the gift of prophecy on people, along with other superpowers like the ability to speak in tongues and the ability to heal.

I listen and listen, and finally, I take the term *symbolic out of body experience* and shorten it to *SOOBE*. Lucas flinches at the acronym like I'm not taking this shit seriously.

* * *

My grandmother, with a bit of help from my grandfather, has

restored order at home, at least partly. Mom and Dad still look constantly wasted, though they are at least functionally wasted. Mom is cutting hair again at Great Clips, and Dad is painting, though one morning at breakfast when we're alone, Grandma tells me Dad has irreparably harmed his career by delivering to an art middleman three shitty paintings he produced, rather quickly, while high.

Grandma likes talking about the family, and I like listening. She must sense this because one day, when I ask about my other grandfather, the biological one and not her husband, she hesitates and grins and asks, *Can you keep a secret?*

I nod eagerly, *Hell yes*, thinking back to when we first heard about Grandma's *indiscretion*, an affair that led to the birth of my father. The story we heard was that my birth father was a nasty piece of work, and no one should contact him, or some serious shit would follow.

He was just a boy, Grandma tells me now. *Even younger than you.*

My eyes must go wide. She battles back tears as she talks about how the boy was a kid named Mike in a group home she ran in 1978 in Washington State.

He was a sweet boy, she says. *Like your father is. He had a good heart, and I wanted to make everything in his life right. Instead, I did something horrible by seducing him.*

I can't believe Grandma is telling me this. It's a shit-bat-crazy story, one that doesn't even sound possible. Then she says, *None of us is perfect. We all make mistakes, sometimes the same one over and over again. But that doesn't mean we are not worthy of someone's love.*

* * *

After hearing I have psychic powers, a lot of heavy shit happens right quick, none of it seen by me in advance: the death of my grandmother from a heart attack, a surprise meeting with a former friend of my biological grandfather at the funeral service, the departure of the grandfather who helped raise me. So, what the fuck is the point of having an alleged special power if it tells you useless shit about some homeless guy but misses the crucial stuff about the people you love?

You probably were given strong clues about all those other events in advance, Lucas would later say, *but you just didn't read the signs properly.*

Right, I would reply sarcastically, refusing to accept blame.

I spend much of the morning before Grandma's funeral service in tears, though my mood improves when I am approached after the service by an older red-haired woman who identifies herself as *Kimberly from Washington State.* She's dressed in a summery pant/shirt outfit that she explains is perfect for the vacation she happens to be on. She's easy to talk to, and I soon discover she knew Grandma from the group home in Washington State. It doesn't take long for me to figure out she was there at the same time as my biological grandfather. When I ask her if she remembers a boy named Mike from her time at the home, she hesitates for only a moment before spilling out his full name, Mike Baker.

I squeal with excitement and explain that this person is my grandfather. When she recovers from the shock enough to ask me how I know this, I debate telling her Grandma's little secret, fully aware Grandma can no longer be punished for her indiscretion, considering she has already suffered the ultimate punishment, death. Better not to go all in, so I say, *Grandma told me she hooked up with him later. You know, when they were both adults. And along came my dad.*

Kimberly studies me, and then my father, and then her eyes begin to drift far away. She suddenly snaps out of her trance and leans in and whispers, *That's not entirely true, is it? The timing, I mean.*

I ask, *How did you know?*

Kimberly smiles, though only with her mouth and only slightly. *Mike was a close friend.*

Perfect. I ask her to tell me all she can about her close friend Mike Baker, and she does, reluctantly at first.

That night I go online and find out all about Mike the Grandfather, spending two hours transfixed by photos of him and more than a dozen stories he wrote from the most dangerous places in the world. A strange familiarity purrs through me. As I learn more about him, it's easy to believe I can start to understand myself better, though it's difficult to explain why. All I know for sure is I am an unreal stalker.

Mike Chapter 10

Missing: Day Six

The Suttons had lived in the Liberty Square area in an apartment building that now boasted a boarded-up third-story window that towered above the tangled remnants of yellow police tape in the shrubs below. I parked across the street; my thinking desperate yet simple: Ashlee may return home at any time. Or not.

Either way, I was running out of ideas, and it was barely mid-morning. Earlier I had returned to the warehouse where I had found and lost Ashlee; it was empty. I had also run through every word I recalled her speaking, writing down much of our conversation before going to bed last night. As far as any hint of where Ashlee may go, only one small part of our conversation stood out, her cryptic reference to meeting me again where the vortex and large cross converge, or words to that effect. On Google, those exact terms had produced a grab-bag of websites selling strange clothing and espousing weird scientific theories, but nothing remotely geographical.

So I sat in my car and brainstormed and overthought while waiting for the appearance of a 16-year-old girl allegedly gripped by mental illness, amazing intuition and more than enough intelligence to make predicting her next move almost impossible.

An hour into my so-called stake-out, a woman stepped from a car across the street and went inside the Suttons' building. Fifteen minutes later, she emerged, returned to her car and began fumbling around in the trunk.

Next, she wandered up the street, a stack of papers and what looked like a roll of tape in her hands, stopped at various telephone poles, bus shelters, almost any free public space, and taped up what looked like an advertisement. She crossed the street to a spot fifty feet in front of my car, and as she taped a piece of paper to a city garbage container, I fumbled for my glasses. The woman moved away, revealing a poster with the red capital letters "MISSING PERSON."

By now, the woman had my full attention as she continued down the street toward my car. I studied her hair, a slightly unnatural shade of red, while trying to look at her face as she passed. I swung around in my seat to watch her out of my back window, and I soon realized what transfixed me: it was her step, purposeful, maybe a little anxious, though full of unstoppable energy.

I climbed from my car and laughed. Last night I had retrieved a single good memory of Kimberly, and now I tried to conjure her in the flesh.

"Miss," I called out.

She stopped, turned around and took a long look at me. As impossible as it seemed, she did bear a striking resemblance to Kimberly, or what Kimberly could look like decades later.

"Hi, Mike," she said in Kimberly's time-battered voice.

* * *

A half-block down the road sat a coffee shop where Kimberly suggested we go after exchanging a long, painfully awkward hug followed by an equally awkward greeting.

"I think we're looking for the same person," she had said, "so why don't we get a coffee and a window table and both keep an eye out for her while we get reacquainted."

When had I last felt this rattled? Less than 48 hours earlier, while in the brief company of the girl we both sought. On the short walk to the coffee shop, I almost tripped twice on ruts in the sidewalk as I tried to examine Kimberly's face like it held clues to her life.

The second time I nearly fell, she laughed. "Better keep your eyes on the road, stupid."

I took her arms and pulled her close, this time hugging her tightly, like the lost decades and all their mass could slip between us if we let them.

This physical contact was not exactly dreamlike. More like a distortion of time in which we had become our former teenaged selves, though trapped inside bodies that had seen and experienced too much. Of course, I was far from the same person inside; what Kimberly was wasn't yet clear.

"It's shocking, Mike, I understand," she said. "More for you than me. I'm aware of your connection to the family, assuming what I've heard is true. Knew it before you did. So, I'm not surprised to find you here. You, I suspect, had no idea I had met any of the Suttons, other than, of course, Ashlee's grandmother a long, long time ago."

We ordered coffees in near silence and took the last window table and, while we caught up, did a strikingly shitty job of watching the street for Ashlee, though some things can be forgiven.

"I've followed your career a bit and snooped online and seen the odd picture of you, so when you called to me on the street, I knew exactly how you looked and how you had aged," she said, grinning. "Gracefully, I think. Growing old, at least physically, is always easier for men."

"You don't look that different," I said. "I was shocked because I had never expected to see you again."

She flashed a smile that quickly faded. "Why did you never come back to Bellingham after prison?"

Always so direct. How did I answer? I shrugged. "Needed to reinvent myself. At age 19."

For nearly an hour, she did most of the talking, filling in all the blanks in her life with only a few surprises. If someone's life can be summarized in one sentence, she had graduated from college, found a job with the Mount Vernon police department, married another cop named Rick, moved to Seattle, gave birth to two now-grown children, grew apart from Rick, got divorced though she still loved him and they remained close friends, retired from the police force, traveled, started working as a private detective and skiptracer, moved to Florida.

I didn't tell her that much of this I had earlier gleaned from Facebook, peeking at her profile from a bogus account I set up. Seeing dozens of happy family photos was enough to keep me from ever again looking her up online. Only her divorce, retirement, new career and Florida move came as news to me.

"What about you?" she asked abruptly.

My eyes moved to the street. "Ashlee could have done a few thousand cartwheels in front of her building and brandished a large sign reading *Here I Am, Fools*, and we wouldn't have noticed."

"I know. Finding people is what I do for a living. Right now I am sucking big time. But you are changing the subject."

I stared at my coffee. "I've worked. Seen the world. Had a few adventures. Maybe done a little good."

"That's modest and brief, don't you think?"

"Not at all."

"I know otherwise."

"Didn't anyone ever tell you to beware of what you read online, especially on social media?"

"Ha," she said. "You don't have a single social media account."

"I'm surprised you know that."

"Don't be. You think I never thought of you over the years?"

I resisted squirming in my seat. "So, anyway," I said. "Sounds like you're happy with your life, what you've left behind."

She sat back in her chair and smiled, maybe at my clumsy effort to shift the conversation away from me.

"Me and Rick managed to raise two great kids and give them

a good life, and I am pretty sure they will one day raise good families too and so on. That's what makes me the happiest. I have a few regrets but, given where you and I started, I am happy with how it all turned out."

I nodded.

"You never got married?" she asked.

I tried not to wince. "Was on the road a lot for work. Never seemed fair to take a wife."

She started to ask another question, which I interrupted. "So, how did you meet the Suttons?"

Kimberly quickly returned her coffee cup to the table. "Okay. Down to business."

She told a story that began a year or so ago when she and a girlfriend took a trip where they flew to New York, rented a car and began driving down the coast to Miami. One night in Savannah, Georgia, Kimberly went online to check social media and spend a few minutes on her usual morbid diversion, browsing *The Bellingham Herald* and *Seattle Times* newspaper obituaries in search of people she knew, a practice that started the previous year after the suicide of two ex-cops she had worked with. It was in *The Herald* she noticed an obituary for Carol Jennings, who had died of a heart attack. She poked around a bit more online and then noticed the same obituary in a newspaper in Jacksonville, Florida, where Mrs. Jennings had most recently lived. Only it wasn't the same obituary. It was slightly different. The Florida one said she was survived by her husband, Don, son Joshua, daughter-in-law, Kacey, and granddaughter, Ashlee, while the Bellingham one only mentioned Don. With the funeral two days away in Florida and Kimberly curious about the discrepancy, and maybe Mrs. Jennings too, she asked her friend if they could time their trip for a short stop down the coast.

Kimberly talked about the small funeral. About approaching Ashlee and saying she had lived with her grandmother in 1978 in a Bellingham group home. And how Ashlee, upon hearing this, asked "Did you know a boy in the group home named Mike?" and seemed to hold her breath while she awaited the answer.

Kimberly laughed. "That was the moment I figured out you were her grandfather. Did I suspect it earlier, and that's why I was at the funeral? Who knows? But the more I thought about Mrs. Jennings, the more the timing made sense. Your involvement with her. The Jennings' sudden departure from town.

"Anyway, I gave Ashlee your name, and her head nearly exploded because she finally knew your identity. We talked and talked, much of the conversation about you, until the funeral director announced the reception would end in 15 minutes, and Ashlee hugged me and said, 'You see, God takes and gives. I've lost my grandmother but found my grandfather.'

"You know, after meeting Ashlee, I thought of tracking you down and phoning you, Mike. I should have. Should have done a lot of things."

I tried to show no emotion. "At some point, you obviously met Kacey Sutton."

"Yes. As Mrs. Jennings' funeral reception wound down, Ashlee introduced me to her mother and father, but before she did, we both agreed it would be our secret that I knew Joshua's father. I told Joshua and Kacey that Mrs. Jennings had raised me for a short time in her group home. Anyway, I continued my vacation, fell in love with the Florida coast, and later rented a small house in Cocoa Beach. Ashlee found me on Facebook and started messaging me, asking more about you, telling me about her life."

Kimberly lifted her long-empty coffee cup and quickly put it back down.

"Anyway, over time, I could tell things were getting bad at her house with her parents' drug use. And Ashlee seemed to be, well, going off the rails. Eventually, I intervened. I contacted child services, maybe partly against Ashlee's wishes. That led to her diagnosis with Cotard's. Do you know about that?"

"Yes."

"Good. I guess. Anyway, they were still a family in crisis, and I stopped hearing from Ashlee. Everything went black." Kimberly let out a long sigh. "You know I am involved in a group that helps exploited children. Called Focus on Safe Situations. Kind of like a strange hobby for me. Some people play pickleball as they grow older. I do this."

She began explaining how kids like Ashlee from the most dysfunctional homes are sometimes exploited, especially if they wind up on the street. Porn, prostitution, an online community of creeps who will pay big money to touch younger kids in the flesh. More than I wanted to hear.

"Unfortunately," she said, "all this makes girls like Ashlee, smart and pretty but completely lost, ripe for the picking. So I was more than a little worried about her. Couple of nights ago, I managed to get hold of Kacey's cell phone number and phone her. She told me the situation."

Kimberly gave me a cop-like look, meaning one incapable of hiding suspicion. "Kacey said Ashlee's biological grandfather was helping and had found and lost Ashlee earlier that day. I was surprised by your involvement. But unfortunately not by Joshua's death, though it deeply saddened me. Anyway, I asked Kacey how you came into the picture. She told me that before Ashlee ran off, the girl had confessed that she knew her real grandfather's identity and that he would soon help the family. Ashlee was badgered into giving up whatever contact information she had for you.

"I agreed to drive down and help with the search. By the time I got here, Kacey, sadly, was dead too."

Slightly breathless, Kimberly stared out the window, still too tough to cry, though barely. "And I once thought we had experienced a lot of shit by the time we turned 16," she said.

"Do you want another coffee?" I asked.

She shook her head and tapped on the table with nervous energy.

My mind began compiling a list of how she had changed since our teenage years. Thicker body, face weathered by sun and time, eyes more guarded though still warm and kind. But still full of all those intangibles that attracted me to her.

"I spent yesterday poking around," she said. "Found those posters in the Suttons' apartment and was starting to post them around here and around the warehouse where you saw her."

"When you were inside, did you put some of your investigative skills to work?" I asked. "Because, you may know, the cops have suspicions that Kacey got a little push through the window."

"Yes. I talked to one of the detectives. They do think it is suspicious. I do too."

"But why would someone do that? And who?"

"Wish I knew," Kimberly said.

"That's the problem," I said. "I didn't know Kacey at all. You barely did. We don't know what she was involved in. Same with Ashlee."

We tried to fill in some of the Sutton family blanks, getting close to nowhere. Were they involved in crime? Did they have enemies? Who was this New Age group offering a $10,000 reward? We agreed we knew next to nothing.

When we fell silent again, my mind began to wander. I studied Kimberly, wondering if my eyes gave off a longing that she could notice. Assuming my eyes were still capable of giving off any emotion.

If they showed anything, she didn't let on. She moved things along, asking, "So what did Ashlee say when you met her? Anything that would help us find her, no matter how trivial it might appear?"

How did I explain a conversation that spun in circles? Of course, I would never reveal to anyone Ashlee's rather personal assertion about my true motives for being in the warehouse. But Kimberly would want to hear the rest of it, especially Ashlee's mention of the cross and the vortex where we would supposedly meet again.

I began telling the story, though a few sentences in, the words began to stick in my mouth for reasons that were unclear.

After offering only the vaguest account of the warehouse encounter, my mouth seized up, and my eyes gaped at Kimberly as if she was an adversary. Or at least someone who could hurt me.

Sure, we had both changed. But in the hour or so we talked, I had begun to believe one thing hadn't. Kimberly was still the same intoxicating free-fall as always. One that always ended in painful reality when my body struck the hard ground.

"Anyway, that's all I remember," I said, aware each word sounded clipped. "We were interrupted by a girl in worse shape than Ashlee, and while I was helping her, Ashlee slipped away. But why don't we exchange phone numbers. I'll let you know if something more comes to mind."

"Sure," she said, the wrinkle between her eyes growing more prominent.

"Guess this means we're working together," she added with sudden enthusiasm.

"Guess so," I said, trying to force an equal level of eagerness into my words.

We agreed I would stick up the rest of the posters around this neighborhood and watch for Ashlee while Kimberly searched around the warehouse. Then we would meet that night for dinner.

We said goodbye, and she hugged me. This time she hung on a little long.

She said, "Sorry."

"For what?"

She shook her head. "Just sorry."

* * *

I did stick up a few dozen posters. Enough to give Kimberly time to leave. I crossed the street to the Suttons' building, climbed the exterior staircase and located their door, which stood behind police tape. The area around the latch plate and strike plate looked like it had been tampered with. I pushed the door, and it didn't budge. I put my shoulder into it lightly, and it popped open, and I ducked under the tape.

Before me stood a messy suite with a cramped kitchen, a small balcony and a living room pockmarked with evidence markers pointing to what probably were bloodstains on the carpet. I didn't want to examine the crime scene, even though my name graced the pages of a police report, perhaps under a heading of "possible suspect." I wandered back to the short hallway with an open door leading to a bathroom and two closed ones that likely led to Ashlee's room and her parents'.

I spent little time in Joshua and Kacey's room, not sure what bothered me more: the broken window that Kacey had crashed through to her death or my surprise son's various personal effects.

I hurried to Ashlee's room, exhaling a nervous laugh over my accelerated heartbeat like I feared the girl stood behind the door with outstretched arms awaiting my arrival. I placed my hand inside the bottom of my shirt, turned the handle, swung the door open, and let out a long breath when the room was Ashlee-free.

If the living room and kitchen looked torn apart, Ashlee's room was worse. Someone, or possibly several people, had ransacked it. It may have started with Kacey, desperate to find a clue to Ashlee's disappearance and gone on from there. Her dresser and end table drawers sat empty, scattered contents on the floor. Same for her closet; its contents lay in a heap outside the open door. She had a computer table but no computer. And no cell phone anywhere in sight.

About all that remained intact were two large photo collages on facing walls. Each comprised several dozen photographs of exotic destinations likely cut from magazines or printed from websites.

I leaned into the first collage and was struck by how many of the locations I recognized. A few were well-known landmarks most people could identify: the Great Pyramid of Giza in Egypt, the Berlin Wall, Trevi Fountain in Rome, the giant Ferris wheel in Vienna, Neuschwanstein Castle in Germany; even the Space Needle in Seattle. Others were more far-flung: Brighton Palace Pier in England, the Piazza del Campo in Siena, the Blue Mosque in Istanbul.

I walked across the room to the second collage, quickly reciting the location of at least a dozen of the photos, reminding myself not to become too prideful of my worldly geographical knowledge. After all, as I had told Kimberly, much of my life was spent on the road.

As I stared at the photographs, the more famous landmarks fell away, leaving the rest, an esoteric mix of city scenes and striking landscapes. My hand rose and brushed over a few of them, and I could feel the blood rushing in my head. I recognized the quaint German town of Dachau better known for the nearby Second World War concentration camp, the tropical beach haven of Cahuita in Costa Rica, the peaceful canals in Colmar, France.

Some photos were marked with identifying captions. Others weren't. But most shared one trait. They were places I had visited.

I returned to the first collage and pored over its content for another 15 minutes. While I couldn't place a few photos, most were images of locations so familiar they elicited memories that brought a wide grin to my face. A cliff-side mountain bar where I shared a dark European beer with a fellow hiker. A dusty desert market where I haggled in broken Arabic for a stone trinket that caught my eye. A tropical waterfall that I plunged into after a long ride by horse. A busy Tehran street where a young woman risked almost everything by knocking on my apartment door with a bottle of rose wine in her hand, her blue headscarf flowing gently in the gritty night wind. The glacier-fed turquoise river where I vacationed with a woman I nearly spent the rest of my life with.

So much of my life, the parts Ashlee would define as Heaven, was taped to these two walls.

The images called to me, almost like Ashlee had assembled them for me. But that was impossible. The knowledge of my trips to these places was etched only in my head, not in vain social media postings or any other record. Yet somewhere on these two walls in this strange girl's bedroom lay a message from Ashlee, and I had no idea what it said, other than the obvious: I feel the pull of these places too.

Who the fuck are you, Ashlee Sutton? I whispered.

I walked to the window and squinted through the glare at nothing, the light's harshness bringing me back to my stark surroundings. After more than 40 minutes in this room, I had done nothing other than get lost in reverie. Lost enough that I didn't see what I had come for, even though my eyes must have passed across it several times. I hurried back to the first collage and hunted for a specific photograph.

When I found it, I let out a nervous laugh. My eyes had earlier skipped over the photograph because I had wrongly assumed it was another place I had long ago visited, a place difficult to force from my mind: Afghanistan's Red City, also known as the City of Screams, a fortress set atop red rock cliffs, all of it likely unchanged in the centuries since being destroyed by Genghis Khan.

But the photograph was actually a magazine image of a different structure built into red rocks on a different continent. The caption read, "The Chapel of the Holy Cross is a Roman Catholic chapel built into the buttes of Sedona, Arizona."

On the browser on my phone, I searched "vortex" and "Sedona," discovering the town's fame came from vortexes or places where energy allegedly swirled like tornadoes.

My phone already in my hand, I should have pointed it toward the image and photographed it. I didn't do that, though. Instead, I reached up and tore the photo from the wall, tucking it in my wallet like a souvenir or perhaps proof the collage existed. Not realizing my mistake, I slipped out of the apartment.

* * *

Late that afternoon, I phoned Kimberly from home to make dinner plans, and when she didn't answer, I left a message. She never returned that or any of my other half-dozen calls or texts. Like years ago in Bellingham on the night before I went off to prison, I heated a box of Kraft dinner, ate alone in silence and wondered if I would ever see her again.

Mike Chapter 11

1982–83 McNeil Island, Washington

The first ferry ride of my life came two days after Christmas on a prison boat where I was handcuffed and my legs chained to a large steel hook fastened to the vessel's floor. Alongside three other prisoners, I struggled to keep my balance on a slippery wooden bench as the boat bumped over choppy water for a good 10 minutes until the McNeil Island Corrections Center came into view. As the ferry docked, I swallowed hard. A guard removed our restraints and led us onto the dock, where the prison, a mix of drab brick and concrete buildings surrounded by high barbwire fencing, rose above us in wretched finality.

Only fourteen months if I stayed out of trouble.

I would learn plenty about the prison and its island in the weeks to come, much of it in snippets from my counselor, a bald man named Larry whom I liked because of his no-bullshit bluntness. I memorized the facts like they weren't attached to a place I would rather forget: 4,000-acre island; last island prison in the United States since the closure of Alcatraz in 1963 and the construction a few years later of a bridge to Rikers in New York; the oldest prison in the country; famous inmates included the Birdman of Alcatraz and Charles Manson; once a federal prison boasting 1,700 inmates; now a state prison filled with garden variety criminals like thieves, sex offenders, killers, and me.

Of course, the most important fact I would discover concerned the skinhead movement. It held little sway within these walls where Hispanics, blacks and Native Americans outnumbered the whites by a wide margin. So much for my glorious tattoo.

My first sense of where I stood came when, after my walk up the road from the ferry through the main gate and to the small processing area and finally to my shared cell, I met my cellmate, a Mexican immigrant with an elegant handlebar mustache who studied my tattoo and made a tisk-tisk sound and remarked, "You don't need to go looking for trouble in this place."

Our cell sat on the fourth level of a five-tier tower. Squeezed inside were two bunks attached to the wall and a small toilet. A thick metal door separated it from a narrow corridor where wire-mesh fencing kept people from throwing items, like each other, onto the much wider ground-floor corridor below. When I would later see how much of the prison sat empty, the double-bunking served as one of the countless annoyances that appropriately made up prison life.

That first night's sleep was restless, especially for my bowels, as I lay awake trying to unload at least some of the responsibility for my incarceration on others.

After a tasteless breakfast, a disinterested-looking guard ushered me into my initial meeting with Larry, who asked if I had any handyman-like skills. When I told him I had worked in a lumber yard and possessed basic carpentry knowledge, he smiled and said, "Good. You just got yourself out of the laundry and kitchen." He assigned me to a work crew that moved about the prison and the island it sat on, one day fixing potholes on a deserted road and the next repairing a leak in a roof. For this, I would earn the standard $50 per month.

Larry nodded at my tattoo and said, "It looks fresh. Let me guess, someone on the outside convinced you that you needed to join a prison gang?"

Of course, he wouldn't be the first to notice. Four nights later while I ate dinner in silence, a prisoner with darting eyes spotted my tattoo, introduced himself as Troy and told me I needed to meet Lou. I followed the man into the recreation building, where Lou sat playing cards with three other guys at a metal table bolted to the floor. Upon introduction, Lou regarded me with a relaxed expression, while his associates studied me with what looked like a mix of hostility, suspicion and, after I was asked to pull down my T-shirt to reveal the rest of my tattoo, what surely was petty jealously.

"Got one question for you," Lou said, his smile offering encouragement that was hard to trust.

On the trip to the prison, I had simplified and massaged my story in my head to make it sound a little more appealing to anyone who asked. This was the short answer I now repeated to myself: "I'm in for beating a pedophile who was assaulting the girls at my group home."

Lou didn't care why I was here. Instead, he asked, "Are you willing to do whatever it takes to protect and serve your brothers?"

Days earlier, I had noticed these men and already knew the role they wanted me to play in their band of fools. Standing body-guard-like at Lou's back during our post-dinner free time, a static action that would make him look important and me stupid. Walking behind him to the showers or prison yard with a few other guys in what I guessed was supposed to look like a military exercise but more accurately resembled a procession of sad-faced clowns. Occasionally taunting other prisoners, especially, oddly enough, other white prisoners. Sometimes providing a little extra muscle for the collecting of debts. And maybe smuggling drugs into the prison, which some inmates claimed was done with the help of a few guards.

All that wasn't what made me hesitate. It was Lou himself. His eyes looked right inside me like I was an adversary he knew or had always known, and he clearly understood I was a desperate imposter who would pretend to be anything or anyone to save his own sorry ass. If this thought sounded crazy, the next one was worse: that his crooked grin confirmed I knew him too, and he was a bigger imposter than me, someone who wielded hate as nothing more than a weapon to gain power.

"Well?" Lou said like he was daring me to out him to his friends.

"No," I answered. "I'm not willing to do that."

Lou sat back and nodded to himself, everything suddenly right in his universe.

"You're dead, boy," spat the tattooed giant to my right whose Mediterranean coloring seemed out of place in this pale-skinned group.

Lou shuffled the cards, his face unable to suppress delight.

* * *

Two days later, an unexpected decision presented itself when Larry called me into his cell-sized office and asked if I was interested in helping him with a project.

"You have your high school diploma, right? You know how to read and write."

"Yeah."

"I've got funding to buy a few dozen textbooks and run a small program to help the most illiterate prisoners learn how to read. I would like you to teach it?"

Now, this was funny. "I have no teaching skills whatsoever. No one here even knows me. I doubt most prisoners would listen to a single word I said."

"But that's why this would work. You have very little history with anyone. A fresh slate. And as far as the teaching goes, the textbooks come with a daily work plan. Three classes a week, 90 minutes long each, for 12 weeks. All of it time that's outside your usual recreational allotment, meaning less time in your cell. Give it some thought and let me know."

Not sure why I said yes. At least the decision was mine to make. Larry gave me a textbook and joked, "Here, you can have a head start."

Five people signed up for my class, which was to be held in a room within the Inmates Services building. Only three showed up: Raymond Williams, whom I had heard led an expansion of a Los Angeles gang into Washington State and promptly got busted by undercover officers in a failed drug deal in Tacoma; his prison friend Jody; and Mark, who at age 57 explained it was too late for him to learn to read, though he promised to listen politely and enjoy the extra hour and a half of "intellectual stimulation."

I suspected he would be disappointed.

Even though the class was small, the intimidation of Raymond's almost savage stare and the knowledge his thick hands could in no time rip the tattooed flesh from my skin left me stumbling over the early parts of the first lesson, until he interrupted.

"Listen, boy, we're wasting our time here if you don't have the balls to do this. Either teach or don't teach, but don't sit up there if you can't do the job."

This bluntest of pep talks worked. It's empowering when the toughest person you have ever met says he's willing to follow your lead, if only for a few hours per week.

I progressed with Raymond and Jody, leaning heavily on one-to-one instruction while keeping to the timeline in the work plans. One day Raymond held his textbook up and said, "Reading this motherfucker is torture. Gets easier every day, though."

His words stayed with me, a mantra for my existence in this place.

* * *

The threats from Lou's group continued, though I did my best to ignore them. I moved with all the defiance I could muster for what it was worth, even trying to emulate Raymond's saunter when he left class. But my true strength amounted to more than some false bravado in my step and a fake fearless look in my eyes. Each day I turned inward for power, never once looking to a feeble group that only weakened each person who joined. High walls weren't only helpful in keeping people in. They could keep people out too.

Even if I tried to make myself look untouchable, it was clear Lou and his gang would come for me. When they did, I would fight with all I had and hope it would be enough.

I also continued to lean on the power of good karma, helping other prisoners when possible. So, when the first 12-week reading program ended, I signed up to teach another. Raymond and Jody both asked if I saw any value in them taking it again, and I said there was.

"I'm getting into this reading shit," Raymond said, cradling the worn hard-cover copy of *The Color Purple* that I would sometimes help him struggle through.

I wound up with a class of six, including Raymond and Jody and four beginner students. Strange as it seemed, when the four newbies sought individual help, their two "advanced" classmates would sometimes pitch in, their faces unable to hide satisfied grins as they teased, "C'mon fool, this shit's not tough."

I even embraced my role as teacher by trying to learn all I could about reading and writing, finding a special attachment to a book called *Associated Press Guide to News Writing*, whose unmarked condition suggested no one else had ever picked it from the shelves of the prison library. In my spare time, I used the book to write short news stories about what was happening in the prison, keeping them to myself, of course.

Spring arrived, and on days I worked outside the prison walls, the island's beauty lifted my spirits. I longed to find a deer trail and sneak deep into the forest like I was back in Bellingham or wander onto one of the empty beaches and strip down and wade into the gentle surf.

One day I received notice of a visitor scheduled to see me that weekend, and Tim Kolchuk crept in on a bright Saturday afternoon, greeting me with "Holy shit, I can't believe the security in this fucking place."

He sat across from me at a table and talked about our hometown and its people.

"Kimberly sends her best," he said. "She wishes she could have come, but you know..."

I did know.

"She gave me this." He held up an envelope. "It was sealed, but the guards opened it, not me, so I don't know what it says."

I took it and tucked it into my pant pocket, and as we talked, I tried to forget it was there.

When our allotted time expired, I stood the moment a guard came by and tapped his fingers on our table, surprised by how discerning my compliance had become. I wanted to hug Tim but was not permitted to touch him, not even shake his hand.

Before he left, he nodded and said, "All of us miss you. Even if you can be a damn stubborn pain in the ass."

A lone guard at his side, Tim walked down a dim hallway that seemed to stretch into a darkness that never quit, and a certainty struck me that we would never find each other again. I started to call after him, hoping to take one last look at a face that comforted me in ways no other could. My shout caught in my throat, and my guard tapped my arm for me to move in the other direction.

Back in my cell that night, I lay on my bunk studying Kimberly's neat handwriting on the envelope. She had wielded power over me, not exactly like so many in this place tried, but it was a dangerous and unshakable force all the same.

I did ache to know what the letter revealed. Did she feel sorry for me or think I got what I deserved? Did she still care for me at all?

The sealed envelope rested in my hands long past lights out, my anticipation slowly withering into disappointment. Lately, thinking about Kimberly in my abundant free time had become like that. Just like fucking all those women in my sperm donor days: a few joyful minutes followed by infinite regret when it became clear nothing else decent would come from it, at least not for me.

It was obvious what I needed to do, assuming I possessed the courage. The walls must go a little higher. Meaning Kimberly must be excised from my thoughts, her lean body forever removed from my memories of walks through the forest, her eager smile and comforting touch wiped clean from any account of my past. For the good of us both, we needed to take different paths where neither one's burdens would slow the other.

Before changing my mind, I gave the sealed envelope a quick squeeze goodbye and tore it into the smallest pieces possible, letting each one rain down into the toilet.

Missing: Day Seven

The special visitor creeps unexpectedly into the chapel, and I am trapped. Sure, I could easily drift off unseen but not Physical Ashlee. And even though I could make her disappear forever, girl gone, problem solved, I am not quite ready to do that. So, I let my accomplice stay where she's planted her little meditating butt on a wooden seat under the holiest of lights in this place where she has gone unnoticed for hours by dozens of worshippers and was only approached by a lone elderly volunteer, who asked, *You sure you're okay, Miss?*

At first, I am pissed to have been followed. Then I remember how difficult it is to hide your thoughts from the world's mind, this great collective consciousness. Information always seeps out and gets shared. Maybe, in this case, the world's just fucking with me. Or maybe I need help. Or someone else does. Who knows? Can't explain why I came here. Just that I did.

When Kimberly rushes over and hugs Physical Ashlee, do others see an emotional stranger embracing thin air? No one seems to notice or care. The two of them sit and talk, a little loud for a place of worship. It is usually a happy occasion to reconnect with someone you love, even if love often puts the other person in great danger. But Kimberly delivers the expected news of a great tragedy, and the two of them shed tears for the past and for a mother who tried her best, more or less. Eventually, they sit in silence, heads tilted back in awe at the large cross.

They need to know we are not safe here in this place of worship. That outside in the mountains of red rocks, the wind shrieks with warnings of danger. That the air around us reeks like blood leaking from a bludgeoned heart. But I don't want to admit that coming here could be a mistake. Even if transcended souls aren't sure what they are doing, they don't make damn mistakes.

I don't alert Physical Ashlee, and in time her visitor asks about the sketchbook in her hand. My counterpart squeezes the book, points to the diary-like words she's reading and says, *This is amazing grace.* She's so right, even if I don't want her to be.

Ashlee Chapter 11

Seven to Two Weeks Before Missing

One night after my grandmother's funeral, my parents start with tequila and end with heroin. They're wrecked, especially my mother, who, at some point after I go to bed, collapses to the floor with a thud loud enough to wake me from my restless sleep.

I stagger to the kitchen and find my father leaning over her unconscious body, whispering over and over, *I'm too fucked to think straight.*

I scream at him, *Do something.*

His eyes start to close before opening wide in a last gasp of salvation. *The Narcan,* he whispers. *Our medicine cabinet.* He slumps back and closes his eyes.

I rush to their bathroom, finding four small nasal spray containers with the word *Narcan* written in bright pink. I take all four and run back to the kitchen, where I peel back the packaging on one and spray the contents into Mom's nostrils. I open another and do the same to Dad.

They don't immediately move, and I run to my room to get my cellphone to call 911. When I return, phone in hand, Mom lies on her side, groaning. Dad begins to sit up. I put the phone down. Soon they're both puking their guts out, and I say, *Serves you right,* even if I don't mean it.

* * *

The next day I call Grandpa, the one who helped raise me, and tell him what happened. *Christ,* he says. *I'm too old for this shit, and you're too young.*

He's old school, and he doesn't make the long trip on the

bus so he can start reasoning with my parents or *enabling them or some shit like that.* He threatens to make sure I become a ward of the state unless they both go into detox. They do, though it takes several rough days before they're gone, and I am pretty sure the results will be less than impressive, even if it exhausts their savings.

While they get help, Grandpa moves in, and I learn something crucial about him: he's losing his mind.

It's dementia, he says. *When your parents are back, I need to take steps for myself. I'm moving to Bellingham and going into an assisted living residence where I can get the help I need. Soon I won't know any of you. And I don't want you to remember me like that.*

As he sits at the kitchen table telling me this, it becomes clear how bad his memory is. He told me the same revelation twice earlier today.

* * *

Kimberly's second arrival in my life is foretold in a SOOBE a few weeks before Grandpa's departure for Bellingham. In this spiritual journey, I stand in a bright red movie theater lobby. On the walls are dozens of posters for upcoming cop movies with ginger-haired female protagonists, each with two words written in cartoon speech bubbles: *Coming Soon.* I return to my body and climb from bed and reboot my computer. It takes no time to find Kimberly on Facebook and message her. She replies 10 minutes later that, yes, she is moving to Florida, and how did I know? Looks like I am starting to figure this shit out. We agree to meet when she gets settled in a few days.

Grandpa says he doesn't remember Kimberly from the group home. Doesn't matter. I arrange a lunch.

We meet a half-mile away in a little café that Grandpa likes because it doesn't serve *that damn ethnic food you can never escape in this city.* All three of us order good old-fashioned American food: a BLT and fries for Grandpa, a grilled cheese sandwich and side salad for Kimberly and, for me, a half-order of really delish nachos, which may not sound American but surely must be by now. From our stools at the counter, Grandpa studies Kimberly while attacking his fries. He shakes his head to himself, no doubt trying and failing to recall her from decades earlier.

While Grandpa may not remember Kimberly, he truly likes her, nodding in satisfaction each time she makes an enlightening and, often, helpful comment about my *situation*. He must trust her too because he confides that he has taken me to the bank and set up a secret account for me with $6,000 in it.

The girl may need to use the money to help pay the rent and buy food, he tells her. *But I warned her never to tell her parents, especially her mother, about the account. She knows how to contact me for more money, but she needs to understand I may reach the point I no longer know who she is.*

Kimberly pays the bill, and we step outside, and before Grandpa and I leave her, she grabs me and hugs me tightly. At this, Grandpa says something that isn't entirely appropriate, like old people often do.

If my son had married a decent, straight-shooting woman like you he wouldn't be in the pickle he's in right now.

Kimberly tries to dismiss the comment with a smile and a wave, but Grandpa continues. *My Joshua never did drugs in high school or university. Never did drugs until he met that woman. I try not to blame her because drugs are a big part of those Caribbean cultures. Those people can't get enough of them. But still, I hate seeing him struggling like this, knowing she will only make everything worse.*

Before he can put down my mother some more, I say, *C'mon, Grandpa.* I wave goodbye to Kimberly and take his hand. He squeezes affectionately, making me wonder if it's funny or sad that Grandpa doesn't see me as one of *those people*, even though I'm just as much like my mom as my dad. To him, I guess I am a white girl who has never visited her aunts in the

Dominican Republic, never learned to speak Spanish, and never got burdened with the black-skin gene that he believes can flare up in Dominican families and, apparently, give its target an insatiable fondness for recreational drugs.

The last time I see Grandpa, at least in person, is at a dinner Mom and Dad host for him before his departure. My parents are already using again, though by now they have become masters at hiding it. Still, Grandpa knows, and throughout dinner, he gives them, especially my mother, a sour face that borders on disgust, his hand gripping his fork like a judge wielding a gavel or maybe an executioner waiting to strike for the jugular.

When it's time for him to leave, we walk out and wait for his taxi. He can still travel on his own even with dementia. Says he only occasionally gets confused but has his wits enough to know that it will only get worse. The yellow cab pulls up, and as he kisses me goodbye, he says, *It breaks my heart to leave you like this. But I wouldn't do it if you weren't the strongest in the family.*

* * *

My smiling dad sits behind the wheel of his car, not a Kia Rio but a fancy bright blue sports car. He's watching a baseball game from a parking spot directly behind the backstop in the front row of the bleachers, which doesn't quite make sense, though what does? As heavy rain begins and the players leave the field, my dad seizes the opportunity to drive across the infield from third base towards first. The turf is soggy, and his car begins to sink, so he floors the gas pedal, leaving two deep tracks in the once-neat turf. As I follow behind him on foot, I can sense everyone's annoyance, maybe anger. The rain's intensity grows, and suddenly we are in an open field where my dad swerves around puddles, which begin flowing into a small creek. The car and my father vanish, leaving in their place a small stuffed animal, which gets caught in the flow of the creek. The stuffed animal dissolves into a soapy cluster of bubbles, which, a voice in my head informs me, is all that is left of my father. *It's the seeds of his essence*, the voice says. I chase the bubbles through the water, watching them dissipate as the creek widens and flows faster. Soon he's everywhere and nowhere.

The next day I tell Lucas about this SOOBE. He has a lot of time for me these days, and I drop by each afternoon after school. From where we sit on the carpet in his office, he listens carefully as he adjusts the collar on his red golf shirt. He usually wears a shirt and jeans and comfortable-looking brown loafers, even though I like to picture him in the cream-colored robe of a guru from the high mountains of India.

Lucas considers my SOOBE and announces, *Maybe it was just a dream.*

Unsure I believe him, I push through his thoughts like someone flipping through the pages of a book in search of a particular line of text. Oddly enough, I sense that he senses me doing this. He silences his mind, something he is a master at doing.

Ultimately, I give up, though I continually check out his thoughts in the days to come, discovering that he never lets his guard down in my presence. Well, maybe once. The time he thinks, in a rush of passion, that he wishes I was a few years older, and he doesn't care whether I know it.

* * *

While my body, like everyone else's, is incapable of evolving and therefore stumbles towards demise, the changes in my soul and mind are spectacular. School can no longer teach me anything. In fact, one night I have a SOOBE where I am at school and several teachers are forcing me and my class to suffocate ourselves by placing our heads inside thick plastic bags closed around our necks by rope-like drawstrings that we are supposed to tug on until we pass out. I don't trust the teachers' assurances that such a near-death experience will make our minds stronger and more creative. I don't trust that they will remove the bags and revive each of us before we die. So, I only pretend to pull the drawstring tight and pass out, and when I'm on the ground, I hear the teachers laughing at our collective stupidity. I understand this SOOBE's heavily symbolic nature, yet it scares me enough that I skip school many days, except when I attend to share my theories with my dwindling group of friends, who begin to roll their eyes the moment my mouth opens. Anyway, after years of getting straight As and being teased as a super freaky nerd and a future valedictorian, I have earned a little break from class.

Lucas isn't always the best source of knowledge either. His lessons often miss the mark, especially anything concerning time and space. Once, he went all Albert Einstein and described time as an illusion because the past and the future and the present, he claimed, all co-exist side by side. There is no *now*, Lucas said, no marker to separate the past from the future.

Of course, what he describes is not exactly what I have experienced, though I don't tell him. I also don't tell him about all the reading I have done on time, most of it written by more progressive scientists who agree time is an illusion. What Lucas teaches resembles the *block universe* theory developed by none other than Einstein and still followed by many scientists. Einstein claimed that his four-dimensional block universe contains a record of all that has ever happened and all that will ever happen.

And while I agree in part, don't my so-called psychic abilities call into doubt the part of this theory related to the future and past? Don't they suggest that I can move forward into some construct where so-called time is different from right now? And that this construct is a possible alternate dimension, one that may come true, or maybe not come true, because I have observed it?

Lucas would argue with any suggestion that the future has not already happened. He would say, *Well, my star pupil, explain how you know what someone is thinking or what someone will say before they speak the word. Doesn't your knowledge suggest that the other person has already thought the thought or already spoken the words, and you have simply found a way to retrieve these thoughts or words from where they have existed for eternity?*

And I wouldn't necessarily have a comeback to give him. Not yet.

For close to six hours one night, I lie on my bed reading every article or paper available on time theories, finally concluding in an unsatisfying nerdgasm that people who claim to have all the answers are full of shit.

* * *

Neither Mom nor Dad works now; they spend most of the day getting high while I hang out in my bedroom, cutting out magazine photos of beautiful and alluring places and attaching them to my walls. When I mention this to Kimberly one Saturday in a text message, she volunteers to come over and see if she can help with my parents or at least save me from boredom. How can I refuse?

It's three in the afternoon, and my parents party with a few losers I don't recognize. When I lead Kimberly into the living room where these supposed friends smoke and drink beer and snort booger sugar, none of them notices me. And neither do my parents.

Kimberly says in a non-judgmental voice, *Looks like quite the party.*

My father glances up and gives her a smile like he has a clue who she is and what she is doing here. *Grab a beer,* he says, adding, *Who are you again?*

It's Ashlee's friend, Mom says.

One of their wanna-be guests musters enough brain cells to stare at me and then at Kimberly and point at us with a jumpy finger and remark, *Isn't one friend much, much older than the other?*

They all laugh, even Mom and Dad. Dad tells Kimberly to grab me a beer too because I am obviously more mature than everyone in the room. More laughter.

Kimberly says, *I'm taking Ashlee out to get some dinner. She's hungry.*

We go to a nearby Thai place and take a seat in a booth. Right away, the huge wall mirror that holds my reflection freaks me out.

We need to find another table, I say, not telling Kimberly why. She wouldn't understand that the sight of my own body repulses me so much I struggle to look in the mirror each morning while brushing my hair or putting on makeup, the latter task being abandoned. She studies me, wanting to ask when I last showered or washed my hair. Or when I had my last decent meal or full night's sleep. Instead, she looks at the mirror and nods.

We sit in the back and polish off large plates of sweet noodles and talk about anything except my parents. Kimberly watches me carefully throughout the meal, and I sense, or know, that she doesn't want our conversation to dwell on the craziness that is my life or, more accurately, my parents' drug use. So she steers the conversation toward me, and in time a new kind of whacked-out world begins to emerge, one that probably scares her more than the piles of cocaine she saw on the living-room coffee table or the way my mother wore a loose-fitting wife-beater shirt with no bra underneath and much of her tatas exposed.

It starts with me explaining to her that I get plenty of breaks from the depressing things at home. *I read the Bible*, I say, not admitting that the extreme violence early in the Old Testament, much of it allegedly committed or ordered by God, made me nearly abandon the book forever. *And when I tire of reading, I go on SOOBEs*, I tell her.

What are SOOBEs? she asks.

I don't need to be a little psychic to see she doesn't like my answer, especially the words, *another dimension.*

I see, she says repeatedly and with concern throughout my description of my symbolic out-of-body experiences.

So how often, how often do you leave your body and go on these little journeys?

I laugh. *I'm getting good at it. I don't need to be lying in bed anymore. I can do it in class at school or while riding the bus to the mall. Or sitting in a restaurant. Watch.*

I close my eyes and tell my true being to leave my body. My limbs begin twitching, and the twitching turns to a full-on vibration, a sign I'm on my way. I will myself to remain in the restaurant and move through a shadow and into the future, ever so slightly, a skill Lucas has encouraged me to explore. When I do, Kimberly and present-time Ashlee appear below, seated at our table and engaged in a deep conversation. They get up to leave and walk halfway to the restaurant's door before Kimberly sprints back to get her cell phone, which she's left sitting on the table. And as she picks it up, it rings, and it turns out to be a scam telemarketer.

Before the weird symbolic stuff begins, I coax myself calmly back down to my body and open my eyes. The clock on the back wall tells me only a couple of minutes have passed, even though I probably traveled 10 or 15 minutes into the future. Time works like that; it accelerates when observed.

Kimberly's own eyes are wide and her hand rests on my shoulder. *Enough with the games, Ashlee. That wasn't funny.*

What? I didn't go far. I was floating overhead.

You were sitting in your seat convulsing as I tried to force you to end the game.

I wasn't pretending, I say.

She gives me her best skeptical-cop look.

So you won't believe me when I tell you I went into the future, just slightly, and that when we leave here, you forget your cell phone and run back to get it? And when you pick it up, it rings, and it's a scam caller.

Now she gives me the I'm-frigging-scared-that-you've-gone-loopy look, and I try to ease the tension by saying, *Of course, now that I've told you that you'll forget your cell phone, you probably won't, though Lucas says a person's future isn't that easy to change, even if she's fully aware of what will happen.*

Who's Lucas?

He's my spiritual teacher. From the Friends of the Seven Signs. Their spiritual healing center is only a few blocks away. I can take you there if you want to see.

Now Kimberly gives me the this-is-fucking-worse-than-I-thought look. *Yes, I want to meet these people. Do your Mom and Dad know about them?*

I burst out laughing. *I told Mom all about them. For what it's worth.*

Kimberly asks for our bill and pays, and we are halfway to the door when she realizes she's left her cell phone sitting on our table. She doesn't turn immediately back to fetch it like in my SOOBE. She freezes and stares at the rather smug grin on my face. To disprove my point, I wonder if she's considering not returning for it. She finally retreats to scoop it up, and as she rests her hand over it, I know what she's thinking. *Is the damn thing gonna ring right on cue?* She pauses, her eyes locked on mine, and when the phone rings, we both jump heart-attack-like. She glances at the number and dismisses the call without answering, and I think, *Maybe the future can be changed, ever so slightly.*

* * *

I introduce Kimberly all around the Friends center. She's clearly equally impressed and alarmed by the way everyone greets me by name. The center buzzes the way it does on those Saturdays when dozens of people return after the crowded spiritual session Lucas leads a few blocks away in my school's gymnasium. More than one cute guy comes over to say hi and meet this lady I'm introducing around. Even Lucas emerges from a small session in a meditation room, takes Kimberly's hand, and says, *Not your mother. Perhaps a close family friend. Am I right?*

Yes, I tell him, and he starts to whisk Kimberly away for a private tour, and when she glances back at me, a slightly amused expression on her face, I hear her thoughts clearly. I call out to her something sure to leave her a little dizzy.

No, Kimberly, you won't find a doomsday bunker in the basement, I promise.

She freezes. Lucas laughs and says, *Careful of your thoughts. That girl has some gifts.*

On the walk home, we wander my neighborhood and soak in the warm night air. Kimberly speaks over the noise of passing vehicles as she describes the impromptu meditation session that Lucas led for her and anyone else still hanging around the center.

I admit I enjoyed Lucas's words about finding enlightenment through letting your mind go free of thought, Kimberly says, *though I liked the yoga part the best.*

You approve?

She gives me a sideways glance.

So, they've never tried turning you against your parents or other people close to you?

No.

And they've never asked you for money, other than for the first meditation class you took?

No.

And none of the guys have… you know…?

Of course not, I say in feigned outrage.

Kimberly gently hip checks me, and we both nearly trip,

195

laughing.

The jury's still out, she says, proof her children are so damn lucky.

We reach the front of my apartment building, and Kimberly looks at her watch. She has a long drive back to Coco Beach. I should let her go. Instead, I say, *Please tell me more about Grandpa. My biological one.*

Kimberly hesitates. *I've told you everything I can remember.*

No, you haven't.

Yes, I have.

Nooooo.

Yesssss. You even got to hear some of the juicy stuff.

Not all. You haven't told me what you said in the letter you sent to him in prison.

I expect her to say goodnight and point me toward my door, but she continues walking, and I giggle.

You're a brat, she says.

Yes, but what about the letter?

She kicks a paper coffee cup blowing on the sidewalk. She looks at me and shrugs like the letter, or what happened with the letter, remains a mystery to her.

You remember how, after you asked, I told you that your grandfather and I never got, you know, physical. How my view of sex was that because of its exploitive nature, it would doom our friendship. Well, the letter I wrote him in prison was to say I was wrong. To say that I had finally concluded the problem with sex did not, in my case, lie with the sex itself but with the partners I had chosen. I also told him I forgave him for the reckless attack that landed him in prison. And that he needed to forgive me for keeping us apart. I told him I missed him badly. I asked him to call me when he returned to Bellingham, and that if he was interested, we could give a real relationship a try.

We reach the relative silence of a side street, and when Kimberly finishes speaking, her breathing is deep and slow.

But you never heard from him again? I ask.

No.

Do you know if he even read the letter?

No. He could have read it and thought, fuck you. Or not read it at all.

I'm so sad for you.

Kimberly smiles, sincere but lacking enthusiasm.

Later I met a great man and had two incredible kids. Just because me and my ex-husband are not together doesn't mean I don't still love him. It just means we grew apart. But I'm more than satisfied with my life. I bet Mike is, too, though that's a complete guess.

I ask a few more questions, but before long, she has switched the conversation in a different direction, perhaps like she planned to do all along. She asks, *How are you really doing, Ashlee?*

A simple yet complex question that's best not to answer.

When my eyes leave hers, she says, *I have a friend who is a Miami cop. I'm going to talk to him about getting Child Services in to do an assessment of your situation. I suspect he can expedite things a little. You may not want this, but it's for the best.*

I don't tell her it could easily cause more problems than it will solve.

Okay, Ashlee?

I shrug.

We walk in silence, like old friends who don't need to fill each second with conversation. When we've circled back around the front of my building, I hug her and say goodnight and start climbing the stairs, fighting an urge to drift off into the moonlit night. I ground myself with the tasks at hand, the ones I can see myself doing in the hour that follows: cleaning up the mess in our apartment, putting Mom and Dad to bed, calling a cab for any remaining so-called friends, and apologizing to the building manager about the noise that of course is the result of my father's struggles with grief over his mother's death.

* * *

One day Lucas tests my so-called *abilities* by repeatedly flipping a coin, so I can guess whether it will land on heads or tails. He does this hundreds of times, scrawling a tick in a small notebook when I'm right and an X when I'm wrong.

You're running at just over 64 percent accuracy, he declares, *so something special is at work here.* Precisely what, he can't say.

What he does say is that he would like to do more elaborate tests. That I possess the oldest soul he's ever met. That I was perhaps one of the first people to walk the earth thousands of years ago, and that my soul has constantly evolved over this time. *You have lived for a near-eternity, each life building on the wisdom of the one before it, each rebirth adding to the world's collective consciousness.*

When I later consider this, a prideful thought overcomes me. That I am on the verge of becoming pure consciousness, a higher being absorbing God's love and power and shooting it back into the world, like water through a pressure washer.

Of course, these grand thoughts can get you in trouble, especially if you repeat them to a state child protection investigator, who is supposed to examine your parents and the neglectful home situation but suddenly takes a great interest in you and your mental health. I soon find myself meeting with a state psychologist who writes on a clearly visible notepad the words *body dysmorphic disorder* before referring me to another psychiatrist whose office is clear across town in South Miami.

Dad, shaken by the visit from the child protection investigator, promises to be in perfect condition to drive me. Of course, he is both high and scared to show it in front of anyone working with the state, so he sends me alone in a taxi.

This psychiatrist, Doctor Gregory, gives me a depression test followed by an OCD test. I try to brush him off by saying my synesthesia, which is well documented, is flaring up, not to worry. But he sees other problems, meaning I am here for the long haul. With nothing to lose, I start talking about my SOOBEs and how I'm beginning to *know* what will happen in the future without even leaving my body. I also discuss my views on everything from God to the Great Evil to what happens when we die and why we are here on earth. I hold nothing back.

Whether I add a little spiritual awareness to his clinical thought process, I can't be sure, even after I try my best to tap into his thoughts. From what I gather, I remind him of his daughter, who struggles with some cognitive dissonance that seems to stem mostly from her lack of willingness to conform to whatever society rigidly expects of her.

It takes three more visits with Doctor Gregory, one of them where, awkward, Sanders drives me at my father's request, before I sense the words Cotard's Syndrome creep into the doctor's mind.

It happens in the seconds that follow my too-honest confession that, with the next death of my physical body, I will evolve to an advanced stage where I no longer need a mortal home to rest my soul. The confession where I also tell him that I don't expect my physical vessel will wait until death to cease to be. A small part of me suspects he already understands this body named Ashlee has nearly slipped away, like an irrelevant and lame cardboard cut-out of a far greater entity. Yet admitting it, at least to me, would of course go against everything he learned in psychiatric school.

Doctor Gregory also bandies about in his head terms like *delusional* and *psychotic depression* and *germination stage*. He tells me he wants to try a drug treatment and requires my parents' consent.

I tell him he's wrong. About everything. *Faith is like a lost desire*, I say. *You need to go find it again.*

As he listens to me, he thinks again about his own daughter and her condition, which must be serious and sad. I want to give the doctor the depression test.

When making my way to the door, I ask him what Cotard's Syndrome is?

Where did you hear that term? he asks.

From you.

No. I don't think that's true.

I shrug.

As I'm going out the door to set up an appointment that will involve my parents, I say, *I'm sure your daughter will be fine. You just need to give her room to be herself, to find her crazy place in this world.*

At this, he jumps.

* * *

Mom attends my next session with Doctor Gregory, and when we leave his office with my diagnosis and prescription and plenty of unanswered questions, we go straight to Walgreen's. I secretly laugh about two things: 1) My Cotard's Syndrome diagnosis, which represents the medical community's attempt to give anything it doesn't understand a name, meaning a specific drug can be applied; and 2) The ridiculousness of me taking my medicine in a household where I am not exactly priority number one.

Yet Mom surprises me, buying a bottled water at Walgreen's and making me take a pill before we walk the rest of the way home, and then, the following day, by dragging herself from bed and forcing me to take a pill before I leave for school. By the time I arrive at school, the thoughts that usually surge through my mind have slowed to a trickle, making me like every other walking zombie. I would run to the washroom and force-puke my guts out if it would do any good.

After school, my parents sit me down in our living room, and we discuss my Cotard's diagnosis and how Doctor Gregory could not give Mom and me an exact cause, even under Mom's anxious, guilt-ridden prodding. A knock to my head when I was eight, bad bacteria in my gut, Lyme disease, a vitamin D deficiency, a predisposition to neural misfiring, poor diet and sleep, brain inflammation, all or none of the above. He had no fucking clue, and I deploy this like a defense attorney to argue that the learned Doctor Gregory is wrong, wrong, wrong about my diagnosis. We also talk about the brain scan he has ordered for me and his plan to try electroconvulsive therapy if the drugs don't work. *Wonder what's next?* I ask the court. *A frontal lobotomy?*

If all this isn't crazy enough, Mom and Dad ask me to repeat everything I told Doctor Gregory, which I do, starting with my ability to leave my body and travel, sometimes into the immediate future. While they drink beer, I regale them with stories about my gift of prophecy, the journeys I have taken, my ability to read a person's thoughts, the predictions that have turned out true. As I talk, they give each other looks that scream, *our little girl really is fucking crazy*, much like Kimberly had when I told her about my abilities. But they nod for me to continue, and as I do, something happens: I sense they want to believe what I say, perhaps because it's better than the alternative.

Mom and Dad go to their bedroom to order pizza, and when they return, they stagger awkwardly, which sucks, though when they resume questioning me, their minds seem more receptive.

Predict something for me, my father says after our meat-lovers pizza arrives.

Like what?

The winner of tonight's Miami Heat game.

Never tried that. How about something else?

Our futures, my father answers.

His words chill me because in the past few weeks, I have tried several times to peek at where they would be in the months and years to come. For my Dad, I always come up empty. And for my

Mom, I at first sense nothing but misery stacked upon misery before getting a glimpse of an older woman wasting away alone on the streets, the Great Evil at her side as she panhandles for change to buy drugs.

How about, I counter, *I predict who will be the next person to walk by our building on the street?*

They agree, and we play this game for the next hour. At first, I detach from my body and tell myself to go forward in time. I watch the street and return and tell them what I saw. A woman in a red shirt pushing a blue stroller. An old man walking with a stoop. After a while, I don't bother leaving my body to go forward in time. I just wait for my soul, the consciousness I share with everyone else, to give me the answer. I am right more than wrong with my predictions, perhaps not the most remarkable success rate but not bad considering the drugs in my system. Either way, my parents love it. They are both happier than a dog with two dicks. Yes, they are high but also impressed.

I sense my father's creative mind working furiously.

Mike Chapter 12

Missing: Days Seven and Eight

My next requested "chat" with Douglas and Sweeny took place on their turf at the Criminal Investigations Unit's offices near Miami airport. Maybe I imagined it, but they both acted a little more formal and less relaxed as they greeted me with a brisk handshake and ushered me into a small meeting room.

"Before we discuss Mrs. Sutton," Douglas said as we took seats around a square table in a private room half the size of my non-palatial suite, "I wanted to update you on her daughter, your granddaughter, Ashlee."

Douglas folded his hands together and leaned toward me. "Obviously, Ms. Sutton still possesses a credit card because she purchased a bus ticket for travel to Los Angeles. By the time we were notified – some of these bus companies are not big on computers – her bus had reached Palm Springs. We had officers board the bus, but they didn't find her. The driver, who had taken over in New Mexico, recalled her. At some point in the night, she got quite upset. But he couldn't say where she got off."

Douglas studied me. He always studied me. "I wonder if she said anything to you that suggested her true destination, assuming it was not LA?"

I pretended to ponder this for a moment, desperately trying to conceal the many excited thoughts swirling through my head at the suggestion she may have traveled to Arizona. Finally, I said, "No."

"Too bad," he said. "She could offer insight into her mother's death and maybe clear everything up. That's, of course, once we tell her. The poor kid likely doesn't know."

Sweeny took over. "So, back to the girl's mother. Still waiting on the coroner's report and the exact cause of death. We have the toxicology report, and it suggests she had enough heroin and fentanyl in her system to kill her. In fact, in her suite we found a spent dose of Narcan, the naloxone used to block the effects of opioids, which suggests she did overdose, and either she or someone else recognized this and acted. Which makes us wonder, Mr. Baker, what her state of mind was when you dropped her off."

The same question they had asked before. "Calm. Hopeful that Ashlee would soon be found. Happy the girl was unharmed."

"Was she high?"

"A little. But functional."

"Did she score drugs on the way home?" Douglas asked. "There's a gap from when you talked to officers at the warehouse until the time you two arrived at the Sutton apartment."

"I had already missed my plane, so we spent more than an hour driving around the neighborhood hoping to spot Ashlee. Kacey did not buy drugs."

"Do you recall touching her purse?" Sutton asked.

"What?"

"Her purse, did you touch it at any time?"

I thought. "Yes. When she insisted on going into the warehouse after Ashlee slipped away from me. She left her purse in the car. I grabbed it for her because it would be safer with us and not left out in that neighborhood."

He nodded, maybe skeptically. "It had your fingerprints on it."

I shrugged. "It would. So, if you did fingerprinting, did you find my prints on the Narcan or anywhere else in the Sutton suite?"

Douglas smiled but never answered. "You had an altercation with Kacey Sutton out by the pool of your hotel a few days back. A taxi driver who brought her to see you witnessed it. Said you were fighting. Said you gave her money to buy drugs and sent her on her way."

I sighed. "I had never met her before. She was there to ask me to find Ashlee though she was too high to make sense. I sent her away with some cash."

"Nice," Sweeny said.

"Finally," Douglas said, reaching into a transparent plastic bag and withdrawing a long black item wrapped inside a second plastic bag. "There is this. You recognize it?"

"It's a tire iron. So what?"

"Doesn't mean anything to you?" Sweeny asked.

"Should it?"

I waited for the two cops to look at one another. Instead, their eyes remained locked on me.

"Officers found it in some bushes outside Kacey Sutton's apartment building," Douglas said. "It has your fingerprints on it. And Mrs. Sutton's."

I blinked, though I warned myself to limit my reaction to only that. The hum of the fluorescent overhead lights grew almost deafening in the room's silence.

My mouth remained shut. After all, I hadn't been asked a fucking question. Finally, Sweeny asked, "Would you mind taking us out to your car and showing us you still have a tire iron in there?"

"Listen, when we went to look for Ashlee, I had a flat tire, and I changed it, and Kacey put the tire iron away for me."

Douglas said, "If true, that explains how her fingerprints got on the tire iron but not how it arrived at the crime scene."

"Can you show us your trunk, please?" Sweeny asked again.

"Looks like I do need a lawyer after all."

* * *

Of course, I checked my car's trunk moments after extricating myself from the two cops who spent a good 10 minutes suggesting my lack of cooperation didn't exactly make me look guilt-free. While I fumbled for my keys in my pants pocket, I considered the closed trunk and wondered if I had an audience at an upper floor window inside the police office.

I opened the trunk, lifted the panel on its bottom, and looked inside to find an empty space where the tire iron should have rested.

* * *

My trip home was kept busy with constant checks in my rear-view mirror to see if anyone followed, almost like I was driving the notoriously dangerous Baghdad Airport Road and not a Florida highway where an over-medicated senior with dementia likely posed the greatest threat. I needed to get away from this city where someone was fucking me over for reasons that weren't clear. Key Largo and its bars beckoned. But for once, I would spend my time searching for options, and there were always options, or so I told myself.

I was nearly home when my choices had been boiled down to this. Sit back and trust Sweeny and Douglas to do their jobs, even sharing my theory that Ashlee was in Sedona. Or put my faith only in myself, meaning I needed to find the crazy girl and listen to what she said about her mother's death, even if it was nothing more than whispers of insanity, which I was learning could be helpful.

As I drove, I tried viewing these two dismal scenarios from all angles, like a dissatisfied artist taking in his own work, and eventually gave up.

Finally, desperation, or perhaps my own bout of craziness, forced me to seek the most ridiculous help available. When I arrived home, I called Maricela over, opened two beers and presented the facts to this unbiased high school-educated arbiter. Her blunt insight, "Even if the girl scares the Hell out of you, you don't want to be hanging around here with your finger up your ass waiting for shit to happen. Someone is messing with you. You need to find out if the girl knows why. And who."

Without a single argument to the contrary, I found myself on a plane to Phoenix later that night. Once there, I rented a car and drove north to Sedona, where I tried to sleep in the driver's seat beneath an unseen vortex and big cross as I waited a couple of hours for the sun to rise and the Chapel of the Holy Cross to open.

* * *

When daylight came earlier than expected, it revealed a surprise: the chapel, its giant cross running the vertical length of the building, sat less than a mile above me on the hillside. The scene looked like the creation of a painter who chose the three most vibrant colors in his palette and decided to go heavy on them. Bright blue for the sky, a deep orange-red for the jagged rock hillside, and green for the trees and vegetation that dotted the landscape. The chapel itself was a dull beige in the middle.

The chapel didn't open until 9 a.m., giving me a couple of hours to search elsewhere for Ashlee. I took the short drive into town, where I found the Greyhound station and asked around about her, in the event she had managed to get on a Sedona-bound bus in Phoenix without leaving a record that police could trace. No luck. I also showed her photo at gas stations, coffee shops and pretty much any business already open, without a single lead.

On the way back to the chapel, I passed a police cruiser and briefly entertained dropping by the police station and identifying myself as Ashlee's grandfather and saying the family suspects she could be in town. But would the local police alert the Miami police to my location?

In theory, only Maricela knew I was in Sedona. I had purchased my plane ticket at the Miami airport ticket counter under my name and got on and off the plane without any problems. But at the Phoenix airport's car rental parkade, I had used my fake Syrian passport, which I had acquired years ago by bribing an official in a part of the country where the government's control was waning. I often used the bogus document while traveling in the Middle East, where being any nationality other than American was safer. That I could speak Arabic didn't hurt either. I had chosen not to use the fake passport to purchase my plane ticket, fearing it might not stand up to scrutiny to fly in this country, though it obviously did to rent a car. So, for the purpose of my rental and my drive to Sedona, my name was Elias Roza.

How long before the Miami cops learned I had flown off to Phoenix? I hoped I could find Ashlee, perhaps even bring her home, before they knew I was gone.

My cell phone rang. Maricela's voice quick and to the point. She said, "It's the cops. They're searching your place. Your car too."

Maybe it was the shock of what she had said. Or the stress, or exhaustion, or something else. But something told me I would never see Maricela again, never again share another conversation with her. So what came out of my mouth was probably the last thing she expected: "Listen, you are fucking smart and really understand people well. You need to go to university. You need to go into something like psychology, or social work, or, I don't know, something that interests you. But don't waste your life."

* * *

At five to nine, I was back at the church's gate, and when it opened, I drove up the winding road to the top parking lot. From there I walked the steep path to the chapel, taking in the spectacular view from the outside before venturing inside. Had

I expected to find Ashlee sitting on a wooden bench staring past the altar at the giant cross in the window and the view of the red rock canyons below? Especially when I appeared to be the day's first visitor. Unsure what I had expected, I sat down and waited, even prayed a little for divine intervention.

By noon, following much sitting and several walks along the path to the parking lot, my faith waned. And that's when she emerged from behind a clump of parked cars. Like the first time we met in Miami, she didn't look shocked when her eyes fell upon me. I considered how this was possible, and the answer, a slew of answers, came quickly.

She slowed, a cautious manner that didn't suit her. Her red hair shone brightly, even eclipsing the rocks that made the stunning backdrop.

This time Kimberly didn't hug me. She half-shrugged and said, "Why don't we sit and talk."

* * *

We found a bench nearby, and before my mouth opened, she said, "Ashlee is safe. She is with people who care about her."

"So, how did you find her?" I asked.

"Well, I didn't find her by myself. I had help."

I stared at her, a little harshly perhaps, waiting for more.

"I located two homeless men who had spent some time with Ashlee in the warehouse where you first found her. They said she planned to go to Arizona. Then the police told me she had purchased a bus ticket to Los Angeles. Finally, you helped us, though you probably didn't know it. After you and I left the coffee shop, you went to the Suttons' suite. From a wall, you removed a photo of this chapel. I know because I had photographed both the walls when I was in her suite. When I saw the missing photo was of the chapel, a place Ashlee earlier had mentioned to friends is always calling her to visit, me and my… my associates took a chance and came here."

She paused and looked off into the distance.

"Seems like a long way to come on a hunch," I said.

"Not for me. You remember that anti-child exploitation group I told you about? We have a meeting in Las Vegas in a few days. To lobby lawmakers and police to finally act on all the children being lured into Nevada and used in child porn videos before being dumped on the street where many become underage prostitutes. So I didn't hesitate to come a little early and drive down here. And I was so relieved to find her."

Kimberly looked at the chapel once again. "She told me God's power is strong here. Before I told her about her mother's death, she described an overpowering awareness of her parents' presence right here."

"Where is she now?"

Kimberly jumped at this question. "I can't tell you that, Mike. It's for her safety."

"You think I'm a threat to her."

"I don't know what you are. Your timing in getting involved in all this… it raises suspicions."

"Who is she with? Who are you working with?"

"People who will take care of her."

"You mean people deluded enough to try and profit from her. You say my involvement raises suspicion. What about theirs?"

Kimberly's poker face had improved since our younger days, though she hesitated at this question and studied her hands.

"Who is she with?" I repeated.

"I'm not going to tell you."

"All that time at the coffee shop, you were playing me. Let's talk about old times, let's work as a team. You are so full of shit."

"You weren't exactly honest with me either. Right after I left, you went into the apartment and found what you thought was a lead. One that apparently confirmed something Ashlee had said to you. But you kept it to yourself."

"Maybe I was planning to share it with you that night at dinner. But you had already skipped town."

Kimberly stood, flustered, and then sat again. "Listen, Mike, none of this matters. Ashlee is safe. Soon she will contact the Miami police missing person unit. And soon, the people she is with will make an application to a Florida court to become her legal guardians."

"So, will she return to Miami for her mother's funeral?"

Kimberly greeted this question with a sour expression. "I've said enough, Mike. You should worry about your own problems."

We sat in silence like we had many times long ago, though gone was the bliss.

Finally, I asked, "What do you mean by 'my own problems'?"

"You know what I mean."

"Yes, somehow I have become a suspect in Kacey Sutton's death. Looks like you already know that."

"Call it a professional courtesy. Detective Douglas."

"Back to Ashlee, it sounds like I'm not the only one with a sudden interest in this kid who no one gave a shit about when her parents were destroying their brains with drugs."

Kimberly's slow, forced breath suggested she took offense. "You're not one to point fingers."

"Is that what you think? That I want to exploit her?"

"I don't know, Mike. All I know is the girl has amazing spiritual power. You've talked to her. You've seen it."

"I've seen madness," I said. "Nothing more."

"Really? Just madness? Nothing else? That's what you think?"

I refused to answer, and we sat in silence a little longer. As an elderly man shuffled up the path toward the chapel, I wondered about Ashlee's family's religious background. Was she a Catholic? Did she even go to church? These questions suddenly revealed a discrepancy in my earlier conversation with Kimberly.

"I was just thinking... When I asked you before about the New Age group Ashlee belonged to, you denied knowing much about it. But how is that possible given you seem tuned in to everything going on around this kid?"

Kimberly leaned forward and studied the ground. "Jesus, Mike. What's your interest here? Do you care at all about the girl?"

What I thought was *Fuck you, Kimberly*. What I said was, *You can't stop me*.

I stood and started walking toward my car. Halfway there, she called out. "Why did you never answer the letter I sent you in prison?"

I should have kept walking. I stopped, my back to her. Footsteps drew near and her hand took mine. "Why?" she asked again.

My eyes drooped under a great weight. How nice it would be to curl up inside my car and sleep until she was gone.

"Why?" she repeated.

"Because I never read it," I said. "It was time to stop torturing myself."

"Is that what I was to you? Torture?"

I shook my hand free and continued walking.

"It's called the Friends of the Seven Signs," she shouted. "Some of what Ashlee knows, the New Age stuff, she's learned from them, from the group's spiritual leader who loves Ashlee like a daughter."

I stopped walking and faced her.

"That's not all, Mike," she said, closing the distance between us. "She does have a gift. You can call it luck, but the fact is she can often sense what will happen next in all kinds of situations. Even sometimes at gambling, something your son Joshua discovered. That's why, and you're right, she needs to be with someone who won't exploit her."

"I'm not convinced that's you or this group."

"You need to trust us."

"Take me to her so I can see she's okay."

"Is that what you want? To see that she's okay?"

"That's one reason," I said.

"What's another?"

"Isn't it obvious? I need to ask her about her mother's death. To see if she knows anything that may help me."

"Or incriminate you, perhaps?"

I shook my head in disgust and climbed into my car, wondering what had happened in her life, or perhaps in mine, to convince her I could hurt a child or, worse, silence a child forever. As I put the car into gear while muttering to myself, Kimberly took up a position at my front bumper, blocking my path.

After I hit the brakes, Kimberly approached the open driver's window and said, "You're not going to let this go, are you?"

When I said nothing, she sighed. "Okay, listen."

Kimberly told me about a bar on the west side of Sedona. How if Ashlee were willing, she would bring the girl, who would answer any questions I had, all under Kimberly's supervision.

"So, she's still in town?" I asked, a hint of unsuppressed excitement in my voice.

"Don't push it, Mike."

* * *

Twice in the hour before the designated time, I circled our meeting place, my windows open wide like the air from the neighborhood would help give my once-trusty intuition a better sense of the situation. The bar was not a seedy watering hole but instead, in true Sedona fashion, a family-friendly bar and grill, which hugged the road in the front parking lot of an aging chain hotel. I cruised the hotel's parking lot, trying to locate the blue Ford Focus that Kimberly had been driving when she left the chapel, the car I had sloppily tried to follow until she pulled over and ordered me to turn away or else the meeting was off. It was nowhere in sight.

I parked five blocks away behind a row of shops that looked too well kept to be called a strip mall and walked the pine tree-lined backroads toward the bar. I couldn't say why I still trusted Kimberly as much as she trusted me.

The jolting sound of a not-too-distant siren stopped me cold. I scanned the street for its source, as well as somewhere to hide, and it didn't take long to notice the grey plume of smoke climbing from a hill to the north. The sirens were probably firetrucks speeding to a brushfire. On I walked, smoke drifting down in the breeze and collected in gaps between evergreen branches.

Before reaching the bar, I veered toward the adjacent hotel, hopping a fence by the empty hotel pool and finding my way into the hotel and out the front door, giving the clerk a friendly nod.

It was 2:40 when I entered the bar and grill, and neither Kimberly nor Ashlee was anywhere in sight for our 3 p.m. meeting. I went to the bar, ordered a drink, threw down a couple of bills and, when the bartender looked away, walked into the kitchen where I apologized to a kid chopping onions and hurried out the back door. I stood in a small alcove, feeling both stupid and exposed, and when a courier truck pulled into the parking lot a few minutes later, I ducked in front of it and continued along beside it until it stopped by the hotel's doors.

Maybe this was a waste of time. Maybe not.

I retraced my steps through the hotel and backroads and minutes later was inside a fast-food outlet, where a window-side table gave me a slightly obstructed view of the bar. I feared Kimberly and her smaller companion had entered while I snuck out the back door. The possibility of them already being inside was pretty much eliminated at five to three when what looked like an unmarked police car pulled up to the bar's front door. Two men climbed out, one positioning himself outside the front door, the other around back. Seconds later, a police cruiser rolled in, and two uniformed officers joined the first man in hustling through the front door.

I hustled, too, jogging the long block to my car and speeding north out of town, constantly checking for police lights in my rear-view mirror. The once bright day had turned into an eerie twilight as wildfire smoke blocked the sun, evoking memories of burning oilfields that transformed the day into night in a distant desert incinerated by war. It wasn't until the outskirts of Flagstaff that I stopped checking the road behind me and took a moment to absorb the sting of another betrayal by the woman who once meant everything to me, who once forced me to travel to the gritty ends of the earth to forget her.

Mike Chapter 13

1991 Iraq and Kuwait

One morning six months after Iraq invaded Kuwait, I sat poolside at the Royal Tulip Al Rasheed Hotel and listened as the journalist I was hired to keep alive sermonized about finding the essence of a story. "Look for that defining moment in each person's life," Peter Clarke said, floating on his back in the pool, a scotch and diet soda expertly cradled in his right hand, his booming voice sharing with anyone in earshot the wisdom he called the tools of the trade. "That moment everything changes. That moment when nothing that follows will ever be the same. Then write about that."

When the bombs began falling on Baghdad the following week, the defining moment in my work-life arrived, thanks to Peter Clarke's sensible aversion to getting killed. And, for the record, he was no coward. Across the globe, Peter had tormented dozens of tin-pot dictators for ravaging their own countries; he had stood up to warlords in the darkest corners of northern Africa, stared down boy soldiers in the Middle East, degraded his health to report on disease and famine in the world's worst economic backwaters. All for a modest paycheck.

And when his own country began its aerial bombing of Iraq on January 16, 1991, to begin the Operation Desert Storm phase of the Gulf War, he was one of few foreign journalists who remained in Baghdad, many of his colleagues having earlier that week paid $200 for taxi drivers to take them to the safety of the border with Turkey.

The attack had started at 3 a.m. Baghdad time when F-117 stealth fighters dropped the first wave of 2,000-pound laser-guided bombs, shaking the city awake. I would later learn that when Peter was roused from his sleep, he had gazed out his eleventh-story hotel window at the flashing lights from the exploding targets and tracer fire, alerted the news service he worked for that the festivities had begun, called his Iraqi and U.S. military contacts and began writing his story. When the power cut out, thanks to a nearby cruise missile strike, he borrowed a working phone from a television news reporter and dictated his story to someone at his news service. Back in the United States, his work made the final nightly deadline for dozens of prominent daily newspapers.

Driving to Peter's hotel early the next morning from my suite in Baghdad's Amil district, all I knew with any certainty was that I had survived the long-awaited first night of bombing, a relentless assault mostly by American planes that mainly targeted Iraq's air force and anti-aircraft facilities. I should have felt giddy not to have been blown into rubble. Or maybe worried I soon would be. Instead, I cruised the deserted streets consumed by a single stupid wish: that my war correspondent boss hadn't fled the city and effectively ended my employment.

When I reached Peter's hotel in its tree-lined neighborhood of foreign diplomats and other non-targets, I went straight to the lobby where he surely would be holding court while awaiting my arrival. He wasn't there, and neither was he in his room or the hotel restaurant. Instead, at 7:10 a.m. I found him floating in the pool's deep end like he did every morning despite the cooler weather, his gentle splashing an almost silly contrast to the distant sounds of war.

I shouted, "You tough motherfucker. Even the military might of 34 nations can't scare you away from your morning constitutional."

Peter gave me a salute, and I envisioned him climbing from the pool, dressing quickly and jumping into my car, so I could escort him out to survey the damage and interview shaken survivors, our adrenaline rushing after weeks of endless buildup to war. Instead, he continued to sip his drink while paddling in circles with his right hand.

"I've made some calls and mapped out four or five locations I think we can reach," I told him, wrongly believing this would get him moving for his towel. "One of Saddam's palaces took a direct hit 20 minutes ago. He wasn't there, but dozens were killed. Why don't we start there?"

At this, Peter began ruminating on the definition of a story as a narrative that makes readers want to find out what happens next and how too many journalists have forgotten this simple fact. "And it shows in spades in their mediocre work," he added.

"Well, yes, but Azir is waiting at my car and he…"

"Do you understand the art of an interview?" he interrupted. "Have you watched me enough to know the importance of asking your subject 'how' and 'why'?"

He lifted his head and took another sip of his drink and studied me and my perplexed look. Finally, he said, "Michael, I'm going to need a little extra help out there today."

I usually did the driving and the interpreting and the pulling out of my handgun at the first sign of trouble. Most days I also helped with research and setting up interviews with whoever could be critical to the story. But I was no journalist. Not sure exactly what I was other than someone who loved the excitement of a foreign conflict and had found someone willing to pay for such a questionable talent.

"So, what exactly do you need help with?" I asked.

"All of it," he said.

* * *

My own journey to Baghdad had its origins in a prison classroom, where the reading lessons I taught were attended by an Iraqi immigrant about my age whose path to McNeil Island in many ways mirrored my own, though his specifically involved violently defending the honor of a sister after two neighborhood idiots called her an *Arab whore*. Kasim enjoyed my class and picked up the required English reading skills so quickly that he found time to return the favor by teaching me to speak a few words of Arabic, a language I was, in contrast, slow to grasp.

More than that, he became a friend who watched my back. After I survived being clumsily stabbed by two drug addicts indebted to Lou the skinhead, Kasim helped me hunt them down one at a time in the weeks to follow and use our fists and feet to discreetly exact a little respect-saving revenge.

When I left prison after serving the minimum 14 months, I didn't journey north to Bellingham. Instead, I traveled south to Vancouver, Washington, with only $80 in cash and the clothes I wore. There I met Kasim's family, who settled me in Kasim's second-floor bedroom, treated me like a valued guest and put me to work in their restaurant below. Kasim's father, Barhoomee, when his eyes first fell upon my tattoo, said, "We Muslims have enough trouble with the Jews without them seeing *that*." So began a long, painful and only partly successful series of treatments to remove it, starting with acid and ending with intense scrubbing.

My Arabic lessons continued with Kasim's family. Over time, I became fluent enough to engage with Arabic-speaking restaurant customers, who looked genuinely puzzled by the pale-skinned kid who more-or-less spoke their language.

Kasim returned home, another bed was added to his room, and he began working in the restaurant alongside me, using the lazy hours between lunch and dinner to update me about the unpredictable cast of characters on McNeil Island, including Lou's death from a fate far worse than violence: colon cancer.

Soon Kasim started taking classes at community college, while I, equating my strange daily contentment to a thick rope cutting off air to my meager brain, began looking for a way to leave my mark on the world in some way other than cutting vegetables and refilling customers' water glasses. I examined what I offered that most other Americans did not, and only two skills came to mind: Arabic and a desire to travel abroad. Five months later, I said a tearful goodbye to Kasim and his family and began work as an Oxfam volunteer at a drought relief project in the Horn of Africa. I toiled for Oxfam in a half-dozen Muslim countries in the years that followed, rarely thinking about my friends, new and old, in Washington state. One day while working in a remote village, I received a shocking message that Tim Kolchuk had been killed in a car crash. By the time I got to a phone and called his father, I had missed the funeral. Ron and I both sobbed through the call, where he gave the barest of details about the crash. A college party. Tim's girlfriend driving them home. A mistake. She survived. He didn't. I learned too that Kimberly had become one of Tim's closest friends, and she was gutted to lose him after, according to Ron, "losing me."

Maybe I should have returned to Washington state. But I didn't. And one day Peter Clarke interviewed me over a beer in what served as a bar in southern Sudan and offered me a job.

By the time the bombs started falling in Iraq, I had worked with Peter for more than eight months. In that time, I witnessed him file countless stories that perfectly captured the complexities of foreign cultures while also revealing the grace that endured in the most harrowing of lives. Some nights I would retreat to my room with a printed copy of his latest article, which I would read aloud under the feeble glow of a tired incandescent lightbulb while choking back a welcome rush of tears. Other nights we would go to bars where he would fall down drunk or make dozens of grand pronouncements seemingly directed at no one in particular though usually built on bits of wisdom that would be useful only to me.

* * *

That first day of Desert Storm, Peter never left the hotel pool as he gave me my marching orders.

"Listen," he said. "The coalition bombs are supposed to be mostly targeting military infrastructure. But anti-aircraft installations can't talk, and neither can bridges and roads, so you need to find the officials who can discuss what's been hit and the people around who have witnessed it firsthand. Are they scared, are they suffering, have they lost someone? We need to put a human face on this fucking miserable story."

He recited a brief list of questions for me to ask and a longer list of the types of people I needed to interview, and before I left, he finally climbed from the pool, dried himself off and accompanied me up 10 long flights of stairs to his room where he grabbed his tape recorder and a spare notepad.

He followed me back down the stairs and through the granite-floored lobby to my car, where the news service's photographer, Azir, leaned against the trunk checking one of his lenses.

Azir smiled when he saw our leader. "Thought you bailed on us," he said.

Peter slapped his back. He liked to slap everyone's back, even in cultures where it wasn't appreciated. "I'm staying until the Iraqi intelligence service or the ministry of misinformation kicks me out. But I am not leaving the fucking hotel grounds."

* * *

Many Iraqis fled Baghdad the previous week when it appeared certain Saddam Hussein would not comply with a deadline to end its annexation of Kuwait. Those who remained mostly hunkered down. So, as we drove through the city, we scanned boarded up homes and shops and empty streets for any signs of life. We tried to give a wide birth to all government buildings, which were either destroyed or deserted in advance of their destruction.

Three times we stopped at bomb blast sites, allowing Azir to take photos while I took notes. Later, we found a group of university students huddled under the bridge, not a good place, and I interviewed them about their wish for peace. I spoke Baghdadi Arabic dialect, and by then, my skin glowed with the same shade of brown as many of the locals, but these students probably knew my roots lay in the United States. When I asked them to deliver a message to America, they didn't hesitate and gave me some of the best quotes I would use. A half-dozen interviews later, we hurried back to the hotel under the hum of constant air raid sirens and the pounding of anti-aircraft guns mounted on the roofs of hundreds of buildings throughout the city.

Peter had me transcribe my interviews and observations into my neatest handwriting. He showed me the information he had gleaned from a dozen phone interviews and an impromptu meeting with an Iraqi general who had shown up at the hotel to talk to CNN's Bernard Shaw. Peter had also lifted Saddam Hussein's "mother of all battles" declaration from Baghdad state radio.

He showed me the structure for a breaking news story as opposed to a feature, throwing out terms I didn't understand like nut graph and inverted pyramid. Then he wrote our story and filed it with both our bylines, his name first of course.

We did the same for another four days, with me each day playing a more prominent role in the writing process. Never were we bombed into oblivion.

On the fifth day, an officer from Iraq's ministry of information arrived at our hotel, found us in the bar talking over each other with slightly slurred voices, and announced Peter and I had been banned from Iraq and had 24 hours to vacate the country or face immediate arrest.

* * *

After the 15-hour drive north through Kirkuk and Mosul and across the Turkish border, we found a hotel in a small agricultural town, and Peter sat on the edge of a saggy bed and told me and Azir that he planned to return home.

I had thought he would become embedded with the U.S. military to cover the so-called ground invasion and liberation of Kuwait, which military sources said would happen in the next few days. Instead, it looked like the war had lurched to an unceremonious end for the three of us.

"God, this Turkish beer tastes like piss," Peter moaned.

He lay back on the bed's bleached white sheets like he floated in a pool at a better hotel. "I talked to the wire service about you two," he said. "They have jobs for both of you covering the ground war if you want them."

I laughed. "I don't think they need me. I'm sure reporters embedded with U.S. troops get a military driver, perhaps one operating a tank."

Peter rubbed his belly. "I should explain. They want you as a reporter, not a driver. They've seen your work for me and want to give you an audition."

* * *

My first story, filed from a desert base in Saudi Arabia near the Iraqi border, was a 1,000-word feature on the preparations by coalition forces, primarily the XVIII Airborne Corps, on the eve of the invasion. I rewrote it so many times every word probably changed at least once. After that, I faxed it to Peter, who would be getting out of bed in Omaha, Nebraska, and had agreed to read "whatever woefully inadequate piece of shit" I deemed fit to send.

While he read it, I paced in the media tent, listening to the small talk of my new colleagues over the hum of generators.

Peter called back and announced, "I'm hungover and you

dump this crap on me. Tell me in one sentence what point you are trying to make."

"How quickly 120,000 coalition troops were assembled in Saudi Arabia for the invasion, which many soldiers believe is imminent."

"Okay. So that much you know. Now that theme needs to resonate in every word of this fucking mess."

He helped refocus and trim the story to 800 words. It read remarkably better.

The next day I filed a piece about the massive operation needed to ship 700 tanks, 1,400 armored fighting vehicles, 600 artillery pieces and countless rations, cots, tents, blankets, and medical supplies from around the world to what was essentially the middle of nowhere.

Peter suggested fewer revisions than the day before.

When the invasion came two days later, my new colleagues and I met up with the 101st Airborne Division and were ferried by Black Hawk and Chinook choppers to a forward operating base more than 100 miles inside Iraq. By the next day, we had traveled about 170 miles into the country, and coalition troops had closed the first of a handful of roads connecting Iraqi forces in Kuwait with Baghdad. Iraqi troops began surrendering en masse to avoid annihilation, and I almost couldn't write fast enough to cover the speed of what would only be a 100-hour ground war.

The following day the U.S. military granted an adventurous request by a group of my colleagues, agreeing to set up a small convoy of trucks and armored personnel carriers that would escort any interested journalists south toward Kuwait through newly conquered territory. Of course, a military public affairs officer would help run the show. The story the U.S. military wanted us to observe and report was simple: the ground war was an enormous success. I could almost hear Peter screaming in frustration. I too recognized it as a public relations exercise.

And an opportunity.

We drove overnight through the desert, unable to sleep, especially as we wound through one battlefield where dozens of Iraqi tanks and personnel carriers lay destroyed or abandoned in the sand. Our headlights and vehicle spotlights illuminated a tragically eerie scene that perfectly illustrated the true horror of war. None of us had any idea that the real horror was still to come.

In the morning, we began hearing reports that the ground war was a rout, and that only a handful of Iraq's 43 combat divisions remained in the fight. Outgunned by more sophisticated weapons, they were being taken down like a hare unable to escape an eagle in the open desert.

As word of a possible ceasefire began to spread, we reached Highway 8, and began rumbling south on the deserted blacktop. Every mile or so our convoy came to a stop as groups of Iraqi soldiers, hungry and dehydrated, approached us from the desert with raised hands, some clutching white shirts, as they tried to surrender. The soldiers with us could only point them north and signal for them to keep walking.

"Why are you on foot?" I yelled down at one soldier in Arabic.

Before an American soldier hustled him along, he lowered his head and began sobbing.

About 10 miles later, our driver, a soldier named Bains, pointed ahead and said "There. What the sweet fuck is that?"

I strained my eyes out the dust-streaked window, unsure what lay on the highway ahead. A soldier beside me stared through binoculars and cursed.

We would later learn that a massive convoy of Iraqi soldiers fleeing Kuwait City in any vehicle capable of being commandeered, many laden with stolen loot, was attacked by coalition aircraft. Bombs were dropped on the front and rear of the convoy, trapping thousands of vehicles in between. And so began the slaughter, with every available aircraft, from F-15s to B-52s, bombing and strafing the convoy for two straight days. Those who didn't escape into the desert on foot were incinerated in what more than one pilot called a "turkey shoot."

As we drew close, our public affairs officer shouted at us to remain in our vehicles as there could be hostile forces in the area. No one listened. He eventually shut up, and the trucks and APCs killed their engines, leaving us only with the sound of boots hitting the road in ghoulish anticipation.

Many of the first vehicles we encountered held charred bodies, skeletal remains of soldiers who likely didn't sense death falling from the sky. A few had stumbled onto the highway's shoulder, their clothes singed to their dying bodies. Civilian cars sat next to tanks, which took a crooked place alongside armored vehicles with mounted anti-aircraft guns that may have failed to fire a single shot. One transport truck held eight meat-charred torsos in its back like they were the actual cargo. The carnage stretched for miles. I started counting the bodies in a 100-yard stretch of highway, determined to extrapolate the loss. Nausea eventually stopped me.

When I had seen enough, I sat down against the back wheel of a truck whose wide-open doors suggested its occupants were among the lucky ones. Around me, I swore the desert still echoed with screams of the dying. That the wind was moist with fallen tears.

I needed to record every detail I had seen. U.S. troops high-fiving one another when they saw every single casualty belonged to the enemy. The Iraqi soldier whose incinerated arms and scorched skull beckoned hopelessly from the destroyed cab of a truck, an image that would be captured by a pool photographer but later deemed too graphic to publish by most American newspapers. The singed man lying face down in the sand with his extended right hand locked around a photo spared by flames of a woman and two smiling girls.

I worried these images would fade before I recorded them in my notebook, not yet aware they would forever be tattooed into my mind, like the swastika symbol still clinging desperately to my neck.

Once my story was written, I was given a satellite phone and the number of a U.S. military censor in Florida who would take dictation and type my story out and file it with my news agency, minus his omissions, which I was sure would include anything militarily sensitive and a handful of emotionally charged words like "extermination" and "massacre."

When I was finished dictating my story, this official let out a long whistle and whispered, "That's fucked up, man." His voice crackled through the phone with something that sounded like heartache.

I suspected this story would launch my career. Of course, I had no idea how right I would be. That word of this attack had already spread, and newspapers and television and radio stations fed by my wire service clamored for any details I could provide. That by the following week, I would be back in post-war Baghdad interviewing sobbing mothers who wondered why their sons had failed to return home from Kuwait.

Our convoy's commander began shouting it was time to move out toward our destination, the newly liberated Kuwait City. I wandered to the edge of the desert, drawn by a curious sight. As I neared, it was exactly what I thought I had seen: the bodies of two soldiers who looked like they had been gunned down while one carried the other to safety. What was unusual was the way they had haphazardly collapsed onto the sand, one on top of the other so their bodies lay intertwined in an almost comically sexual position. I needed to pull them apart and position them side-by-side with their hands across their chests. It was the decent thing to do. I knelt beside them but hesitated. I rubbed at the grit that had settled in the corner of my dry eyes and considered the level of detachment needed if I wanted to continue doing this job.

I stood and turned away, leaving the men where they lie.

Up ahead, a soldier impatiently signaled me to return to our small convoy. The desert wind whipped up silently as I trampled over the sand, and even before becoming adept at traversing an endless expanse of death and ruin, I knew to cushion the deafening crunch of my retreating footsteps, like a grave robber heavy with spoils.

Missing: Days Eight and Nine

The holy light falls away and its opposite, the garish glow of greed, soon replaces it. I laugh at where Physical Ashlee has been taken. It's a reminder of how the mind-made world spins in circles. Rinse and repeat. All so predictable. All so human.

Lucas arrives full of smiles and hugs. He offers condolences too and tells the physical body standing before him that it has a second family, large and loving, to lean on in its time of need.

He throws out memories of the time he repeatedly flipped a coin while the not-yet-transcended Ashlee guessed if it would rest on heads or tails. He says we are in a perfect place for more tests on Ashlee's powers; a place where an exact value, specifically a dollar value, can be applied to the results. With that in mind, he asks the girl-shaped body to pick the winners in a handful of baseball and basketball games for him. He hands over a printed list of games and a pencil. Through Physical Ashlee, I glance at the list and sense each game's outcome, quickly instructing my subordinate on what teams to tick off. Lucas looks alarmed by the ease of my selections and spends the next 10 minutes explaining how each of the one dozen bets is for $50,000 and he has taken a second mortgage on his home to raise the money for his life's work and how the bets must be taken as seriously *as life and death*.

As if.

He can see that even Physical Ashlee is not buying the testing bullshit. Yet he still pushes ahead, asking that the 12 selections be made carefully.

I stand by each pick and later win nine of the 12, including two long shots.

He delivers this good news to my room with a Starbucks hot

chocolate and cranberry muffin and watches with delight for a few moments as my side-kick picks away at the offering.

When he leaves, Kimberly says, *He sure is smitten with you.*

What exactly do you mean by that? I ask through Physical Ashlee.

Kimberly gives off the same ferocious look my mother occasionally did. *It means you need to be careful around him.*

I'll be okay, I tell her.

I know you don't believe that.

Why?

Because, she says. *You always bite your bottom lip when you are anxious. When you are bothered by something. It's like a tic. You are biting it right now.*

She is right, at least about that.

* * *

Maybe to kill time, Physical Ashlee spends hours writing in the sketchbook, recording everything that appeared to happen from the moment I supposedly went missing. I can't be bothered by her shallow interpretations, so I don't look over her shoulder as she writes. When she's finished, she flips back to the last thing I wrote *before* leaving home. It's something I don't want to read either. Not sure why I put such a sad fucking story on paper unless I had been desperate to rewrite history and spread the blame around.

We all have our addictions, and mine is reliving my mistakes. I lean in and read along, reminding myself not to get too wrapped up in my own words.

We are only a few words in when I am struck by a premonition of what will happen the moment we finish reading. Physical Ashlee will put the sketchbook down and bury her face in a fluffy hotel pillow. I will order her to pick up the damn sketchbook and toss it in the trash bin under the bathroom sink, unsure she will listen because I swear she's gone rogue. At first, she will refuse. Then she will scream. Finally, she will cry. But she will do what she's told. Through her sobs, through an explosion of snot, she will whine, *That's all I have left of them.* Maybe I will want to comfort her. I won't, though. Because she needs to understand that survival depends on finding strength in yourself, not others.

Ashlee Chapter 13

The Week Before Missing

Dad claims he's good to drive, though conveniently, or perhaps inconveniently, he no longer owns a car. He sold the Rio to pay a debt to the man with long sideburns named Cheech, who I suspect is Dad's drug dealer. So, we take a cab.

I tell Dad I can only do what he wants if I skip taking my antipsychotic medication today. His eyes turn sad like he might cry. But he nods and smiles tightly and says it's okay because I don't need the medication, not with my strong mind. It's tempting to say, *How would you know?* He never once met with Doctor Gregory, leaving that task to Mom, who asked almost no questions other than, once she heard everything was confidential, *So is all this the fault of me and my husband and our... little problem?*

The taxi crawls east on Highway 836 in the late afternoon rush hour, and Dad gives me a nod like isn't this a cool adventure, a little quality father-daughter time. *Sure, Dad, we are really living our lives now,* I think with no shortage of sarcasm. I can't remember the last time I left our apartment with him, so I suppose this is what progress looks like.

The casino sits back from the highway at the end of a long palm tree-lined road. Dad pays the driver and takes my arm, a little awkwardly, and leads me inside. He's been here before and knows the layout of the building and the various vantages of the casino floor that holds hundreds of slot machines. We wander down a hallway toward the video arcade, and he whispers, *Stop anywhere you want and do your thing. Then point me to the best machine. Preferably one of the five-dollar high-roller machines.*

He doesn't fully understand how my so-called *thing* works or that the antipsychotic drugs I took yesterday and the day before and the day before that are all still in my body, turning my energy flow to a trickle, like water frozen in a pipe. He just knows our family is in debt, and he *needs this one thing*.

Once I glean enough about the casino floor layout, we go to the video arcade where I sit at one of those race car driving games and search my true being for the location of not one but two winning machines. The answer comes quickly, like knowledge I was born with. Then I let my soul wander into the future, hoping to confirm what I know. I observe a grey-haired woman go into a noisy, denture-chattering frenzy after a big win. Then a second person, a wrinkled man in a cowboy hat, also hits a jackpot at a nearby machine, though this one is not in the high-roller area. Anyway, both machines are the exact ones my soul had moments earlier singled out.

Of course, there is a gaping hole in all this logic. Like if I already knew which machines were the winning ones, and I intended to tell my dad so he could get there first, it should be him I see winning. And if so, who the fuck are the grey-haired woman and the man in the cowboy hat? Did my mind invent them as visual support to what my gut, or my soul, told me? Or am I changing the future by inserting myself and allowing Dad to win? It's a rabbit hole best avoided.

I take my dad to the edge of the casino floor and point to the machines, which both sit unused, and he gives me $40 for the arcade and a kiss on the cheek and says, *Tonight we do it big, girl.*

I hear myself giving him the only advice I have, based on a slot machine website I visited in the cab. *You need to be patient on the machines*, I tell him. *It will take time to hit it big.*

More proof, ha-ha, that I'm psychic because it turns out to be one of the longest nights of my life. Over the next three hours, Dad doesn't win much but doesn't lose much either, perhaps a sign he's following my advice to be patient. I tell him that if he wants to stay here forever, he needs to get us a room in the hotel above and let me order from the room service menu. And that's what we do, and just before midnight, he glides back into the room where I watch television, his face still frozen in a look of utter shock, and gives me the biggest hug ever. He tells me how I am a game-changer for a family in debt as he unveils a cheque that, minus withholding taxes, is for $23,000.

Finally, my father puts the cheque on the bedside table and flashes some bills that he claims add up to $600, a suitable amount to drop on a poker or roulette table before bed, before a few solid hours of sleep and perhaps one more good jackpot tomorrow, with my help of course. I know better than to trust him alone in the casino and its many bars with that much cash, but I don't want to be a downer on this happiest of nights.

Don't stay out too late, I tell him like a stern parent.

Text your mom the good news and tell her we'll see her tomorrow morning with two large cheques, he says kissing me on the head and spinning toward the door.

My journeys that night are cracked-out, medication-fueled events that make so little sense they must be dreams and not SOOBEs. I remember commanding, *I don't want to dream,* before a tarp of blackness pulls itself across my head.

Yet a man in a gold suit appears at the foot of my bed, his apologetic voice repeating the word, *Miss.* To his right stands a man in a black-pant, white-shirt security guard uniform, his hands behind his back for lack of a better place to rest them. And crawling across the other bed toward the pillow is my completely trashed father, who slides the pillow under his face and groans once before going still. The clock radio reads 4:11.

The man in the suit speaks. *Sorry to intrude, but this man says he's your father.*

I nod and ask, *What are you doing in my room?*

He was wandering drunk in the hallway trying his room card on all the doors and waking people up. We almost threw him out of the hotel. But in his pocket, he had the slip that the room card came in

with this room number written on it. We want to make sure you know
him and that everything is okay.

It's fine, I say. *Thanks.*

Both men stare at me. In my grogginess, I misunderstand their
expressions and body language as that of suspicion. Do they
think I am a young prostitute or something? Slowly I understand
that the source of their distaste isn't some misperception. They,
in fact, see the situation exactly as it is. That the passed-out man
is my father, and he really did bring me to the casino while he
gambled and got fall-down drunk and lost $600. They don't,
however, know the small role I played in the epic dysfunction,
that of driving the Bronco.

Either way, I don't need their pity, so I turn my face away,
and that's when I see the cheque for $23,000 is missing. No. No
way. One of them must have taken it. At last, the truth comes to
me like a giggle from the darkness.

* * *

At 8 a.m., it takes all my will to drag myself from bed. I stand
in a beam of light coming through a gap in the crusty-looking
brown curtains, trying to ignore the offensive racket of my
father's snoring. I close my eyes and contemplate drifting far
from this life and into a mundanely boring one where I could be
a girl doing all the stupid yet amazing things a teenager should
do. Of course, to be that girl, my parents would both need to
disappear, taking with them the many burdens that should
never have fallen on me. For the smallest possible measure of
time, I ache for them to be gone. Or for me to be gone.

I let my over-air-conditioned skin wallow in the sun's
warmth, extending my pity party until it becomes unbearable.
Downstairs I buy one coffee, one bottled water and two breakfast
sandwiches at the coffee shop and two toothbrushes at the gift
shop. Back at the room, I shake Dad awake and scold him for

stealing the cheque and losing our money.

I didn't steal it, he argues weakly a full 10 minutes later when he's returned to earth. *The cheque was made out to me.*

I stare at him until he looks away and says, *I know. I screwed up.*

I tell him to eat and that I called Mom and she's on her way. At the mention of Mom, his chewing slows like he's about to be sick. I leave to brush my teeth, determined not to feel sorry for him.

When Mom arrives, the two of them huddle in a flurry of harsh whispers. They book another night in the hotel and get a cash advance on their credit card to give them money to gamble with and to buy me a bathing suit so I can go to the pool and hot tub and perhaps pretend we are on a family vacation. We return to the room with a plan for me to journey ahead to select a slot machine for them. I move confidently through the room, assembling a bag to take to the pool, slightly giddy by my power over my parents as they await my pronouncement. I say nothing and grab a room key and my bag and head for the door. Do I sense them holding their breath as I turn the knob and pause?

When I spin to them and say, *The progressive machine two to the left of the one you won big on last night*, the relief on their faces is instant.

In the hot tub, I close my eyes and pretend the creepy man with a large belly hanging over his too-tight bright orange trunks isn't watching me intently. As the jets massage my back, I know Dad will hit the full progressive jackpot and Mom will quickly take his seat so it will be a little less suspicious when she wins big rather than him for the second time in less than 24 hours. This time, I also know, the cheque, minus $200 for our cab ride home and some groceries, will be made out to my mother, who will tuck it into her purse. At home, I will show her how to use her cell phone to deposit it into her bank account and how to pay off their credit card balance online. Next, we will go to the supermarket and shop for the week, and when we get home, Mom will make all three of us appointments for teeth cleaning and checkups with the dentist. Later she will assemble a tasty seafood pasta dish, and we will all sit down as a family before she and Dad disappear into their bedroom to celebrate their good fortune of having brought blessed little me into the world.

When it all happens pretty much as I saw it, right up to Mom and Dad both kissing me on the top of the head before retreating to their bedroom, I rise and do the dishes. I ignore the voice accusing me of enabling a larger and more dangerous drug habit. Instead, I cling to thoughts about my mother paying three months' rent in advance for both this apartment and Dad's studio. How that represents stability more than anything else.

The dishes done, I listen at their door and am relieved to hear voices, and I pray their drug of choice isn't heroin or meth or anything too strong. I sit on my bed and phone Gina, and we talk about what I missed in school today, though I'm distracted by a distant voice warning, *It's coming.*

In the past few weeks, I have spent hours with Lucas receiving one-on-one training to improve my abilities, though much of what we do is stretch on bright purple mats as he tells me life secrets, at least as he sees them. Lucas likes to explain God and Satan don't exist in heaven and hell but in each of us. He will take my hand and stare intently into my eyes and tell me he's never encountered someone so full of God's presence. Of course, he's a big believer in dualism as it relates to the mind and body, although not in any way that involves good and evil. He will say, *God and Satan are not equally opposing forces; God is much stronger. But never underestimate the Great Evil, which is always attracted to the Great Good. So, you, more than anyone must be vigilant.*

Is it this power of suggestion that makes me believe the Great

Evil lurks barely out of sight each time I journey away from my body into the future or each time I sense my mother or father twitching in anticipation of a needle or pill or powder they can no longer resist?

After saying goodnight to Gina, I challenge the Great Evil to leave the shadows and confront me. I call it a motherfucking cocksucking coward, though in a hushed voice, my eyes turned down.

* * *

At school, I smile at how perfectly I understand the day's new algebra lessons, even if it's obvious this pleasure of mastering a new task is really the contentment of returning to a familiar one you perhaps mastered, or at least grasped, lifetimes ago.

I start thinking about what Mom and Dad are doing now and whether they will want to try another casino with me tonight like they did the previous two. It would be better, I decide, to stay home and have a leisurely dinner again as a family, even if the images that come to mind of us joking around the kitchen table are themselves a little delusional. It is while I am lost in these artificially happy thoughts that cognition strikes, a breath-stealing kick to the ribs. *No, no, no,* I scream. I rise, forgetting to grab my books, and stumble out the door, ignoring classmates' murmurs and my teacher's puzzled voice.

I run down the hall and out the front door, my mind devoured by a single thought: that it's all my fault, the dipshit who days earlier wished them out of my life, the dipshit who gave them the financial means to leave.

A block away, I stagger past Maria Perez, who stomps out her cigarette and surprises me with a look of sympathy and not a grin that would reveal her as an agent of the Great Evil.

My fingers shaking, I phone Mom's cell phone, and when she answers she shrieks like someone's torturing her with a sharp knife. She pleads, *Don't come home, my baby girl. I don't want you to see him like this.*

Maybe she doesn't know I witnessed his end weeks ago and was too stupid to understand that the vision of my father disappearing into a soapy cluster of bubbles was no random dream but a foretelling of his rebirth.

Something inside me cracks and comes apart, releasing a voice that screams this is my fault, that everything is my fault. I want to float into the sky and drift back into a past where my life isn't such a screwed-up mess, though such a time and place doesn't exist. Instead, I collapse to the sidewalk, my elbows and knees saving my face from the hardest and bloodiest impact.

Maria Perez kneels at my side, her ring-heavy hand resting almost gently on my trembling back, and through my tears, I nearly laugh at her kindest stab at comfort, until the raw truth in her words connects with me. She says, *Remember, whatever it is, it can always be shittier.*

* * *

Mom shudders beneath a tear-dampened blanket on the couch. I curl up on the floor at her feet. And this, at least, brings us closer, for now.

* * *

I stand beneath the colored lights of two giant amusement park Ferris wheels in a city I am sure is Vienna. In my arms rests a grinning pale-skinned baby whose large head and chubby body stretch the inside of a pale green jumper. How many teenage girls get to cradle their newborn mother? Of course, I know the answer. It happens all the time, even if almost no one realizes that people who love each other always, with a little outside help, find one another in the next life. After all, humanity's collective mind does enjoy a damn good love story.

The wonder of seeing my mother wrapped in new purity dims, at least for a moment, the stark light that shines on the other half of the equation. That before rebirth comes death.

I pull myself back from the future and onto my bedroom floor. I creep into Mom's darkened room and make sure she continues breathing after taking an assortment of pills, mostly legal, that she assembled to plunge herself firmly into a fantasy world where her daughter didn't kill her husband.

From her bedside, I drift into her future once again and see a vast nothingness. The peek into her next life in Vienna was a gift that comes only once.

It's no small task I face. It's hard enough for a person to change her own path; changing someone else's is nearly impossible. But I will try, or at least I tell myself this.

Let's do it, girl, I whisper. Obediently, I rise and find my thickest hoodie and snatch up my cell phone, ID, credit card, small sketchbook and all the cash in the apartment, tucking most of it into my knockoff Louis Vuitton purse. Into the night, I vanish. The Great Evil is close behind, barely out of sight, like the worst kind of stalker. It, of course, has no idea of my destination because I have no clue either. All I know is that if I can lead it far enough away, my mother might have another chance in this life.

A helpful voice inside me argues. It reminds me that Mom looked happy in her next life, where she will grow up to have a solid and inherent aversion to drugs, and that I could more easily move into a permanently-out-of-body existence if she weren't here suffering through her current life. It's not a point I wish to argue, so I strangle the voice into silence. Another voice arises right away, suggesting I seek help from Lucas and my friends at the center. I strangle this one, too, not wanting to waste more time with those who are captivated by my abilities but even less knowledgeable than me about how to use them without killing my own damn father.

I stop at a traffic light in an unfamiliar neighborhood. Two muscular teens with backward baseball caps eye me from a bus stop, and I don't shrink back. I meet their gaze, and they both flash unconvincing grins. They sense it. The malevolence in me. The ability to do something horrible and walk away without a care. They turn so all that's visible is their muscled backs, like even they want no part of me.

Sirens sound. A convoy of four police cars screams through the intersection. No one seems to notice; not the bus-stop boys, not the drivers in a handful of stopped cars. It gets me wondering if the world I create has become larger than that of everyone else, those tired masses who live in a universe shrunken by fear and conformity. Maybe if they too were not afraid to set their minds free, they would inhabit a world bursting with loving consciousness, with wide symbolic spaces unrestrained by physical boundaries.

It's a nice thought, this. Ashlee the fearless. Ashlee the explorer. Ashlee the transcendent. It's a nice thought if you ignore a few niggling details. Like how fear has replaced the wonder in my most distant out-of-body travels, leaving me as hesitant as a small child who's wandered far from home. And worse, how the unenlightened people around me could be right: that a mental illness and all its delusions propel me not only on these psychedelic trips but throughout the rest of my day, making me just like my parents only without the recreational drugs. There's one more question, the worst of all, that I don't wish to consider. Aren't I really leaving Mom to spare myself from having to watch her die the same horrible, inevitable death as my father?

All these misgivings swirl around in my head like a sticky goo until, finally, the real question, the only one worth asking, floats to the surface: Do I need to keep suffering through my current physical life, this life that has gone so wrong? Or put another way, why wouldn't I want to expedite my transformation into a higher being by snuffing out the flesh and bones that weigh me down?

Mike Chapter 14

Missing: Days Eight and Nine

In Kingman, Arizona, I turned north and watched the landscape slowly return to desert, the way it would remain until the Nevada border and the Colorado River, better known as the Grand Canyon. It wasn't until the sprawl of Henderson, Nevada, that I felt safe enough to exit into a gas station and empty my aching bladder with a near euphoric groan. After refueling and buying three pieces of questionable fried chicken, I drove a few blocks to a strip mall and sat in my car eating. I had no idea whether Ashlee and maybe Kimberly were anywhere near Las Vegas. But when desperation prevails, you give life to any low-hanging theory, and so I did, searching the web on my phone for a group, if I remembered Kimberly's words correctly, called the Friends of the Seven Signs.

The situation looked simple: When Kimberly gave me the name of the New Age group, she had already decided to turn me in by contacting Douglas and informing him I was in Sedona and would be meeting her at a certain bar at 3 p.m. She had probably also told Douglas her group had found Ashlee, perhaps even arranging a conversation between the two. One phone call, multiple loose ends tidied up. Did Kimberly suspect I had hurt Kacey Sutton and maybe wanted to silence Ashlee? Did she believe I was like my son, Joshua, someone anxious to get Ashlee under his control before her gambling luck ran out? Either way, she had known one phone call to Douglas or Sweeny could see me locked in a Sedona jail until everything was sorted out.

The Friends of the Seven Signs, at least according to its website, did exist, in the form of a group of "3,800 spiritual explorers dedicated to serving their highest purpose," whatever the fuck that meant. Their website made no mention of Las Vegas or Ashlee. I thumbed through their Facebook page, with its 4,800 Likes, and their Twitter account, with 8,220 followers. They both contained workshop information and so-called inspiration phrases. Again, no mention of Ashlee or any connection to Las Vegas.

It was on Twitter that a six-hour-old tweet caught my attention. It read, "Ready for four days in the desert with my New Age buddies." The hashtag FriendsoftheSevenSigns and a photo of a pair of dice accompanied it.

For close to an hour, I dug further down into Google. My eyes ached from reading small print, my back hurt from hunching over, and I grew tired of fighting a desire to check into a hotel off the strip and lose myself in a hot bath followed by a long sleep. After, of course, a foray to the closest bar. The Google searches had started to stray off-topic, throwing up links to the television show *Friends* and an episode involving Phoebe's uterus. I would try for another 10 minutes. As that time ticked down, I finally stumbled upon a cached page on a chat board that mentioned the group having held a spiritual retreat two years earlier at the Tropicana hotel in Las Vegas.

I removed the battery from my cell phone, and forty-five minutes later, I had checked into the Howard Johnson hotel a block away from the Tropicana. I showered, changed my clothes, fought an urge to collapse into bed, and walked along my hotel's dreary street, unfittingly named Duke Ellington Way, toward the glitz of Las Vegas Boulevard and the pretend New York skyline in the distance and the many-stories-tall Tropicana sign a block away.

The resort's conference rooms were at the back of the sprawling property. There, I checked a room list for any mention of Friends of the Seven Signs, finding nothing for earlier that day or that night. I zigzagged through the casino and lobby, walked through a couple of restaurants, loitered in the lobby, and finally ordered a beer in the lounge.

It was after 10 p.m., meaning Ashlee would more likely be curled up in a king-size bed in an air-conditioned room above me, rather than wandering the not-overly-kid-friendly resort. At this thought, a burst of hysterical laughter rose from my gut because her most likely whereabouts was far from here. I ordered another beer, listened to a Hawaiian band play '70s music and tried not to ask myself what I was doing here, even if it became obvious when I had knocked back three more beers and three shooters with ridiculous sounding names I would be too hungover to remember by morning.

* * *

When artificially bright sunlight squeaked through my room's stiff curtains, I awoke and showered, selecting a can of nuts from the mini bar for my breakfast. I checked the Friends of the Seven Signs website and social media accounts without finding anything new or interesting and returned to the Tropicana, this time starting my search at the casino and restaurants in the front and working my way back to the conference rooms.

There on the menu board were the initials FSS beside the time 7 p.m. and Ashton Room #3.

* * *

While the discovery of the promising initials had convinced me to stay away from the Tropicana until that night, restlessness again prevailed, and I plotted one quick afternoon pass through the resort. I put on my sunglasses and the baseball cap I had purchased from a store in front of the MGM and studied myself in the mirror long enough to laugh at my poor disguise.

This time I avoided the casino and instead sought out places with views of the pool and restaurants. I settled at a bank of penny slot machines in a wide and open corridor. Soon I had a beer in my hand and then another. Ashlee slipped from my mind, and it was while I debated treating myself to a steak dinner that she materialized on a set of outside stairs beside the swimming pool. Or at least it was someone who could be Ashlee. This person came to me in a rapid series of short bursts as trees and huge ornamental columns and, finally, a high poolside wall all obscured her moving body for long moments. I pieced the glimpses together and determined it was Ashlee, who wore a dressy pair of shorts and a blouse that looked purchased from the hotel's gift shop.

By the time the girl climbed another set of stairs and entered the restaurant, I had abandoned the slot machine that held my meager winnings and was hurrying down the hallway. At the restaurant, a curious and slightly distant sight greeted me. This person who had transcended her earthly body and never ate had taken a seat at a table on the terrace that overlooked the pool, her face pointed at a menu. And stranger still, across from her sat Kimberly, the other woman who haunted my life.

I began taking long and sullen strides toward their table, telling myself, fuck it, let Kimberly call the cops again because by the time they arrived, I would have all the required answers from my granddaughter. As I approached, I waited for them to turn and spot me, their faces consumed by surprise, mine by petty satisfaction. At the last second, a more cautious approach asserted itself, and I veered off, taking a seat at the restaurant's inside bar, which offered a partial view of the two of them. Perhaps, it would be better to talk to Ashlee alone, assuming such an opportunity presented itself, and not to reveal myself to Kimberly just yet.

I sipped a margarita, aggressively perhaps as it was gone in minutes, and watched them talk easily like a couple of old friends. When their food arrived, Ashlee pushed her plate away. Kimberly gently coaxed her, holding up a single French fry, a fork of lettuce. My view and eyesight weren't the best, though I swore Ashlee grinned as she rejected each item.

Mostly, Kimberly ate while Ashlee talked, making me long to be within earshot. I ordered a second margarita, then a third, not wanting to look suspicious. While I licked the salt from my lips, I half expected Ashlee to glance up and point to me, her psychic abilities proven once more. She never did, though, leaving me almost disappointed.

Kimberly paid their bill, and they lingered at their table, their bodies alert but relaxed, their eyes closed like they were meditating. Kimberly was demonstrating she could take a considerable dose of crazy for her New Age team, which was suddenly boosted in size by the arrival of two men. The men spoke briefly to them, and all four left the restaurant, me throwing down some cash on the bar and following.

I expected them to turn left toward the hotel rooms, but they walked through the casino floor to the concierge desk, where they appeared to ask a single question before proceeding back through the casino. On the way, one man peeled off and took a seat at a roulette table, while the other accompanied Kimberly and Ashlee to the Starbucks coffee shop in the hotel, where they sat on stools.

A few moments later, Kimberly placed an order with the barista while Ashlee, prompted by the man, closed her eyes like she searched for a single thought. She spoke a dozen or so words to the man, who then texted on his phone. For an observer like me who suspected what they were attempting, it all looked ridiculously silly, these adults believing that whatever spilled from a mentally ill girl's mouth had some bearing on what would happen seconds later at a roulette table a hundred yards away.

I stood defiantly in the open, the disbeliever that no one cared to see. I would be spotted soon by either Ashlee or Kimberly, assuming they hadn't noticed me already. Slowly I turned, making my way to an almost empty roulette table where I settled in two spots down from Ashlee and Kimberly's friend and purchased $100 in chips from the dealer.

My lone roulette companion looked to be in his mid-20s and fit. Behind him stood another man I had never seen before, and the two started talking like a couple of buddies in town for a long weekend.

"Are you winning, James?"

"Nope," James replied.

But that would change.

What I knew about a roulette wheel, with numbered pockets from 1 to 36, plus 0 and 00, was that if you try to pick the exact number where the ball will stop, your odds are 38-1, usually paying out at 35-1 to give the house a slight profit. So, if you bet on an exact number instead of a group of numbers, you had a less than three percent chance of hitting it.

My pile of chips slowly shrank, as did James's, until he scored a direct hit on number 11. He didn't win on the next two spins, but the one after rewarded his bet on number 32. I watched him play, his friend hovering behind him as he talked on his phone while occasionally squeezing James's back with encouragement. I bought more chips. James continued winning, mostly betting on red or black or on even or odd. His friend never left his side, never put his cell phone down. As luck went, it was pretty good, good enough to bring the floor manager to a spot behind the dealer where he began observing this man wearing a red golf shirt that neatly matched his growing stack of red chips. Only then did James begin to lose, though only small amounts that hardly dented his winnings.

My chips gone, I returned to the Starbucks, where Ashlee had grown bored. She argued with Kimberly, her hands flying like she conducted a large orchestra, and then she stood abruptly. Her voice grew nearly loud enough for me to hear. A few customers turned their heads. That was when the man sitting with them took Ashlee's wrist in his hands and gave it a slight twist. The face she claimed to no longer inhabit grimaced, and her eyes flashed a look of fear, followed by anger and then flat-out defiance.

Kimberly pushed the man, and Ashlee pulled her hand free. And just like that, the girl was gone, Kimberly and the man on her heels, the man shouting words of apology to Ashlee in a display of full-out dysfunction. I hurried to catch up, having seen enough. Ashlee plunged into a crowd entering an elevator, with Kimberly and the man steps behind her. I could hear the elevator doors closing and ran to catch up. I expected to see the doors bump open at the last second, the man dragging Ashlee out for some more profitable tests on her psychic ability. I could see what would happen next: my fist hitting the man's face hard, him going down, me standing over him and punching away until others stepped in and stopped me.

But psychic power, it seemed, was an ability that didn't extend through my entire family. The elevator closed, the digital display above its doors flashing with a half-dozen different ascending numbers.

* * *

For 45 long minutes, I waited at the elevator's base, hoping Ashlee or someone in her group would materialize. When no one did, I returned to the casino floor, where my roulette partners were gone. I approached the front desk on the chance Ashlee or Kimberly were registered under their names, which they weren't. I tried to find out what floor the Friends were staying on but was met only with a suspicious gaze. I paced the lobby, undoubtedly looking like one of those agitated nutcases people report to hotel security or the cops. Finally, I had the sense to leave.

I walked down the Strip to a drugstore near Planet Hollywood, purchased two disposable phones and called Detective Douglas on one from a sidewalk crowded with a hopeful throng of glassy-eyed gamblers marching from one casino to the next.

The detective answered curtly, though his demeanor improved once he knew it was me.

"Mr. Baker, how is the weather there in Arizona?"

"Really nice in Sedona, but I had to leave quickly."

"Really? Well, I hope you found what you were looking for."

"I was going to ask you the same thing. I hear you were in my apartment. And car. You finally got a chance to check for a tire iron or something."

"Yes, or something," he said laughing, and for a minute, I thought he must be nearly psychotic enough to enjoy his job.

"So, I guess I should be concerned when you send officers to arrest me?"

He laughed again. "You mean those officers who were asked to stand there while you phoned me so you could answer a few more questions while I encouraged you to return to Miami."

"Why is it I don't believe you?"

"Doesn't matter what you believe. Because here we are talking, which means I can finally ask you the questions."

"Don't you remember? I'm lawyering up."

"Well then, who is your lawyer?"

"Still looking for one."

"Your search has taken you far. All that way and did you even get to talk to the girl?"

I considered my answer. It didn't matter because Douglas said, "I got to talk to her. To Ashlee. Your old friend Kimberly put her on the phone."

"You're sure it was Ashlee you talked to?"

"Pretty sure, yes. I questioned the girl for a good 30 minutes. Her friends are bringing her home tomorrow. She didn't seem to know anything about how her mother died, though it was an interesting conversation all the same. I asked her about you.

She said she told you in that warehouse where you met that she had foreseen her mother's death. She said you thought she was crazy."

This I found interesting. "Don't you?"

"I think the crazy person is the one who flees during a police investigation. It's time you returned."

"What did you think you found in my apartment or car that you would send officers to arrest me in Sedona?"

"You're too suspicious," he said. "Everything's fine. Assuming you return home so we can meet. With your lawyer present, of course."

"Maybe you need to stop looking at me and start looking at the group that's gone psycho over a 16-year-old girl."

With this, I ended the call.

* * *

In the half-dark, I sat on the bed in my hotel room, my breathing shallow, my fists knotted. It wasn't the conversation with Douglas that bothered me. Our quick chat, at least the way I read it, had convinced me of two things. That I was still a suspect in Kacey Sutton's death, despite his assurances otherwise. And that as far as the police were concerned, Ashlee Sutton was safe. The first point should have bothered me the most. But it was the second that lodged itself in my head.

If she was safe, should her arm have been wrenched like it was in the casino? Just reliving that moment sent emotions tearing through me, as did thoughts of what would happen if I met up with her assailant.

I needed to push this aside. Focus on one thing: figuring out who was fucking with me, though it could be argued a certain group staying across the street checked off more and more boxes by the hour. This thought was interrupted by another flash of rage.

I loathed this anger and what it said about who I was, just like I loathed my growing emotional attachment to a girl who, yes, was blood but was also little more than a stranger. Someone I had met once in my life and inexplicably traveled across the country to meet again.

Over the past few days, I had grappled for the source of the girl's emotional power over me and more than once considered the obvious possibility: that Ashlee resembled my long-dead mother. In my entire life, I had possessed only three photos of my parents. Two I had abandoned with everything else I owned when going off to prison. The third, the one of my 17-year-old mother standing in a creek cradling me, had met a wet ending years earlier when I discarded it in frustration in a body of water that never matched the photo. The years since surrendering those photos had stripped away any memory of my parents' faces, especially my mother's.

I closed my eyes and tried to conjure my mother's face from some deep-buried brain cell. Twenty minutes later, I stood from the bed and kicked a small metal garbage bin in frustration. From the hallway came a woman's laughter, loud and mocking.

* * *

I paid for another night in the hotel, knowing it would not be needed. I threw my belongings into the trunk of my car and sat behind the wheel, staring nowhere in particular until finally, my mind emerged from the loop where it was stuck. I pulled my car out onto the street, found a parking spot facing Tropicana Avenue, and climbed out. As I walked to the Tropicana Resort, I picked up the only decent weapon available, one I had noticed earlier that day lying in a clump of discarded beer cans and escort service flyers. It was a brick, dislodged from a small garden wall outside the neighboring casino, its color a slightly duller red than the hills around Sedona.

I didn't walk through the Tropicana's main entrance or the casino, my brick in hand. Instead, I cut through the parking lot toward the conference rooms. I checked the time on my phone, inhaled sharply and squeezed the brick with the same anticipation as years ago when I held a large rock on the beach in the moments before clubbing a little fucker named Jimmy.

When I entered the conference area minutes from now, the first swing of the brick, and maybe the next few, would be saved for a man whose name I didn't know.

I told myself that what was about to happen was only me getting answers, nothing more. Then I walked on in the most unnatural glow of lights, my steps mostly measured, the brick partly concealed in my fist.

Mike Chapter 15

Sept. 11, 2001 Seattle, Washington

She paced the sidewalk outside our apartment building, her elegant fingers twisted in anxious knots, her face turned down 11th Avenue toward Seattle University, the place I jogged to each morning before turning around and faithfully coming home. From across the street, I stretched my hamstrings on the curb and watched Jennifer through passing traffic for long enough to realize something was wrong. I needed to go to her. Right now. Yet I hesitated, wondering if it's true that we reveal much about ourselves, maybe too much, in the most trying moments of our lives.

Finally, I stepped forward, and Jennifer looked relieved when she saw me. It was like I had returned from a dangerous far-off country, as I once often did, and not a safe neighborhood blocks away.

"My God, Mike, you haven't heard yet, have you?"

"Heard what?"

"We are under attack. America is under attack."

"By who?"

"Terrorists. Come inside and see."

She unlocked the front door to our building, and as we climbed the stairs to our second-floor suite, she said, "You've had two calls already. Associated Press and Reuters. They want to talk to you about going there."

"Where?"

"I guess wherever the terrorists are based."

Inside our suite, CNN blared from our television. I watched open-mouthed, forgetting to take a seat. It was 7:53 a.m. on a beautiful late summer day in Seattle, and both towers of the World Trade Center had fallen.

"Are you going to go?" Jennifer asked.

I didn't turn away from the television until I stumbled upon footage that showed objects, which likely were people, falling from the towers' upper floors as an inferno bore down.

Jennifer repeated her question. "Sorry, what?" I asked. "Go where?"

She stood between me and the TV. "You know. To wherever they want to send you."

I squinted at her, perplexed by how she expected me to answer before hearing the offers. My eyes drifted to the window and the bright morning sun.

When my gaze returned to Jennifer, a business-like expression had taken over her face. "Looks like we both need to make some phone calls," she said.

* * *

Jennifer phoned her law office and arranged to work from home. I called both news services, listened to what they had in mind, and promised to get back to them.

"So," Jennifer said, a forced casualness in her voice, as I hung up the phone after the second call.

Such a diabolical two-letter word.

* * *

We had met a few months into the new millennium while both serving as panelists at a Rwandan genocide conference in Seattle, a city where we both lived. The genocide was a topic familiar to me. Six years earlier in the small African nation, I witnessed the brutal horror the world had seen coming and refused to stop.

During a short break after the session where I spoke, a panelist who worked for the United Nations approached, told me she had appreciated me sharing my experiences and asked what lessons I thought we as a society had learned from the ethnic slaughter of as many as one million people in that tiny country.

My answer: "The same lesson as always. One that, in Rwanda, we chose to ignore once again: That people with a little power can do horrific things if other people with a little more power refuse to stop them."

We talked, and it didn't take long to discover we had visited many of the same countries. I suggested we discuss our travels further over coffee or a drink.

As she considered my offer, her eyes glowed with wonder usually reserved for a precocious child. When she said yes and suggested a place, I was so focused on the way her words flowed with the gracious humanity often missing in my travels that I would later struggle to remember the bar's name.

We found a corner table, and, over the robust voices of a bachelorette party on the other side of the room, she told me her special interest in Rwanda came from her genetic roots, one-eighth Rwandan on her mother's side, "the rest pale white European." She looked mostly Caucasian to me, though her brown hair and eyes and full facial features hinted at a heritage a little closer to the equator. She went on to describe her jet-setting work as a lawyer for the human rights office at the UN. One month in France fighting a case at the European Court of Human Rights, the next in the Middle East investigating a shocking tale of abuse. In between, she would return to Seattle, the city where she grew up and owned a condo.

We talked late into the night, and I only half-remembered saying, "I can't believe someone blessed with your intelligence was also given so much beauty."

She asked if I was flirting, and I asked if she wanted to see me again to talk about something other than genocide.

In the disjointed series of events that formed my life, meeting her would become the luckiest moment. And the unluckiest too, for she was a pleasurable and thought-provoking book I couldn't put down, even though it would disrupt my busy life, and hers, in every way imaginable.

Our relationship started slowly, an ideal situation for two people on the road so much. Often, we would spend long hours on the phone from whatever cities our assignments took us. Three times when we shared the same continent, we hopped on planes and met in a romantic city somewhere in the middle. Occasionally, I would return home from an assignment and be amazed to find her waiting at the airport, my favorite Starbucks coffee blend in her hand, her eager smile hiding nothing as she explained she managed to work a break into her schedule. Somehow in our weeks or months apart, she failed to find a more suitable replacement in a world teeming with them.

When we were both in town, I shaped my empty schedule to hers, meaning we spent much of our spare time together, often exploring new restaurants around her Belltown condo, discovering walks in unfamiliar parks and urban areas, and occasionally, hanging out with her shockingly large group of friends.

That winter, we both took extended work breaks. Almost every day we walked the three-mile trail around Green Lake. One Sunday afternoon, a northeast wind blew Arctic air across the city. Grey ice covered every inch of the lake, though signs every few hundred yards warned it wasn't thick enough to walk or skate on. Leafless tree branches chattered together as we walked quickly by, her arm tucked in mine, our heads twisted away from the cold. When her parked car came into sight, we ran for it, laughing. At her apartment, we threw off our clothes and raced for her bed and its heavy covers. She pressed the coldest parts of her body against my warmest, and I kissed her hard. Soon she straddled me, the covers thrown to the floor, and stared intently into my eyes.

"This shit's starting to get real," she said.

It was delivered as a breezy, throw-away line, yet she had put into words what we both felt: a tumbling forward that left us both exhilarated and uneasy. We had walked far out onto that thin ice where heartbreak could come from any direction.

One day in the spring of 2001, Jennifer suggested I move in with her and rent out my condo. I tried not to look terrified.

"We aren't in town that much," I said.

She smiled. "All the reason not to have the cost of two apartments."

I nodded, panicked that a better objection failed to present itself.

"I have a second proposal too," Jennifer said.

And before she spoke, the ground felt like it was shifting between my feet.

Jennifer knew I had a standing job offer through an editor friend who worked for the Seattle Post-Intelligencer. General assignment reporter. Decent money. Regular hours. She had mentioned numerous times that she had similar offers from local law firms seeking a civil rights lawyer.

"Why don't we both take a position in Seattle, commit to one year, get a rest from years on the road, and see what we both think?"

"You've got your dream job," I said, hoping not to sound desperate. "I couldn't ask you to give it up."

"We both have our dream jobs. But I think it's time to try a dream relationship for a while."

Weeks later, I surprised myself by accepting the Seattle job and moving my meager belongings into Jennifer's apartment. Maybe I was calling her bluff because there was no way she would ever give up her UN job. But she did.

We unpacked my clothes, and I told her she must be a kind witch capable of controlling others through powerful spells. Her eyes went wide, and as she helped hang my shirts in a cramped closet, she regaled me with stories about her Rwandan grandmother who had been a seer and folk healer who could supposedly make people better with herbal remedies and the power of suggestion. Jennifer said with a chuckle that she shared some of her grandmother's gifts because she had twice dreamed about an older me being vexed by a precocious dark-haired teenage girl who was much smarter than me.

After making love to Jennifer on our first night in what would become our place, I wandered into the living room and sat naked in the dark, my body filling with cortisol and with thoughts about how the person sleeping in the next room was so focused on parenthood that she was dreaming a teenaged daughter into existence. This shit *is* getting real.

* * *

We spent much of the morning on the day known as 9-11 huddled in our apartment watching CNN. I had been scheduled to start work at 3 p.m. but would go in a couple of hours earlier to help with the biggest story of the new century. In the air, more than one deadline hovered like a missile-armed drone.

"So, when do you need to let the news services know?" Jennifer asked.

"By late tomorrow."

"You're not even six months into the one year you committed to the PI. That you committed to…"

"The bosses will understand. This is a huge global story. A modern-day attack on Pearl Harbor."

She turned down the television's sound, working the remote like someone choking a small animal.

"A commitment is a commitment."

"Sometimes circumstances force changes."

"How long would you be gone?"

I explained about leaving soon for Pakistan. About the uncertainty of where the story would go from there.

"So, how long?"

"Months."

"And then you'd return to your job at the PI?"

"Not sure I would still have a job there."

Jennifer sat back on the sofa. The energy she usually moved with had vanished nearly as suddenly as New Yorkers' sense of security. With an unusual lack of enthusiasm, she said, "I imagine there are certain reporters out there who almost welcome this attack. An international blockbuster story. One so big the news services will throw all kinds of resources at it. Get them off whatever mundane stories they had been covering."

I let the remark slide.

"It's my birthday next week," she said almost absentmindedly. Almost.

"I know," I said.

"Thirty-three. I'll be thirty-three if you can believe that. How fast the time is flying by."

Was it too early to report to work? "Listen, I won't be gone forever. Just long enough to cover the biggest story of the century."

She threw out a sarcastic laugh. "It is only 2001. There will be other big stories this century."

We sat in silence until she said, "We always talk about it. It's always there on the horizon. 'Maybe we'll start trying next month, or maybe in the new year or in the spring.' But we never actually get there, you know. We never actually start."

The television replayed the twin towers' fall in a seemingly endless loop, cutting away to the expressions of horrified onlookers.

"Today's not the time…" I started to say.

"It's never the time, apparently."

She took my hand, something I wished she hadn't done. Usually, I longed for her touch, but sometimes, unexpectedly, she would rest her head or a hand on me, and instead of soaking up this open affection, I would be overwhelmed by a desire to squirm free.

I stood. "I feel bad not being in the newsroom right now. I think I should go."

"If you went... overseas I mean... when would you leave?"

"Right away. The day after tomorrow maybe."

"The hotel we've booked in Portland this weekend is prepaid, and we'll lose the $350 if we can't go," she said.

I shrugged. The Portland hotel was part of our pleasing routine of spending weekends exploring the Pacific Northwest, sometimes driving north to Vancouver or west to Ocean Shores or east to Moses Lake. Jennifer knew how I longed to become uncoupled from my usual surroundings, and I think she too loved sharing these moments when we would explore a new city or chunk of wilderness, returning to our hotel each night famished for a large dinner and each other's touch. Late one afternoon, she kept her sunglasses on as we made love in a sun-drenched hotel room in Birch Bay, and even hidden behind her Ray-Bans, I swore her eyes wondered: Is this enough to keep us together?

Now her uncovered eyes bore down on me.

"If you accept one of those assignments with a news service, one of those very risky assignments, you need to give me a date when you'll be back. And when you return home, you need to stay here and focus on us."

I went to the window yet really didn't look out. My eyes felt they had instead turned in to see my thoughts, to review Jennifer's words, or should I say ultimatum.

"Did you hear what I said?" Jennifer asked.

I nodded. "Sorry. I'm a little distracted today."

"So you understand what I'm asking for?"

I sat next to her, my eyes returning to the television. This time I took her hand but said nothing.

"You work in communications," she said. "So communicate.

261

Tell me what you're thinking right now."

Not possible. Because what I thought was how this moment shared the same sense of asphyxiation as many of my worst foster home memories, and most of those ended, mercifully, with the sweet-yet-temporary relief that followed me dropping from a window ledge and running into a dark, empty street.

"I can't tell you exactly when I would return home from overseas," I said. "Just that I would return. That I always come home."

"And when you come back, you would stay, right, with me, for longer than a few months?"

"Yes, of course… unless something else big came up and I needed to leave sooner. Or unless you took your old job back with the UN."

Jennifer rose, and if a simple straightening of one's body could be labeled as hostile, this one could.

This shit's getting real.

"You know," she said, "there is no going back. To the way it was before when we carried out our long-distance relationship. It was good, great even, but it wasn't sustainable. For any number of reasons."

I said nothing, but she did. "You know that, right?"

"Yes," I said.

"So you need to choose. Either us or your overseas job."

"Both. For now, it's got to be both."

"How long is this *now* you keep talking about?"

"I don't know. Not exactly."

Jennifer moved to the window, where she put her back to the wall and studied me from this short distance. She did this when she sensed a conversation going in circles. Watch me like my movements would reveal some hidden insight, perhaps some encouraging sign she had missed. It always made me wish her job hadn't made her so good at seeing through people who attempt to hide behind the ambiguity in their words.

I waited for her to rip my words apart. Instead, she turned away, and when she glanced back a minute later from the kitchen, she said, "I'll make you a turkey sandwich for lunch."

I should have drunk in the relief. I had again bought more time in that unsustainable world she talked about. Yet instead of slouching back into my seat, I remained rigid. Tense. Like a great threat still hovered around us.

When she was finished with my lunch, Jennifer placed the bag at the end of the kitchen counter, where I would grab it on my way to the bus. She remained in the kitchen, and though I could sense her stare, I knew her once-hostile eyes were now calm, like a sudden storm had passed. The transformation should have been shocking, but it never was.

I joined her in the kitchen, and she leaned forward on the counter, her fingers before her like in prayer, and when she spoke, her words sounded like a pep talk, though not for me: "Okay. You go, and we put our plans together on hold. Not forever, but until you return. Until you think you can stay for a little longer."

I gathered my wallet, keys, cell phone and lunch.

"We will figure out a game plan tonight after I get home," I promised.

She nodded and smiled. "We always do."

Jennifer stood by the door, her hands resting gently at her sides, her eyes swelling with forgiveness and maybe faith that all things can change.

I turned away from her, just for a second, and glanced at the television footage of office-attired New Yorkers staggering from a towering grey wall of dust and debris particles as an anchorwoman stretched her vocabulary by using the word "audacious" to describe the attack.

Outside our apartment, the sunshine beckoned. Somewhere in the distance, the next bus approached. If I left right now and hurried across the park, I could make it in time. I saw too how the rest of my day could unfold if I let it. If I took that first step.

At work, I would be asked to write a Seattle-endures-911 story or some other ridiculous piece that ignored the larger picture in favor of parochial reverberations. Once it was filed, I would go into the managing editor's office and tell him I was quitting. Later, back in our apartment, I would be greeted by Jennifer's always expectant smile, her patient touch as she helped me pack. While I was gone, she would consume herself with her work, the work that never entirely satisfied her. And in the weeks and months to come, I would find myself at home in whatever far-flung place served up the most newsworthy international strife, this rousing time overseas punctuated by increasingly shorter return trips to Seattle, where the loving, compromising face awaiting at the airport would slowly take on an indomitable distance.

This imperfect yet desirable version of my life would all be set in motion by that first step toward the bus.

"It's so horrible," Jennifer said, her eyes, like mine, once again affixed to the television set. "They started their day like any other, and then this happens, out of nowhere."

Words not intended to stir debate. Words I needed to ignore as I said goodbye.

"The terror attack wasn't a complete surprise," I told her. "It wasn't audacious. Not at all. There had been any number of clear signs something was coming. There always are. But they were ignored."

Her fingers clenched softly. "I can't believe you'd say that. You think New Yorkers should have been prepared for the brutality of this?"

I shrugged. "Maybe not exactly this. But something. They're not living in a fairy tale. They should have seen something coming. They should have at least expected change, which in itself is not always all bad."

"So, are you blaming them for not taking precautions?"

"No. There was little they could have done."

Jennifer moved past me into the living room and picked up the remote, squeezing it gently until the television went black. I wanted to step toward her and take her hand, maybe even convince her of something that wasn't true. When I didn't, she turned to the window, her body shaking, her eyes traveling across the street toward the playground in the park where mothers watched children too young and sheltered to comprehend the devastation unfolding not so far away.

My fingers remained clenched around my lunch. I put the bag back down on the kitchen counter.

Ashlee Chapter 14

Missing: Day Nine

Kimberly sits on a king-sized hotel bed, her legs crossed in an impressive display of flexibility for someone her age. She imagines she sees Physical Ashlee lying on her stomach next to her. She imagines she hears my voice entering her ears, even if it simply resonates in her heart.

No, I lie. *I want to go with you, but I can't.*

Why can't you? She asks this again and again.

Kimberly can't understand why someone with my ability to look into the future is unable to see everything that awaits. I am not sure myself. Maybe we aren't meant to see all things or have all the answers. Maybe some are meant to reveal themselves as surprises, forcing us to respond on the double from the heart.

Kimberly wants me to go with her to *someplace safe*, wherever that may be. She thinks my grandfather, who evaded the police after Kimberly set him up, could be a threat. If not him, someone else. She can feel the danger with her cop gut, which is why she believes I am safest with her, the one who cares most about me.

I, too, sense danger. But unlike Kimberly, I know that the longer she stays with me, the more it threatens her.

I ask Kimberly if it was hard to betray a friend. She says doing the right thing isn't always easy. But it must be done. That's why I don't tell her what I believe: my grandfather is nearby. He has watched me more than once, and he's coming for me tonight. I plan to go with him.

Kimberly phones Lucas and tells him I don't feel safe, and tonight's event must be canceled. They argue. Kimberly hangs up, curses and tells me that Lucas said it's too late to cancel, but that he will personally look out for me. Kimberly has, of course, already given up on Lucas. She dislikes the gambling he has involved me in, suggesting it has crossed an invisible line in some unhealthy way, as it did for my mother and father. She says I have nothing to prove, and the Friends don't need the money. She's right, though I don't tell her I gave up on Lucas and the Friends long before she did. Everyone forgets that I never invited anyone to find me. I am only here because it is a necessary step in my mysterious journey somewhere else.

Kimberly leans forward on the bed and asks again if I will leave with her, slipping away before tonight's meet-and-greet and speeding off in her rental car.

We can be out of here in ten minutes, she says.

If she knew how much I wanted to say yes, she would keep pushing me. That's why it's better she hears me answer, *I think going with my grandfather may be the correct path.*

Is it?

Yes. This answer isn't a lie. It's also not the complete truth.

The complete truth is something better not shared with anyone. Especially not the chatty little Physical Ashlee. What would this little tagalong do if she knew I were only going with my grandfather because he would be easier to ditch than Kimberly, especially once he has asked me the questions he wants to ask? She would blab, like always.

I also tell no one that once I ditch my grandfather, I will find a quiet place to go. Not to die but to say goodbye to my physical self, to finally embrace my full transcendence.

Kimberly stares hard at the worldly entity before her and asks, *What is it you really want, Ashlee?*

I want people I care about to stop going away.

She nods. *I was just a few years older than you when that was all I wanted in life. First, as you know, Mike left for prison and never came back. And then our close friend was killed in a car crash. One. Two. I was devastated.*

Tim, I say.

Kimberly looks puzzled. *Yes, Tim... How did you know that*

267

name?

I must have heard it somewhere.

I don't know where, she says.

Kimberly shrugs, no longer sure about anything. Then she lurches across the bed, her hands gently taking hold of the girl she first met at a funeral, her long red hair partly concealing her own tears. All of us possess some psychic power, and Kimberly's has told her she will never see me again after tonight. That someone else will leave her life forever, or so it will seem.

Mike Chapter 16

Missing: Day Nine

Assuming my base assumption was correct, I knew exactly which Tropicana conference room held the Friends of the Seven Signs and a private session with their new prophet or whatever they called someone with Ashlee's illness. I moved toward it quickly, the thick carpet doing little to soak up the recurring anger in my steps. From the room next door, overweight conference-goers wearing bright golf shirts and drinking from champagne glasses spilled out into the air-conditioned hall. None noticed me or the brick tucked in my right hand.

The door to the FSS's room was closed, with no one standing outside. I pushed a few last-second doubts aside and burst into the room where what happened next left me, at least for a moment, too stunned to move. The three-dozen or so eager-eyed dupes, who sat in a semi-circle of chairs facing Ashlee and a handful of devout men, turned to me and applauded.

As I stepped toward Ashlee, she stood, the grin on her face bordering on sweetly goofy, and said, "Granddad, I just told all these people you were coming for me. Then the door flew open and look who wandered in."

A few people murmured approvals of sorts. All that changed when my eyes found the man who had twisted Ashlee's arm.

As luck would have it, it was this man who approached me, a little cautiously, with the roulette player who went by the name James trailing behind.

"Good, so we now ask that you wait outside until our meeting is over," he said, stepping forward to shepherd me out the door.

I swung the brick, catching him on the forehead, sending him to the ground. The audience's adoration diminished instantly. As the man struggled to one knee, I struck him again, barely stifling a grin. I moved toward James, who backed away.

With my brick-free hand, I motioned for Ashlee to join me, and when she took a single step toward me, I hesitated, perhaps because deep down I had expected my violence to drive her away. I took her arm, gently, and spoke the same words as in the boarded-up warehouse in Miami: "We need to go."

She took a slightly distressed look at the bloody man on the floor, who groaned as he pressed his fingers over his open wounds. She nodded, whispering, "He'll be okay."

The man to her left, the aging hippie with grey skin whom I had seen pictured on the group's website in a write-up about its spiritual leader, reached out for Ashlee's other arm with two wrinkled hands that surely had touched Ashlee more than once. I raised my brick, and he fell off his chair, cowering. With Ashlee, I began moving toward the door.

From the floor, the group's leader did what leaders do, shouting for people to dial 911 and find hotel security. "Stop him, please, Kimberly," he called, and that was when my eyes settled on a familiar presence at the back of the room, her arms folded before her in a defiant pose often presented to me as a teenager.

Ashlee moved in step with me, and when we passed by Kimberly, my old friend looked from Ashlee to me and sighed, like what I had done had been far too predictable, even to non-psychics like her. Yet she made no move to stop me.

Soon we were hurrying across the Tropicana's vacant back parking lot, only slowing enough for me to peek over my shoulder for pursuers. In another 30 seconds, we reached Tropicana Avenue and rushed past the casino next door, where I returned the brick to where I had found it. Soon my car would come into sight on the side street outside my hotel. Not long after we would be on the road, with Ashlee safe, and she would tell me everything, and while it might not all make sense, between the two of us, we would know what to do next.

Ashlee squeezed my hand and grinned almost shyly when she noticed me studying her or taking in this physical presence she claimed was an invention of my less-developed mind. Ten lanes of traffic pulsed by. It would have been nice to take this first walk in the distraction-free silence of the open desert, where there was no chance she could suddenly disappear from my side.

Fifty feet from my car, Ashlee's footsteps slowed. She looked up at me, her face again beset by hesitation. Her mouth went wide. She said, "I'm so sorry, Granddad, but I didn't see this coming."

"What?" I asked, wondering if I heard her right.

The door to a cargo van flew open, and out jumped three men wearing green windbreakers emblazoned with the word POLICE. I tried to speak, but before the words left my mouth, an object pushed against my chest. I heard the buzz of electricity, felt a razor-sharp pain surge through my body. My limbs went dead. Another man caught me before I hit the ground and pushed me into the van. Unable to turn my head or call out, my world contracted to the tiny patch of floor where my face came to rest.

Ashlee Chapter 15

Missing: Day Nine

When the curtain finally lifts to reveal all the actors, good and bad, one thought swamps me: transcendence doesn't make you immune to stupidity. Again I have missed another vital detail and misread the source and perhaps the strength of the danger, meaning I have imperiled yet another person.

Detective Douglas doesn't watch in satisfaction as his men shove my grandfather into the van. That's because his eyes almost bleed with savage hunger as they lock onto my physical representation. My true being starts shaking, like when a younger me would first leave her body. Suddenly, I am a little girl who wants to escape within herself from everything harmful around her. I start rising, a few feet at first, then a few hundred, and soon the dusk sky consumes me. Below, the Strip looks like a string of Christmas lights stretched out neatly on a front lawn waiting to be hung on a sweet-smelling pine tree. I drift into my future, seeing nothing but the same cold darkness that greeted me when I explored what lay ahead in my parents' doomed lives. Sentimentality's grip must be strong because my body heaves. *Don't be scared*, I tell myself weakly. My mind recalls a childhood kite on the end of a string. A string anyone could control.

Detective Douglas speaks my name. He touches the elbow on the imaginary physical body that people call Ashlee. With this contact, a connection is made, like the completed electrical circuit that brings the Times Square New Year's Eve ball to the ground. Down to the street my essence falls under the weight of earthly heaviness. My boots touch the sidewalk, leaving me spiritually handcuffed yet again to the ugly mess of flesh and hair and pimples people see when they think they look at me.

Detective Douglas reminds me who he is, his words confident and full of deceit, like he's sure that I don't see what he's doing. Like he's sure I have nothing to teach him about faith and sacrifice and the power of love. Thinking I care, he delivers a fauxpology for making a potentially dangerous take-down in my presence. He reminds me of our phone conversation. He explains how the danger has mostly passed, as if, and begins ushering the body he sees before him toward the open door of the van that holds my grandfather. I know I must follow. When Physical Ashlee is inside, my true being with her, the van door slams shut, and we begin moving.

My grandfather lies on the floor, his hands bound together behind his back, Detective Douglas hovering up-in-his-shit over the top of him. The lights of the towering signs outside the MGM Grand flood through the windshield where two men sit in the driver and passenger seats. From where I linger, my grandfather's eyes are hidden, yet I know they're filled with hurt and betrayal. He thinks I gave him up. He will soon learn the true situation is much worse than that.

The van hits a pothole, and my grandfather's head slaps against the floor. He groans, and I should go to him. My mother's presence whispers to me from inside the vehicle. I can smell the scent of cinnamon on her sweaty skin from when she would bake cookies in the stuffy kitchen of the apartment where we once lived. She leans towards my presence and says, *Be careful, my baby girl.*

I smile at the words *baby girl* because just as nothing remains the same forever, many things reverse places at some point in time.

Being careful is for pussies, I whisper, confident she doesn't understand the full extent of my power, which is another way of saying she doesn't grasp the depth of my love.

I wait for her to laugh and tell me I'm a little shit, but she doesn't. She feels it, too: the darkness around us in this confined space, in this glittering city bewitched by greed.

Now that I am safely in his control, Detective Douglas speaks freely. "So, my kind girl," he says, "I understand you've been on the most amazing winning streak. Let's hope your luck has not run out just yet."

My grandfather twitches when he hears these words. He is no dummy. Finally, he starts to realize how much trouble he is in.

Outside, a dirt-streaked windshield looms the gaudy lights of an Eiffel Tower that any supposed teenage girl would see as a lame lie. As the van leaves the bright glow and bustle of the Strip, the loudest sound soon becomes my grandfather's painful groans as his circulation returns.

Detective Douglas studies the items he's taken from my grandfather: A cell phone, car keys, passport and wallet. He laughs at the passport and studies my grandfather. *Well, Mr. Roza of Syria, I guess this explains why tracking you was much harder than I anticipated. Very clever. Once a criminal, always a criminal is what Detective Sweeny said about you just the other day.*

Like Douglas is one to talk.

The van plunges deeper into the darkness, and I try to light it with God's love, which of course flows through all of us. If I could, I would summon up a harmful force to strike down the Great Evil, though everyone knows this isn't possible. You can't use good for bad.

Detective Douglas gives me that hungry look again, something I counteract with another thought about love. My so-called vision falls on Physical Ashlee's hand, the one my grandfather held sweetly moments ago. It shudders like a baby left helpless in the cold. I wait for it to disappear into my hoodie's pocket. It doesn't. Instead, it coils into a fist.

Missing: Day Nine

The city's bright lights faded, and with them went any hope our destination was a Las Vegas police station. The feeling in my arms and legs slowly returned, only to be cut off by straps around my wrists and ankles. I lay on my side facing Douglas, who sat on the floor, his back against a side wall, his eyes focused intently on something out of my vision. It could only be Ashlee he stared at like a teenage boy engrossed with his wildest fantasy.

My brain felt useless, like soft clay squeezed together in a choking motion and then stretched out to reveal its many weaknesses. I struggled to speak. When my voice eventually crept back, I threw curses at Douglas, followed by threats and finally pleas to let Ashlee go. He laughed. Time also became jumbled. Had I screamed at my captor or only imagined the need to do so?

I wanted to call out to Ashlee, confirm she was okay, at least for now. After a hazy internal debate, I decided to wait until I could actually see her, assuming that happened.

"Where is Sweeny?" I asked Douglas, my words sounding like they came from underwater.

Douglas nodded. "He's back in Miami working while I flew off to Ohio for a few days' bereavement leave. Dead uncle and all that."

"It will be your own funeral if you hurt the girl."

He smiled at this. He did have a sense of humor, as sick as it might be.

"So, Kacey Sutton's death...?"

Douglas put a finger over his lips. "Be a little sensitive, Mr. Baker. Her daughter is right here. But I guess you must be happy to finally have your answer."

Did Ashlee follow the conversation? Didn't matter. Douglas was soon trying to draw her in with a question. "Look into the future, my prescient princess. How rich do you make me?"

Ashlee would spit in his face. Or at least lie. When she spoke, it was easy to imagine her grinning, like in the warehouse when her strength made me fearful. She said with cool indifference, "I will make you rich in every way that means nothing."

* * *

We stopped only once on the trip, and as we pulled off the road into a parking lot, I caught a glimpse of a lighted sign atop a tall pole that contained the words *super market*. Douglas and the man in the passenger seat surprised me by telling Ashlee they needed to make a quick stop with her.

Then Douglas added: "If you attempt to run or alert anyone to your situation or fail to obey any commands I give you, your grandfather will suffer horribly before paying the ultimate price, understand?"

"I'm not stupid," Ashlee said as she moved toward the van's open door. Douglas took her arm in his hand, and the sound of their steps faded away.

The door slid shut, and I slowly began sliding my feet closer to it so I could kick it with all my might. The man in the driver's seat anticipated this and said, "Don't bother. This part of the parking lot is empty. And if you make me get out of this seat, I'll take it out on the girl when we get where we're going."

* * *

We bounced along a quiet, pot-holed road in total darkness. Whatever our destination, it looked isolated.

Douglas leaned forward. "Almost there. The girl will go to

work soon."

"So that's all this is?" I asked. "Pure greed?"

Douglas considered this like it represented more than a rhetorical question. "Greed, yes, of course. Extreme curiosity too. When Mrs. Sutton contacted the police with her fears that the family's newfound good fortune had led someone to hurt her husband and your son – which no one had because he simply overdosed, end of story – I took a look at his finances. Several large cheques from local casinos, a whole bunch of sizable cash deposits. All of it adding up to more than $100,000. I was more than intrigued. Then when she let it slip that Ashlee was the one with a thing for gambling...

"Have you heard of Karl Jung's theory that all coincidences stem from synchronicity? That life is not a series of random events but an expression of a deeper order of everything that is about to come. It's all right there for us to read, though only a rare few find the ability to read it. Or find the signs that point them to the door leading to something more. It does happen occasionally, though."

Douglas would stop there. But, apparently, this was a subject he loved. He took a deep breath and said, "In 2012, the best poker player in the world walked into a New Jersey casino with an accomplice and walked out 17 hours later with $4.8 million dollars. Now, this guy seemed to have the touch. He had in his life already won more than $25 million playing poker, much of it online. That night he would win close to $5 million, not playing poker but baccarat. And how? By what's known as edge-sorting. In this case, by taking advantage of the almost indistinguishable aberrations in the designs on the back of the playing cards. His female accomplice had the most incredible ability for noticing, on a quick glance, the minute differences that helped her identify each card. Few people in the world could look at those cards from across the table and identify, in the seconds before they were dealt, the tiniest imperfections.

But she could."

He looked at Ashlee.

"That woman was out of my grasp. You weren't."

Douglas turned his eyes back to me.

"When the universe speaks, most of us ignore it. But some are crazy enough to listen, to see patterns in plain sight. And they discover they can understand it. Because what is madness if not everything that science has not yet managed to prove? Thousands of years ago, no one thought you would ever be able to accurately predict the weather. Or an eclipse. Even though the necessary information was all right there. Every time someone figures out the patterns, the cause and effect, they are literally diagnosed as crazy, at least at first. Like Ashlee, who is not crazy but brilliant at effortlessly piecing it all together. She is someone who can let go of every restrictive thought in her head. People like that can look at someone's face and know his thoughts, even what he may do next. People like that can, I sincerely hope, look at a computer screen and know which cards are about to be turned over in a poker game. The girl is open to believing everything is possible. And so it is. But she is not clairvoyant, not someone with special powers, like an open third eye chakra. No, no, no. She is simply prescient, at an extremely heightened degree, meaning she is bursting at the seams with knowledge of what will happen next. The girl doesn't *see* the future so much as *understand* it."

A strange sound rose from the darkness, and it took me a few seconds to identify it as Ashlee laughing. When she spoke, the words and tone she used with Douglas came as a second surprise.

"What the actual fuck are you talking about?" she asked, any sweetness long drained away until the person left sounded more like her mother.

"Yes, patterns exist," she continued, "and, yes, they are important, and, yes, God has put them everywhere in plain sight for us all to see, and, yes, they reveal themselves to those whose consciousness is in tune with the universe, those who have faith. Aren't you clever? Yet what do you focus on? Not the mysteries of life and death and love. You care only about games of chance. Child's play. Because that's all you are. A greedy little boy."

Now Douglas laughed, his spilling forth with delight. "Please tell me more," he said with excitement he could not suppress. "I do want to hear."

"You don't scare me. I've seen into your future, and it sucks, just like you, because you are a fucking cowardly cocksucker who does all his nastiness in the shadows. Yet there will be no hiding from the God of the Old Testament, who will make you pay for your sins."

His smile strong as ever, Douglas signaled for her to continue, which seemed to catch Ashlee off guard.

She hesitated, only for a second, before plunging forward, much of the emotion gone from her voice. "Einstein was wrong in his theory about the block universe because we do have free will, with God's grace, to determine our future, and I will make sure my future doesn't include you. And you should be very scared, because when I look into the future, I'm also changing the future, ever so slightly, by being the one to witness it, by being the one to interpret what I see. Our inner worlds, our thoughts and emotions, are connected with the outside world, the so-called real world. And in my inner world, I feel so much hatred for you that it is bound to bleed into your small, pathetic existence."

She began explaining concepts like how the universe is aware and shares a consciousness with each of us, though most don't know it. Sometimes she used words so foreign they sounded like a different language, often deploying them to explain why Douglas should be fearful. Douglas tried to follow along, though he too gave up, declaring to whoever could hear that you do not need to know how a car worked to drive one.

Ashlee pushed on, her voice stern like that of a judge delivering a verdict to the worst offender. Douglas, who clearly had experienced too much of a good thing, turned to me and said, "You know I should duct tape the girl's mouth shut for our sanity, but I don't want to curb her genius."

Douglas sat back and, for the next few miles, sang an old song, "Don't Stop Believin'," by Journey at the top of his lungs, trying to drown Ashlee out, perhaps demonstrating he could out-crazy her.

How had I gotten myself trapped in this madness? When the obvious answer popped straight into my head, I struggled to suppress my own insane laughter. Somehow I had forgotten the lesson violently etched into my mind years ago: that the biggest threat we face comes from those who are supposed to care about us most.

Mike Chapter 18

2003, Afghanistan

On a morning thick with car exhaust and dust clouds, I met Aarif on the teeming sidewalk outside my war-scarred hotel in Kabul, and the moment we shook hands, I began comparing him to myself of 15 years earlier: did he understand the story I worked on, could he navigate the roads easily, was he reliable, did he speak the required languages, was he enjoyable to be around, could he be trusted, was he fearless?

Aarif, 23 years old and already a father of three, had come highly recommended by a friend of none other than Peter Clarke, my mentor back in the days when I was the local guide and interpreter. Now Aarif would do the same for me as we traveled west to a small city called Bamyan, where I had arranged to interview four women about how their lives had changed in the months since NATO forces drove the ruling Taliban from their country. Of course, these weren't just any women. A human rights group working with battered women had helped place them in a shelter and told me their stories typified the hardships still faced by women throughout the country.

As we left Kabul, Aarif navigated with confidence the mix of cars, bicycles, carts, beggars and pedestrians going in a million different directions on Zargona Road, which had no marked lanes. This gave me hope he would at least get me in one piece to the city that lay a questionable four-hour drive away.

"The family we will stay with tonight is wealthy by Afghan standards, though you may find the accommodations not as acceptable as you would like, perhaps not exactly like a Holiday Inn," he told me with a grin.

"So you covered the American invasion of our country in 2001?" he asked.

"Yeah. Went back and forth between here and Pakistan for nearly ten months."

"And your interpreter back then?"

I hesitated, though only for a moment. "He was killed one morning coming to pick me up. Ambushed near his home by a group of men who knew what he did and who he did it for."

Aarif showed off his crooked teeth with a wide smile. "Let's hope I am a little luckier than him."

On our journey, we passed through three Afghan National Army checkpoints, the soldiers in green camouflage uniforms and black boots moving nervously as Aarif and I approached confidently in his beat-up Toyota Corolla. While some sections of the highway were nothing more than a bumpy gravel road, others were newly laid black asphalt that weaved between steep red rock hillsides that reminded me of nothing back home. I took in the scenery, slept in short spurts and bombarded Aarif with questions about how his country's security, economy and cultural conditions had changed in the past few years, nodding each time one of his answers surprised me with its depth.

By the time we arrived, light rain fell in Bamyan, though the city still hummed with life. We joined a slow parade of vehicles along muddy streets, passing kids pushing wheelbarrows full of grapes, sandaled pedestrians stepping through puddles while balancing monstrous bags atop their shoulders, even a man slapping a donkey on which rode a woman wearing a full bright purple burka.

Aarif pointed at a hillside to the north. "This city is famous, not just because it's at the center of the ancient Silk Road trade route between China and Europe, but also because of what's up there, the two huge statues of Buddha that the Taliban blew up back in 2001. If we get time, we can drive there. On the hill below is Bashir Navid's home. I am friends with his son Pamir from Kabul University. They are good and influential people."

The home looked non-descript except for a bright blue door,

which opened the moment we pulled up. Bashir Navid and Pamir, each wearing a traditional perahan tunban that flowed down to their knees, greeted us with bows followed by warm handshakes and invited us inside, where our host's wife and two daughters had laid out a feast of rice dishes, meatballs, soups and flatbread.

The seven of us sat cross-legged on pillows, and I ate far more than I ever dreamed possible.

Bashir Navid, fluent in English, spoke about his business trips to New Jersey, where he sold nuts to an American health food company. The discussion shifted to politics and the tenuous rule of Hamid Karzai and even Donald Rumsfeld's announcement earlier that year that major combat was over.

"So, Mr. Baker," he said. "You are writing a story about how our country's women are prospering, or maybe not, since the Taliban were expelled from government? Well, you can see in this household, they do very well, judging by all the food they consume."

His daughters gave each other an amused look and smiled politely. They wore head scarfs and seemed at ease in the company of two male guests, a situation not common in this country.

Later, while the women carried off the empty plates and bowls, the men sat and talked for another hour until our hosts finally rose and said goodnight. As we readied for bed, I glanced across the hallway into Aarif's room, my guide taking a small handgun from his overnight bag and checking to see if the safety was on. The sight of a weapon seemed like overkill in a place where polite conversations could stretch late into the night. I turned away.

* * *

In the morning, we rose to a busy house and another communal meal before setting off for what passed for a women's shelter. Aarif struggled to find the place, despite detailed directions given to him by my contact in the human rights organization, a woman whose name I knew only as Donyaa. The shelter was tucked in an unmarked house on a street lined by high mud walls. When Aarif found what he believed was the right door, he knocked tentatively, and a woman opened it, studied us and said to me, "Mr. Baker?"

For most of the day, I spoke, through Aarif's translations, to a series of women from mostly poor, uneducated families who told stories of forced engagements at age 14, marriages at 16 to older men, beatings from family members for disobedience, long days of work instead of education, despair instead of hope, and continued isolation in the post-Taliban era, in part in the form of burkas worn when they ventured out in public, which was in itself rare.

Their stories were, of course, heartbreaking and no doubt all too common, the exception being that rather than living in continued misery, these women were fortunate enough to have found help from an outside agency.

The last woman I would interview, Jamila, was the youngest of all, and unlike the others, she spoke English. Donyaa escorted the 17-year-old into the room, and if she had been dressed in jeans and a hoodie instead of the loose pants and long-sleeved tunic and dark green scarf she wore around her head, she would have reminded me of a typical American teen. Jamila greeted me with a smile and a nod and a simple "Hello." Her eyes fell on Aarif, and she looked at Donyaa and back at Aarif with uncertainty. She nodded politely to him while saying his name.

Donyaa apologized to me and led the girl from the room. I turned to Aarif.

"Yes, I know her," he said. "She used to live in this very town like I did years ago. She was friends with Pamir's younger sister until she ran off. I didn't know she was one of the women you would interview today. No one has seen her in months."

Donyaa returned alone, sat down and addressed me. "That was unfortunate. We have tried to protect the identity of these women from the outside world. Jamila is from here in Bamyan, and that is why she has been staying at a shelter up north. So no one would recognize her. We brought her down last night, thinking it was important for her to tell her story."

She turned to Aarif. "I appeal to you for your confidence in this matter."

"Of course," he said.

"If Jamila's English is good, why don't I interview her without Aarif in the room?" I suggested. "Maybe that will make Jamila more comfortable."

Donyaa shook her head. "I think it's better she returns to the north while we still have some daylight."

I should have agreed. I did have enough good interviews and could do without one more. Yet I found myself gently pushing for time with Jamila, for reasons I didn't understand.

Donyaa sighed. "Jamila is a very spirited girl. I will see what she says."

Jamila agreed to return. "She claims that this is her path," Donyaa told me, her words slightly dismissive.

Jamila soon sat across from me with her hands folded together on her lap. She glanced nervously around the room, bit her bottom lip, rested her eyes on Donyaa and in clear English said, "I am ready."

I began with simple warm-up questions, mostly about her country in general, and when she answered, her eyes remained on the comforting face of Donyaa. It didn't take long before she at least began glancing at me, her pale face gaining a little more color each time she did. Slowly her answers grew big, ambitious even.

"Our country is filled with more natural beauty than people can imagine, but war is a cancer that devastates everything in its path," she told me.

Soon I began questioning her about herself, and with this shift, she finally made sustained eye contact and in doing so began describing hardships, including an arranged marriage to a 43-year-old, an imposition she tried to resist, triggering savage beatings from her father, mother and two older brothers.

She spoke with a strong voice that was betrayed, only slightly, by the way she nervously clenched her fists so hard that the skin beneath her fingernails turned white.

"Even my younger brother, Kamal," she said. "When he was nine, my parents wanted him to whip me, to share in the condemnation of my disgrace. He would not do it, and he was beaten alongside me."

I asked where she had learned English.

She laughed for the first time since entering the room, and it was a beautiful sound that almost made her jump. Her eyes darted playfully between Donyaa and me.

"That was the one teaching I received from my near marriage. The man I was to marry. He was politician. Diplomat too. His fortunes, they improved much when the Americans invaded. He equated English with a prosperous future and spent to have me tutored each day in what he called the language of the world. On his courtship visits, he would speak only in English. So this new language I learned."

"And that helped lead you to Donyaa and her group?" I asked.

Jamila and Donyaa exchanged a light-hearted glance.

"It was God who led me to my salvation," Jamila finally said. "A divine voice from within me one day instructed me to go to the bazaar immediately. I was terrified. Confused. But I did what I was asked. And as I wandered between stalls, I overheard two aid workers talking in English about a group that helps women flee from abuse. From my invisibility beneath a full burka, and much to their surprise, I spoke up, knowing exactly what to say: 'Where is this group you talk about?' And here I am."

Jamila flashed a shy grin and added, "How would you say it in America? 'There's no damn way I'm ever going back.'"

Maybe it was the heat, a lack of sleep or an insane desire to applaud any woman who had displayed a single shred of defiance in this country, but I found myself stifling the strangest, and most inappropriate, longing. One that whispered for me to get up and hug the young woman like she was an old friend I hadn't seen in years.

* * *

After packing for the trip back to Kabul, I walked out the next morning to an empty kitchen. My shouts of hello went unanswered, and a quick search showed the house was empty. Later I would look back at that moment and its latent sense of foreboding and wonder why I didn't treat the home's silence as a signal to run. Instead, I checked out a few empty rooms and tried to recall when Muslims pray. It was a Friday, and the schedule for this day was different, and I used that fact to convince myself the home's silence carried nothing ominous. I phoned Aarif, who was to meet me here in a half-hour, and he didn't answer.

I ambled the halls and soon stood in an empty courtyard breathing in the scent from an unfamiliar tree. The sound of approaching vehicles announced itself from the street. Even before they skidded to a stop, I had begun looking for a place to hide.

The men carrying rifles searched the house until they found me crouched in the wardrobe closet in Bashir Navid's room, my phone pressed tightly to my mouth while I left another frantic message for Aarif. They all wore turbans or other head coverings, and I feared they were Taliban until I noticed only one with the customary beard.

"Come," grunted the bearded man.

I climbed out and stood but didn't move forward, and two men pointed their rifles toward the floor and pulled me along by my arms. Before leaving the house, they tied my hands behind my back. Minutes later, a blindfold enveloped me in darkness.

Fear distorted my sense of time as we bounced along, mostly uphill, for a half-hour or so. I comforted myself with the thought that dozens of kidnapped Americans, a few of them journalists, have been returned unharmed after a ransom was paid; that if these men wanted to kill me, they would have done so the moment they found me.

When the vehicle jerked to a stop, my story was rehearsed: my employer would pay handsomely for my release but only if I remained unharmed.

They pulled me from the vehicle and led me, still tied and blindfolded, along uneven ground before pushing down on the top of my shoulders and head, a command to sit.

In the distance, voices argued. One sounded like Aarif, a thought that echoed with the hollowness of wishful thinking. Somewhere closer, a woman screamed and sobbed until what could have been a slap brought silence.

My blindfold was removed, and my eyes adjusted to the sun's glare, revealing what looked like a quarry but more likely was a rocky plateau outside Bamyan. The mountains that surrounded us were a stunning bright red, and somewhere in those distant cliffs were, probably, the ruins of the Red City, an old fortress I had driven past two days earlier.

My attention quickly shifted to a man who stood before me in a chest-high hole, using a short shovel to remove chunks of dirt from the rocky ground.

"No," I groaned, sure my eyes took in my final resting place.

A woman's screams rose again from behind me, this time closer. I tried to turn to see. A man beside me pounded the top of my head with the heel of his hand until I again faced forward. In English and Arabic, I began reciting my story about my employer paying a huge ransom for my safe return. No one seemed to react, making me wonder if they understood. A few minutes later, the reason for my presence here became clearer when two men led, and then dragged, a woman into my field of vision so that she stood beside the hole.

I knew who it was before I saw her. As they dragged her from somewhere behind me, her fingers reached out and brushed my back, flooding my mind at once with images of Jamila.

Seconds later, our eyes met.

She no longer wore the same colorful, embroidered dress and trouser combination as the day before. Instead, she was in pajamas like she had been wrenched from bed. A red rope bound her hands in front of her. Her bottom lip was red with blood, either from being struck or biting it herself.

Instead of angrily bombarding me with the guilt I deserved, she pleaded to me softly in English, "Please, help me."

Her captors formed a circle around her. Yet it was me she watched as if to say she would control the one thing she could: she would make sure the last face she saw would be the lone one filled with compassion for her.

An older man began speaking a language I didn't understand. He pointed at Jamila and yelled, possibly delivering the most vigorous denunciation possible. At one point, he shook his finger in my direction. Two men stepped forward and began wrapping Jamila in white cloth from head to toe. She fought, hopelessly, and more men joined in, one of them using a long rope to bind her in place beneath the cloth. I thanked God I could no longer see her face or understand her desperate pleas.

The men lifted Jamila into the hole. Half of them held her down, while the other half filled the space around her with dirt and rock. When they finished, all that remained was the outline of her shoulders and head beneath the cloth.

At the feet of those who surrounded her sat piles of stones. Stories of public stonings under the Taliban were well known. The rocks used could not be so large as to kill the victim quickly or so small as to make the execution go on for more than one hour. The perfect size was that of a small apple.

The man who did most of the talking cast the first stone. I would learn later he was Jamila's father. The rock struck with a hollow thud on a spot that was probably close to her collarbone. Jamila began shrieking.

Next came Jamila's mother, her stone skipping off the ground before striking her daughter. Then the two older boys, the first one catching Jamila below the top of the head with such force it silenced her, for a second, until her wails echoed into the hills.

The last family member, I later discovered, was Jamila's younger brother, the one who would not whip her when asked. Did he now hold a grudge against her for running away from the family, for leaving him alone? He threw with a strength that belied his age.

Soon everyone, everyone except the men on my sides and me, held a stone and they let fly in rapid succession, filling the air with a sickening combination of sounds: Jamila's high-pitched bawling and the thump of stones striking her, each noise struggling for sick dominance.

I tried to look away, and several hands forced my head back. When I could stand it no more, I closed my eyes, which only intensified the sound. I asked God to take her life quickly, and my prayer went unanswered. It took dozens and dozens of throws to savagely silence Jamila, to tilt her head unnaturally to one side.

A hand suddenly covered my mouth, and another sound disappeared from the air. I had been screaming.

In the minutes that followed, another 40 or 50 rocks struck Jamila's body, ensuring the job was done.

The white cloth had turned red. A woman reached between a

gap in it, fumbling around Jamila's neck for a pulse. The woman nodded, and, slowly, people began to drift away, shuffling along like peasants weary after a long day of physical labor.

The bearded man signaled for me to stand. I couldn't. They lifted me to my feet and dragged me to the back of a truck, where I was blindfolded. They tossed me in, and we drove. Rough hands later dragged me off the truck and onto the ground. Someone kicked me in the nuts. Would the barrel of a gun rest against my head before they pulled the trigger?

Instead, all that struck me was the sound of vehicles starting and pulling away. The ensuing silence echoed with a cruel shame, like everything decent had been stripped away.

Footsteps crunched on gravel. Hands tugged at my blindfold. A soft voice, Aarif's, said, "They are gone, Mr. Baker. We are safe."

He untied my hands and helped me stand. I forgot to breathe, and in the time it took to suck in a large gulp of air and force it back out, my hands wrapped around Aarif's throat, and we tumbled to the ground. He was smaller than me and couldn't shake free, meaning if I didn't stop, I would kill him.

I released him and rolled over and closed my eyes, and in a pattern that would surely repeat itself every day for the rest of my life, I relived in my head the brutal story I wanted the world to hear but could never share with a single person.

When Aarif found the strength to speak, he groaned. Instead of making excuses, he said something surprising: "I will never forget the words she kept repeating until she could no longer speak."

"What? That you're the one who got her killed? Because you couldn't shut your mouth?"

He winced. "No. How do you translate it to English? Something like, 'Family is a blight on our gracious souls.'"

Mike Chapter 19

Missing: Day Ten

The area where we stopped in the early morning darkness smelled like shit, probably some far-flung farming community. My captors helped me from the van and cut free my legs but not my arms. The two men pushed me toward the shape of a dark building, perhaps a house, and when I tried to kick one of them mule-like in the nuts, and missed, the jolt of the stun gun knocked me to the ground.

"Stop hurting him," Ashlee yelled before a light in what looked like a farmhouse popped to life, and they yanked me to my feet and herded us inside.

In the basement, our accommodations awaited beneath the glow of an LED lantern. Two mattresses on opposing walls, a toilet, a water tap positioned over a drain in the floor. Two thick chains, dozens of feet long, each attached to a metal peg cemented into opposing walls.

Ashlee was chained up first, the restraints wrapping around her tiny waist and neck like a cobra, before being locked in place by two heavy padlocks. She was shoved onto what would become her mattress and told she could sleep for a few hours. I received similar treatment.

"Night, night," Douglas said in a mocking tone before turning off the lantern and climbing the stairs.

So this was how we would spend our time while Ashlee attempted to make three men rich? Like caged animals whose final freedom would come only when our value faded to nothing.

Of course, I was extraneous to their plans. Once I, brick in hand, had extricated Ashlee from her New Age friends and inadvertently delivered her straight into Douglas's greedy arms, I was of little use. Unless I was meant to serve as spirit-raising company for Ashlee or as someone to torture if she chose not to cooperate. Or more darkly, as the body of an on-the-run killer that would be found next to Ashlee's in a supposed murder-suicide after these men had seized every penny possible, assuming Ashlee could do anything for them.

I knew little about luck, other than good fortune or bad fortune seemed to attach itself to certain people. When I considered Ashlee, despite her gambling success, all I could see was the worst of luck: losing both parents, being exploited by nearly everyone she knew, all while battling a severe mental illness. So, what about the way she could "sense" the future? All I saw was a brilliant yet naïve girl who could take the facts and extrapolate the likely outcome. Sometimes. And perhaps someone with such great empathy that she could look at a man and see he hurt and understand why, a skill you could argue was no gift at all but more like a curse.

As for her ability to predict which number a roulette ball would come to rest on or which slot machine would pay off, this was inexplicable luck that always came and went, usually quickly, and when it did, so would everyone's use for her.

"Are you hurting, Granddad?" Ashlee asked from the darkness.

"I'm okay."

Did I hear her chuckle to herself?

"So you do believe you're my grandfather?"

The question surprised me. "Yes."

I struggled to my knees.

"What are you doing?" she asked.

"Seeing how far the chain reaches."

On all fours I crawled, discovering enough chain to reach the toilet, the tap, though not my companion's mattress, limitations, I guess, that were the same for her. A shuffling sound came from her corner of the room. When her cold hand contacted my face, I assumed she sought comfort. But her graceful fingers only grazed my skin without clinging, suggesting otherwise.

From upstairs came heavy footsteps and furniture being moved and voices thick with the excitement of a bold plan taking shape. I recalled the question I had wanted to ask in the van about how she wound up imprisoned next to me when she had seemed to sense what was about to happen on the quiet street outside my hotel. How she had time to turn and run but chose not to.

When the only answer that made sense finally came to me, I considered it with disbelief before reaching for her, my appreciative hand outstretched into the darkness. She had already disappeared like she was never there.

* * *

When the first light of dawn swept into our dungeon, I moved to the light source, our room's lone window, a two-foot by two-foot pane that opened inward because on the outside, attached to the house, was a set of bars. The window sat about five feet from the basement's sunken floor, though on the outside, it was about one foot above the ground. Flat green fields stretched off in the distance. The cargo van rested on nearby gravel.

Maybe the sight of the van put a wishful idea in my mind because I swore I could hear the distant sound of tires on gravel.

I turned the window latch and tugged on the window, and nearly jumped in surprise when it swung back. I placed my face against the bars, the cold air reviving me, and began screaming the word "help" over and over.

Several minutes later, Douglas spoke my name from behind me. I turned to see him watching me passively while the two men, whose names I would learn were Nick and Thomas, unchained Ashlee after first using a key attached to a yellow rubber duck keychain to undo her padlocks.

"There's no one within miles, so knock yourself out," Douglas said. "And I appreciate your enthusiasm. I had planned to start Ashlee's workday at 8, but since we're all up now…"

* * *

In the morning light, I scoured the room for any item to pick the padlocks, finding only a two-inch long screw I managed to extract from a board behind the toilet. It didn't fit into the locks in any way, though I tucked it beneath my mattress just in case. I checked the window repeatedly for signs of anyone, searched my chain for a weak link, tried to use my body as leverage, or at least dead weight, to pull the anchoring bolt from the cement wall, and finally attempted to bend and slip my body loose from the chains, an exercise that only rubbed my skin raw.

I opened the window and shook the bars, which rattled like they were loose. I used the palm of my right hand to jab away at the top-right corner, where the bars seemed to give the most, and heard the squeak of a screw. Encouraged, I pounded away until my hand was bruised and bloody and, soon, swollen with what felt like a million broken bones. Then I pounded on each corner, and my grunts soon turned to laughter, hysterical laughter, because the bars twisted and then toppled forward and fell flat on the ground, bits of rotten wood still attached to its screws. I stared out at my escape route and laughed once more because my chains, of course, prevented me from taking it.

A few hours later, the man called Nick, a good-looking guy in his early 20s, came down the stairs carrying a sandwich wrapped in plastic, a water bottle and an apple. He nodded for me to move back and tossed them on my mattress.

He looked at my bloody hand and then around the room. He smirked when he saw the window was now free of bars.

"You okay with committing double murder for a few dollars?" I asked as he moved toward the stairs.

I had hoped my words would catch him off guard. Maybe plant a little doubt in his head.

He turned back and said, almost with blind enthusiasm, "From what I've seen, it's gonna be a lot more than a few dollars."

A half-hour later, he stood outside the window examining the area where the bars had been attached. Behind him sat a heavier set of bars that he had taken from somewhere else on the property. He positioned the new bars over the window and adjusted them a half-dozen times before giving up and walking away.

He returned to the basement with Douglas, who held the stun gun and ordered me back. I sat near the toilet and watched as Nick held the bars over the window and nodded to himself before going to work with a drill and electric screwdriver. Apparently, exhaustion was getting the better of me because mixed in with the drill's whir was a noise that sounded like a girl screaming, though it stopped when the drill stopped.

The newly installed bars covered an area three times larger than the window and required five of the eight screws to be drilled into the foundation's cement wall, with only the top three going into the soft wood of the house. Both men seemed to like this.

"Excuse me for worrying, Mr. Baker," Douglas said before he left, "but I fear you may possess some lock-picking skills I'm not aware of."

I didn't explain that all I possessed was the rawest of desperation.

* * *

A little later, Ashlee was given a lunch break on her mattress, chains and all. If a face can look disheveled, hers did. Is there a bruise forming under her left eye? On her wrists? She ignored my questions, as well as the food placed beside her. She stood facing me in the same grey hoodie and jeans as when we left the Tropicana. Maybe the dwarfing effect of the chains was to blame, but she seemed smaller and less weighty than in the warehouse, though she continued to strike an irrational fear in me that every abhorrent thought ever crossing my mind would soon be revealed. That she was able to see all my thoughts because she controlled what went on in my head.

I didn't know exactly what to say, so I went with the obvious. "I'm sorry," I told her. "I thought I was taking you to safety."

She stood watching me with amused incredulity, like our conversation in the warehouse had never ended, only taken a dizzying break in which my world was turned upside down and shaken.

"Please don't say you came to Las Vegas to help your crazy-pants granddaughter. Because we know what that would be. The. Biggest. Lie. Ever."

My body shifted slightly. "Okay. I also had wanted to talk to you about, you know, your mother's death, because somehow suspicion had fallen on me. But I did want to get you away from those people."

She tilted her head slightly like she had caught me in a lie.

I began moving the conversation in a different direction. "We need to, we need to work together to get out of here."

The girl gave me a smile that was easy to detest. "Like family? Work close together like family, is that it, Granddad?"

"Sure," I said.

"Because it's never too late, right, Granddad? And you do love being part of the fam, don't you?"

"Okay, listen. I really didn't know I had a granddaughter or a son until a couple of weeks ago. And I am sorry for that. But we need to get past that."

I waited for her to turn away in anger like a petulant child. Some petty part of me wanted her to be consumed by rage and all the unpredictability of a mental illness. Instead, she kept her eyes calmly focused on me.

"Are you sad, Granddad, that you never got to speak to your son? Has that thought haunted you in the days since you learned about him?"

Not the type of question anyone wants to hear.

"Why don't you sit down and have something to eat," I said.

"Why don't you stop telling so many fibs."

Ashlee didn't sit down, or more accurately, stand down in any way, but she did look away from me and toward the upstairs where she had spent her morning. Finally, mercifully, she said, "For all the good it will do, here's what you want," and she heaved herself into a narrative of Douglas's online betting strategy that employed multiple computers and dozens of accounts playing games of chance, like poker, on a handful of legal websites in Nevada, and even more games like slot machines and roulette on illegal ones overseas.

Then she talked about his accomplices. Thomas, she said, was the computer expert who made his living gambling and owned this house and the surrounding land.

"Detective Douglas arrested him years ago in Florida for a slot machine scam that didn't work and says he 'kept him in his sights' since then," she said. "He's also the one who almost grabbed me off a bench in Miami after I disappeared. The one who sounded very convincing, at first, when he claimed to be a cop. So, Thomas is the smart one. The other guy, Nick, he is the muscle. A crook who's not a rat. A so-called stand-up guy. The detective brought him with him from Miami. He was the one wearing the Seattle Seahawks shirt who walked into my building, so you would look guilty of hurting Mom."

The number of details she had consumed and the ease with which she effortlessly recounted them was impressive. How long had it taken Douglas to put this all together?

Ashlee leaned closer. "I heard them talking. We're near

Logandale, Nevada, in case you were curious."

She described the house's layout and its isolation, how the men treated her, how much she was winning. For nearly 10 minutes, Ashlee spoke about the matters related to our dilemma, and some small part of me tingled with optimism that she fully understood the danger we faced and that she, and only she, could extricate us. Then I pointed again at the food on her bed, and our conversation began its slow descent into craziness.

Her eyes regarded the sandwich like a bad joke. "Come on, Granddad. We talked about this before. The physical body you see before you does not exist, so there's no need for it to eat."

"How about I turn around so you can use the bathroom," I said.

She smirked before saying, "Someone's not listening."

She did sit, though, her legs crossed and her arms and hands resting on her thighs with her open palms facing the sky like they awaited a great gift. Maybe they did because her eyes closed and her face took on a serene expression. I called her several times, and she didn't answer.

Five minutes later, her eyes opened.

"Ask it," she said.

"Ask what?"

"The question you're dying to ask."

"I don't know what you're talking about."

She grinned. "Yes, you do. I just drifted into the future, and you do ask the question, after much going in circles, so come on and ask it straight away."

I spat out a bitter laugh. "I probably have a million questions, like what the fuck was with those photo collages in your bedroom, but I'm not sure I want to hear your answers."

"You liked the pictures? Those were just places I'm pulled to, places I want to visit or perhaps already have."

"So you've traveled a lot with your mother and father?"

"No. We never left the country."

"Not sure what to say to that."

"Don't change the subject," she said. "Just ask the question."

I urged myself to direct her back to the task at hand and away from this bullshit, yet I found myself posing a question like a wooden dummy on the lap of the most obnoxious ventriloquist ever born. "Okay, if you can peek into the future, do we both make it out of here alive?"

Her smile grew wide. "See. That wasn't so hard."

She raised her arms into the air as if stretching. "Remember, I'm not here physically," she said, "so this body you see before you, is in no real danger from the Great Evil, though my true being could be because I have chosen to stay at your side and help you."

She paused like she would say nothing more. After all, our conversation veered close to revealing a gaping hole in the logic of her so-called beliefs.

"You, on our current path, do not make it out of here, though I'm working to change that," she said finally.

I lifted my chains, shook them, and tried to point out the absurdity in her answer. "If you really do have these powers you claim, you could have maybe steered us from this place."

At this, she laughed. "You've been headed straight to this basement for years. There was no stopping you."

I wanted to object, though she may have been right about this one thing. "He will kill us if we can't find a way to get out of here," I told her. "So, when you're upstairs, you need to look for a way to escape. An open door. A cell phone in reach you can grab to call 911. A weapon like a knife or scissors you can smuggle down to me. The stupid yellow rubber duck keychain with the keys to these padlocks."

She smirked. "A key? C'mon, Granddad. If only it were that simple."

"You have a better idea?"

"There are better ways to defeat the Great Evil."

"Such as?"

Ashlee folded her hands together and looked skyward, big delusional, happy thoughts no doubt swirling through her head like a teenage girl about to announce to her best friend forever, *I met this cute guy.*

"By having faith," she said.

I could no longer stand to hear her speak, yet she continued, almost as if in spite.

"All you need to know is that death is not the end," she said. "Our consciousness exists outside of our brain function and continues on after we die. We don't fade to black. Instead, we are placed inside newly born bodies with our existing knowledge and level of consciousness but with almost no knowledge of our previous lives, a fresh start, though not really, because the past, it speaks to us if we choose to listen. And in our new bodies, we continue our work toward our purpose on earth: improving humanity and our planet."

I didn't try to hide my disbelief. She responded to my doubt with what resembled a soliloquy, one filled with short phrases like "pure energy" and "the true reality" and "out of body experiences" and even a description about the intricacies of moving through space and time.

To grasp the depths of her illness brought me sadness, followed by more desperation, because any chance of escaping depended on her, the one our captives sometimes unlocked. I lay on my back and stared at the unfinished ceiling. "You need to keep your strength, so can you eat your lunch, please?" I asked one final time.

"If you show some faith, Granddad, and imagine you see your conjured-up Ashlee eating her lunch, the lunch which I hate to say you've conjured up too, well, that is exactly what you will see."

I begged myself not to look in her direction and give her any insane satisfaction, but I couldn't help myself. I turned to her and watched as she picked up the sandwich and took a bite and another and another until only crumbs remained.

A sudden wind whistled through the window I had left ajar, pumping more cool, damp air into our cramped space. I closed my eyes and lay back again, despair washing over me with the force of the rainstorm outside. "I want to live." I heard myself plead those almost-foreign words to anyone who would listen.

From the other side of the room came Ashlee's voice, chilling in the way it made me doubt my own beliefs. "I told you, Granddad, stop telling so many damn fibs."

* * *

Ashlee was escorted upstairs shortly after finishing her lunch, and when she hadn't returned by the time the sun slipped low, I feared her luck had run out. But Nick escorted her down the stairs a short time later, resecuring her chains a little more gently than the time before. From a plastic bag, he pulled more sandwiches and fruit and threw them onto our mattresses and said, "Enjoy."

As he climbed the stairs, I said, "The girl gets her gift from me, and I see all of this ending badly for you."

His footsteps didn't slow, and he was gone.

Ashlee took a seat on the mattress and started going into her trance-like pose. I interrupted by asking, "What did you see up there? A way out? Something useful you could grab?"

She ignored this question and others for the next 20 minutes. If the chains were longer, I might have gone over and shaken her. Finally, her eyes opened, and she announced, with a hint of triumph, "Granddad, I have good news for you."

Her words, of course, still resonated with a trace of madness, though it didn't matter. She was all I had. I leaned toward her and whispered, "Was it a weapon left unattended? Or maybe a phone?"

In the dying light, her grin pushed forward. "No. Something better. I have determined your path away from here."

My body slumped.

"It's all set. The day after tomorrow. Maybe the day after that. I found the answer in the beautiful cleansing rain falling outside."

"Uh-huh," I said, not even trying to hide my disappointment. When she started speaking, any last bit of hope slipped away. She rambled on without me stopping her.

"You can't hide your disbelief, and that's okay," she said. "You've been tricked by evolution, Granddad, like almost everyone else. You're hardwired only to see what you need to see to survive. And that means you don't see what you need to see to really live."

She told me the craziest theory on the nature of reality. How everything we saw and touched and smelled and heard and tasted was not real but only icons in some virtual world. She talked about how she had transcended on the day before she met me at the warehouse. How she had stepped through the door, or perhaps behind the curtain, and into the actual reality that remains hidden from almost everyone.

Again, I couldn't resist: "So what did you see?"

She smiled a less crazy smile than usual. "Light. Lots of light. I saw the glorious light of our shared consciousness, which is all around us, even if few can see it. And in that light was the truth: that everything else we see is an illusion we create out of fear."

"Not sure how that helps us right now."

She laughed. "This consciousness is full of infinite wisdom. It has helped show me what will happen next. I won't explain it because it won't be easy, and I don't want to scare you. It will be spectacular, though. A preacher might claim it's the hand of God magically rescuing you, but that would be a lie, given that God always leaves us to get out of our own messes. A New Ager might say it's psychokinesis, the ability of the mind to affect matter, the product of inner reality being used to change the outer world, but that's not exactly right either."

When I said nothing, she continued. "So what will happen? You'll see, and then you'll know."

She paused. "Are you listening, Granddad, because there's more?"

"Yes, I'm listening," I said, sure she would spot the lie.

"You have more important work left to do in your life, in this life. I can't see what it is, but it's important, so it's not time for you to go to the next one. Not yet. So when it's time to escape, you'll know it, and you'll need to fight with everything you have. You can do that. But you'll need to believe with everything you have too. And that's way harder."

* * *

Outside the house, a vehicle's engine sounded. Could be the one that brought us here. Could be another. I went to the window and screamed "help" repeatedly, just in case.

Douglas, lantern in his hand, came to fetch Ashlee for her "night shift." He looked at me and seemed to roll his eyes. He unchained the girl and sent her upstairs, where I could hear Thomas's voice calling down, "Here she comes, the world's finest gambler."

At least she seemed to be winning, which would buy us a little more time, though I questioned how much this mattered if she refused to consider any means of escape other than the hand of God or telekinesis, or whatever she had mentioned.

Douglas turned to me. "She loses a lot, but she wins a lot too," he said. "And the wins eclipse the losses by enough of a margin. Three percent. On most games of chance, that's how little you need to improve your odds by to go from losing to winning. And the girl is much better than that."

He paused. "Did you know most of these gambling websites

have built-in algorithms to detect anything unnatural, like someone trying to cheat or manipulate the system? That's what makes the girl so perfect. What she does is as natural as the beginning and the end of time. It's not perfect like a computer program. Instead, it is built with the flaws of humanity."

I only half-listened. I focused instead on where he stood and how I needed him to take two more steps forward. Just two more to bring him into my chain's reach. But like me, he had obviously drawn an imaginary line. And he was careful not to cross it.

"I am sorry, Mr. Baker, your fine life as a globe-trotting journalist will end in a shithole like this. And the girl, even more of a shame. I wish I had the ability and the time to study her mind, to unravel all the secrets of her soul that even she doesn't understand. Time is too finite, as always. A precious gift doomed to run out."

At least this sounded honest. Most of it.

"No, you're not sorry."

"Well, okay, you got me. Niceties and all. But I will make sure no one suffers. As long as the cooperation continues."

"If I get loose, there's one promise I can make. You will suffer."

His deep laugh resonated through the darkness. "Well, I better make sure you never get loose."

Ashlee Chapter 16

Missing: Day Ten

I follow Nick and his lantern down the stairs and into the damp darkness like a loyal pet at its master's heels. At least, this is what he must believe. He even thinks he is chaining me up like a dog or maybe a trained monkey. An animal that's not dangerous but prone to wandering off. An animal he's free to abuse. My true being doesn't make him aware of how dangerously wrong he is.

Somehow my grandfather has fallen asleep in my supposed absence, and he now gives off a pained snoring sound.

Granddad, I say through my thoughts once Nick has left us to the blackness.

My not-so-loving elder snorts back to life and mumbles, *Yes. I want to tell you something.*

Okay.

There is a long silence, and he must wonder if I have drifted away into an exhausted sleep as he had. He has no idea how much I'm struggling with what to say and whether to say it. Not just about what's happening upstairs. But about everything.

I will start slow, seeing where my words lead me. I say, *The universe is part of us, not the other way around, meaning we have both God and Satan in our hearts, in each and every cell. Most people are ruled by God's grace and some by Satan and others by neither. Satan, the Great Evil, is strong in Detective Douglas. But Detective Douglas is not the Great Evil like I once suspected. He's just a weak man who does evil things.*

Tell me what happened? Granddad says.

I don't answer. My newfound thoughts about the bad detective swirl around me. Mostly how I was wrong to think that I would be meeting the source of all the universe's evil. What I encountered was only a pitiful person full of greed and the lowest and simplest desires known to man. It makes me wonder what else I have gotten wrong. What other ideas I have allowed to become too grand.

What happened? Granddad repeats.

These next few moments are critical. All I need to do is shut my mouth and let time pass. Simple. Only it's not. Words have a way of clawing into the daylight, where they fall to the ground and explode like bombs.

Can you sleep? my grandfather asks. *You must be exhausted.*

And with this shift in the conversation, the dangerous moment passes. Relief churns through the air beside a playful voice that asks, *Do we need to discuss this again, Granddad?*

He forces a shallow laugh full of defeat. I've already told him about finding the path to our salvation, one that does not require locating a weapon or an unguarded cell phone or an unlocked door. He doesn't believe it. Maybe because he senses doubt in me. Which makes it a good time to change the focus of our conversation to something else.

Do you want to know more, Granddad? I ask. *About how this universe really works.*

He hesitates and says, *Well, you do have a captive audience.*

But do you want to hear? I ask again.

Sure.

He doesn't sound convincing, but that's okay.

In the darkness, I get him to raise the palms of his hands to the heavens and feel the universe's love flowing into his body. I get him to place his hands over his heart and feel his outward flow of love to the universe, his glorious contribution to humanity. We talk about life's biggest mystery, where consciousness comes from. I even give him the answer. Our amazing souls mixed with God's love. Each word I drench in hope, maybe enough to make him ache for me to be right. We talk about many things but mostly love. Never the vengeful Old Testament God who enforces morality. Always the loving New

Testament God, the one who each day proves that God is love, like the verse from John. When I need an example about love, I include stories about my father, the son that my grandfather has never thought to ask about.

Reality nips at my words like a stray dog that needs confronting.

There's one final lesson, Granddad, I tell him. *And it's this: Because time doesn't exist, there is no future to worry about and no past to regret. Not really. All that should matter to you right now is this very moment.*

I add, *You need to appreciate this moment alone with your granddaughter like it's all you have or will ever have.*

It's hard to appreciate anything given the danger we are in, he says.

Neither of us is in any danger this very second, are we?

Well, not this very second.

Good, I say with enthusiasm.

My grandfather will surely call me out. He will say my expressions of love and togetherness are bullshit, given I am the girl who fled from everyone and traveled almost clear across the country. He knows how much we are alike. That I, too, am an expert at pushing people away. But he remains silent. Maybe he has dozed off again on his filthy mattress.

Like I am reading him a bedtime story, I press on with more tales about the mysteries of our world. If he's not already asleep, he will be soon. The supposed voice he thinks he hears is growing heavy and hypnotic as it fights to stay awake. The darkness around us fills with the light of bright bulging flowers on poppy plants that my grandfather is winding his way through on a twisty path in a hostile foreign countryside. From somewhere close comes the impossible sound of light snoring from the lips of a young woman kept safe from the darkest of nights by the comforting images in her head.

I gasp, and the snoring stops.

Missing: Days Eleven and Twelve

The pattern repeated itself the next two days. Ashlee spent large chunks of the waking day upstairs helping three men find untold riches. On her breaks, she would be returned to the basement. And instead of enlightening me some more about the ways of the world, she had me tell her stories. About growing up and meeting Kimberly and the violent incident that tore us apart. My time in prison, in the Gulf War, in Seattle, in Afghanistan. She listened carefully, the wheels turning in her head, sometimes nodding like everything made perfect sense. I talked and talked, hoping to draw her into my world, the real world, where our only hope for escape lay.

With a little prodding from me, she continued to eat, though she grew paler and likely weaker, as if the physical Ashlee she claimed I imagined was fading like a hologram powered by a slowly draining battery.

But while the days fell into the same hopeless rhythm of a death march, there were rare moments when the will to fight trickled through me. I would coax her to look for a way out, suggesting she ask to use the upstairs bathroom and then bolt out the open door. Of course, she always told me this wouldn't be necessary. I would be free soon. Hadn't I been watching out the window for the signs?

To this, on what would be our last day here, I finally spoke the words she needed to hear, though they likely came too late. Speaking the truth felt wrong, like breaking some rule she had created.

"You have a mental illness, Ashlee, and it is preventing you from seeing the truth. That I'm powerless to help us, and we will both die very soon if you don't either escape or find a way for me to help you escape."

She ignored me.

"Listen, you are delusional. All these things you say make no sense. They aren't reality. They are lies your brain tells you to help you cope with everything you've lost in your life. To ease the pain of the uncertainty we all face."

The door at the top of the stairs creaked open.

Ashlee leaned forward and said, "That's the real crazy talk, Granddad. The person who believes in nothing and understands nothing, telling me that my answers are all lies. But I forgive you."

In her absence, I thought of nothing but whether I had upset her so much that she wouldn't be able to perform the one task that kept us alive. When she returned for her lunch break, she calmly took a spot on her mattress and waited for our captors to leave. In her fingers dangled a set of two keys.

"What are those?"

"Your car keys. They went and got your rental car from outside your hotel. Parked it out of sight in the barn up the hill." She began to whisper. "I think that's where they would like us to be found. You know, dead in your rental car miles from here."

"I would rather have the keys to the padlocks, but it's a start. Toss them here. I want to try them on the padlocks on our chains."

She did, and they landed in my hands, solid and undeniable. Of course, both keys were identical and didn't come close to fitting, which didn't stop me from playing with them for most of the afternoon, listening to the steady rain, thinking about how my only hope for the future rested with a girl who had so little left in this world that she pretended she had already moved on.

* * *

Douglas brought Ashlee back at dinnertime, chained her up and patted the top of her head in the most condescending manner possible. "We love our lucky girl, but the luck is starting to wear off."

Of all the words Douglas could have spoken, those were the ones that shook me most.

"Well, maybe it's more a case she's getting bored. Maybe she needs a pep talk from her grandfather, you know, to put her back on track. I could stop at any moment as a rich man. But richer is always better, and a longer winning streak gives you two more of an opportunity to become acquainted. And besides, we haven't yet reached our goal. If we do hit it, we plan not to let greed overcome us. We will have a modest celebration and quit while way ahead."

He took a few steps toward the stairs. He swung around like a thought popped into his head. "You know, the night we took you and the girl out of Las Vegas, we made that one stop at the supermarket. I had her select numbers in the Powerball lottery. The odds are 292 million to one, a huge long shot, but I thought, give the girl a shot. If she hits it, we won't need to spend as many days in these questionable accommodations doing the online gambling thing."

He looked at Ashlee and leaned close to me, though not close enough. "The draw was last night. You know how many numbers she hit, in total, on six tickets? Not a single one. Sucking that badly is hard to do for someone like her. Nearly impossible actually. So, I asked her, *What the hell?* And she said, *God was not ready for you to win so much so soon.*

For the first time, his voice couldn't suppress a trace of hostility. He said, "I love that freaking girl, though sometimes I could… Well, you can imagine."

When he was gone, I asked her, "Are you getting tired?" I didn't ask, *Is your lucky streak finally running out?*

"You know the answer about whether bodies that don't truly exist get tired," she said, though with only a fraction of the playful enthusiasm as before.

"The car keys won't do anything to these locks. I've tried."

"Don't worry. Just have them in your pocket when the time comes."

I waited for my anger to rise at her absurdity. Nothing came. I nodded solemnly and said, "Yes, I'll be ready for our big escape early tomorrow."

Did my words echo with bitterness? Maybe not, because in the fading light, Ashlee gave me a sweet smile, the kind that could break a person's heart if they really had one.

"Very early tomorrow. That's right," she said.

The next time Douglas came down the stairs could easily be the last. My time together with Ashlee, however short, drew to a close, and instead of treasuring each moment like she had suggested, I found myself debating where the largest share of the blame should fall.

* * *

Nick emerged behind a flashlight's beam and unlocked Ashlee without speaking. As he ushered her toward the stairs, he shone a burst of light across my body for a moment, in perhaps the way a man without a soul said goodbye.

* * *

In the dark, another outpouring of fight spilled from my body. I angrily prayed to God, shouted out the open window, struck the padlocks on the cement floor, pulled on the chains, twisted inside the chains, screamed at the chains. I sat with my arms around my knees and, in the steady beat of the rainstorm, tried to convince myself I had lived a good life, a sometimes-unselfish life, even if it always seemed like a penciled sketch still awaiting the warm colors of a painter's soft brush.

The question of blame arose yet again, and by that time, I had given Douglas a free ride. He was simply doing what criminals do. The real blame fell on either me or Ashlee. So where should most of my expanding hostility be directed: the delusional girl who wrapped people up in her web of illusions or the stupid man who, by getting close to her, ignored everything he knew to be true?

As these cruel thoughts cycled through my mind, the sound of shouting burst through the room. The source lay upstairs and was all male. And joyous. The jubilant noise continued for what seemed like hours, coming with the depth of a party that seemed to involve more than three people. A champagne bottle popped open, people laughed and talked excitedly over one another and someone, probably Douglas, loudly pontificated.

I pictured Ashlee taking in the festive scene before her. Did she understand one of the cardinal rules of games of chance: with winners came losers?

In time the upstairs grew quiet, and I could almost hear Douglas whispering in my ear some theory about how time is not inexhaustible. A female voice cried out, followed by silence, making me wonder if the sound had been the wind.

Outside the cellar window came the crunch of tires on gravel. Maybe more than one car, maybe close. Laughter rang out too. Outside the window, the dark shapes of two men, probably Thomas and Nick, could be seen sharing a cigarette, or more likely a joint, beneath a sky that had finally stopped shedding water. They exchanged words more frequently than whatever they smoked, though exactly what they said never reached the basement window.

I sat on my mattress and waited, aware only one more chance would present itself: when they removed my chains to take me to wherever I would supposedly blow my brains out. For that moment, I needed to be ready and calmly focused in the hope they made a mistake. My hands made a terrible weapon, but they were all I had unless something better could be found, perhaps something sharp and larger than the keys or single screw in my pocket. Something in my mind clicked together, and I stood at the window, my heart pounding wildly, my forearm parallel to the glass. As gently and quietly as possible, I pushed on the pane with my arm, frustrated when it wouldn't give. Nick and Thomas were gone from the van, though they were likely somewhere outside and within earshot. Time ticked down. Finally, I slammed my forearm into the window, and it gave with a pop.

I waited about a minute to see if Nick or Thomas or even Douglas would investigate the sound, but no one did. I reached out, pulled in a large piece of glass, placed it on the cement floor and tapped it with the heel of my shoe, hearing it further shatter. In the darkness, I groped for one long, sharp piece. Finding one, I placed it on my mattress. The rest I picked up, somewhat carefully, and threw beneath the mattress. I sat, the dull end of the glass shard in my right palm, the sharp end hidden by my wrist, and waited for the pounding of footsteps on the stairs and the glow of a lantern, knowing that with them, everything would come to a quick conclusion, one way or another.

The footsteps never came.

Instead, after what felt like another lifetime had passed, a low rumbling noise made itself known over the anxious internal chatter in my mind. My body began to shake. No surprise, really, because I had every reason to be terrified. Yet something about this was different. I reached back and rested my left hand on the wall and felt a vibration that could have stemmed from my hand, though that didn't seem right either. The shaking intensified enough to erase any doubts that the source was external. Within seconds the ground convulsed under my body hard enough to bounce me off the mattress. The once-distant rumble transformed itself into a deafening roar. From outside came a cut-off scream, and as my brain tried to wrap itself around what was happening, the house heaved like a giant had charged at it with his full weight.

The impact flung me awkwardly forward, and in the dark, my moans of terror were drowned out by a cacophony of destruction: breaking glass, splintering wood, heavy objects tumbling. A wet substance poured on me through the overhead window that I had broken minutes earlier. As I struggled to my knees and finally to my feet, the door at the top of the stairs exploded inward, followed by the rush of a waterfall.

The water, syrupy like earthy molasses, began quickly filling the basement, rising to my waist. I screamed Ashlee's name, heard nothing and called out again.

Near the stairs, the ceiling gave way with a thundering explosion. Seconds later, it opened directly above my head, sending a suffocating wave of water pouring down upon me, knocking me to my knees and immersing me. I struggled back to my feet, the water reaching my neck.

"Ashlee," I screamed into the darkness, into the abyss.

Her name would be the last word out of my mouth. In the time it took me to draw one more breath, the water rose above my head. I clamped my mouth shut and ordered myself not to panic. I tried to swim up, my chains pulling me back down like an anchor, their force as unyielding as the twisting, exhausting current.

As my consciousness withered along with my body's oxygen, my mind filled with a jumble of disjointed thoughts, twisting and tumbling. How, if I managed to resist taking a breath underwater, I would pass out before suffering the agony of drowning. How Ashlee was only 16. How she believed something more awaited us all. And how that probably meant nothing to a non-believer like me.

In a spurt of clarity, I managed a single thought about the girl, about what she was experiencing, assuming she hadn't already been swept to her death. *You're not alone*, my mind whispered to her, a hopeless declaration kept from her by water and muck and splintered wood and countless other barriers. *You're not alone*, my mind repeated, wishing it hadn't waited so long.

I began drifting upward in the current's pull, the chain's weight becoming irrelevant. The roar of rushing water and a disintegrating house fell away, a placid humming taking their place. In some back corner of my brain came a sense of serenity.

A weight crashed clumsily into my head and chest, or perhaps me into it. Something grabbed at my face. Fingers maybe. An arm went around my neck and pulled without moving me. Hands shook at me, tugging furiously, imploring me to follow. My body needed to tell my mind to swim, but instead, it asked a single, useless question: How long had passed since my last breath? With this thought, I inhaled involuntarily, water filling my mouth and windpipe and producing pain as sharp as a full stun-gun jolt.

The pain led to a reflex-like surge of panic, which prompted me to kick my feet, to reach forward with my arms, even if only at the same glacial speed of a cement statue come to life. The hands pulled at my shirt, and I tried to follow, the current helping a little. I inhaled a second even more agonizing underwater breath, and as I did, my face and hands smashed into something that could have been the iron bars over the window. Water poured from the basement out the opening that once held glass, and I closed my fingers around the metal and used the bars to push my body up.

In the blackness, my head broke out of the water with such a dizzying force that I didn't understand to take a breath until my body did so involuntarily for a third time. Then came the gasps interspersed with coughing fits until a hand grabbed my face and a small voice shouted in my ear, "I told you, Granddad."

I reached up, and my hand struck the ceiling, which shook with rage. The noise was at once more deafening. Ashlee placed her lips against my ear and screamed something about the key to my padlocks. Her hands pulled at my chains underwater in the dark. She needed to wait, to not risk dropping the key. The flow of water would soon stop, and we could survive in our narrow gap of air. Before I could tell her this, a terrifying groan closed upon us, and I let go of the bars and wrapped my arms around the girl, letting our weight and that of my chains pull us down.

Even underwater, the noise resonated like the end of the world. The current that had barreled out through the window immediately reversed course, and I hung onto the girl as we were torn across the room until the chains went taut and recoiled slightly. How long could I hold my breath for a second time? How long could I hold on to my granddaughter?

And for once, an answer came. The current slowed, and we kicked our legs and broke through the surface. Yellow light in the ceiling caught my eye, leaving me confused. The girl laughed, and I knew what she knew. It was the moon.

* * *

In the heavenly light from that three-quarter moon in a sky still heavy with clouds, the shape of a small rubber duck materialized in Ashlee's hand. The rush of water through the basement had slowed to a trickle, and she had my padlocks off in seconds. I slipped free from my chains, and we used the iron bars, which were still attached to the basement's cement lower wall, to climb from our watery near-tomb.

I collapsed to the ground, Ashlee beside me. In the distance, sirens sounded. Off to my left lay a house, its sides crumpled in like a cardboard box that had collapsed under its own weight in a rainstorm. It softly creaked and groaned.

Ashlee, her legs and feet bare, looked wide-eyed into the distance, where the departing water still rumbled along on a downhill route.

Ashlee Chapter 17

Missing: Days Eleven and Twelve

We stumble up a hill to the barn. It takes all Granddad's strength to slide open the heavy wooden doors.

Granddad's rental car sits inside. He fumbles in his pockets with swollen fingers until, to both our relief, he pulls out the car keys. He collapses behind the wheel while my being takes up the space beside him. He turns the heat on full and drives forward, and we wind our way up the steep driveway to the road. We can only turn left because the road to the right, which he will later tell me was built over a now-collapsed earth dam, is gone.

A few minutes later, we pass a fire truck. And then another. He nods at an approaching police car. No. I repeat this word to him, and we keep going. I can't explain why we're still not safe. Like so many things, I just know.

My grandfather's clothes, skin, and hair are super caked in earthy muck, which he brushes from his eyes. With this simple motion, I wonder if he will return to his predictable old habit of forcing everything to conform to what he believes. But as we drive, he doesn't even try to put words to what he saw at the farmhouse. Instead, he takes a single deep breath full of relief and wonder, like nothing more needs to be said.

And the strangest of thoughts forces its way into my head. How pleased I am to share with him these last few days, these precious moments swelled heavy by lifetimes of living.

Mike Chapter 21

Missing: Day Thirteen

We entered a small town, and when we passed a sign pointing to the interstate, I followed it. At the highway, I took the onramp heading east, and we began stacking up the miles in silence. I pulled off at a highway rest stop and turned on the interior light and searched the car, finding my Syrian passport and credit card in the glove compartment, where Douglas likely left them as two more damning pieces of evidence against me. In the trunk sat my travel bag, its contents looking like someone had torn them out and chaotically stuffed them back inside. My real passport and credit card and two $100 bills remained tucked away in a sock, probably where Douglas decided to leave them to be found by police.

I removed a T-shirt and a pair of boxers from the bag and told Ashlee to change into them. She gave me her look, and I laughed and said, "Humor me again."

I asked her if the rushing water had ripped her jeans and shoes off, leaving her in just her shirt and underwear. She shook her head and told me Douglas had made her take a bath, and she was getting dressed when the waters from the burst dam struck. She had heard him scream but never saw him when she emerged from the bathroom into the chaos. She grabbed the rubber duck keychain from where Nick had left it on the kitchen counter and fell into the rush of water that tore through the house. "The rush of water," she added, "that swept me into the basement, into the blackness, and straight to you "

While she changed in the passenger seat, I stripped down in the darkness behind the car, not caring if another vehicle pulled off the highway and stumbled upon this strange scene. We had caught up to the storm once again, and rain pounded down, cleansing my naked body. I stared up at the sky, fighting an urge to scream in euphoria. With my fingers and the falling rain, I combed more muck from my hair. I pulled on a clean shirt and boxers and jeans, my last, and forced my wet feet into a pair of sneakers.

Back in the car, Ashlee had changed and tucked her knees beneath my shirt, stretching it out.

"I thought imaginary bodies never got cold?"

"You mean that imaginary body that only you see?" she asked. "It's probably just curious how much it could stretch your shirt."

* * *

We reached the desert town of Mesquite before daybreak and drove the empty streets past small casinos and fast-food outlets and RV parks while I pondered our next move. Ashlee had fallen asleep, or so it looked, a sign we needed rest.

I still didn't want to use a credit card containing my name, real or fake, so I pulled into a gas station/truck stop and dug out one of the hundred-dollar bills to gas up and buy an assortment of packaged breakfasts, snacks, bottled water and a pint of vodka. And a pair of cheap flip-flops, size unknown, a pair of navy-blue athletic shorts, size small, and a hairbrush.

I located the most run-down motel in town and decided to try to negotiate a cash deal to stay until the morning of the following day.

The clerk hobbled from the back office on a bad hip, wiped the sleep from the corners of his eyes and told me to come back in the afternoon. My stiff fingers thrust out a hundred-dollar bill.

"How about a room right now until noon tomorrow? Cash."

He looked at the money before turning back to me.

"You look like shit. And let me guess. No ID? And no

vehicle?"

"My car's out front," I said.

He walked to the window, pulled aside the dusty drape and looked out, no doubt spotting Ashlee's young face in the first hint of daybreak. He returned to the counter grinning, took my money and gave me a key. He flashed a mouth full of crooked teeth in what resembled a smile and proclaimed, "We don't judge 'round here."

Ashlee Chapter 18

Missing: Day Thirteen

My slightly overcautious grandfather parks the car two blocks away from the motel on a back street in a sketchy industrial area. Imaginary Ashlee, who apparently didn't get washed away when the dam broke, slips on the hilariously ugly shorts Granddad bought, as well as the three-sizes-too-big flip-flops, and we three shuffle along the shoulder of the road through a pounding rain that's a blessing, given it means no one is out to witness the horrible fashion crime being committed.

As we cross a swollen creek, Imaginary Ashlee looks down in dismay at dozens of dead fish floating on the surface, their white bellies facing skyward. Granddad turns his eyes upstream and surveys the business operations that border the narrow wash, most notably an auto wrecking yard and a dump where stacks of used drywall rest under several feet of water.

We're killing ourselves, Granddad.

He nods and takes Imaginary Ashlee's hand to get us moving toward our hotel's shelter. *I know*, he agrees. *Each generation doesn't always leave the planet in better shape for the one that follows.*

Imaginary Ashlee stops abruptly, and even she's determined that he understand. *No, Granddad. There is no next generation. There is always just us.*

Our room, like every no-tell-motel in the movies, contains one queen-sized bed as well as a musty smell of dampness and not-so-long-ago cigarette smoke.

We need to get some sleep so we can think straight, Granddad says.

A smirk rises from my soul. *I'll watch you sleep, Granddad. We are safe. For now.*

He tugs back the covers and drops heavily onto the bed.

Imaginary Ashlee surprises us both by hesitating for several seconds before diving in on the other side and inching her tiny body back until it touches his. *What a little rebel*, I whisper to myself. Then comes a second even greater surprise as my grandfather lifts an arm around her and pulls her close, taking in her warmth, feeling with contentment the rise and fall of her lungs beneath her slight ribs.

And, oh, this is what I have missed the most since saying goodbye these past few weeks to almost everyone I love. A kind and gentle touch that seeks nothing in return. I want this again more than anything, even if just for the very, very tiniest of moments.

I am watching the two of them from an angel's vantage high above the bed when my longing transforms itself into action. I begin falling into that imperfect form that is still capable of housing the lightest of souls. As my soul settles in, the girl's body sinks a little deeper into the saggy mattress. My grandfather's loving arm squeezes us tighter, like a muscle that contracts out of habit.

Just for the very, very tiniest of moments, I tell myself again.

* * *

We sleep most of the day and awake to an almost delicious feast of powdery donuts, muffins and pastries. *How sweet is this*, I think while licking sugar from my lips while stretching out on a mattress a thousand times cleaner than the ones at the farmhouse.

Yes, it looks like I lied when I promised myself to only very temporarily re-inhabit a space inside Imaginary Ashlee or Physical Ashlee or Whatever the Fuck You Want to Call Her Ashlee. Instead, I'm like the distant relative who moves into your home and won't leave. Whatever.

Granddad takes a shower. I stretch and quiet my mind

through meditation, which is perfect because so many questions are trying to gnaw at me.

When Granddad finally emerges in a puff of steam from the bathroom, he tells me I should soak in the bathtub before we plot our next move.

Pure energy never needs a bath, I say, unsure why I won't admit returning to my old physical companion.

The dried mud left on the sheets suggests otherwise, Granddad says with a kind grin.

When I don't budge, Granddad goes into the bathroom and turns on the water. A few minutes later, he calls, *It's just right. C'mon.*

When again I don't move, he comes and takes my hand and leads me to the tub, probably waiting for me to point out with questionable yet grating precision that the hand he holds isn't technically mine. I say nothing.

Okay, undress and get in the tub, he says. *I want to try to find the local news on the television.*

He leaves, closing the door behind him, and I stand staring at the bath. From the other side of the door, Granddad's distracted voice asks if I'm in the tub yet. I step forward and think of Mom, of the way she taught me to check the water's temperature with my elbow before jumping in. *Pain isn't an enemy,* she would say, *but a helpful signal. One that can warn you away from a much greater danger.*

I lean down and place my elbow in the tub. It's just right. I strip and step in but don't sit right away. I am too busy marveling at these silly bodies we are given. How they can recognize when our true being is in danger, sometimes from our own selves. How they can help concoct the most amazing ways to keep us safe.

I sit and begin scrubbing.

When I am drying myself off a little later, the sound of the television being clicked from channel to channel reaches me from the other room. Then the plastic wrapping being removed from a cup and water being poured into it. And then some other liquid, probably the vodka Granddad bought.

I shout out, *If you're making this imaginary body do this, you need to untangle its hair.*

Granddad's almost-scared voice comes back. *What? Why?*

I smile. *Because you do.*

I can't come in there when you're in the bath.

The body is out of the bath. It's wrapped in two towels, so you won't see anything. Just its shoulders. And its hair.

I can picture him standing there perplexed by what to do. This physical body tingles with love for him.

You're needed in here, I repeat, almost welcoming in my tone the slight whine Granddad surely believes accompanies the speech of every other 16-year-old girl.

Okay, he announces like a general preparing for battle. *I'm coming in.*

I sit on the edge of the bathtub, one towel around my waist, another around my chest, and when Granddad enters the room, I don't look at him. I don't have to. I know what he sees in the areas not shielded by rough white cotton: every vertebra in my spine, every rib on my side, every bone and knot of muscle throughout my shoulders and neck. He stares until I turn my head and his sad eyes meet mine.

I nod at the hairbrush in the sink and explain how to tackle my hair, starting with the bottom six inches and working up and finally attacking the roots and working outward again. His hands are much gentler than Mom's, maybe too gentle for the job, but I don't care. I long for one of my mother's cringeworthy-long hugs, my father's bird-peck to my forehead.

Did you know, Granddad, that physical bodies don't evolve as quickly as our souls; that's why they often need to be replaced with new ones, through what some call reincarnation? To keep up. So it's the soul, the soul, that's most important, not the body.

Makes sense, he says, his voice slightly sleepy again.

Granddad moves my hair off to one side, dampens a towel and begins attacking spots of mud on my back and shoulders. Then he goes back to work with the brush.

Done, he says, rising with both knees cracking. *Why don't you fill the tub and soak some more?*

As he turns to leave, I stop him with a few words I don't want to speak, in a direction I don't want to go. Not really. *Detective Douglas gave this body, this surely imaginary body, a bath. At the farmhouse. Twice.*

Something in his breath catches.

It doesn't matter, but he washed between its legs and all around its chest. He touched himself and made this body's hands touch him. He said she was his dirty little girl.

* * *

Through the bathroom door comes sounds of my grandfather flipping absentmindedly through dozens of television stations in search of the local news. At one point, and for more than a minute, a goofy kid's program serenades me, showing how deeply he's fallen into his thoughts. Eventually, he finds a newscast, which leads with a story about the rainstorm that caused an earth dam near Logandale, Nevada, to fail, sweeping two people to their death. A third person, the anchorwoman says, survived.

Twenty minutes later, I emerge from the bathroom wearing Granddad's T-shirt and boxers.

He doesn't seem to know where to look or what to do. He rushes forward and takes me in his arms and squeezes hard. I half expect some of my ribs to pop.

He's coming for us, I say.

Who?

Detective Douglas.

Granddad doesn't look as alarmed as he should. *Is that an educated guess or one of those... prophecies, visions, I don't know what you call them?*

Doesn't matter what you call them. I just know.

He nods.

So you believe, Granddad?

Yeah. I do. And more than anything, I want him to come.

* * *

We sit on the bed, and my grandfather tells me his plan. It's a violent plan, one that could make everything worse. One that will take a toll on him even if it does work. We are both in disbelief that after all we've gone through, little has changed. I say, *I think it's doomed to fail because the only way to defeat darkness is by bringing forth more light.*

I expect him to crack up at this. But he actually considers what I say, and he nods, almost smiles even. He squeezes my hand and says, *Just trust me.*

Twenty minutes after Granddad presents his plan, we heave shut our hotel room's saggy door and start walking to the rental car. The so-called dangerous voice, the one that has been absent since the broken warehouse in Miami, settles gently in my mind, like a bird touching down after a long journey. I freeze, not wanting to scare it off until I have taken a good look. Until I confirm that it has changed with the imagined passage of so much time and so many miles. It no longer suggests I am too weak to endure the loss I have encountered. Instead, it asks, simply, honestly, and in my father's voice: Do you have the guts to choose life over death? Ten words, that's all, but ten words that need to be answered before anything else.

Granddad looks back with eyes that are patient, familiar. I hurry to catch up.

Maybe it's the exhaustion, but a weird sense of contentment

rushes over me. I wish this short walk could go on forever or at least until the sun loses its warmth. When did I last feel like this? The answer comes quickly and with regret. It was not that long ago with my parents, the parents I had foolishly and selfishly wished would go away. Apparently, my prayers were answered, lucky me. I see, too, the mistake I made leaving Mom in those last days. How I failed to understand that I was stronger when I was with her, like I am with Granddad. Too bad it didn't work the other way too. That they were stronger with me, with the girl who was given a great and dangerous perception but not the fucking manual on how to use it.

As we near the creek teeming with dead fish, Granddad takes my hand and gives me a big smile, maybe to distract me from the death that lays belly-up in plain sight. Even if the timing of his smile is forced, it is still beautiful, not just an act of love but a more-than-ordinary act of creation. I smile back, strong, the kind of smile that announces he doesn't need to shield me from life's brutal truth. As we walk on, I consider this, the way we have chosen to find something other than despair, given the shitty tasks that holler from up ahead and the tragedies that call mournfully from behind.

My too-big flip-flops snap against my feet with purpose, and I squeeze my grandfather's hand with all my strength, hoping together we will manage to conceive a world where this won't be the last time we share a sugary-sweet moment.

* * *

Mike

At a department store in town, I bought Ashlee a green hoodie, jeans, shirt, underwear, pair of black boots and a cell phone, putting it all on the credit card tied to my fake identity. On the way to the car, we passed a bookstore, and she insisted on going inside. When she finally emerged, she clutched two books.

We drove up a hill to the Mesquite police station, which sat near the edge of town in an industrial area carved from desert. It wasn't an ideal location, but it would need to do.

I pulled over on the street a half-block up the road. We looked at each other, unsure.

She said, "I don't think the God in us likes this."

"Does He have a better idea?"

"*She* wants to know why you can't come inside with me?"

"I can't. What if I'm arrested? How could I keep you safe?"

Of course, I had no idea whether I remained a suspect in Kacey Sutton's death. My gut told me no. That Douglas had tortured Kacey in hopes of finding out Ashlee's location, and when he realized she didn't know, he had thrown her through the window to silence her forever. That he had planted my tire iron after the fact and it hadn't been used in the attack on her, a detail the coroner's report may have already revealed. But I wasn't certain. I also wasn't certain what would happen if it became Douglas's word against mine and Ashlee's, and I didn't intend to gamble with Ashlee's life to find out.

Ashlee studied my face, and as she did, I tried to keep my thoughts on the logical parts of the equation, like the reasonable man I hoped she saw before her. If she managed to peer deeper into my heart, into the black recesses that struggled to hide the violent rage crying out for appeasement, she didn't let on.

My granddaughter reached over and placed her arms around my neck and hugged me harder than you would expect from someone her size. It left me woozy, confused, because it was the type of hug that made you yearn to be a better person, not one that made you do what I was about to do.

"Do you remember what I told you to say?" I asked.

"I'm not stupid."

And with this, she opened her door and climbed out. As she walked toward the building in her new boots, each step seemed to lack the same blind enthusiasm as our getaway from the

Tropicana. I pulled away, my mind drifting back to the story Kimberly told me about the unenlightened cops who greeted her when she reported her sexual assault more than 40 years earlier. How three or four men had gathered around and looked skeptical as they made her recount the attack in great detail, each one taking turns prodding her to admit she had simply gone a little too far with her boyfriend and now wanted to blame someone else. And how she had, in typical Kimberly fashion, reached under her sundress and pulled her panties off and threw them at the cops, saying, "The blood is mine, the cum is his."

I hoped much had changed.

* * *

I drove to the hardware store on the main street and purchased several items, most of which a clerk with arthritic fingers loaded into a paper bag. Rain fell lightly fifteen minutes later when I parked my car on a residential street and walked across a golf course in the dark and up a sand hill, from which I could see the police station across the street. When I could hear no automobile sounds, I crept across the street and found a spot in a drainage ditch beneath a nectarous-smelling tree where I hunkered down and waited.

My grand plan amounted to this: Ashlee would go inside the police station and give her name and say she had been abducted in Las Vegas by a Miami police detective who took her to a rural area and sexually assaulted her over several nights. No mention of her having transcended her body and having psychic abilities that could make people rich. The only reference to me would be Ashlee saying I had removed her from the Tropicana to return her home, only to have Douglas, in turn, take her violently from me. She was to say she didn't know what happened to me. Only that she escaped the farmhouse after the dam gave way and hitchhiked until she was far enough away to feel safe, and only at that moment had she decided to involve the police. I had helped her come up with enough details to hold the story together.

Assuming Detective Douglas had survived and was hunting for Ashlee and me, the Mesquite police would contact him and ask him to come in. He would ask why, and they might vaguely tell him it was about Ashlee, being careful not to spook him. He would surely ask if she was alone. Then one of two things would happen. He would flee, going into hiding with all three shares of the riches, and Ashlee would never be safe. Or he would come here to clear his name by discrediting Ashlee, a task he surely believed he could fulfill, given her diagnosed mental illness.

I wanted him to try the latter.

Because he wouldn't expect me to be right here waiting for him.

The police cruisers used a gated parking lot out back, and each time one came or went, I ducked from the glare of their headlights. It was impossible to see inside them, and if Ashlee had been driven out in one, I wouldn't know. Visitors parked in the front parking lot 50 feet away from where I waited and, now that it was night, each one rang a buzzer to be let into the station. In my almost two hours here, only two people had entered.

The tree that sheltered me became rain-soaked, and water began dripping steadily down upon my head and back. I reached into my jacket pocket, removed the small vodka bottle and drank some down, telling myself it was needed for strength. Soon a familiar contentment pushed forward, taking me back to my Fort Lauderdale hotel's sun fried pool deck, where not long ago, there had at least been warmth in the nothingness of my life.

In the distance, a car's horn sounded. In my head, a pesky thought suggested Douglas had already slipped past me and into the police station where he had managed to wind up Ashlee enough that she talked up a storm. Even if such a thing happened, there was no way the cops would release her into the custody of the man she had accused of harming her. I hoped. One thing was certain: I better not fuck this up because when it came to having Ashlee's back, I was all that she had left.

Then another strange thought stepped forward, only to be quickly pushed aside. She was all I had left too.

Mike and Ashlee Chapter 1

Found: Days One and Two

Ashlee

The wrinkled lady behind the police station counter is nice, same as the detective who returned to the station to take my statement, a half-hour after she had gone home at the end of her shift. She is full of questions, and each one spawns at least three more, which leads her to make a really smart decision. She orders Chinese food for the two of us, plus Candace, who is the woman behind the counter, and Officer Jackson, the uniformed cop who called in the detective shortly after I said I had been abducted and sexually assaulted by a cop.

The detective, who told me to call her Louise, asks me to start my story at the beginning, the very beginning, which Granddad warned me about. He told me not to get into anything too far-fetched, using his definition of far-fetched, which he explained in great detail. Just stick to basic facts. Cops like that. I ran away from home after my father died and my mother's drug use flared. Some family friends tracked me to Las Vegas, and I was with them when my grandfather showed up to take me home. Then I was kidnapped by a Miami cop I had never met before, and he took me to a farmhouse where I was sexually assaulted. *Don't tell them about the gambling*, Granddad coached. *Tell them about the sex assault. It's more believable.*

I try to be vague, though Louise's forehead creases like she knows I am hiding all kinds of shit.

When I describe my escape after an earth dam broke, she says, *Wait a minute. Are you saying you were in the farmhouse in Logandale that got swept up in the earth dam collapse?*

She studies me carefully. *That could explain all your injuries.*

This was the point where she called detectives in Logandale

and confirmed the names of the two men who died and the one who survived. The names, of course, had not yet been released to the public, yet I had given them to Louise. She had made that first phone call right in front of me in an interview room where we chowed down on sweet noodles and lemon chicken. Maybe she heard something in that call that she didn't like or was sensitive. Because the next call she made in a private office, before returning and telling me she had talked to Detective Douglas, and he had volunteered to come in for a friendly chat.

Don't worry, Ashlee, she says. *You won't see him, and he won't harm you, I'll make sure of that.*

Something changes in her face. *To tell you the truth, I doubt he will come in. The detectives in Logandale are keeping him busy.*

Before I can ask what that means, she says, *The two men who died in the dam collapse. Thomas Fisher and Nick Hargreaves. What can you tell me about them?*

Of course, the question is a landmine, given I am not supposed to talk about the gambling. So I describe them, their personalities, how they abducted me and stun gunned my granddad, leaving him on the sidewalk, without detailing how they were involved in online gambling.

Louise, like always, prods me for more details. Then she studies me some more until I squirm.

Two detectives from Logandale are coming down here early tomorrow morning to talk to you, she says.

Why?

I think there is more you aren't telling me, Ashlee.

For once, I do something clever and shut up.

Fisher and Hargreaves, she says. *Both are known criminals. Fisher, some computer crimes related to gambling. Hargreaves, a string of assaults. Both are sex offenders too. Each has been charged in the past for abducting street kids in various cities and using them in violent child porn. Offering them up to rich men. Never convicted. That's why they aren't in jail.*

Louise rubs her eyes before continuing. *One of the Logandale detectives said that in the debris from the house, they found a high-end video camera.*

My hands are shaking, and I slide them under my butt. *I don't know anything about that. Just about Detective Douglas touching me and making me touch him. Like I told you.*

Louise takes a deep breath. *Detective Douglas says he was at the house investigating Fisher and Hargreaves. An unsanctioned investigation, he claims, meaning on his own time, which itself is highly unusual. Says he has for years suspected these two were grabbing street kids from Miami and abusing them and forcing them into child porn videos and selling them to pedophiles. Says he was doing surveillance on them from a spot on the property when the dam broke.*

Just another big lie, I say.

Well, Louise says, *I guess the cynic in me could argue that Douglas wasn't investigating Fisher and Hargreaves but instead involved with them, maybe even recruiting for them, given his access to police files involving at-risk kids.*

Louise keeps talking, though I begin tuning her out. Sounds like Douglas is in deep shit for hanging out with a couple of nasty criminals. Maybe so much shit that I am the least of his problems. Except I know he's coming. Urgently. Because he needs to discredit me before I say too much.

Louise sighs, maybe in frustration, and then pours more soy sauce on her noodles. *You are safe here with me, Ashlee. No one is going to hurt you again. But you need to trust me enough to open up.*

She passes the lemon chicken, and we review my story about another thousand or so times, even discussing both my parents' recent deaths. I try to stay on topic. She keeps pulling me into another narrative. The one in her mind where Nick and Thomas haven't yet moved on to gambling and are instead involved in child porn, in forcing kids on pedophiles. It's an unsatisfying conversation for both of us.

Anyway, it's pretty clear Louise believes Douglas assaulted me. Not so much the rest of my story, especially how I managed to avoid the various first responders after the dam broke and hitchhiked to her town, where I've been hanging out at fast-food restaurants, too nervous to enter a building populated with cops. She asks if she can scroll through the phone she sees tucked in the back pocket of my jeans; I tell her I just bought it and haven't made a call on it, which again produces a skeptical look from her.

She's also skeptical about what happened in Las Vegas because my New Age friends never filed a police report after granddad violently removed me from the conference room. She asks me why they didn't report it, and of course, I can't answer. She has me write down Lucas's full name and phone number.

She asks about a half dozen times if I know what happened to my grandfather after Detective Douglas and his men stun gunned him and why, if he was okay, he never called the police. She repeatedly asks about the brick incident and why my grandfather felt he needed to use violence to separate me from my New Age friends.

Aren't you worried about your grandfather? she asks.

The question startles me, leaving me struggling for an answer. Yes, I am very worried about my grandfather, though in no way she can imagine.

Do you think he never called the police because something prevented him from doing so? Are you sure they left him behind when they grabbed you?

I answer her with a question. *You think he's hurt or dead?*

I was wondering if you have any reason to believe that?

I should just say *no* and let the conversation move on. Instead, I hear myself say, *Of course, I do. Seems like everyone I care about winds up dead. It's like I'm cursed. Or like I curse others.*

She shakes her head. *I'm sure that's not the case. Could your grandfather have approached someone else in your family for help?*

Maybe asked them to call the police?

No. There's no one left but the two of us.

Well, your grandfather is lucky to have a true survivor like you on his side.

Don't be so sure. Because great light attracts great evil.

If Louise notices me venturing into an area Granddad had warned me to avoid, she says nothing. She squeezes my hand and starts telling me there's no evidence something terrible happened to my grandfather, though the tightness in her mouth suggests she isn't so sure.

Louise leans forward and nods at my two new books, which sit face-down on the table. *What are you reading?*

I turn them over. One is the same book of quotes that my former favorite therapist once asked me to scan for a single great inspirational sentence, which of course, helped lead to my Great Awakening. The other is a novel about a teen girl who becomes pregnant after getting raped.

Louise studies the novel's cover and winces slightly before saying, *But of course, Ashlee, you were never raped, right, and I am sure you don't think you will get pregnant after what happened to you, do you?*

I feign outrage that she thinks I am naïve enough to believe touching could lead to a baby.

Good, she says. *Just checking.*

I just bought that book because... well, because it's a story about forgiveness and finding the strength to accept your life and get on with living it. At least according to the back cover.

Louise smiles, picks up the book of quotes and starts leafing through it. I consider telling her about its significance, about Picasso's epic *Everything you can imagine is real.* The quote that's like a safe harbor in a storm or anytime you feel you could drown in your own chaotic doubts. But I say nothing about it.

Instead, I point to the background photo on Louise's cell phone, which rests on the table between us, and try to change the subject. *Is that your husband and kids?*

She gives her phone a warm look. *That's them. I like having that photo where I can see it. It reminds me how much I have to live for and that I need to stay safe because I have three people waiting for me to return home.*

The words aren't even out of her mouth before her eyes go wide and her mouth clamps shut.

Sorry, she says to poor orphan me.

It's okay, I say, asking for a break to empty my bladder and stretch my legs. Of course, Louise thinks this is the best damn idea she's heard all night. She says she needs to make a few more phone calls anyway and suggests I make myself comfortable in the staff lounge until she comes looking for me.

As I get up from the table, Louise stops me with a question that is clearly a trap, one obviously sprung by something Detective Douglas said to her.

When I come get you, I'll give you a rundown of exactly what will happen next, with victim's services and a social worker, and where you'll stay tonight and the nights after that as we work through this, she says.

Then she waits for me to say something like, *No, how about I tell you what will happen next. After all, I am the clairvoyant one.*

I keep my eyes grounded and humbly say, *That would be great.*

She seems to accept my response and then does something unexpected. She predicts my future. *You know, it may not feel like it now, but in the years to come you will meet someone who will fall hard in love with you, and you will get married and raise a family and probably have a brilliant career and be swept up by so much happiness.*

It's probably the kindest thing anyone's ever said to me, but it's impossible to tell her this because the tears are coming. I force a smile, and as I start rushing off to the restroom, I pass Candace, who says something to Louise about the video she's awaiting finally arriving in the online Dropbox.

I wash my face at a sink and try my damnedest to look into

my future. Not years ahead like Louise claims to have done, but even just 20 minutes. All that comes is an image of a girl staring out of a window into a vast darkness. I give up and wander through the deserted glass building, pausing in the staff lounge, then pacing the halls restlessly.

Louise's office has a large interior glass window with open blinds. When I walk by the first time, she's looking at her computer screen, her eyes wide, her face twisted like she's about to be sick. When I pass by again a few minutes later, her head is in her hands, and she's sobbing, almost with forced restraint, her shoulders rising and falling softly. Alarmed, my thoughts go to her kids. Her husband. Something that's gone wrong at home. I want to go in and comfort her, maybe show her the Picasso quote, though she first needs time to pull herself together.

Downstairs, the front desk area where Candace works still smells like fried rice. She signals for me to take a seat next to her behind the counter, which I do. My thoughts are still consumed by Louise and whatever crisis has snuck up on her. That's when I notice a large screen fed by six surveillance-camera feeds from around the station, including one facing the parking lot outside the front door. I think about my grandfather's plan and how he's doomed to get caught because Candace likely uses the screen to monitor each nighttime visitor driving into the parking lot.

Candace shows me photos of her two Labradoodles. She talks about her kids who have married and moved away. She talks and talks, yet barely a word reaches me. All I can think is how Granddad will soon be added to the list of people I have cursed.

The phone rings. Candace answers and begins dealing with a noise complaint. I move to the window and peer into the darkness where Granddad promised to hide. I bet, true to his word, he's out there huddled from the rain. That he didn't pass the crazy girl off to the cops so he could get out of town lickety-split. Does he understand his decision to stay with me in an act of vengeance and protection will likely end with him going to prison or, worse, getting killed if he fails to surprise Douglas? Even if he gets away with his plan, I can picture him forever living with murderous regret.

I can't stand to get another person hurt. I consider running out the door to my grandfather and sending him away. Or charging upstairs to Louise and telling her everything, so she can go outside and stop whatever's about to happen.

Candace promises to have a patrol car dispatched. She puts the phone down, but it rings immediately. She says Louise's name. They seem to be discussing calling at least one patrol car and two officers back to the station until their shift ends.

As they talk, a car's headlights break through the outside darkness, probably a cop returning at shift's end. That is until the vehicle drives past the station and turns to circle back. My whole body starts to shake.

You okay, sweetie? It's Candace, her phone call ended.

For months I have renounced time as meaningless. But now I have run out of it, and I can't stop whatever comes next.

Sweetie? Candace repeats.

My thoughts go to Granddad huddled low on the ground somewhere. Maybe ducking down in the wide ditch beside the parking lot. How I have always tried to coax him, and so many others in my life, to look skyward and see the same awesomeness as me, never realizing sometimes they first needed a helping hand to get to their feet.

Physical Ashlee's strength surges through my soul, hard and sharp like teeth, and I step forward, positioning my undeniable mass in front of the video surveillance screen. Then I reach down for all the charm I can muster, hoping it will be enough, unsure what will happen next. And I am almost left breathless by the unexpected jolt of power as my spirit and body finally work together instead of trying to undermine one another.

I tell Candace, *I'm so tired. Can you show me where the coffee is kept?*

She smiles and says, *How about I go get you a cup.*

She turns and leaves. I move toward the glass front door, not in the direction of the person I hate but toward the one I am destined to love through all eternity. Yet under a fluorescent light at the door, it's the man I despise most who first comes into sight. He parks his SUV and steps out, and when his eyes fall on my smirking face and his body goes rigid, it's clear he senses his own future.

* * *

Mike

The SUV turned into the parking lot and took a space near the door. If this was Douglas, he had not been far away. I bit down on my lip and scooped up my hardware store purchases. I couldn't see inside the vehicle, even when its door opened and the interior light came on, and by then, I was more than halfway across the parking lot. Out stepped a man who looked toward the police station and froze.

I moved in behind him. Maybe he heard my footsteps. Detective Douglas whirled around, and before his face could register surprise at this strange man approaching in a painter's mask and gloves, a short-handled shovel came down on his head hard enough to kill him.

* * *

I opened the SUV's back door and, with difficulty, heaved him inside. I threw the shovel in the back and climbed into the driver's seat, removing two zip-ties from my pocket and reaching back and double binding his hands behind his back.

I turned my attention to the police station, its windows tinted and dark except for those around the front door, and I prepared to surrender if someone had witnessed my attack. Someone was watching. Ashlee stood in the light, her right hand patiently signaling for me to leave, as if in the saddest of goodbyes.

I slipped the car into reverse and began winding down the hill.

Under a streetlight near the highway, I stopped and searched Douglas's pockets for his cell phone, tossing it out of the window. The vehicle was an aging Ford Explorer that I believed had been parked behind my rental car in the farmhouse barn. It was likely too old to have a built-in GPS tracking system, though who could be sure. In the SUV's middle console sat a stun gun. I picked it up and checked to see if it worked. A spark of electricity lit the darkness. I reached into the back seat and jolted Douglas long enough to elicit a burning smell so putrid I needed to open all four windows to stop gagging.

He didn't move.

* * *

I drove west on the interstate into the darkness, the rage that allowed me to take a shovel to Douglas's head draining away. What flooded in to fill the void was unwanted.

Forty minutes out of Mesquite, I turned off on a two-lane road skirting around the Valley of Fire State Park. I reached back and grappled around for Douglas's neck. A slight pulse, maybe, ticked through an artery. I cursed and gave him another jolt with the stun gun.

When the state park lay to my right, I slowed and searched for one of the gravel roads typically used by ATVs and other off-road vehicles. I found one that looked passable and took it.

In Mesquite, I had purchased a disposable cell phone and browsed the web for large tracts of nearby government land that likely would be deserted and not prone to being bulldozed by property developers anytime soon. When my screen filled with dozens of Google images of this state park and its stunning red-rock scenery, I stopped searching.

The vehicle bumped along the trail. I desperately wished Douglas would quietly slip away in the back seat, assuming he hadn't already. If not, I would once more need to muster enough fury to strike a living person with a shovel, though this time, that person would be helpless.

A couple of miles along, the terrain turned hilly. The road trail ended at a steep gully, forcing me to backtrack. I turned onto a flat stretch of desert, driving for another few hundred yards.

I chose a flat, non-descript spot that, once the sun rose, would likely prove to be surrounded by scenic clusters of rock formations. It was a shame I would never see this area's beauty in daylight when the red sandstone formations caught the sun in what, according to various websites, looked like a dazzling display of fire.

The second I slipped the SUV into park, a low groan rose from the backseat. A similar sound moved up my throat in reply.

* * *

Hard to say how long I dug. The task swelled when, with my first few shovelfuls of earth, the ground proved to contain as much rock and clay as soil and sand. Of course, the act of digging a grave can never be easy and, unless you are a man like Douglas, it will quickly take its toll.

Some people claim time moves differently in the desert. Something about the solitude. Perhaps that explained why I struggled to determine the exact moment the shape of the hole began to change. I only knew this decision came sometime after the first few shouts rose from the SUV, followed by several kicks to the door. My flashlight's beam showed the hole I dug no longer looked like a typical grave. It was deep and narrow, more vertical than square or horizontal. Or, in other words, the hole was shaped so a body could stand to face the heavens in judgment.

I pulled Douglas face-first from the back seat and dragged him to the edge of the stoning hole. Perhaps staring down into that abyss brought him to life. His shouts became desperate pleas, and his pleas became phrases and even full sentences that, for the most part, could be understood.

"You don't want to do this," he said, his words sluggish as if the blow from the shovel had knocked his mind into a lower gear. "It will haunt you forever."

I knelt, knowing his mouth needed to be gagged. Instead, some cowardly part of me let him speak.

"At the farmhouse," he said, his words taking forever. "What we saw. It was a powerful act of God. And he chose life for you and me. We could split the money. A fortune for each of us. A just reward for two tireless public servants."

"And what about the girl?"

"Forget the girl," he said.

"So, you're saying you will leave her alone?"

Douglas took a deep breath and said, "When the Mesquite police contacted me about her, I warned them. That she was a mentally ill runaway with knowledge of her own mother's murder. That she would do anything to stop me from finding her because maybe she was involved. Get a hold of her psychiatric report, I told them. I imagine they have by now. They will see she gets the help she needs. So, yes, I will leave her alone, as God intended."

Part of me had to admire him. He could look you in the eye and spin lies effortlessly. He had surely lied to the Mesquite police about Ashlee being involved in her mother's death. Just as he was lying to me about leaving her alone.

I tore away a long piece of his shirt, and before I could tie it tight around his mouth and the back of his head, he began screaming: "Wait. The money. I wrote down my gambling and banking accounts and passwords from memory. The list. In my pocket. You take it. All. Just untie me before you go."

Not sure why I looked. Maybe to prove to myself the depths of his deceit. I did remember feeling a wallet in his front pants pocket when I searched him. With my foot, I turned him over and pulled out a brand-new wallet. It contained no ID, just a few bills and a small piece of folded paper. My flashlight's beam revealed a neatly handwritten list of account names and numbers, as well as passwords and dollar amounts, pretty much as he had described.

Douglas watched me and his face twisted into what could be considered a smile. "Do you have cell phone reception?" he asked. "If so, try one out. Log in and make an online transfer to your bank account to see that I am not lying."

The piece of paper and the writing on it felt fragile in my long, dirt-caked fingers. Even the slightest mishandling could destroy a fortune. The night seemed to freeze while my eyes studied the paper. The soothing trill of a cool wind whistling through the creosote bushes faded away. So did the distant hum of diesel engines and glare of fast-moving headlights where the interstate highway assaulted the still desert a few miles away. All that remained was Douglas's breathing, heavy with desperation.

I crumpled the paper and tossed it into the hole. Then I knelt and tied the strip from his shirt tightly around his screaming mouth.

His words and grunts soon became mush. I positioned his feet over the hole and pushed him in. With the shovel, I filled the empty gaps around him with dirt and rock to trap him in place with only his head and shoulders and chest exposed.

Did Douglas know about my parents' violent past? Probably. He seemed to enjoy taking the time to figure out what motivated his prey. If so, maybe he wasn't surprised that whatever savage legacy they had left for me was about to come to life once again. That whatever good came from my lifetime of work would soon mean nothing, like I always feared.

I stood over him and let my flashlight fall on a ground littered with dozens of rocks the perfect size. A rush of urgency churned in my gut, telling me to find a more expedient way. To get this over right now. My mind agreed, and within seconds, I lifted the shovel high in the air over his trembling head.

* * *

I couldn't do it.

The hate rattling around my chest should have been enough to send the shovel crashing down. It wasn't. I paced behind Douglas, unable to forget what he did to Ashlee, unable to make him pay for it. And worse, unable to make Ashlee safe from him. From beneath his gag, Douglas expelled noises that were almost words, each one probably intended to form part of some reasonable argument.

I sat on the edge of a boulder and stared at the night sky, surprised to see the clouds had rolled away. I cast my eyes at the clear moon and thick scattering of stars and asked God for the strength to take a life.

My thoughts turned to Ashlee, who had earnestly explained in our farmhouse dungeon that God and Satan live inside all of us. That the universe is part of us, not the other way around, meaning no one is ever truly alone. For one heartbeat, I looked inward. Then for another. And another. I reached deep inside for a solution, and when it finally presented itself, I couldn't be sure whether it came from me or a more powerful source.

I picked up a large stone, its weight tearing at my arthritic wrist the longer I held it. This was how it was with people, too, especially those closest to you; the pain they caused grew with the passage of time, with the diminishment of our lives. But could the opposite also be true? Could those closest to you be used to help shoulder a burden? Could love, assuming you were fortunate enough to find it, become a heavy weapon you could let fly in your darkest moments?

I counted out 21 stones.

I caressed each one, drawing from its collective strength. The first stone was for Joshua, the son I never met. The next one for Kacey. Then Ashlee. The next 11 the children I fathered in Bellingham. Then Kimberly and Jennifer, whom I loved in different ways. One for the baby, or family, I had denied Jennifer. One too for Maricela, who represented the many people in my life I tried to keep distant. One for each of my parents, whom, if nothing else gave me, I hoped, the courage to commit a most difficult act. And, finally, the last one for me.

This was my family, whether embraced by me or not.

I shut off my flashlight. The light of the moon was enough.

My mind once again slipped back to Jamila's stoning. How more than half the stones missed her. I always wondered, did some of her executioners possess terrible aim or a last-second conscience?

None of my 21 stones would miss its mark if I could help it.

With a trembling hand, I picked up the first one and felt its power. Even in the near darkness, horror wrenched through Douglas's twisted, howling face. I raised the stone, first to my chest and then high in the air, and threw with all my love.

* * *

For more than an hour, I dug the stoning hole into a deeper and wider grave. After burying Douglas and smoothing the ground over his body, I lowered my head and said, "Please forgive him."

I didn't ask for forgiveness for myself.

The dull thump of the stones striking Douglas, the sense of the heat and the life leaving his body. They were sensations that could never be forgotten. And neither should they. Because like joy, pain is a reminder we are alive; that perhaps we possess something worth losing.

I sat on a boulder and watched the first inkling of daylight turning the black rock formations in the distance into a bright and recognizable sight. With it came the sense I had been here before. That part of me would never leave.

I waited to plunge into a well of regret so dark and deep that no decent man could find his way out. My emotions were well known to me. Or so I thought.

My fall never came.

A small plane flew overhead, a reminder to get moving.

I picked up the shovel, placed it behind my seat in the SUV and drove roughly halfway back to the main road before stopping and getting out. Into the desert I walked, shovel in hand, determined to leave it nowhere near Douglas's grave. I considered chucking it into a thicket of brambles, but that felt wrong. It deserved more. My mind swelled with expressions and symbols of love, like the wedding ring Jennifer wanted or the vow of chastity Kimberly thought could preserve our friendship. A shovel, perhaps, was the strangest of all, but love came in unexpected ways, especially when you were determined not to find it.

I lay the shovel in a slight wind-forged indentation on the desert floor and used my foot to gently cover it with reddish sand.

Mike and Ashlee Chapter 2

Found: Day Two

Mike

On the outskirts of Mesquite, the sleepy throes of what passed for morning rush hour loosely gripped the highway: the odd clump of cars inexplicably bunched together and the occasional motorhome or truck rumbling along in the slow lane. Up ahead sat the exit leading not just to the police station but the nearby McDonald's restaurant where I had promised to meet a certain teenage girl for breakfast, assuming she had managed to slip away from her law enforcement chaperones or, more likely, her newfound social workers. My bloody task complete, all I needed to do was engage my right-turn blinker and ease the Explorer into the exit lane. Yet hesitation clenched down upon my hands and arms.

I forced out a small laugh at the absurdity. Without being debilitated by fear, I had spent chunks of my life traveling thousands of miles through areas ruled by the most dangerous and ruthless people on the planet, or worse, by no one. And now, a two-mile journey to usher a 100-pound girl into the debatable safety of my presence left me nearly immobilized.

I recalled Ashlee telling me in the warehouse that my small-minded perceptions of the world kept me locked in my own tiny, prison-like reality. Her words had angered me, even if her smirk had fallen away and she delivered them with kindness, almost pity, like she was regarding an abandoned old dog that had found a way to survive alone in the wilderness for so long it would never again seek a place in a loving home.

The SUV began drifting over to the exit lane, almost on its own. I brought it back to the highway and hit the gas pedal, blowing past the exit. In no time, I had crossed the state line into a small corner of Arizona.

With each mile, my insides rattled with a sense of disobedience, like a naughty Grade 6 student writing one joke answer after another on an important exam. At the same time, Ashlee's grip on me fell away, as if each inch I traveled weakened the spell of this sweet sorcerer who could control my every move and, worse, my every thought.

An hour later, I was in Utah, where pockets of green stripped the desert of some of its harshness. Only then did I exit the highway.

* * *

Ashlee

The morning's first rays of sunlight strike me through an open window at the shelter for battered women where I was given my own hotel-like room and told to get some sleep. Which I did. Until something startled me awake. My eyes are drawn outside to a distant series of hills that are perfectly flat like colossal tabletops, as if a giant had sliced their peaks off with a mighty sword. Granddad crashes into my thoughts. I sense he's out there in those hills, his dirty job complete. Does he, too, wield a sword? One he used to cut himself loose from me and the story only I could tell. I also sense he's come up with his own happy ending, like he's already forgotten what he's learned.

Mike and Ashlee Chapter 3

Found: Day Two

Mike

I parked the Ford Explorer in a shady spot in a rest area that sprawled around a cement restroom building with a blue tin roof that looked nothing like the sky's color. Soon I leaned against the vehicle's dust-streaked back door, feeling a welcome stretch in my hamstrings.

A week earlier, I had committed Kimberly's cell phone number to memory. I punched the numbers into my phone and waited.

"Hello," came a voice sounding both hesitant and distant, like she had already returned to the safety of her home.

I wanted to whisper, "Thank God." Instead, I said, "It's me. I need your help."

"Where is Ashlee? Is she safe?"

"We got grabbed the moment we left the casino. We eventually got away. Though not until she went through hell. She's with the police now. She's okay, I think."

"What do you mean, you think?"

And so it began.

I told her the bare-bones story once, quickly identifying Douglas for who and what he was, though keeping details to a minimum. When I described the earth dam collapse and how Ashlee and I had survived, along with Douglas, she exploded.

"What the fuck, Mike, you think she's safe even at a police station with that man on the loose and determined to silence her and without you there.

"I took care of it," I said.

"What do you mean by that?"

"I mean, he can't hurt her ever again."

Silence. Then, "My God, Mike."

A few moments later, she asked, "Why didn't you let the police handle it? Why did you…?"

"Because it needed to be done my way."

"Oh, Mike."

"So," I said. "The favor I need is for you to go get the girl. To take her home with you. With you and only you. To look after her until she can look after herself. I know it's asking a lot."

A noisy diesel truck crawled by, and I anxiously pressed the phone to my ear.

"Where is Ashlee?"

"In Mesquite," I said. "I bought her a cellphone. You can text her, and she'll tell you where she is. My phone's been buzzing like crazy. Probably her texting me."

"And where are *you*?" she asked.

"At least 60 minutes away. In Utah."

A second truck rumbled by while I awaited her answer, my fingers wrapped tightly around the small phone. Without Kimberly's help, and in the absence of mine, one didn't need to be psychic to see Ashlee's future: group homes possibly followed by mental hospitals and heaps of mind-numbing medication. And finally, the street, the last dumping ground of those incapable of conforming in most ways, especially financially.

"You know I would do that, Mike, but…"

"But what?"

"But that's not what she wants. She wants to be with you, her remaining family."

I had my response prepared and laid it out as bluntly as possible. "She shouldn't have to live with someone who just committed the worst crime imaginable."

"You didn't commit the worst crime imaginable. Douglas did. And besides, is that the real reason you're not taking her to wherever you're going?"

"Yes."

"If she was on the phone right now, I know what she would say. She would call you a fucking fibber."

"Where are you?" I asked.

"Still in Nevada, in my car driving. I'm at least an hour away from Mesquite. But listen. Take a few minutes and tell me about what happened to Douglas. About whether you took precautions and about whether you are on the run. About where you'll go next. About why you weren't damn smart enough to let the police handle this, because they would have gotten to the bottom of it eventually."

I laughed. "It was the *eventually* part that scared me. Anyway, I'll answer every question. Just promise me you'll turn your car towards Mesquite."

"Already on my way. But..."

"Yes?" I asked, relieved that Ashlee had at least one person she could trust.

"There's a reason why I call you stupid."

"You know, you were right," I told her. "About Ashlee. There is something remarkable about her. Not just her ability to endure so many terrible things. But something far more. Something I couldn't even begin to explain."

"Of course I was right. Haven't I always been a good judge of character?"

* * *

When our conversation ended, mostly at my insistence, I leaned back and drank in the relief of knowing that Kimberly, at this moment, was doing exactly what was best for Ashlee. Maybe not for me. How long would it take for a police cruiser to show up beside me in this parking lot or on a nearby stretch of highway if Kimberly decided our shared secret about how I stopped Douglas grew too heavy for her to bear?

I stared off across the highway into the desolate countryside, flat and brown and empty except for the occasional patch of scrub brush. It invoked images straight from western movies of solitary travelers becoming lost and disoriented, their bones in time becoming part of the barren landscape.

By now, the slight boost of adrenaline from talking with Kimberly had faded, profound exhaustion taking its place. I grabbed the gloves from my pocket and put them on and climbed back inside the Explorer, where I reclined my seat. A 15-minute catnap would give me enough energy to drive hundreds of miles. Around the Grand Canyon and then south. I had shared with Kimberly my far-off destination. How I could get there through Mexico and live cheaply on the money from my Syrian accounts and not return home until ready, perhaps after making some subtle inquiries with her about the status of the separate investigations into Douglas's disappearance and Kacey Sutton's death.

"Years ago, I visited this beautiful seaside village in Costa Rica," I had told her. "It's called Cahuita. A friendly place full of backpackers and students and former hippies."

I shifted in my seat in the Explorer as I relived my two months there. Renting a bungalow a few blocks from the beach, learning Spanish from an 80-year-old local woman with crooked teeth and a broad smile, and each day walking the trails of the national park, where a thick rainforest ran right up to the edge of the most stunning white-sand beach. And the damn monkeys. Small and grey with long arms and tails, they would swing endlessly from branch to branch over the ceiba and coconut trees that reached out over the ocean.

As sleep embraced me, I saw myself walking the beach in loose flip-flops, only I was no longer alone. Ashlee walked next to me, our bellies satiated by the tropical breakfast smoothie I had made in our cottage, our attention skyward as we looked past the darting monkeys for the sloths that hung high in the trees beyond the reach of predators.

It was strange how Ashlee had begun to bleed her presence into my distant memories. But was it the past I really saw? Because time was a long, looping road, one where you could become turned around and unsure if you stared off at the horizon in anticipation of what was coming or back in the direction where you had been.

I sat up wide awake and gripped the steering wheel to calm the shaking in my hands. It didn't work. My whole body jerked violently like I was sobbing hard without the tears. Like I didn't have it in me to cry for what was being left behind. I forced myself to close my eyes and tilt my head back and soon found myself playing the distracting game of trying to guess what scent, other than diesel fumes, the wind carried through my open window. Perhaps it was the smell of a distant rain that had fallen in a nearby desert canyon where no one was present to see it.

* * *

My peaceful slumber at some point turned into a nightmare, one in which the blackness surrounding me took on the empty darkness of a deep grave. My mind replayed images of Douglas's battered body crammed into a hole dug through rock and sand. The gatekeepers of sleep smiled at the appropriateness of where I now found myself trapped.

My torment didn't last long, especially not compared to the sentence handed to Douglas. In my nightmare, I poked at the wispy blackness above me, like a man buried alive. In mere seconds I forced my head from the ground and emerged into the grassy area outside the restrooms in a Utah rest stop where my sleeping self lay less than one hundred yards away in a parked Ford Explorer that belonged to a dead man.

From somewhere distant came the call of her voice. My

eyes moved across the near-empty asphalt parking lot and saw Ashlee motioning to me with one excited hand. I began moving, more of a glide really, toward the spot where she waited, the highway's roar falling away, replaced by a similar but more natural sound coming from the girl's direction. Before I reached her, Ashlee turned, her body first rising over a short hill and then disappearing in descent. Cresting the hill, I saw what had captured her attention: a wide creek, its current flowing fast and clean around an assortment of grey boulders.

"C'mon, Granddad," Ashlee shouted from a steep trail winding down to the water and the small gorge that held it.

When I caught up, Ashlee stood on a large rock jutting out over the water, her gaze directed downstream to where an elderly couple, dressed in loose-fitting white baseball hats and matching red jackets despite the heat, threw a stick for a yellow dog.

My granddaughter turned to me and said, "Isn't it beautiful."

We watched the dog repeatedly charge into the shallow water after the stick, always emerging with it downstream and carrying it proudly back to the couple. The repetition of the simple action, the couple's encouraging words, our shared presence under the warm sun. It all felt hypnotic, my nightmare now a heavenly dream. Once I had dreamed about meeting Ashlee in a damaged warehouse, but this dream seemed different, even if it too felt eerily real. In the first one, she orchestrated every movement and word. By contrast, this one felt strangely unique to me, like she was another player in my life, in the failed dark comedy called the Mike Baker Show.

The man gave the stick a harder-than-usual toss, forcing the dog further into the current, which caught him in its rush and plunged his head briefly underwater before he scrambled onto three large rocks that formed a small, safe island. The couple began calling his name, Frank, their voices increasingly urgent as the dog refused to budge from his sanctuary.

With me right behind, Ashlee made her way to the bank, where the couple paced helplessly. The journey to the dog didn't appear overly onerous for a teenage girl and her able-bodied companion, though it would have been all but impossible for the couple.

"We'll walk out and get him for you," Ashlee said, her words, it appeared, almost making them, and perhaps me, cry with relief.

I slipped off my shoes and rolled up my pants while Ashlee removed her black boots. Her jean legs were too tight to slide up on her calves, and they became wet the moment we plunged in. She didn't care. The rocks under our bare feet weren't slimy, though the current was strong and constant. We needed to be strong too, and adept and smart enough to change our path when necessary. In less than a minute, we navigated to where Frank, a puppy on closer inspection, sat wagging his tail.

Ashlee scooped him into her arms, his tongue shooting up to her neck in appreciation, his wet fur soaking into her shirt. She stood cradling him, the flowing water separating itself around her legs, her immovable form. She repeated his name in a soothing whisper, her wide eyes reassuring him before turning briefly away to trace the safest route to dry land. Her fingers' grip remained gentle and fiercely protective. She glanced up at me, her grin bashful at the affection she poured into the four-legged stranger.

Her expression beamed with a dizzying familiarity. My head whirled. Time distorted and collapsed. And before me, I no longer saw a teenage girl holding a dog but one cradling a baby that was surely me as she stood in a Bellingham creek whose exact location had remained obscured in mystery. A maternal love radiated from her touch, its energy strong enough to sustain a person through the most grueling lifetime.

Time contorted again, and my mother rocked her sleepless baby in a cramped nighttime kitchen. Then she sheltered me from a summer rainstorm beneath a canopy of cherry blossoms. The locations rushed by in the background, almost superfluous. A busy bank. A doctor's office. A back alley where her cocaine dealer lurked. But as whatever existence she constructed raced past, she remained steadfast, with me tucked faithfully in her arms. Time twisted again, and my mother's mother appeared before me, an ever-familiar smirk as she raised her baby toward a blue sky so flawless it could never last. Then her mother, lifting her maternity dress to dip a bare foot in an ancient canal. And her mother, screams of labor piercing a dusty village in the shadow of a red rock mountain.

It was a glimpse of eternity that hinted at all life's answers, one that told a story of distant places and cultures that forever changed for better and worse, even if the faces taking them in never did. And in this never-ending panorama, a greater truth screamed to be heard: that something far more precious was being squandered with each passing second, with each rush of wind and water.

Maybe Ashlee was right that we all get to choose our own reality. Because suddenly I was back with my granddaughter and the puppy, desperate to hold on to this single moment with someone I had found the faith to love, knowing it really could be all the time I would have with her.

Far too soon, Ashlee turned and took her first step toward shore. Frank, his tail slapping her chest with a steady rhythm, blocked Ashlee's view of her footsteps through the submerged rocks. My steadying fingers wrapped around her arm, and we began soldiering along together, the way it was always intended.

* * *

I awoke unprepared for the exhausting emptiness that abruptly follows every dream, this gift we allow to slip away by opening our eyes. My gloved fingers brushed at my damp forehead, pushing away the strands of hair that stuck to it. Was I still dreaming? The pain in my bladder and the harsh reality of the sun in my eyes convinced me otherwise. My phone told me nearly two hours had passed. It also told me I'd been texted and called dozens of times by the phone I had bought Ashlee.

I threw open the SUV's door, dropped my legs to the pavement and cursed the tightness in my lower back, which made the quick walk to the restroom something more. It was at a urinal at the edge of a piss-covered floor that whatever old perceptions I clung to began to shift, as if they longed for a new shape that could fit into the craziest of spaces.

When I returned to the truck ten minutes later, my hands juggled two bags of salted nuts, an assortment of chocolate bars, two bottles of water and one flavored energy drink. I longed for something stronger. Something soothing.

I needed to phone Ashlee or Kimberly and admit my mistake, but that felt wrong, like a shortcut you know will get you lost. I sat and stared across the parking lot at the short hill I had climbed with Ashlee in my dream, the trail that ended in the heavenly creek below. This hill looked different. It was dissected by a grey strip of crushed gravel trucked in from God-knows-where to construct a smooth trail that rose to the ridge's peak and disappeared. I considered walking to the trail's mouth and listening for the low roar of moving water. This, too, felt like cheating.

Morning turned to afternoon. My faith never wavered.

My bladder aching, I made another trip to the washroom, emerging minutes later amid a late-afternoon flurry of arriving vehicles that made the once-sleepy rest area an almost-bustling oasis. Groups of travelers, some grasping babies squirming in bursting diapers, raced past while others stretched and sunned their tired muscles, their bleary eyes resting on a tree's soft green leaves. My eyes turned to the supposed trail that led to the supposed creek. Would my dream-fixated imagination push forth a bright and familiar flash of red and yellow right before my eyes? It didn't. But was it conjuring something better because a familiar voice called out to me?

I stopped and scanned the parking lot, cursing the line of cars and trucks cruising in search of the most convenient parking spot. When my eyes settled on the treed area where the Ford Explorer sat, a girl waved her arm at me in a semi-circle, her thin body shimmering in the heat rippling off the black pavement.

I stepped forward, close enough for my imperfect vision to confirm it was my granddaughter who leaned against a bright red sedan. She wore the same boots, jeans and green hoodie as when we said an anxious goodbye outside the police station. When I waved back, she flashed a victorious grin. From inside the car, another person watched, no doubt pleased with her front-row seat to the coming reunion.

Before reaching my granddaughter in the middle of the parking lot, I knew what would happen.

* * *

Ashlee

We come together in an awkward hug, the only kind my grandfather knows. His shaking arms pull me close as cars, RVs and even a damn bus squeeze by in opposite directions. He is like a sturdy shelter in this precarious outer realm, on this solid yet exposed patch of ground where together we amount to so much more.

Granddad nods at a hill that's split in two by a gravel trail. This man that I have for days bombarded with the universe's strangest and most amazing secrets laughs and says, *Now I have one for you.*

He tells me he believes that over the short ridge are two people and a furry companion who need our help. And that, maybe, there's something else over there, something more than the beauty and sadness constantly orbiting us all. I spin away and plunge forward, no time to waste. He plods after me, a step behind as always. Halfway up the hill, I turn back. He flashes a contented, unhurried smile that tells the world he finally gets it. Because he, like his granddaughter, sees that the true wonder that sustains us won't be whatever spectacle awaits on the other side but what came moments before in our simple embrace.

Author Biography

Jeff Beamish is a fiction writer, former journalist and author of the novel *No, You're Crazy*. His previous novel, *Sneaker Wave*, was shortlisted in 2014 for a national fiction award in Canada. He has had short fiction published in four literary journals, *The Nonconformist Magazine, Consequence Forum, Litbreak Magazine* and *Free Radicals*. As a journalist, he has written and edited thousands of news stories and features. He has been fortunate to find inspiration in the stunningly beautiful scenery in the Canadian province of British Columbia, where he lives and works.

Note to Readers

From the Author: Thank you for purchasing *No, You're Crazy*. My sincere hope is that you derived as much from reading this book as I have in creating it. If you have a few moments, please feel free to add your review of the book to your favorite online site for feedback. Also, if you would like to connect with other books that I have coming in the future, please visit my website for news on upcoming works, recent blog posts and to sign up for my newsletter: http://www.jeffbeamish.com.

Sincerely, Jeff Beamish

Acknowledgments

Thanks to the British Columbia Arts Council for its financial support while I wrote this novel.

ROUNDFIRE
BOOKS

FICTION

Put simply, we publish great stories. Whether it's literary or popular, a gentle tale or a pulsating thriller, the connecting theme in all Roundfire fiction titles is that once you pick them up you won't want to put them down.
If you have enjoyed this book, why not tell other readers by posting a review on your preferred book site.

Recent bestsellers from Roundfire are:

The Bookseller's Sonnets
Andi Rosenthal

The Bookseller's Sonnets intertwines three love stories with a tale of religious identity and mystery spanning five hundred years and three countries.
Paperback: 978-1-84694-342-3 ebook: 978-184694-626-4

Birds of the Nile
An Egyptian Adventure
N.E. David

Ex-diplomat Michael Blake wanted a quiet birding trip up the Nile – he wasn't expecting a revolution.
Paperback: 978-1-78279-158-4 ebook: 978-1-78279-157-7

The Cause
Roderick Vincent

The second American Revolution will be a fire lit from an internal spark.
Paperback: 978-1-78279-763-0 ebook: 978-1-78279-762-3

Blood Profit$
The Lithium Conspiracy
J. Victor Tomaszek, James N. Patrick, Sr.

The blood of the many for the profits of the few… *Blood Profit$* will take you into the cigar-smoke-filled room where American policy and laws are really made.
Paperback: 978-1-78279-483-7 ebook: 978-1-78279-277-2

The Burden
A Family Saga
N.E. David
Frank will do anything to keep his mother and father apart. But he's carrying baggage – and it might just weigh him down ...
Paperback: 978-1-78279-936-8 ebook: 978-1-78279-937-5

Don't Drink and Fly
The Story of Bernice O'Hanlon: Part One
Cathie Devitt
Bernice is a witch living in Glasgow. She loses her way in her life and wanders off the beaten track looking for the garden of enlightenment.
Paperback: 978-1-78279-016-7 ebook: 978-1-78279-015-0

Gag
Melissa Unger
One rainy afternoon in a Brooklyn diner, Peter Howland punctures an egg with his fork. Repulsed, Peter pushes the plate away and never eats again.
Paperback: 978-1-78279-564-3 ebook: 978-1-78279-563-6

The Master Yeshua
The Undiscovered Gospel of Joseph
Joyce Luck
Jesus is not who you think he is. The year is 75 CE. Joseph ben Jude is frail and ailing, but he has a prophecy to fulfil ...
Paperback: 978-1-78279-974-0 ebook: 978-1-78279-975-7

On the Far Side, There's a Boy
Paula Coston
Martine Haslett, a thirty-something 1980s woman, plays hard on the fringes of the London drag club scene until one night which prompts her to sign up to a charity. She writes to a young Sri Lankan boy, with consequences far and long.
Paperback: 978-1-78279-574-2 ebook: 978-1-78279-573-5

Tuareg
Alberto Vazquez-Figueroa
With over 5 million copies sold worldwide, *Tuareg* is a classic adventure story from best-selling author Alberto Vazquez-Figueroa, about honour, revenge and a clash of cultures.
Paperback: 978-1-84694-192-4

Readers of ebooks can buy or view any of these bestsellers by clicking on the live link in the title. Most titles are published in paperback and as an ebook. Paperbacks are available in traditional bookshops. Both print and ebook formats are available online.

Find more titles and sign up to our readers' newsletter at
http://www.johnhuntpublishing.com/fiction

Follow us on Facebook at https://www.facebook.com/JHPfiction
and Twitter at https://twitter.com/JHPFiction